Praise for Kim Michele Richardson and *Liar's Bench*

"This glorious debut novel is one of an unexpectedly fine cro of recent and new Southern fiction. *Liar's Bench* succeeds on ma levels. As a coming-of-age story, it is splendidly realized and lifting. As a portrait of a Southern community painfully stum into the age of racial and gender equality, it is penetratin convincing."

—*Southern Literary Review*

"A well-crafted, beautifully written novel."

—*News-Gazette* (Champaign, Illinois)

"Satisfying . . . with thought-provoking historical element
—*Historical Novel Reviews*

Books by Kim Michele Richardson

Liar's Bench

GodPretty in the Tobacco Field

Published by Kensington Publishing Corporation

GODPRETTY
in the
TOBACCO
FIELD

Kim Michele Richardson

KENSINGTON BOOKS
www.kensingtonbooks.com

KENSINGTON BOOKS are published by

Kensington Publishing Corp.
119 West 40th Street
New York, NY 10018

All Kensington titles, imprints, and distributed lines are available at special quantity discounts for bulk purchases for sales promotion, premiums, fund-raising, educational, or institutional use.

Special book excerpts or customized printings can also be created to fit specific needs. For details, write or phone the office of the Kensington Sales Manager: Kensington Publishing Corp., 119 West 40th Street, New York, NY 10018. Attn. Sales Department. Phone: 1-800-221-2647.

Kensington and the K logo Reg. U.S. Pat. & TM Off.

eISBN-13: 978-1-61773-736-7
eISBN-10: 1-61773-736-4
First Kensington Electronic Edition: May 2016

ISBN-13: 978-1-61773-735-0
ISBN-10: 1-61773-735-6
First Kensington Trade Paperback Printing: May 2016

10 9 8 7 6 5 4 3 2

Printed in the United States of America

For G. J. Berger,
dearest friend and quintessential
Jerry Rice in a pass–catch duo

and

For Stacy Testa,
my patient voice of reason and wonderful
word keeper and story cobbler.

I adore you both.

The soil is the great connector of lives, the source and destination of all. It is the healer and restorer and resurrector . . . Without proper care for it we can have no community, because without proper care for it we can have no life.

—Wendell Berry

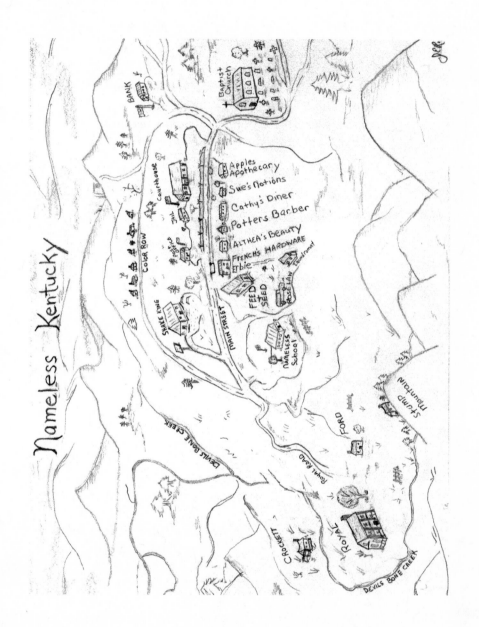

Chapter 1

As sure as ugly is found in the morning addict waiting to score in the parking lot of a Kentucky Shake King, there is GodPretty in the child who toils in the tobacco field, her fingers whispering of arthritic days to come.

My uncle, Gunnar Royal, says I'm that child and that I'll find Salvation if I work hard enough. But it's doubtful. I've been working these fields since knee-high, and ain't nothing but all kinds of GodUgly keeps happening around here.

Now, every time we pass the Shake King my uncle points to the whores and hooligans who hang out there. That's what he worries on—what I might become and what my insolence could bring. That's what makes him pour the bitter herbs into my mouth, and why he sends me out to work the tobacco rows at daybreak. Gunnar says at fifteen I should know better, should have learned better, being that my sassy mouth-of-the-South has earned me buckets of punishment from his tincture of biting herbs steeped in moonshine.

When my uncle took me in ten years ago, I learned the widower scriptured his Jesus with moonshine, and he made it his sole purpose to chase out my parents' devils. If anyone could, I reckoned it'd be Gunnar. A feared man in these hills, he'd served as executioner and strapped no-telling-how-many Kentucky prison inmates into the ol' Sparky electric chair during the forties and fifties. And although it's 1969 and Gunnar's nearing sixty, lordy-jones that man can still set a full field and cut a look that's meant to do a'hurtin'.

Outside, a July rain dropped softly onto mountain shadows as the fog rolled through. I waited to be done with his latest by turning to the little windup clock on my nightstand. Keeping time to the soft ticks with steady taps on my knee, I glimpsed into childhood memories, searching for distraction from the mounting pain Gunnar'd dished out.

I studied my parents' photograph on the nightstand, my daddy looking on as Mama playfully wrapped the frayed cloth cord around me while pretending to talk to him on the toy telephone. A cottony memory whisked through my thoughts, easing the pain a little: She'd lightly poked my ribs and laughed softly into the tin mouthpiece. "Yes . . . uh-huh, me and the kid's on the way . . . Right, snugbug?" Mama had tickled me and put the red receiver up to my ear. "Tell Daddy we'll see him at the tent revival, sugar. Talk to Daddy, RubyLyn," she'd coaxed. I grabbed the old toy, raised the cord, and shook it at her, hissing like Daddy's church snakes.

"Little Miss Preach!" she'd teased, catching me by the ribbon of my dress. My toddler's giggles had lit across her singsong as she pulled me into the soft folds of her satin slip.

I'd found the family photograph tucked inside Mama's old pocketbook along with her tube of Rattle-My-Tattle red lipstick, a few coins, and a homemade paper fortune-teller that we had made together.

I slipped my thumb and forefingers into the worn paper pockets of the fortune-teller, opening and closing it several times. I ran a finger over the tiny penciled portraits she had sketched of us on two of its triangle flaps. The third folded apron showed her sketch of a tobacco leaf. She had saved the last blank spot for me. Resting a fingertip on the faded red heart with the strange streak through its center, I thought about my daddy's missing portrait, what could've been—and should've been.

It was a sad broken heart that I barely remembered coloring onto the empty space. But, yet, it was my crayoned drawing from a time before memories could snug root.

I clutched my chest and rolled slowly over to the side of my bed, dropping the fortune-teller onto the bedspread. A shadow spilled under the closed door and I cast a prayerful eye toward it and stood. He went on into his room.

I wiped a bead of sweat off my upper lip, the pain crawling into my head and sliding down my throat. If he didn't let me out soon, I feared I would never swallow again, talk again. I began to pace in front of my open window, forcing myself to breathe in the fresh air. Some days the bittersweet vine rooted with patches of morning glory that had been hugging this big old house since 1857 gripped more than the white-columned porch and paint-peeling boards. You couldn't escape it—him. Not even from outside. Especially like now when the heavy fog burdened, and the cradling mountains squeezed a little too tight.

Sinking back down onto the bed, I punched the mattress again and again, glancing back at the clock and fighting the nerves whittling me down. Reaching under the pillow, I pulled out my mama's snakeskin purse with its kissing-lock closure. I rubbed my fingers over the biscuit-colored skin, trailing the diamond paths darkened with age and oil from my smooth tips. *Such a fine thing.* I knew from town talk that my daddy had it made for her and the skin had come from one of his church snakes.

I flicked open the golden clasp and dug out her lipstick and streaked the red paint across my puffy left cheek and imagined a mother's velvet kiss left its sweet mark.

Once more, I eyed the clock, slapping my fist on a jiggling knee. I picked up the fortune-teller again, tracing the paper's speckled grain that had been produced from the pulp of the tobacco stalk, questioning . . . Refusing to believe like some of the townsfolk—that there was anything magical in my fortune-tellers. Believing would mean I'd somehow heralded tragedy with this broken heart long ago. . . .

Gunnar rapped on my bedroom door. I slipped the fortune-teller into her purse and shoved it back under my pillow. Cupping a hand over my face, I opened the door.

He frowned as I pushed past him down the hall and into the

bathroom, my cramped jaws near splitting. Quickly, I spit out the mouthful of elixir he'd made me hold for fifteen minutes, the tang of moonshine burning my gums and widowing my sass— until the next time.

I touched my cheeks where the fires had leeched to tender skin, rubbing my tongue over the blistered lining of my jaws.

I spit again, blood this time that had me screaming. "G-Gunnar!" I looked at the sink in horror.

Gunnar rushed in beside me. "Good Lord," he said softly to himself, before going to get the goldenseal medicinal he'd concocted.

"Please," I cried. "I need to see a real doc. It's bad—"

"Rinse." He pushed the jar into my hand, watching me swish the antiseptic around in my mouth. "I've warned you not to use my paper for those sinful witch fortunes you call art," he chided.

"See what you made me do, Gunnar? *See?* . . . You old . . . executioner . . ." I spit out more blood.

He backed out into the hall. "You're not going to waste my good paper making vulgar scrawls."

"And you're"—I spit once more—"you're not gonna execute me that easy . . . *dammit.*" Tears splatted down.

"Quiet that serpent tongue."

"Gunnar, help . . . *God, please help me. . . .*"

"Only the GodPretty in the tobacco field. Only the *God-Pretty,* RubyLyn."

Gunnar's bedroom door clicked shut on my pleas.

Chapter 2

Ugly . . . I sucked on the cold cloth numbing my swollen tongue as dawn crept slowly into Nameless, the mountains holding the nights longer in these old hollars and dark hills. I'd sure found lots more of it ever since my daddy, the sin chaser and snake-handling pastor of Nameless, Kentucky's Mountain Tent Tabernacle, died when I was four, and six months later when Mama passed, too. You wouldn't think it could get any uglier than that. But I keep finding more of it in this hollow town that folks said wasn't worth naming—these tobacco fields where I'd toughened my Kentucky soles and sharpened my bluegrass-green eyes on the passing of seasons—from the long winter months of field preparation, my sneakers oozing in cold mud, to the summers of sticky-sap leaves scratching at my sun-burned face, to the tobacco worms hitching onto my skirts, and Gunnar's mean potions leeching onto raw skin.

It weren't no surprise I had to dig for the pretty in these fortune-tellers. Making them helped me feel alive, kept me closer to Mama, and made me feel like the artist folks whispered I'd be one day.

I pulled up the edge of the mattress and looked at the books I'd hidden there—the beautiful art on worn covers. A thimble of hope bubbled. *"Artist. My ticket out of here . . . one day . . . one day soon,"* I said fiercely, and dropped the mattress, afraid if I didn't poke the words they'd never see light.

Despite it being the Lord's day, and Gunnar's punishments, I was going to keep at the fortune-tellers—this time by looking to discover who I'd be swapping that important first spit with. The thrill of discovering who that might be made it that much more daring; the chances of it favoring my absolute true love made it real.

Stepping over to my bedroom windowsill, I slipped the latest fortune-teller I'd made into Mama's purse and parted the curtain. Below, Rainey Ford, our black field worker, carried two big bundles of tobacco sticks into the barn and dumped them. He walked back out, pausing to pet the old mama cat circling him. Rainey pulled out something from his jacket, likely a piece of chicken or some scrap he always thought to save for her, and dropped it. The cat hunkered down over the food, then snatched it up and took off into the barn.

Over the past ten years, when I wasn't looking, grace had snuck into Rainey's bones and muscled him into a fine man, tall, strong, but with a softness that made my heart sing.

As if snagging my thoughts, he peered up at the two-story window. I dropped the lace curtain. Shamed because he saw me and shamed because he'd showed up on Sunday to work for me again.

When Gunnar'd caught me drawing in the barn instead of helping clean it, Rainey stood up for me, saying, "It's only a minute break out of a very long day."

But Gunnar didn't care for Rainey's lip. "Been hearing a lot of fireball-sass this past year from my field worker since he's turned eighteen," Gunnar'd bit to Rainey before doubling his chores.

I peeked back out. Rainey tossed me a small, crooked smile. It was the same one he'd been giving me for years, but this one was different somehow. More grown-up than boyish, like there was a secret in it.

My eyes went to the bureau, sought out the keepsake that had once belonged to Daddy. My only memento of his, and a fitting spot to keep promises and secrets. I stepped over to the dresser and opened the small, hinged box. Daddy's snuff was long gone, replaced with memories: a tiny nest of rescued threads from Mama's clothes, along with the dried tobacco leaves and blooms that Rainey had given me with his promise.

We'd first met when he was eight and I was five, practically growing up together. When he turned ten he came calling with a pink tobacco bloom in one hand and a looped field clover blossom he'd fashioned into a ring in the other.

Boldly, he'd asked to marry me and then smacked my cheek with a kiss. Gunnar'd puffed up at that, and said, "Don't touch her kind, *ever*." And then he'd swatted Rainey's tail all the way down the tobacco rows, across the field, and parked him on his own front porch. Despite that, Rainey had stood up and, with a trembling lip, shouted out a promise, "My bride, my RubyLyn."

For a long while after that, Gunnar'd kept a watchful eye on us, harping on "social standing," cooling Rainey's declaration, with me tucking those blooms and leaves inside the keepsake.

Now, even before the day could catch its fire, I could hear Gunnar outside, breathing his own, needling Rainey for news on his tractor part he'd ordered from the traveling trader last month. "Miss Law's gotten a mite big for her girdle, taking her sweet time getting back to these parts. Should've been back with it yesterday," he said.

I rubbed the tobacco tin with shaky hands and anxious thoughts of escape. I inspected the dead clippings. Feelings for the land I'd loved, just as dead. Spent youth scattered in an old rusting tin—my destiny doomed, reflected in its pitted brass lid—my draining breaths spent on dying dreams of getting out.

A few minutes later the screen door slapped. Gunnar's feet hit the bottom landing, and he yelled up the stairs, "Hurry it."

I closed the lid on the tin and went over to the closet to grab my church dress for Sunday service.

Downstairs, Gunnar barked louder for his breakfast. Tossing the dress aside, I went down in my nightgown to light the oven.

He had an old wooden toolbox sitting on the table, still gnawing for his tractor part, biting for Rose's whereabouts.

"Not like Rose to be late," I said. "Hope she's all right." I glanced at him tapping the wrench against his long johns.

"Humph, even Satan wouldn't wrestle with that woman."

A loud horn poked the morning light. I ran to the front door and flung it open and saw the rusted jalopy coming down Royal Road.

"There she is now," I called to Gunnar. "Rose," I hollered out the screen door, waving. "*Rose . . .*" I grabbed my sneakers from the foyer and pulled them on before barreling outside in my gown. Running alongside her big old green 1941 Dodge Canopy Express wagon, I ignored Gunnar's demands to stay put and fix his breakfast.

It had been nearly a month since I'd last seen the traveling trader. Rose Law was born in Nameless, and everything about her felt exciting and grand and what I imagined I'd find in the city. Miss Rose had a warm smile and a soft touch. Not a bit stuffy, when we'd first met, she'd pulled me into a hug and insisted I call her Rose, same as all the other youngsters.

Rose climbed out of the truck, shucking off her travels. She hiked up her skirt, peeling back a half-slip with flame-colored blooms and a lacy scalloped hem. She played with the suspender clips on her girdle, tugged at her drooping nylons.

"Hey, kid," she greeted, patting her haystack-high hairdo, wriggling down the gathers in her carrot-orange shimmery skirt and matching blouse.

Rose's arrivals were big, bright. She looked like one of those she-devils on the paperback covers that she kept hidden in the back of her truck and wouldn't lend me—what she called her "excitement books."

"Running a day late. My truck broke a belt in Louisville and I had to wait," she prattled, "but I got Gunnar's tractor part and—" Rose stopped and inspected my face. "Oh . . . looks like you've been drinking the Jesus juice again, kid."

Heat curled around my face, licked at my ears and scalp. Every time Gunnar punished me with his homemade elixir, the insides of my cheeks and lips would swell an' tell for a week or more.

Rose gritted her teeth and muttered a curse.

"Gunnar's been growling for that tractor part since yesterday morning." I tried to change the subject.

"Been growling for a'smackin'," she chomped. "*Lord,* sometimes that fool man reminds me of my grandpap."

When Rose was thirteen, her parents were shot during a moonshine raid. Her drunk granddaddy took her in. But when he began beating her, Rose ran off to the city and stayed for ten years, coming back only after he'd passed.

"Come on round here, honey." She guided me to the back of the Dodge. "I got something at the Woolworth's to take care of *your* parts, too."

I helped her lower the tailgate. Rose dug through her boxes of books, secondhand clothes, stacks and cartons of many sizes, and then passed me a small paper bag.

I looked inside and gasped. *A soft brassiere, satin undies, and a book.* The daffodil-colored underwear had *Wednesday* embroidered across the front.

"New, too," Rose said as I held the undies. "The woman in the shop said the package split open during shipping. Grabbed the only one left for ya, kid."

"I saw these in one of your old catalogs . . . Never owned any Days of the Week undies before," I marveled. "Thank you, Rose." I glanced back at the house for Gunnar, expecting him any minute to slip on his overalls and come out. "I'm going to get these on first thing. . . . Reckon God won't mind if I wear these Wednesday undies to church today," I whispered.

"Don't reckon He will care much about toting *Wednesday* on a Sunday prayer bottom, honey." She nudged her chin to the countryside. "He loves Himself some pretty, too. Here, have a gander at the brassiere. See if it'll fit," Rose rushed.

I pulled it out and saw the white cotton fabric had a pretty pink rose in the center. Smiling, I pressed it to my chest. "I can't wait to wear it," I squealed. "This ol' one's been driving me mad, cutting into my skin for a long time."

"Heard tell a girl having mad boobies is worse than contracting the mad dog sickness," she snorted, and patted her big chest.

"It sure is pretty and all with the flower." I held it up to me, studying. "Perfect, Rose."

Slyly, she tapped the bag. I pulled out the book, *The Great Gatsby,* by F. Scott Fitzgerald. "Rose, oh . . . oh, this looks great!" This didn't look like one of her *excitement books.*

"The cover is torn off the back, so I couldn't really sell it." She shrugged an excuse.

"It looks practically new. Oh, it's the love story you told me about—the girl who's a Kentucky flapper."

"Yup, that's Daisy."

"I can't wait," I said, running my hand over the dark blue cover, tracing the haunting eyes floating over the sparkly city. I studied the naked women the artist drew inside the eyes. "It's odd," I declared. "Look here, Rose, wonder how the artist made it so mysterious and pretty . . . I want to draw like this one day."

"Oh, I have something else." She pulled out a creased sketch pad. "Maybe you can practice your own on this," she said.

"Do I ever need paper . . . Thank you!" I tucked it under my arm, then went back to the book. Thumbing through *The Great Gatsby,* I stopped at a poem. Smiling, I shut my eyes and inhaled the ink. "This is gonna be the best one ever." I kissed her cheek.

Chuckling, she brushed me off. "Better hide that one from Gunnar real good, honey, or he'll use it for kindling."

Behind us, the screen door banged a warning, and Rose quickly snatched everything back, stuffing the book and clothing into the bag.

I held on to the sketch pad.

"Hello, Gunnar," she called out, "brought your part. Would've had it yesterday, but this old truck of mine busted a belt. Anyways, found it at Clyde's Tractor Parts in Louisville just like you said it'd be."

She set my bag on the tailgate and pulled out a small package and handed it to him. "Got your order of thick rubber gloves in there, too."

"Thank you, Miss Law." Gunnar studied the receipt taped onto the box and fished inside his pockets for money.

"Say, Gunnar," she said, "State Fair's coming up next month. RubyLyn's gonna need a ride"—Rose pointed to the tobacco fields—"for that winning tobacco exhibit."

"Sure am." I pulled myself up. "Best crop ever."

Gunnar handed Rose payment, then scratched his neck, taking a spatula to the idea over his own mulish thoughts.

"I think it'll win the two-hundred-dollar prize." I worried for an answer. "And you said I could when I prepared the field this winter and—"

"And we know you've been doing little of that lately." Gunnar shot out an accusing finger.

"Been working twice as hard, and waiting all my life," I reminded. "You told me I could when I turned fourteen. Done made it to almost sixteen now. It's time—"

"There's no time for fairs and foolishness," he snapped, "or that." He glared at my sketch pad.

Rose stepped in front of me. "I'll tote RubyLyn up to Louisville and have her back in the field the next day. Won't cost any extra to have her along. And she'll get to show her tobacco, see all them fine crop exhibits . . . and them new tractors I told ya about last year . . ."

At the word *tractor* something passed over Gunnar's eyes.

Rose licked her painted lips, then glanced down at my feet before continuing. "Sure would be a big help, her setting up my wares in the booth. At forty-four years old, these ol' bones . . . *Lord,* these ain't like they used to be." She lifted a limp arm, jiggled. "Don't think I can manage without help this year. Nah, sir, can't . . ."

Dogged, Gunnar stared out to the fields, his mind working some more. After a minute he quipped, "She'll work for her share of the gasoline . . . and you make sure she does."

"Lotsa work to do, ya hear?" Rose lectured me for Gunnar's sake. "Takes a mess of hard work to set up a fair booth . . ."

"Yes, ma'am," I said, not imagining anything harder than breaking your back in the tobacco.

"Gunnar"—Rose pulled her small frame up and pushed—"I brought some nice shoes back with me. Might find a pair in there for the kid, seeing how hers is—"

"Not till fall," he growled.

"The fields have worn them out," I protested.

Gunnar didn't make much off his small tobacco patch. And money for selling the crop only came in the fall. He wouldn't take a draw, and as far as I knew the damn government didn't care considering the sorry state of my shoes and the ugly ankle-length dresses he picked out. He called it being frugal and proper, but I knew he didn't pay attention to my growing and was too tight to buy new things and too stuffy to buy anything colorful.

Gunnar never once peeked inside the town's Feed & Seed's mail-order catalogs that they carried. Instead he went behind the store where Rose parked the traveler and went through her secondhands she'd picked up in the city thrift stores.

Rose frowned. "Fair prices . . . Come take a peek, Gunnar."

I rolled my worn sneaker in the dirt, remembering when I was seven. In the back of Rose's traveling trader I'd found a spanking new pair of red patent leathers and some ruffled anklet socks that fit like a fairytale.

I have no idea why, but I'd begged for those shiny shoes, promising God and Gunnar (and there weren't much difference at that point) I'd work twice as hard if I could have them.

Rose had put her hands on her wide hips to chide him to spend one more dollar, but Gunnar fixed her with his cold executioner's stare. When she sighed and cut the price to a measly two dollars, Gunnar smacked the shoes out of my hand and reached for a big plain pair of boys' sneakers that cost one dollar less.

When I got home, I saw that Rose had packed those boy shoes with a half bottle of her Faberge Tigress cologne. Thrilled, I'd dabbed the cat perfume all over myself, toes included, and waited for an exciting transformation. I'd practiced purrs and roars, swelling my sentences with them. Nothing happened and no one noticed. Instead, the cologne gave me an elephant-sized headache, and Gunnar had sneezing fits that shook the panes. For three days the bees chased me through the fields, finally sending me off to a creek bath. Soon enough, Gunnar found the perfume, poured out the pale yellow liquid, and buried the bottle under the dirt floor in the barn.

*   *   *

"No shoes till September," he repeated to Rose, "and not a day sooner." Gunnar nailed a warning finger to me.

Rose raised a brow. "Your niece's brassiere and panties . . ." She ceremoniously waved the small sack with them and the book inside, hoping he wouldn't look, and that the mere mention of female unmentionables would have him hightailing it back to the house.

I held my breath.

Gunnar fished inside his pocket, pulled out another dollar, and shoved it into her hands for the clothes.

"A gift." Rose tried to give the money back. "Young lady needs herself a good-fitting brassiere—"

He held up his hand. "Dammit, woman, this is the Lord's day!" Gunnar spun around. "RubyLyn, fix my breakfast and get ready for church," he roared from halfway across the yard.

Rose snorted and I choked down a giggle.

"We're going to the State Fair, kid!" she declared with a hug, and handed me my package.

"*The 1969 Kentucky State Fair,*" I barely breathed, thinking about the prize money that could get me a new life.

All day long I felt like one of those girls in the Sears, Roebuck & Company catalogs. Wearing the new underwear, holding on to Rose's declaration, and peeking at the glorious new book, I steered clear and refused to let Gunnar spoil it.

That night I leaned out the window, hoping to see Rainey. I couldn't wait to tell him that I'd be going to the city. But the barn shadows stood quiet.

A half hour later, I heard him playing his violin. The soft, airy notes coming from his porch brushed across the tall tobaccos and rose into the quiet countryside. His old-fashioned draw tickling and teasing the summer breeze that mewed through leaves. " '*Wake up, wake up, Darlin' Corey, tell me what makes you sleep so sound.*' " Rainey sang "Darlin' Corey" in a sweet measure that deepened with the notes. One of those naturals, he'd picked up his daddy's violin when he was four and his mama said that in no time he was making that old fiddle spark magic into the nights.

Like always, he finished with "Sweet Kentucky Lady," the honeyed ballad he'd first sang for me when I came to live with Gunnar.

A gust of cool mountain air lapped at my skin. I pulled on the quilt jacket Rose had made for my thirteenth birthday, crawled into bed, snuggling into the fabric she'd pieced together from a few of my mama's old clothes that Rose begged from Gunnar after Mama's death. "Hard things can happen in a house without a mama . . . girl should have one close at this age," Rose had said when she surprised me with it.

I lingered my touch over the fraying seams and faded patches of Mama's dresses, lazed a crooked arm across my eyes. Sometimes when my mind let me, from one patch or another, I'd catch a glimpse of something she'd worn: the swish of her pale-green dress, a wrinkle lying along a daisy-splattered sleeve, the willowy blue sash on her hip, my little hands clumsy and clinging to them, my face pressed into the folds of soft, rain-washed cottons when she held me.

It was like she was still with me. And every thread that had worked itself loose from the jacket and fallen, I'd scoop up and save inside Daddy's tin. Not able to throw any more of her away, or bear to lose another piece of her.

I brushed a sleeve lightly over my hurting jaws and more hard things I knew were headed my way.

Chapter 3

For Penance, Gunnar sent me to work the back rows of the tobacco alone. But with the State Fair only a month away, I welcomed the Salvation. Quiet field work let me visit loud thoughts of the city I'd soon live in. I'd be sixteen in September, and if Rose made it there at thirteen, imagine what the extra years and prize money would do for me. These were just a few things rattling my brain.

I gathered tobacco seed from the blooms for next year's planting while Rainey worked the rows alongside Royal Road. I was a little relieved Gunnar'd separated us, being I didn't have much talk in me still because of my sore mouth. Not to mention I was embarrassed for Rainey to see my puffy cheeks and swollen lips.

Still, I missed him. Every time my eyes set upon him, worked shoulder to shoulder with him, or heard him humming three rows over, my heart got lighter and my mind rested some.

Shortly before suppertime, I took the hoe to my own tiny tobacco rows, careful not to disturb the prized plants. The last thing I needed was my small patch competing for sun and growth, getting crowded out by Gunnar's tobacco.

After an hour of weeding, I dropped the hoe and looked over at Gunnar's land. Fifty acres of the best in these parts. A breeze rippled over his separate five acres of tobacco, leaving a standing shiver of green rolling toward the east. Gunnar grew some of the finest burley on the rich bottomland, and still left a big plot for vegetables, letting the surrounding acres rest for crop rotation. I dropped my hoe and examined my work.

When Gunnar parked his tractor for the day, Rainey joined me to inspect the leaves.

"I will surely take home the prize money at the State Fair next month," I slyly announced to Rainey.

"Gunnar told me." Rainey grinned. "And he wants to send me, too, so I can check out those new tractors he's been hearing about. Rose can tote me in the back."

"Oh . . . he did? It's going to be swell, Rainey."

"Swell," he bounced back.

"Yeah . . . The city—us there, the lights, the people," I chirped. "I can hardly wait—"

Across the field, Gunnar rang the porch bell.

Happy, I slapped the dirt off my hands and looked over to the big porch aglow from a grayish orange ruffled sunset. "I best go get supper on the table. It's later than I thought."

"I still got some time," Rainey said, picking up my hoe.

"You go on, and we'll finish this later."

He lifted the bandana from around his neck and wiped the beads above his lip. "Just another hour, girl." Low sunlight sparked his smiling eyes.

I stared at him, thinking how hard he worked. How he hung around extra to help with my burley. How much he acted like my uncle when it came to putting tobacco above everything else—and even the way his hands talked like Gunnar's when he was excited. My uncle had rubbed off on him good.

"You've stayed till eight o'clock every day this week, Rainey Ford. And you've more than earned your five dollars from Gunnar today. It's Thursday night and I bet your mama has a mess of fine fish on the table waiting. Go on and get." I hiked my thumb to his small house on the other side of the field.

"You know August is coming fast," he said.

"Only July 24. Sure wish it would come faster," I said, thinking about the fair.

Rainey shook his head. "*Only?* You know with folks running

toward the easy draws, instead of field work or to the coal mines, it'll be hard for Gunnar to get his crop harvested with only the two of us."

"That's what Gunnar says, too, but he's talked to the Newtons."

"Now, Roo." Rainey teased out my nickname. "You know the Newtons ain't gonna work the field beside me . . . not many folks in eastern Kentucky would, I imagine. Hell, Jenks showed up last week and hightailed it back out of the rows when he saw me."

He was right. Not many would, and most said they'd load muck in the coal mines before working alongside a field nigger.

"What about Mr. Thomas and his son?" Rainey asked.

"They might pitch in." I studied. "They told me last month they're not taking a draw and said they'd come by as soon as it's housing time."

When I first came to live with Gunnar, he'd kept me inside and busy with housework—and only taking care of the big house, refusing to let me work in the fields, unless I was being punished. But after President Johnson came to Kentucky and declared his War on Poverty, Gunnar couldn't get men to work the rows. He swore he'd lost money when he had to reduce his crop. And when my punishments started adding up, he gave me a fulltime hoe to go along with my dust cloth, sassy mouth, and sins.

Him being a former government man and all and having experience as a hardworking state executioner employee, I reckoned that was his way of working the devils out of me and getting free help at the same time.

Rainey said, "Hope so. Seems everyone around Nameless is thinking up easy ways of doing jobs other than *work*. Even Statler's saying his cow has to be babysat seven hours a day or else she won't milk."

"Statler clan is always claiming something, mostly pickpocketing good folks' hearts for whatever they can get."

"Damn government sure 'nuff gave him the draw."

Gunnar clanged the bell again.

"Sound like ol' Gunnar," I mused. "Go home, Rainey, it'll get done. We'll make it, we always do."

"Just a few more minutes, Roo."

"Well, bye, then, I need to go over and get squash from the garden."

"Hear, now. We don't have to say good-bye." Rainey reached for my little pinky with his, tugged. "Thought we agreed never to say that." He lit a soft smile.

There was that smile again. More and more it was something I needed at the end of the day to get me through to the next.

"Oh," I laughed, "so tired I nearly forgot." Because a "good-bye" seemed too sad and forever, and we'd both had our share of that with family, me and Rainey had made a secret pact nearly a decade ago, a childish pinky promise to never say good-bye to each other. Instead, we'd always call out our partings with a pinky squeeze and sweeten it with a "good night." Morning or night, it was our saying, and the cracked-open door that meant we were always with each other.

"Real glad you're going to the fair with me and Rose. Good night, Rainey."

Rainey grinned. "Good night, Roo." He squeezed our pinkies together, holding on a bit longer than usual.

I pressed back. "Don't stay too long now."

He went back to hoeing. I watched him a second, wondering why everything felt so confusing around him lately. Mostly I'd forgotten the silly childhood promises, but recently, I couldn't stop thinking about them or him . . . and what his grown-up kisses were like. I couldn't help wondering if he was thinking of mine. . . .

Rainey glimpsed over his shoulder. "Need something else, Roo?"

Red-faced, I mumbled good night again and hurried across the field to the garden. I grabbed two squash and headed to the house. Stopping at the pump, I washed up, then stepped over to the clothesline to pluck off linens, stuffing them into a basket.

I toted the basket up to the porch and set it down, surprised to hear a woman's voice inside. I slipped inside and ran upstairs to my bedroom. Below, Gunnar called for me.

Hurrying, I stripped off the old shirt of Gunnar's that I used to protect my arms, and changed out of my heavy work dress into a clean one.

In the kitchen I found Henny and Baby Jane Stump and their mama seated at the table next to Gunnar, who was studying papers.

Henny was my best friend, well, besides Rainey, my only friend who lived close enough to claim. She was sixteen and the oldest of ten kids. Her little sister, Baby Jane, was eleven.

The Stump family lived on the mountain behind us where rocks gather and the pines straighten up scrawny for breath. Gunnar'd been renting some of his land to Mr. Stump so he could grow food to feed his family. Gunnar would hire Henny for field work—when she'd show up.

"Hi, Mrs. Stump. Lena's baby come yet?" I asked about her fifteen-year-old daughter, and tossed a smile to Henny and Baby Jane. "Hey, Henny . . . Baby Jane."

Baby Jane scrambled up from the table and wrapped her small arms around me. She pressed her face to my chest, squeaking a sob into my dress.

I patted her head and glanced over to the table.

Mrs. Stump's face was packed loosely with folds of hard times. Henny's fragile cheekbones were tight and tear tracked. Henny didn't answer about her sister. Mrs. Stump wouldn't answer, just cut Baby Jane a look.

Baby Jane scurried back to her chair.

I wondered why they were here and what had them so upset.

"RubyLyn," Gunnar interrupted.

"I was only—"

Gunnar had his spectacles on, studying a letter of sorts in front of him. "You're late," he said without looking up. "My supper should've been on the table an hour ago."

I eyed the skillet he'd used to fry himself up a bologna sandwich while I'd been working. "Your bones ain't broke," I huffed. "Look at this mess. No one thought to wash the skillet?" I said fussier than I'd intended and knowing I was the only "no one" doing chores in this big house.

The Stumps shifted in their seats. Gunnar stopped reading and knitted his snowy eyebrows together.

I set my lower lip in defiance until Gunnar pierced me with his summery green eyes.

"Ru-by-Lyn," he shoved the syllables through his teeth.

Even in front of company I knew Gunnar would never give. He was one of those people who don't splinter—who grow stronger from others' fractures. He splayed his hands in the air—those loud hands that never seemed comfortable to rest and you wondered where they might land.

"Cleaning and dishes is women's work," Mrs. Stump admonished quietly.

"Set some extra plates for the Stumps," Gunnar said, rising from the table. Chairs scraped against the checkered-green linoleum as Gunnar and Mrs. Stump headed into the sitting room.

Baby Jane rushed back to my side, and whispered, "N-n-need some help?"

"No." I bumped the oven door shut. "What are y'all doing down here anyway? What's wrong?" I rested a hand on my hip and looked over at her sister. "I thought you weren't feeling good, Henny."

"Pa's worked out a deal with Gunnar and we's just delivering on it," Henny said, looking away and fidgeting with the collar of her dress.

Before I could ask what type of deal, Gunnar came back into the kitchen with Mrs. Stump. He eased down into a chair and asked for coffee.

They drank mostly in silence while I melted butter in the skillet and tossed in the chops. Mrs. Stump talked a little about fall crops while Gunnar listened with grunts. I sprinkled salt, pepper, and parsley onto the meat and tried to listen, too. When I finished, Baby Jane helped me out by setting the plate of meat in front of Gunnar. Quickly I added a couple teaspoons of vinegar and flour to the butter in the skillet and stirred it into a gravy that Gunnar liked.

Dusk scratched narrow tracks across the walls by the time I put the basket of biscuits on the table. I was hungry and bone tired.

"Iced tea," Gunnar mumbled as I pulled out my chair to join them.

I banged on the aluminum ice trays, filled five glasses, setting one in front of each of the plates, then plopped into my seat.

With closed eyes, Gunnar leaned into his prayer-clasped hands, and said, "O Lord, if able, bless the weak who share our table—lead, guide, and direct our Sinner who prepared this dinner. Amen."

The Amens tightened on the Stumps' lips. Gunnar grabbed the plate of cucumbers that I'd prettied atop a pink lettuce-laced plate.

I peeked over at Baby Jane gripping her silverware. Her fork shook and fell onto the plate, clattering. "Ain't . . . ain't hungry, ma'am," she whispered sideways to Mrs. Stump.

Surprised, I raised my brows. The Stumps were always hungry.

Gunnar poked her with a mean glare.

Mrs. Stump pulled Baby Jane up from the table, smacked her face, and dragged her out of the kitchen and onto the porch.

Henny kept her eyes downcast. Gunnar had another helping of cucumbers. Mrs. Stump returned with a twitching mouth.

After a hushed supper, I collected the dishes and took them over to the sink. Gunnar and Mrs. Stump pushed back their chairs.

"Bring some coffee into the parlor," Gunnar called over his shoulder.

I got out a tray and two china cups along with the creamer and sugar bowl. "Here," I said, pouring the coffee and then handing Henny the tray, "help me carry this into the sitting room."

Henny walked turtle-slow out of the kitchen and into the long foyer. She glanced at the wall of sour-faced Royal ancestors and then up at the gleaming chandelier that she always loved and said she'd have someday. To me, it was one more useless thing to be dusted in this house of old things.

Henny's cups rattled on her tray as we entered the room and she fixed her eyes on the carved box on the mantel that I'd told her about.

Mrs. Stump and Gunnar sat side by side in two flowery wingbacks, waiting. Me and Henny breathed in the cool air of the window unit. I took the tray from her and set it on the small table in front of them, then nudged Henny to follow me out.

As I closed the pocket door behind us, Henny bubbled. "Sure is a pretty room. A family could live in a room like that. Y'all sure do keep it clean and all."

"Gunnar makes me keep it extra prissy for visits like today." Though there hadn't really been a *today* for at least a year that I could recollect, unless you counted the preacher . . . And I couldn't recall a time when Mrs. Stump sat *anywhere* but in the kitchen until today. More than anything, Gunnar wanted it pretty for visits with his departed wife.

"What's going on in there, Henny?" I asked when we were back in the kitchen and out of earshot. "Gunnar doesn't share a meal without good reason."

Henny picked up a dishtowel and wadded it in her hands. Dead air filled the room; then her shoulders shook. "It's . . . th-the well. It's gone dry again," she sobbed. "And Sister's baby is due this week. . . . We've plumb run out of space now that we're burstin' with twelve. Pa says a four-room house ain't made for thirteen and he's not about to bring bad luck down on the Stumps by giving it one more brat."

That was true. Everybody knew Jesus's thirteenth dinner guest was Judas and how that turned out . . . Even though Gunnar had helped Mr. Stump build a sleeping alcove onto the back of his cabin a few years ago, it was damn near hard to borrow air with twelve others stirring it.

"That damn well . . . it's *always* going dry," Henny cried.

"Oh, Henny, use ours," I offered. "The water truck stopped by last week—our cistern's full and our well has plenty. Heck, we have enough for the whole population of Nameless." *All 592 of them, if you counted the potheads and the Shake King dirt,* Gunnar would always say, adding, *we're surely living like royals*—a feeble joke about his last name and the middle name my parents had given me.

"It's hard, Roo. Pa won't help. Baby Jane's working for the Millers, and the little ones can't help. I have to tote the water back up the mountain all by myself. And 'sides, Gunnar don't like to share much. I can see it in his eyes when he catches me out there filling a bucket." She bit on her nails. "So Pa's been doing some big thinking."

I took the towel Henny was holding, and asked, "What'd that crazy daddy of yours do now?" Even though I was positive I didn't want to know.

A clap of the screen door and the fall of footsteps outside on the porch steps interrupted us.

"What's going on, Henny?" I yanked on her arm. "What's Gunnar and your mama up to?"

Henny turned to the window. "He's . . . Oh, Roo . . . It's Pa. He's sold Lena's baby." She blubbered and then latched on to me, squeezing tight enough to pop off my sun-bleached freckles.

Chapter 4

Outside, secrets gathered and piggybacked onto winds that raced under a heavy Kentucky moon.

I pried myself loose and leaned into the window. Henny's mama had her head bowed with Gunnar's, both of them whispering as they stopped along the back path. Head tucked low, Baby Jane lagged behind, spilling into their shadows.

Mrs. Stump took a paper from my uncle. Half-bent from years of baby making, she grabbed Baby Jane's arm and ambled slowly into the fields toward Stump Mountain.

I turned back to Henny. "W-what do you mean *sold?*"

"Pa . . . he's done sold Sister's baby to a Louisville couple who can't have kids, so he can buy an acre from your uncle. They're picking up the baby soon as she drops it."

"Dammit, Henny Stump, that's nothing to joke about." I scowled.

"Cross my heart." Henny dragged a big X across her chest, making her boobies pouf out like she always did when she wanted me to know she was a little older and trying to be smarter because she had me beat by time. Though, in truth, most everything around here was older in hill time. She held up her palm and traced two more X's to punch the swear, then lifted her hand and pressed it to mine.

I broke away. "Sold—"

"It's true, Roo. Pa's fixin' to have Ma work out a deal to use the three hundred dollars they pay him to buy land from Gunnar. We need more food, and the money can pay off our Feed Store credit and some things Pa needs . . ."

"Things?"

"His stuff." She shrugged.

His booze, I thought.

"Ain't his fault, Roo!" She read my eyes. "Them damn government men got his nerves all skinned up. He needs it, and just last week Baby Jane got a fever again and spread it to the babies."

"I can give her some of Gunnar's Bufferins," I said.

"Ma made her up a tonic of shine and wild cherry. But Baby Jane still won't eat and Ma had to fetch the granny woman."

"What's wrong? What did Oretta say?"

"She said there ain't enough fat on Baby Jane's bones. *Feed her more.* Used to be Ma couldn't keep her from eating. Now, she's having to whip her to get her to eat and stop spreading the fevers. But there ain't enough food, Roo. And it was only yesterday that we finally got the electricity turned back on. Ol' Kentucky Electric weren't gonna do it, but then we put it in one of the babies' names 'cause Pa done used up mine with 'em."

"Lordy . . . lordy-jones." I stacked my prayers.

"The baby'll be here soon . . . Coming on Lena's birthday."

"July twenty-six," I said without thinking.

"Twenty-seven," she corrected, and shot me a suspicious look. "Sister's birthday ain't till this Sunday."

Henny rested her head on my shoulder, sighed. "I'll never know my baby niece or nephew. The baby'll be doomed and won't ever have a sister 'cause the city folk can't have themselves babies. Oh, I can't imagine not having a sister, can you?" Her words spun in the air before crashing.

"*Sister.*" The word bruised my heart. Henny and Baby Jane were the sisters I never had. And Henny failed a grade, so we even shared the same teacher when she'd show up for school. But in the looks department, I didn't come close. Henny had curves like a stretch of Sunday road and a long, satisfying wiggle to call up a wolf whistle in a Saturday crowd down at the Feed & Seed. She was in a regular brassiere by ten, while I was still padding nothing more than a trainer, two months shy of turning sixteen.

About the only thing I had going for me was a pair of pretty dancing feet and a deep set of bluegrass-green eyes. "Same as my mama's," Mrs. Stump had said, and both "about as useful as a skipping stone in a collection plate," she'd added. Which Gunnar'd made sure to remind me after I'd dropped my prize rock in there one Sunday as an offering when I was six.

Henny patted my back. "I don't mean you, Roo. We'll always be sisters."

I thought of my sister, Patsy. What could have been if she had lived.

"Oh hell!" Henny said, seeing my face. "Look what I've done. Got ya thinking about her. I'm sorry, Roo."

I brushed off her apology and stuffed back the thoughts of Patsy.

"We's sisters. *Always,*" Henny said. "But it's bad this time. Every time Pa ends up in the pokey, he comes home with another big idea. This time he met up with another feller in there who told him about the baby-buyers. Pa says he won't take another twelve years of the government making him walk us kids to school. And Ma can't do it with the babies clamped to her teats."

"But he has to," I insisted. "Your littlest brother, Charles, and this new baby and the others can walk the paths together when the time comes. Maybe the baby's daddy can—"

"Nope, Sister still won't name the daddy, but she swears he'll take her and the baby away if Pa'd let her. But Pa told her no, that he wanted her around to help with chores when he gets his quit pay. Said he's quitting 'cause his hip bones have been scratched thin from walking the ridge. He's been having me write his letters again . . . Says them damn government men are gonna have to give him a donkey and disability pay 'cause it's all their fault."

Like most in Nameless, Mr. Stump had been in the "Happy Pappy" work program ever since President Johnson came and made jobs for the unemployed daddies and other hurtin' men around here.

"Maybe he can get another job with 'em," I said.

"Just 'cause Gunnar landed a good government job a'killin' convicts don't mean everyone can get so lucky, Roo."

I winced. I didn't think he was that lucky. Gunnar hardly talked about his old executioner job, not as a job anyway. Instead he talked about an old hanging—and how Kentucky was always messing up its executions. Talk that just seemed to make him more testy, and a little more bitter.

"I bet that city couple has a big house and there's a school on every street corner," I cheered, picking up a towel to dry the pots. "Maybe it's not such a bad thing for the baby . . . maybe even lucky." I glanced at her bare feet and hand-me-downs.

"What do you mean?" She flipped back her long wheat-colored hair, narrowed her sparrow-brown eyes.

I shrugged.

"I know'd you've seen more. Tell me—"

"No, I just forgot Lena's birthday. It's—"

"It's the Granny Magic, ain't it? Ya done seen something in one of your fortune-tellers about—"

"Don't say that. I've told you I am not a granny woman." I shivered at the thought of babies—childbirth.

I tried long ago to tell Henny about my fortune-tellers, the good guesses, the easy money from the kids wanting them—leaving out that I always folded the sheet of tobacco paper counterclockwise, drew on the pictures, and then put it inside Mama's snakeskin purse alongside her fortune-teller overnight to let it cure. Only then would bigger thoughts flow onto the fold-out paper designs I'd made.

No one had ever seen Mama's original, not even Gunnar. For years I'd missed it, then one day I cleaned out the purse and found me and Mama's fortune-teller sewn into a double layer of hidden lining. Still, Henny didn't listen, didn't want to believe my fortune-tellers weren't full of the woo-woo magic. I'd told her a dozen times that the only thing I could see was my own future out of this town that couldn't afford to claim itself properly on a map.

Last week, Henny'd begged for one of my fortune-tellers for the new baby. I'd sketched tiny pink and blue daisies all over the back of the paper, and a portrait of a swaddled baby in its center before folding it. Running out of thoughts and getting sleepy, I'd crimped the folds and tossed it into my mama's purse to cure. The next day, I'd looked under the four blank triangle flaps and drew a blue heart under the first, a fat pink heart onto the second and third, and then on the fourth apron fold, too. *Not* 'cause I had a premonition about the baby being a girl; not for any other reason than for running out of blue ink.

"Know ya want a fancy art place in a big town, but even Oretta says you've got the knowing," Henny said softly. "Hate to talk about it, but you ain't scared 'cause of what happened to your sister and ma—?"

"I don't care what that old granny witch says! I'm not going to be a hill charmer tethered to herbs and rock, staring at women's cooters, waiting for a baby to fall out," I grumbled. "Hoodoo won't buy you Honey Girl slips, you know . . . ?"

"Slips," Henny snorted.

"They've got them down in the Feed's mail-order catalog for two dollars and ninety-five cents. Didn't your mama ever have one?"

"C'mon, Roo, stop talking crazy. Ya know Ma wouldn't wear the devil's underwear. She says they look like what you'd dress them naked girls with on them little matchbook covers—"

"Important people wear them . . . Lady Bird . . . And, Rose said that elegant movie-star lady, Elizabeth Taylor, wears the prettiest slinky slips in the big motion pictures. It was in a movie picture called *Cat on a Hot Tin*—"

Henny crossed her arms. "Pa says Rose Law ain't nothin' but a dirty gypsy, and that 'spectable females shouldn't be sellin' trash out of the back of an automobile like that—"

"She's *not* dirty! She's a trader, and works hard. Rose has some nice things and really good books. And just the other day she gave me *The Great Gatsby*. Last month it was *Grey Maiden* by Arthur D. Howden Smith. After I read it, I gave it to Rainey and he liked it so much he read it twice."

"Ain't that the book you said had them swords—and them swashbuckler peoples?"

"Yeah, it was great. Rose gets the *best* books."

"Books is silly, Roo. Ya ran around here like a swashbuckler for a week and then got in trouble with Gunnar again when ya topped off more than the tobacco heads." She frowned.

"I gave you *Charlotte's Web* after Rose gave it to me. You said you liked it."

"Weren't nothing special." Henny rolled her eyes. "Some *stupid* pig, that's what Ma said. I say *some stupid spider*."

"Yeah, but you don't kill spiders anymore. And what about your '*oh, Danny, I love you*' book you couldn't stop reading?"

Henny's cheeks flamed. We'd found the *Man Hungry* paperback by Alan Marshall when Rose asked me to toss a box of junk into the trash down at the Feed. Henny had been with me, spotted the fireball novel and snatched it up for herself.

"You sure like Rose's ol' excitement books, and your Mama sure likes those wool long johns she gives her for the babies every year."

"Humph. Ma said Rose Law is so dumb she can't even catch herself a man. Now tell me about Sister's baby—"

I cringed. "Don't say that. Rose is smart and knows plenty about *everything*—books and movie stars and—"

Henny's eyes lit up. "Ma saw her, ya know? Saw that Elizabeth Taylor on a poster once when she visited my auntie over in Beauty, Kentucky. I sure would like to go see a real movie picture with you-know-who."

"Who?" I asked, relieved to talk about something other than Rose and babies.

"Carter Crockett." She smiled secretly.

"Crockett? Henny, no, he's a nineteen-year-old troublemaker. You know he quit school in seventh grade."

"That's because he's smarter than them old lesson books."

"What about his missing fingers?" Long ago, Carter's older brother, Digit, had cut off his trigger finger, then his middle one to dodge the draft. Weren't no time when brothers Carter and Cash decided they'd shuck honor and best their older brother: Carter sliced off both of his, then cut the tip off his left pinky, telling the officials a tall tale about corn pickers. Cash cut off his left pointer. And when Digit got out of prison with his hourglass tattoo, Carter'd tried to best his brother again, inking himself a big clock face with no hands across his arm, though Carter had never done anything big enough to do time in the big house, just the troublemaking stuff to land him into little town hoosegows. A little too much jaw-hawing out at the Gravel Road Lounge off Old Road 3.

"He's so brave." Henny sighed.

"I've told you that boy and his two brothers are tomcat mean. Their daddy killed Rainey's daddy and—"

Henny snapped her shoulders back and flared her nostrils for my attention. "Everyone knows that was an accident with Rainey's pa. Beau Crockett said it was the color blindness—he thought he was shooting a deer in them woods."

I shook my head. Gunnar thought different. He wholly despised the neighbors who lived on the other side of our farm. There'd been bad blood between the Crocketts and Royals for a long time. They were a low-life bunch, Gunnar said, and eighteen years later he still believed Beau Crockett intended on shooting Rainey's daddy because Gunnar gave the black family two acres of his land instead of selling it to the Crocketts.

"Carter is the cutest boy round these parts." Henny's pale cheeks spotted. "And just look what he gave me." She reached down under her collar and pulled out a necklace.

Beside his two other brothers, Carter Crockett had been the "cutest" until he turned twelve and dangerously handsome. Then something seemed to split off him inside, sucker out, and sprout straight *ugly*.

One hot Sunday when we kids took to the creek for an after-church social, Carter teetered along the bank watching. Nobody'd taught him how to swim, and he hated anyone who could, throwing his skipping rocks out, nipping skin if he could.

He'd sit on the grass, souring, him with a bunch of raccoon pecker bones dangling around his neck—showing off the newest hook-shaped charm that he'd gotten from his latest coon hunt—looking over the younger girls to favor one with the sweetheart gift so she'd hang it from her own neck and be his gal. He had at least five of those nasty coon penises hanging from a piece of old leather rope around his neck.

One particular kid, Billy O'Brien, took to water like birds take to sky. He could do a perfect backflip from the wooden plank nailed to the tree, and swing from the old knotted rope higher than anyone before flying out and landing in the deep end.

That day Carter lit a cigarette and paced back and forth, muddying a grassy path. After Billy did a double backflip, Carter called out, motioning him up to the bank near a thick knee-high stump.

Carter asked him to prove who was the toughest and waved his cigarette in front of him. But Billy brushed him off with a laugh. Carter insisted, taunting him with names; then he promised, "You win, Billy, I'll give you one of these here." Carter pointed to his necklace, lifted the longest coon bone, coaxing. "Look at the hook on this coon's pecker, boy. This here is my biggest and you can have it if ya beat me." Carter knelt down and laid his arm across the stump, wheedling an invite.

Billy had never learned to hunt, but he was sweet on a certain girl, so he took him up on the dare.

We gathered around as Carter clasped Billy's long, muscular forearm beside his bony one, squeezing them close. Then Carter took his lit cigarette, puffed hard, and snugged it between their joined arms, sizzling flesh.

Billy jerked. Again, and then again. Carter never blinked once. Billy screamed a few seconds in, jumped up, and scrambled into the creek, cursing and nursing the burn on his limp arm. But not Carter Crockett, nuh-uh, he was just getting started. With a hard smile, he picked up the cigarette, took a long, hot drag, and put it out atop the blistered hole on his arm for a good three seconds more.

* * *

Henny dangled the yellowing bone from a piece of twine. "Ain't too many boys can get you one of these." She flipped back her hair and I saw a fresh bruise on her neck.

I thought about Rainey and his red-blossomed clover ring.

Henny rubbed the necklace across her lips. "Can't wear it around Pa, but we's going together now."

"But he hits his girlfriends, Henny."

"Mary deserved that busted lip—"

"Like you deserved that?" I pointed to her neck.

She pressed a hand over the bruise, covering. "She deserved it, ya know she did. Carter said she made sweet eyes at another boy down at the Feed & Seed. And even Ma said she'd asked for it . . . And this"—she rubbed her neck—"is what I get for nagging. Now, c'mon Roo, ya got to tell me what you've seen about them baby-buyers." She stuffed the necklace back under the collar of her dress, patted.

"What? No, I-I'm trying to tell you I don't—" I looked into her hopeful eyes and hung my protests with the iron skillet on its nail board beside the stove, clattering the pots next to it. "Okay . . . okay, don't tell, but maybe I've seen something," I lied to cheer her. "City stores that have big bins of food, and giant buildings—buildings bigger than the Feed & Seed—as big as barns maybe. Everyone dresses pretty like—"

"*Lady Bird Johnson!* Oh, to be a First Lady of this here big ol' United States . . . Imagine." Henny sweet-toothed the thought.

I giggled. "Uh-huh, and with long, pearl-stitched gloves," I added, recalling a scene I'd snuck and read in one of Rose's excitement books in the back of her traveling trader next to the stack of girlie magazines and tonic cures.

"Will the baby grow up with two of everything?" Henny asked.

"*Two.*" I stretched my arm, wiggled an invisible glove over my rough, gum-stained hands. "And if it's a girl, the people will get her *two* Honey Girl slips . . . with Chantilly lace trim. Oh, and some soft nylons," I said.

"*Girl!*" Laughing, Henny raised the hem of her stain-spotted dress, rocked a bare leg, and teased out a silky line from Margaret Whiting's "The Money Tree." " '*That beautiful, lovely, wonderful money tree.*' " Henny whipped out an arm.

I hooked mine onto hers and we grabbed each other's waists, circled and sang.

Gunnar walked into the kitchen and slapped rubber gloves down onto the table.

"I wonder if they buy teenagers filled to the brim with sin," he said.

Chapter 5

W hat had gotten into me? By the look on Gunnar's face, I may as well have been do-si-do'n on the kitchen floor with Satan.

Fire flicked my ears at the thought of him overhearing my talk about unmentionables.

"I best go catch up with Ma." Henny colored, too, as she made to move past Gunnar.

"Not so quick," Gunnar said, sidestepping to block her. "You'll want to take these, Miss Stump." He picked up the rubber gloves. "Go ahead, take them with you."

"But Henny's still on laundry duty at the creek because she's been green with the 'bacco sickness," I protested. I knew Henny didn't like to work in the tobacco, and she was delicate and lately had gotten a touch of the greenies from the work. It didn't bother me much. But some folks said working tobacco was like smoking fifty cigarettes in one hour. And every time the dew was thick on the leaves, Henny claimed the moisture soaked her skin and made her head and belly hurt something awful.

Myself, I couldn't wear the gloves, any gloves. They sweated and chafed my hands, left 'em fiery hot and looking worse than the tar that stained them.

Henny took the gloves and nodded vigorously. "Yessir, I've been sick."

Gunnar pointed to her arm, reddened and tracked with tiny bumps. "Your mother said this was the only thing ailing you. A plain old poison-ivy rash."

Henny tucked her arm behind her back.

"You've been running my property lines with that Crockett boy," Gunnar said, "when I have been paying you to do field work. Since that doesn't seem to have any effect on your health, tomorrow morning you'll begin clearing that plot your pa's buying from me. Seven o'clock sharp."

Henny has been faking the tobacco sickness with poison ivy?

"So, is Mr. Stump selling the new baby?" I blurted.

Gunnar jerked his head toward me. "You would do wise to keep a *GodPretty* soul when your *weak* mind is tempted to meddle in others' affairs."

Henny clutched the new gloves, slinked past Gunnar. I heard her pounding down the porch steps.

Gunnar watched her from the front door. "That girl's got a mess of trouble on her tail. You'll not have her in the house anymore."

I gasped. "But, Gunnar, she's my best friend—"

"She's trash. Keep *it* outside."

I ran to the back porch. Henny was in a full run heading toward Stump Mountain. I stood there under the star-packed sky rubbing the panic pricking my flesh until I couldn't see her anymore.

When I came back in, Gunnar had gone off into the sitting room. I paused in the doorway and peeked in. He was talking to his wife, again. All five pounds of her. The weight of her ashes inside the hand-carved box he had sitting on the mantel, and I reckoned about the same weight as a bag of the Colonial sugar in the pantry. I'm sure he was souring Aunt Claire on his many, many disappointments in me.

I stepped back to go up to my room.

"RubyLyn," Gunnar said without turning. "Coming up on August . . . Do you think the tobacco needs a dusting, or is it too soon?"

Surprised because he never much asked my opinion, I said, "Reckon it could. It's been sixteen days since I did the last poison. Rainey's been seeing more of the hornworms. And I saw flea beetles moving up the stalks the other day."

"Why don't you oversee it."

"Yessir." I waited for any other instructions he might have, again surprised he wanted me to oversee anything.

"Those Stumps . . ." he began. "I've been helping them ever since I inherited this house. When it was just my folks' five acres. And I worked damn hard to buy up more land. Still do. But those Stumps"—he wagged a finger—"stopped working after the president came to Kentucky."

A lot of things had *stopped* around here. Gunnar'd stopped taking care of the house, stopped painting the boards, and stopped fixing up things inside.

"The Stumps," he said quietly, "will do better without an added mouth." He worried a finger along the edge of the wooden box before running his palm over it, straightening it just so. "Time for bed."

Upstairs, I pulled out the snakeskin purse and dug inside for Mama's fortune-teller to study my crayoned heart with its wiggly break struck through the center. *Why did I draw this when I was five? Maybe Henny was right . . . I'd been cursed with the Granny Magic. No . . . not true, dammit. . . . It was my art that would lead me out of this cursed town. And if that meant playing woo woo with the fortune-tellers, selling 'em and acting as matchmaker, I'd damn well continue. . . .* I bit the vow into my pillow.

I spent Friday alone in the tobacco field while Gunnar and Rainey drove over to the next county to look at a tractor. Henny still hadn't showed up in the fields. And on Saturday when Rainey hadn't made it over to the rows by seven, it looked like I might be working by myself again. I took the hoe to the vegetable garden, digging up weeds as fast as I could, then started over in the tobaccos, topping the flower heads.

It was eight thirty when Rainey finally showed up, whistling a tune, eyebrows reaching for the morning sun in an I've-stashed-a-secret sort of way. He put the catch bucket on the gathering table.

"Someone's in a light mood," I fished.

"Mm-hmm."

"And a little late," I said. "Done made it to the third row while I was waiting for you. I didn't spy any hornworms."

"And if you had?"

I grinned, happy to see him. We both knew I hated picking worms and fell into a puddle of wriggles if I had to touch one. It was the rules. *Our rules.* I'd easily toss out the field snakes Rainey was deathly afraid of, any snake, and he would pluck off the slimy green hornworms and throw them into the catch bucket for me. My daddy had lived with snakes and was never afraid of them. I guess that's why they didn't bother me much, and I could tell from the shape of the pupils and the coloring which snakes to take a hoe to and which to reach down for. Yet, I truly and fully despised touching the little hornworms.

"Did you see Henny in the backfield on your way over?" I asked.

Rainey looked over his shoulder toward Stump Mountain. "Sure did. What's that about?"

"Her daddy is buying a back acre with money he's supposed to get from some baby-buyers who live in the city." I dropped my voice to a whisper. "Henny said he's going to sell Lena's baby. I didn't want to believe it, but there she is, clearing Royal land to make it Stump land."

"Sell?" Rainey puzzled. "I thought I saw the midwife's truck going up Stump Mountain when I left this morning. *But hell . . .* selling a baby? Don't seem at all right."

"Midwife?" I looked anxiously toward the mountain. "Oretta's up there now?"

"Sure 'nuff . . . Humph, it's hard to believe Gunnar'd sell them land, but then I suppose it's better than letting it go to seed."

"They sure can use the food. Still, Gunnar's not talking and he's split me and Henny up. He got wind of her seeing Carter Crockett and decided he'd task her with setting her daddy's new plot. Likely be back there forever."

"*Crockett.* Ma said the sheriff was over there yesterday."

"That makes twice this week." I frowned.

"She saw Sheriff drive by with Digit Crockett in the backseat this time. Said the boy looked pretty busted up."

A garter snake slithered out of a row of tobacco to hunt and bask. Rainey startled and I stomped a foot to shoo it away. I knew snakes didn't hear like people, they felt their noise. I stomped twice more to scare it with the thumping. The creature flattened its head, forked a tongue, then took its sweet time to slide back into the plants.

"Those Crockett brothers are dumber than hornworms and just as slippery," I said.

Everyone knew the Crocketts scrapped at any excuse, their porch railings and boards bloodstained, full of jars of shine and piss beer—the brawls teetering, just begging to spill out into the muddied yard, lick the mountains with drunken curses.

Anytime the law went out to pick one of them up on a warrant, the rest of the Crockett clan lazed on their stick-railed porch, stoking, rooting the family member on to prove his namesake, until the lawbreaker would sidle up to the sheriff or his deputy and murmur the obligatory poke, "Ain't nothing personal, Sheriff, but you know I'm gonna have to fight ya before I can let ya take me to the can."

Rainey and I would slip over there and watch.

The sheriff might flip a coin with his deputy to see which one of them would roll up their sleeves. Other times, Sheriff would tease out the talk: stuffing himself a fat chaw of Red Man, fussing about not wanting to tear his clean britches, jawing on about the weather and such, or asking about each of the Crocketts—and how the rest of their kin were doing. Then Sheriff would wipe the tobacco spittle off his jaw, grin, and roll up his sleeves. The fistfight would be on while the rest of the Crocketts would sit back on the porch, hooting, sparking it further. After the scuffle, the offender would brag his injuries, surrender himself to the sheriff, and bid good-bye to his family.

"At least you don't have to worry about Cash anymore," Rainey teased.

I blushed at that. Cash was the only Crockett kin to get his full learning. His teacher even tried to get him into a college when he finished high school two years ago, but Cash wouldn't go.

Cash got sweet on me when I turned thirteen and decided to come calling. Flattering, since most girls three-mountains-wide were hot after him, but Gunnar wouldn't have it, even though Cash tried to get his permission first. And after chasing Cash off the land three times, Gunnar'd had enough.

My uncle took the pellets out of a shotgun shell and repacked it with rock salt. Then when he caught Cash sneaking around the house, softly calling for me again, Gunnar took his gun after him. Cash was the faster runner, but not faster than the rock salt stinging his hiney.

After that, Cash took off to the city.

Rainey stared off and turned quiet. I needed to get him back to his whistle.

"So"—I gently bumped his shoulder—"are you going to tell me where you were? It's not like you to be late."

His soft laurel-green eyes lit up and he reached inside his back pocket. Pulling out a long envelope, he tapped it across his hand. "Got my official greeting letter from the president. The postmistress had it waiting for me this morning, along with a package of catgut I'd ordered for my violin."

"Oh . . . that's . . . What did Abby say?"

"Even Ma can't boss the president, and she doesn't know yet. But if I know her, and I do, she will sit down and write him back a letter, giving a dozen reasons why my black hide can't go."

I nodded weakly, knowing Abby would.

"I'm outta here, RubyLyn. Ain't it swell? Says here I have to go get my army physical at the Nichols Army Hospital in Louisville. I can't wait."

"That's just . . . swell, Rainey. Swell." The cheer limped off my tongue.

"California, here I come."

"California?"

"Uh-huh. Going to Fort Knox for my basic, then I'll get my special training at Fort Ord on the big Pacific Ocean. That's where I'll train for jungle combat." He paused to study me.

"California's a far way from Nameless—Louisville—us," I whispered. *Us.* I tinkered with feelings. It felt right—a lot like my parents and what I remembered from them. The time they'd kissed. Mama'd swooped me up into their hug, and said, "There's nothing meaner than a bad man, and nothing sweeter than a good one, snugbug. When one as fine as your daddy comes along, you best latch on to him and get all God's goodness."

Even though I didn't understand most of it back then, I knew she thought my daddy was that fine one. And more and more I couldn't help thinking Rainey was mine. I suspected it long ago when he gave me the marriage promise. I felt it last winter when he brought hay bedding and milk for the gray barn cat's new litter, and I knew it every day in the long hours he worked, the strum of his violin, and the smile he saved for me. Now Rainey was off to other worlds that could only be seen inside Gunnar's old encyclopedias.

I glanced at Rainey, and said quietly, "I've read about other big towns. Even heard where a white woman and black man can hang together, where the black can shop with white folks, pray together, and even . . . marry and live together and stuff." My face flushed.

"Hard to believe." Rainey wrinkled his brow.

Hard to believe how big my feelings were growing for him. . . . Weren't no paper fortunes talking. It was my heart a'knockin' at something I didn't quite understand.

"Rose says it's true," I said.

"She would know . . . Be nice not having folks fuss at you— be like living a fairy tale, I imagine."

Then something else stirred. "Rainey, I've been hearing about all the foot soldiers coming home in coffins—the living ones missing legs, blind even—lots of bad stuff. You think about that?"

Rainey shook his head. "I think about getting away from Nameless more. Hell, girl, none of that stuff is gonna happen to me. They say they got bigger weapons and teach our soldiers how to fight even better now."

The look on Rainey hadn't changed. He believed all of it.

He peeked over his shoulder, then leaned in. "We both know staying here is as good as being dead . . . I'll get a leave after two months, Roo. Going to spend it in Louisville. And I'll have me some good pay, too."

"With my prize money for the 'bacco, I aim to live in Louisville. Maybe we can meet or . . ."

He reached out and snuck a breezy finger to my jaw, lighting skin, dizzying my mind. "I've been thinking about us lately— you," he said softly.

I searched his face.

Rainey tilted his chin down, put a hand on my shoulder. "I want to ask you—"

"RubyLyn! *Roo*," Henny hollered from behind us, silencing his question.

For a split second Rainey tightened his grip on me; then we broke apart, turning to see Henny running toward us from across the fields, flailing her arms.

"Roo . . . oh . . . hell . . ." She bent over and rested her hands on her knees, blowing out tiny breaths. "Sister's baby . . . the baby . . . it's coming. C'mon, Gunnar said to fill the buckets and help me get the water up the hill. Th-them baby-buyers are up there waiting—and we still don't have water."

"Lordy-jones!" I said, feeling sick and legs filling with sap. I sat down in the field. Henny jerked on my arm. "*Come on*, Roo, hurry!" she cried, shaking me out of my collapse.

"Roo, you okay?" Rainey stepped forward, concerned.

I found my legs, and we ran to Gunnar's barn and hauled out the buckets to the pump in the side yard. After we'd filled them, Rainey toted two, and me and Henny lagged behind him carrying one each up the mountain.

That no more than fifteen-minute walk uphill turned into thirty minutes, what with trying to keep our water from sloshing out of the buckets along the narrow rutted trails. The new baby, Rainey's lost question, and what lay ahead kept me company.

The hill swelled under our feet as we dragged ourselves

through scents of pine, damp leaves, and ragged breaths of silence. At the first switchback we passed a shiny green station wagon with wood paneled doors parked next to the old pickup that belonged to midwife Oretta. We stopped to stare a minute and flex our hands.

Out of the corner of my eye I saw Mr. Stump over on one of the trails. I wondered if he was hunting squirrel or rabbit for his family's supper.

Gunnar said Mr. Stump wasn't much of a worker, or hunter for that matter, just a blowhard mostly. Mr. Stump liked to boast that the government worked it out to let him draw the "Pappy Pay" after he groused once too often about the one-and-a-half-mile hitch his kids had to walk to get to school. And when they couldn't get a school bus to ride up his ridge, he'd flat out told them his kids weren't going. Mr. Stump spent most of '68 being fined, and when he didn't pay the fines, jailed. This year the government came up with a "solution" to feed the Stump bellies and brains: *During the school year Mr. Stump would get up at six to walk his children to school and then collect them at three.* This made for one happy pappy, who earned just shy of three hundred a month for walking his kids to and from school and idling around moonshine stills along the way back home.

Rainey bumped me lightly, pushing me onward.

When we reached the Stumps' house, Henny's brothers and sisters were playing loudly on the long raised porch propped on stilts.

I climbed up, stepping high over the tall weeds shooting out between each board. I set my water down near a broken porch board and the kids swarmed the bucket, cupping their hands to dip up water, slurping, splashing, and taking turns to stick their blackened feet inside.

Baby Jane stood back from the others, wiping a puddle of worry off her face. I motioned to her. She rushed to my side. "Best get, Baby Jane." I squeezed her shoulder and gently pushed her toward the steps. Unsure, she clutched my skirt.

"Go on." I nudged again. Reluctant, Baby Jane took off.

Beside the ratty screen door, a man wearing glasses with a dark jacket hanging over his arm and polished black shoes and a woman wearing a yellow summer dress sat on wood crates. The woman had one of those fine city faces, like a Hollywood movie star in Rose's magazines. She held a small green knitted blanket, her hands balling up an edge, over and over, while the man sat with one leg perched over the other, kicking at the air.

Two bony dogs, long robbed of their tail wags, shared the shade of the porch, not bothering to rise to sniff a greeting.

Mrs. Stump pushed open the screen door, stepped out, and clapped her hands, shooing away the noisy kids. One of the toddlers rubbed his sunken belly, crying for food. The older ones scattered off into a cluster of scraggly pine, and the tucked-tailed dogs skittered away.

Rainey set down his buckets and helped three of the smaller, barefoot and bare-butt kids off the porch. One of them slapped away Rainey's hand and tumbled headfirst onto the ground. When the boy screwed up his red face to croon his injury, Mrs. Stump raised a warning finger. He took off wailing toward the woods.

Rainey said, "Best get back to work now."

I nodded readily. "Me too."

"Let's go," Henny sang out.

Mrs. Stump shook her head and pointed. "Henny, stay put. *You* go, boy. And, *you*"—she stabbed a finger my way—"c'mon inside and haul one of them buckets in with ya."

Henny kicked a protest into the dirt.

"Me?" I asked, wanting real bad to hightail it straight out of here, far away from any business of birthing and baby-buyers.

"Roo"—Rainey looked at me—"want me to wait for you?"

More than anything I wanted him to.

Mrs. Stump lifted a hanging metal cup off the tarpapered wall beside the screen door and shook it at Rainey. "Keep your ass to the rows, darkie. Ain't got no business around us white females!"

I winced, knowing most folks around here felt that way, even the ones who the town thought beggarly. Once, Mrs. Stump whipped Rainey with a tree branch when she spied him rescuing one of her daughters after the little girl took a bad tumble in the creek. Gunnar saw it from his tractor and hurried over with me running alongside him. He snatched the switch out of Mrs. Stump's hand, then swatted Rainey once on the behind with it, then again, saying, "I'll take care of him, Mrs. Stump."

He gave a tongue-lashing to Rainey on touching white females, then on the way back, Gunnar'd quoted President Johnson like he always did, mumbling more to himself than to me or Rainey, " 'If you can convince the lowest white man that he's better than the best colored man, he won't notice you're picking his pocket. Hell, give him somebody to look down on, and he'll even empty his pockets for you.' "

Gunnar'd looked at me, and said, "Mighty knowledge in that, maybe even some of the Lord Almighty's thoughts in there," and then he'd repeated them twice more as we walked back across the field, and every time Rainey ran afoul with white folks like the Stumps.

Mrs. Stump banged the cup against the wall, startling the man and woman. "Git," she snapped at Rainey.

I snuck a finger toward Rainey's tucked hand. "See you back at the rows."

Rainey didn't dare touch it. *Good night,* he barely mouthed, a faint wiggle in his pinky.

Mrs. Stump glowered, then looked at the couple who now had their round eyes set on me. "Mr. and Mrs. Emery, it won't be much longer now." She handed them the mug. "Fetch yourself some water if ya need to." Looking around, she yelled, "Henny, where'd ya go? . . . Git in here!"

Out of the corner of my eye, I watched Henny slip into the woods.

Chapter 6

Mrs. Stump caught the folds of my long cotton dress and pulled me inside before I could protest. Not four feet from the screen door, Lena was stretched out on the floor atop a stained tick-striped mattress, whimpering. Another long mattress butted up to the far wall, and a sagging brown couch missing a leg hugged another. The little air in the room was soured with mash, hotly baked, and stirred by the youngest Stump boy, Charles. The one-year-old slobbered out a lost tune as he crawled back and forth across the blackened wood floor.

Above, a single bulb added to the harsh light spilling across the kneeling midwife, who hovered over Lena. She dabbed at Lena's mouth with a whiskey-soaked rag and spoke softly. "C'mon. You gotta let this baby go, girlie. *Push*," Oretta urged.

Lena cried out, "I ain't giving away my baby. I ain't—" She lifted her head, clutched her belly, and grunted. "No—"

Mrs. Stump bent over Lena and hissed. "Wouldn't have to if you'd drank the pennyroyal I brewed ya—"

"I couldn't kill it, Ma," Lena sobbed.

"Humph," Mrs. Stump grunted. "Do as Oretta says, or we'll lose you both. And we sure don't need no law snooping round up here."

As far as I knew, nobody had come meddling around here or even cared about the three baby graves set out back marked with tobacco sticks, and the one full-sized grave that showed up in the spring that no one talked about.

Mrs. Stump knelt down behind Lena's head and slipped her hands under her daughter's back, pulling her up to a half-sitting position. "That baby's gonna have a birthday *today*. Push."

Oretta scooted down to Lena's feet, grabbed her ankles, and shoved her legs upward.

"No!" Lena screamed, kicking, crossing her legs tightly. "He—he's coming back for us, Ma. *He is.* . . . We's getting hitched, Ma, swear. I'm getting a dress—"

"You'd be trading that hitchin' dress for a mourning dress if I get ahold of him," Mrs. Stump spat.

"Where's Pa? He said . . . he said maybe I could keep it. I'll find it food," Lena breathed. "I will."

Mrs. Stump bared her broken teeth. "Your pa's busy working hard to feed ya—and you can keep it all right: long enough for it to get outta there and get its starch. *Push.*"

Little Charles stopped crawling, sat up, and began to suck earnestly on his thumb.

I moved closer to the door. I'd seen animals give birth: Gunnar's barn cat, even a field mouse birthing nine mice no bigger than my pinky, but never a woman other than my mama. I didn't see it exactly, but I was close enough that day to feel it in my dreams at night. And over the years folks had done enough whispering about Mama dying after she tried to give me a baby sister.

Some blamed Daddy, and hushed talk around town was the Scripture had sent her to an early grave. But Scripture never killed anybody back then . . . not since the Crusades anyway. Still a few said that a broken heart took her after Daddy got to handling a demon bigger than his nasty snakes. The only thing I knew was after Daddy died, Mama seemed to be sleepwalking during the day, and sometimes no matter how hard I yanked on her, or cried for her to stop, I couldn't shake her awake.

Lena thrashed, gusted out a tight yelp between her teeth. Terrified, my knees knock together. I rested my forehead against the doorjamb, trying to gulp down more air.

Oretta closed her eyes and chanted a prayer of sorts. For a second I caught a foggy glimpse of my daddy's long-ago tent revivals, the frenzied prayers swirling, hissing. When Mrs. Stump joined in, I felt myself buckling.

Oretta rushed to my side and pressed a cloth full of sharp, smelly herbs to my nose, burning, shooting me back upward.

That the Stumps were using prayers to birth the baby instead of the old town doc and his medical bag scared me for reasons I couldn't understand.

I pushed Oretta away, flattened my face against the door to shove back the darkness.

"RubyLyn, this ain't the time for hysterics! Tell Lena 'bout that couple out there," Mrs. Stump ordered.

"Huh? What?" I tried to shake myself out of the haze.

"The premonition!" Mrs. Stump bit. "Where's Henny? *Henny!* . . . Henny gave us the fortune-teller and done told me what ya saw—said you even seen it'd come today—now tell Lena about the Emerys."

"Today's July 26? *Oh!*"

Lena moaned and looked up at me with a dirty, tear-soaked face.

My eyes filled at the thought of her losing her baby. "No, Mrs. Stump, I—"

Lena blew out a string of yips.

I peered out the screen, into the tree line, and took several short breaths. "Uh . . . well, the Emerys and the baby . . . er, the baby *girl* . . ." *Like Patsy,* I thought. *Is it a lie if I wished it?* I tried to get a glimpse of the couple by pressing my face flat to the screen, but all I saw were the man's and woman's legs shooting up and down. "The Emerys have lots of food," I said softly, squeaking open the screen and sneaking a better look. "Lots."

Mr. Emery held up his glasses, wiping the lenses with his hankie, inspecting, rubbing, then inspecting again. Mrs. Emery leaned out from behind her husband and locked eyes with me. I couldn't get a sense of anything, except maybe they were wondering if they really wanted to take this baby, take it far away from this place.

Lena screamed out again, twice, and a third time. Oretta sang, "Good, good, good," at each holler.

I heard a baby's faint cry.

"A girl," Oretta announced, lifting up the baby. "Nubs all here and the mama'll be fine." The midwife tugged at the baby's toe. The baby girl let out a strong squall as if in agreement.

I sagged against the door, relieved.

Mrs. Stump moved over to Oretta and took the baby.

"Ma, give me my baby." Lena sniffled, raising her arms. "My baby . . ."

Mrs. Stump carried the baby past her daughter, into the kitchen's doorway, and quickly dipped her into a bucket of water.

Then Lena's mama smacked the baby's behind and brought the crying infant to me. "Give the baby to its ma and pa."

My hands were dirty, stained from the fields. I pressed myself against the screen.

"Git on with it." Mrs. Stump jerked her head toward the porch, shoving the tiny, naked baby into my arms.

The baby felt cooler than the hot air and slippery like a horn-worm. Shaking, I pushed open the screen with my knee and slipped out.

Lena began weeping softly behind me.

Oretta said, "You ain't done just yet, girlie. Push a little more to get the rest of it out of you. C'mon now."

I stood still on the porch in the softness of a warm mountain breeze, feeling everything and nothing. The shade and silence numbing. The baby mewed and thrust up her tiny pink fist.

Inside, Lena cried out, "My baby, *my baby*."

The couple got up off the crates. Mr. Emery slowly put on his glasses. Mrs. Emery had her wide blue eyes fixed to the baby.

Lena's cries grew louder, turning into broken sobs, pleading, "Let me just hold her, please, Ma, let me see her . . . just once. Just one kiss. Oh, *please* let me hold her just one time."

Mrs. Emery opened the green blanket toward me and scooped the baby into her arms. "She's perfect. *Perfect.* Let's call her Eve," she whispered, lifting up the baby to her husband.

With a hesitant hand, Mr. Emery touched the baby's hair, then leaned over and kissed his wife's cheek. "Eve," he echoed.

They stood there together, huddled over Eve, laying soft words between Lena's sobbing ones. "RubyLyn, bring me back my baby. *RubyLyn . . .*"

Clutching long sticks, two Stump boys wandered into the yard with their two-year-old sister tagging behind. The boys stopped under the half-broke birch to poke holes in a hanging hornet nest.

"Please . . ."

Baby Jane sat on a rotted log, waiting, tearing at her nails. She jumped up and ran to my side, clutching my dress. Blindly, I shook her off.

"Oh, please . . ."

Ten-year-old Ada Stump walked out of the woods, striking matches and throwing her lit sticks toward the cabin.

I stepped off the porch and set out onto the downhill trail.

"Nooo . . . RubyLyn . . ."

I turned around and looked at the shack built with its loose-lip promises and dreams that wouldn't carry past its tarpaper walls—sitting there wedged between rock and a shallow well and the stinking two-seater outhouse in the woods.

Overhead, a hawk called out and quieted. Lena's pleas bubbled out of the tiny house and stirred the still mountain.

I didn't stop when I spotted Mr. Stump, half-hidden, slumped against a tree, tipping back a bottle of Old Crow.

Halfway down the mountain, I glanced back once. Mr. Emery and his wife and new baby followed behind me. Protectively, Mr. Emery wrapped an arm around his wife's small waist, hitching the hem of her pretty yellow dress.

A slinky slip the color of skin hung a few inches below it.

Chapter 7

I'd never owned anything as fancy as a yellow dress, but a snip of her apple-green one sewn to the left pocket of my quilt jacket reminded me Mama'd worn one just as pretty to his tent revivals. And when both my folks still had the starch to stand upright, Mama would swish those green skirts my way and teach me the Patsy Cline songs to sing to my sister. Her, always declaring when the child was born, the baby would have her favorite singer's name. I remembered Mama had insisted she could tell it was a girl early on by the way her belly hung.

I had been so excited that I'd paraded around, crooning those songs in my prettiest five-year-old voice so I could sing them real good for our Patsy—especially the "Walkin' After Midnight" song, Mama's favorite. And even after Daddy left, I kept singing.

The day Patsy was born, an old woman pulled me off the porch where I'd been waiting and rushed me into Mama's dark bedroom. Teary-eyed and looking more sleepy than usual, Mama'd cocked her head to the tiny bundle in her arms and made me promise I would always look after Patsy and sing sweet songs to her. She quoted a Bible verse about *giving joyful noises to the Lord,* asking me to quote it back, and then said, "Remember, the strongest prayers are in song."

Seeing Mama's tears like that made me cry, too. And I'd hugged her and given my promise right away. Then the old woman shooed me from Mama's side, pushed me out before I had a chance to hold my sister.

A cord-cutting not unlike what Oretta had done minutes ago.

Weren't no time after Mama's passing when a small lady in a severe dark dress and veiled hat showed up and took me and my sister away to a big shadow-filled building called County Catholic Orphan Asylum.

Inside, the lady gave Patsy to someone else who disappeared with her. I'd screamed for my sister until the black-veiled lady ended up switching my legs till they burned.

They said Patsy died in her sleep the second night there. Gunnar came for me and took me to her and Mama's funeral.

At the graveyard, the preacher called upon prayer, then after a bit of quiet, talked about Mama and Patsy and more prayer. When he told the small crowd of folks to "fill the parting with joy," I tried to sing loud, wildly crying, shouting Cline's melodies into the dirt for her and Patsy like she'd taught me—making the *joyful* noises and hoping to rouse them.

The preacher'd stopped the service and looked to my uncle. Gunnar hissed something and jerked on my shoulder. I tried to hush, but the song kept bubbling up inside.

My sister and Mama never heard, only a bobwhite that called back in low whistles. When it was over, Gunnar pointed to his truck and I lagged behind with the Cline song low in my chest, kicking up the clay and the bobwhite who'd burst into flight and carried it off for his own. I watched the gray-mottled bird lift its fat body into the sky until Gunnar yanked my arm and pulled me to his side. It was the last time I'd sung Patsy Cline.

After their funeral Gunnar dropped me back at the orphanage.

For two more weeks I lived with a bunch of other kids in the orphan asylum. I'd cried buckets until one day Gunnar came back.

"Is there no one else, Mr. Royal?" the same lady wearing the same black dress pushed.

I sat on the hard chair next to Gunnar inside a small office, swinging my nervous legs.

"I am someone, and the *only* one," he answered.

She asked him lots more questions about church—religion—

and faith healing. With each of Gunnar's answers, her mouth cramped until it looked like her stretched lips might crumble like bad bricks.

"We feel she should be baptized Catholic right away—the one and only true faith," the woman said. "It's your duty and the only way to rid her of her parents' demons."

Gunnar's jaw twitched on his reddening face. "No better than serpent faith. I'll raise her as I see fit," he growled, "and not with your idol-worshiping statues, hoodoo candles, and Latin tongues!"

My knees slapped each other, hammered up and down. Faster and faster. The room got quiet; then the lady flattened her bone-white hands on the desk. She asked for "papers" the way Gunnar sometimes talked about having a title paper for an automobile trade. Without missing a beat, she'd grabbed a switch beside her chair, reached over, and lit my wild legs with it. Gunnar slammed his fist down on her desk and stormed out, leaving me bawling.

A long week would pass before he returned with some papers that he gave the lady in exchange for me.

I remembered being a little scared and curious about the tall man I'd only glimpsed a handful of times. But that day, I clutched his big hand, eager to escape the grim-looking lady.

Even though living with Gunnar had been a nightmare, those weeks inside the orphan asylum proved no fairy tale either. Still, I had to wonder if it might've been better if he'd left me.

Right away his big house struck me as too big for only him and me. Mama and Daddy had a small home with useful things that didn't have a particular place. Gunnar's house was high and mighty with stuff collecting a gray dusty death in darker spots. Flashes of fancy linens, silver and china in fancy floral wall-papered rooms that nodded a power over the visitor, but never got used. Worse was the firefly quiet, no radio, no song, supper chatter or laughter, just grunts and grumblings, his heavy footfall, and the clinking bourbon bottle. Wasn't but a week in his house when I'd started to miss the sound of the other orphan kids.

* * *

Picking up my step, I tried to put more distance between me and the Emerys.

I caught myself humming "Walkin' After Midnight" as I swept down the mountain's second switchback, pounded the verses down and around the next, and another, until I was helplessly screaming the chorus past the Emerys' shiny automobile and all the way to the bottom of Stump Mountain.

I couldn't stop now that I had it back. The song looped, grated the rawness inside me like the day I'd lost them forever and the graveyard bird had stolen the old song for good.

" '*I'm always walkin' after midnight searching for you!*' " I barked on Royal land until hot tears bent me over, slapped at my rocking shoulders.

I thought about Mr. Stump slowly dying from the drinking same as my daddy.

I prayed for baby Eve to live.

I wondered if Lena would forever feel the cord-cutting like me, and where her angry fist would land someday, somewhere, on some other road out of here.

Lifting the hem of my dress, I fanned my hot face, wiped my eyes. Blinking, I caught a glimpse of rustling through the trees on the side. I straightened, shaded my eyes against the sun's glare, and spotted Carter Crockett's red ball cap bobbing, flashing against the leaves like a lightning bug.

Henny called out to me and came running from a thicket in the other direction. She latched hold of my arm. "What happened?" she asked, out of breath. "Tell me about the baby—"

I jerked away. "Not telling you nothing, miss mouth-of-the-south. You told your mama, and *I* got stuck with the cord-cutting! How could you?"

"Cord—what? I swear I didn't know she'd make ya stay like that. I knows how scared you is of birthing after your ma died of it and—"

"Shut up, Henny! You don't know nothing—NOTHING—slinking off just like your no-good daddy."

Mr. Stump wasn't worth two hoots and I was beginning to wonder if Henny would ever be.

"I-I'm sorry." Henny touched my shoulder.

I pushed her hand off. "I can't wait to get away from you and this damn town." Fresh tears stung my eyes.

"C'mon," she pleaded, "we's sisters—"

"Don't." I pointed at her. "*Don't* talk about sisters when you weren't even there for your *own*."

"Listen, Roo, I had to tell 'em. *Had to*. Sister—"

I narrowed my eyes.

"L-Lena said she'd run away. Run—"

"Like you did with that no-good Crockett today?"

She tossed a guilty glance over her shoulder. "It's true, Roo. Lena said she was fixin' to run off. Pa couldn't have her doing that, 'cause then the law'd be up there and ya know how the law is? So I thought if I told her how nice them baby-buyers was, ya know, that pretty fortune-teller, what all was on it . . . well, she'd see differently—"

"Well, Henny?" I said, scissoring my fingers in the air. "I'm predicting you ain't never gonna see your baby niece, Eve. *Ever!*"

"Roo . . ."

The Cline song punched in my chest, snuck back into my throat, vibrating the dangly grape that hung there. I took off as fast as I could, winding myself before it could roll off my tongue, ignoring her shouts close behind me.

When I spotted Rainey and Gunnar talking in the tobacco, I cut through the rows closest to the house and ducked inside to the bathroom. I couldn't let them see my face. And knowing about Rainey leaving would make it worse. Resting my hands on the sink, I bent my head and thoroughly damned the song, the day, and everyone in it.

I was still spotted and red-faced when Gunnar knocked on the door about ten minutes later. I reached for a cloth to dry my face, stopped and thought better of using my aunt's pink company's-coming towels. Using my arm, I wiped my eyes, and said, "A minute, Gunnar."

"Hurry it up."

"Okay."

Not three seconds later he was back at the door. "*Hurry it.*"

I walked into the kitchen.

"You've wasted enough time at the Stumps'," he grumbled over his coffee cup.

"Wasted?"

He raised his brow slightly.

"I worked all morning helping the Stumps, Gunnar."

He set down the cup and glared. "You *wasted* all morning on the Stumps."

I squinted back at him. "I can't wait to get out of here."

"You'll get back to your chores."

"I broke my back toting water up the mountain and then I had to—"

He shot his hand into the air, and railed, "I've been breaking my back teaching you this land day and night so you can go to agriculture college in Lexington and take over one day."

I flipped inside. He'd never told me . . . all this time acting like I was a work mule, *a stupid work mule.* "You've been working me to a death closer than my time, Gunnar. I can't even stop and draw a little, or read none—"

"*I* will assign your reading."

"Done read every book on your shelf. Even the encyclopedia ones, twice. You get to read your *Old Judge Priest* books . . . many as you want, even." Gunnar loved the old wisecracking Kentucky author, Irvin Cobb, who'd written the funny stories. And he'd collected almost every one of his sixty books, stacks of 'em. I knew when he was reading them in his room, too, because I'd catch him chuckling late at night when he said he was turning in early to brush up on *The Good Word.* In the morning, I'd make his bed and find one of Cobb's books shoved under a tossed blanket.

"Gunnar, I like to read funny stuff, too, different stuff, and my teacher said *all* reading makes you smart and—"

Pinking, Gunnar smacked the table with his open hand. "You'll not read trash and you'll not use good paper on trash."

He slammed the jar of bitters down onto the table. And like always when his hands went smacking and thumping, I knew trouble was coming. I shrank back, and he grabbed my arm and shoved me into the kitchen chair.

I covered my jaws with my hands. "My . . . Gunnar, no, my jaws are still burning from the last time," I said, shaking. "It'll eat a hole in my tongue—"

"Hope to God it'll nip the sass in it this time."

"M-my teacher says my art is good, and I'm going to take it to the city one day—"

"Art . . . ?" he snickered, shaking his head. "Is that what you call those damn fortunes you make, all about who's going to kiss whom and far worse? You're going to end up like your snake-charmer pa if you're not careful."

"I'm going to *end up* far away from you," I lashed back.

I hated when he talked like that. My daddy weren't no snake charmer. He was a good preacher, folks had said, and despite Gunnar telling me he was a drunk.

My daddy was smart enough to make snakes lie down quiet. I pushed back the squeaking thoughts that said otherwise. *Why couldn't he have done the same with his demons?*

Chapter 8

Idyll days of August brought no peace to my bone-jumping demons. Nightmares of babies wouldn't stop. And the idea of Rainey leaving me here alone in the tobaccos was more than I could stand. The notion of him coming back wounded or worse, unbearable.

Evenings, I stretched the daylight into dark, escaping the bad dreams by working on my sketches, drawing cities and everything I imagined there. I studied book covers and thought about the piles of books I'd pored through in the back of Rose's truck. One morning I got up the nerve to show Gunnar my new drawings. I thought if he saw them on Rose's official artist pad, he might soften some, maybe even like them a little. But he'd pushed me away, calling them ugly, and I turned back to the fortune-tellers.

When I was sure Gunnar was asleep, I stole downstairs into the sitting room to get the tobacco paper for the fortunes.

Tonight, I eased open Gunnar's secretary drawer again. I looked over my shoulder at the tall bookcase beside the fireplace. Gunnar loved to see me reading, as long as it was the Bible or what he thought I should be reading. He called himself a learned man after getting one year of college in before his mama passed—the doing that brought him back to Nameless.

I snatched sheets of the tobacco paper out of his secretary, pressed them to my face, inhaling. Old man Graydon Turner made the paper for us once a year, pulping some of Gunnar's tobacco stalks to produce it. He'd let me watch him once and then gave me a stack of my very own, despite Gunnar objecting and saying it would be wasteful for my silly drawings.

We'd gone into Mr. Turner's barn and watched him chop up the stalks and mix it all into a huge vat. He cooked it like soup, stirring, fussing over it. After, he would strain dirt off the stock, then mixed in a little bleach to whiten and some starch to size. He poured the mixture into large screened pans where he let it dry with a woodstove and fans. Mr. Turner delivered the first rolled-up batch to Gunnar and sold the rest to the Feed & Seed. I loved the light brown speckled paper, its rich pipe tobacco smell.

I tiptoed back up to my room and snipped out a square to make myself a kissing fortune. I peered out the window. Gunnar's old tobacco barn sagged to its shadows and seemed to buckle into the earth. I drew the barn, detailing and shading just right, down to the tender poppies that hugged its weathered oak boards.

I cut out another square of paper for someone else. I crimped the creases counterclockwise. Carefully, I sketched another barn and an automobile, adding chickens onto the special fortune-teller with some pretty tail feathers, fat wattles, and fancy combs. I drew a tiny basket onto the last fold. After an hour of shading and perfecting the hens and basket, I pressed it to my heart, then put it inside Mama's pocketbook to cure along with mine. All my heartache seemed to disappear with it, leaving me lighter, and the tangled thoughts of the baby business and Gunnar's meanness gone.

Moonlight painted soft stripes across floors and I placed the purse on the sill to bask in its beams. Gunnar dared not come into my room. He considered it a breach of Southern manners, and had never once crossed the threshold since he brought me here. Knocking or yelling from outside the door was his calling card, but still I had to be careful; you never knew with a smart, eagle-eyed executioner.

I fell asleep only to wake hours later in a sweat of tightly tangled sheets. I sat up and rubbed my face. It was wet from tears. I'd been dreaming of Patsy and heard her crying, and in the background there had been another noise: hens cooing.

Despite it being the first night of August, I pulled on my quilt jacket and buried myself deeper under the covers.

Before the first sparrows could gather in the bushes, I slid out of bed, wishing I could slide right back in and take what my dreams had cheated me of. Shaking off the slumber, I dressed, smiling as I stuffed a tiny cheesecloth-wrapped package full of seeds into my pocket. Then I took Mama's purse off the windowsill, pulling out the fortunes I'd made.

My finest, especially the one with the chickens. I felt hopeful. And as usual, more thoughts flowed and I took my pencil to each of the flaps, writing two names on the one I would keep and only one name onto the other I would give. I slipped them under the seeds in case Gunnar had his sneaky eyes on.

But Gunnar was gone. He must've left early to work in the barn, so I hurried into the kitchen, grabbed a piece of bread, slathered on butter, and downed it. I buttered two more pieces, then stuck them inside my old Three States tobacco tin that Gunnar'd given me to scrub and use for my lunch pail.

Dawn gathered in the hills as I sat down on a quilt next to a tobacco row and worked the latest paper fortune-teller I'd made, stretching my thumbs and pointing fingers inside the four-pocket slits. Every minute or so I would stop, cock my ears, or look around for my uncle.

Landing on number six, I opened the triangle flap and peered inside at the boys' names. *Rainey*, it predicted. "Bur Hancock, three, Rainey Ford, four," I whispered, and let my fingers gallop the folds again. I blew wisps of hair off my sticky forehead, the humidity making them clump. "Rainey, six, Bur, five," it read.

"One more Rainey . . . c'mon *seven*." I closed my prayerful eyes and mumbled, lighting into the fortune-teller again, knowing I wouldn't be satisfied until I reached my favorite number—seven—feeling foolish and carefree, but enjoying the tiny break before another long working day.

Startled by the sound of rustling grass, I twisted around. Baby Jane Stump circled a tobacco stalk. The sun rose over the mountain behind her, sending fog-soaked rays tumbling to the fields.

I blew out my breath. "You scared me, Baby Jane." I squinted up at her, gathered Gunnar's old shirt tight across my chest. "Quit sneaking around like that. I thought it was Gunnar. Lordy-jones, you nearly popped the hairs off my head." I smoothed down the apron covering my long dress and picked at the fabric with shaky hands. "What are you doing down here so early on Saturday? It's not even eight yet."

I stuffed my fortune-teller into my pocket, annoyed that I'd been interrupted before landing on "seven."

"I h-have to be at the Millers' early now. They told me to come early starting in August. And I—I wanted to be sure and see you 'fore your uncle made it out."

"How's Lena?" I couldn't help asking.

She looked away nervously. "M-Ma says Sister's got the baby weeps."

It looked like Baby Jane had been crying, too. She dropped her empty basket beside me and sat down.

I reached inside my pocket and pulled out seeds I'd been waiting to give her. "For your mama's fall garden," I said, placing the tiny cheesecloth package into her hand. "Tell her there's twelve rutabagas. And ten turnip seeds and fourteen carrots." I had to fib to Gunnar and tell him the price for feminine protection went up at the Feed & Seed.

Baby Jane stuck them inside her pocket, and murmured, "I like the rutabagas, 'specially like you cook 'em, mashed and all."

"Grow 'em and I'll make you another dish."

Baby Jane tapped my shoulder, dangled a rubber band. "Do my hair today?"

I took the rubber band. "Don't I always do your hair? But you need to learn to do it yourself, Baby Jane, in case I'm not here . . ." I thought about the city.

"You do it best, RubyLyn." She turned around, swept her light brown hair over her small shoulders.

"Are you hungry?" I asked, combing my fingers through her locks. "Brought you some buttered bread."

Baby Jane coughed and shook her head.

"Heard you had the fever. Feeling better?"

"Uh-huh. Ma gave me the coal oil."

Mrs. Stump couldn't afford the town doc and relied mostly on concoctions of coal oil mixes and homemade brews from the bark of wild cherry trees and roots she'd have Henny dig up.

Gunnar preferred his medicine potions of bark, root, and coal oil, too, over the doc's visits. Most hill folk did. Once when I was little and couldn't shake a bad cold, Gunnar'd fed me heaping spoonfuls of coal oil and molasses for two weeks.

I brushed bangs away from her eyes, wishing I had a pretty ribbon. Scooping her hair up into my hands, I began braiding it for her like I did most mornings. When I was done I reached into my dress pocket and pulled out the special fortune-teller I'd made for her last night.

Baby Jane's eyes widened and a smile rosied her cheeks. "My own kissing fortune," she said.

"Too young for kissing fortunes, and this is way better," I fussed. "You're barely eleven and there's a reason I mark them G for grown-up. See?" I pulled out my own fortune-teller, turned the paper upside down, and showed her the "G" I'd written in red.

She bobbed her head. I shoved my own fortune-teller back into a pocket.

When she was older I'd put a few more suitors in the fortune like I did for the older girls around Nameless, but for now there would only be one for her.

Baby Jane fished three pennies out of her dress pocket. "Been saving, but here, want you to have it," she said solemnly, holding out the coins.

"That's good you're saving," I said, pushing her hand back, "but I don't sell my *special* fortunes."

Her eyes rounded. "Is it bad luck?"

"Something like that." I tugged gently on her braid.

"I love it lots, RubyLyn, thanks! And I'm gonna save enough

money so I can buy me a hen just like the Millers . . . b-buy a nice dress and get myself a man so I can leave," she said real quiet.

"Man?" I asked.

"Uh-huh, I aim to have me my marriage bed by the time I get my fourteenth birthday. Aim to get away 'fore they . . . they try and sell me . . . or lock me away up there . . . like Sis—" She dragged her words into a sob. Her face tightened and a fat teardrop fell from her wide honey eyes onto the three pennies.

"What? Oh, Baby Jane"—I pressed her head to my shoulder—"no one's gonna lock you away or sell you." I stroked her long braid. Though I wasn't too sure of anything lately.

A trembling cry caught in her breath. "B-been selling some of the eggs I get for workin' for the Millers when Pa ain't countin' too hard." She wiped her watery eyes with her tiny fists. "Don't tell no one."

"I promise." I reached over and pulled my lunch pail onto my lap. "Hungry?" I asked again, trying to cheer her.

Baby Jane licked her lips, swallowed hard, then looked away. "I—I ain't hungry," she denied. "Don't need much to eat, neither." She pressed a hand into her small belly, pushed.

"You love the butter and bread. Made you two today," I coaxed.

Stubbornly she shook her head. "They see me eating, they might . . . s-sell me, too."

The weight of my heart doubled and felt hot. At least I had food. And there was my land to bring to a marriage bed. I looked over at my own tiny patch in the five acres that would be mine someday. "Not yours yet," Gunnar had said when he'd showed me the deed long ago, "and doesn't include all of mine," he added. He'd tapped the paper. "Fully and legally on our daughter RubyLyn Royal Bishop's marrying day, or eighteenth birthday, whichever comes first," my parents' Last Will instructed.

But I wouldn't be tied to the land like Gunnar. I was going to be an artist. Rose said it could happen. And Mr. Parker even hung one of my barn drawings up at the Feed & Seed. Weren't no time before he sold it to someone passing through for a whole five bucks. I had my tobacco to get me out of here, my art to keep me there. But Baby Jane . . .

"Long day. Here, eat." I nudged, pulling out the slice of buttered bread and handing it to her. "And stop by this evening or in the morning. I'm running low on eggs."

She sniffled, took a small nibble, then gave it back. "You are?"

I frowned and put it back in the lunch pail. "Yeah. And don't be worrying none about those baby-buyers and marriage, okay? Keep this fortune close." I curled her hand over the paper and pressed.

Baby Jane looked anxiously up at Stump Mountain, then slowly opened the folds of the tobacco paper, running her fingertip over the drawings. She pressed it to her chest with a lopsided grin. "It's so beautiful, RubyLyn."

"Special ones are." I smiled.

"*Special.*" Her face lit as she inspected the folds of the paper fortune-teller, tracing the basket and chickens. She peered curiously at the name *Frank* and looked back up at me.

I nodded.

Baby Jane blushed.

I tapped the drawing of the chicken. "One day you'll have fancy chickens."

"Chickens," Baby Jane marveled.

"Sure will." I couldn't help sending up a prayer. "The best birds in all 'tucky."

She stared at her chicken fortune-teller, then leaned in, wrapped a sweaty arm around me and squeezed tight.

"Oh, thank you, RubyLyn!" she exclaimed. "This is the prettiest fortune *ever*. Even better than the pictures in the book you gave me!"

I laughed. When Baby Jane was five, I'd found an old book on Gunnar's bookshelf, *The Little Red Hen*. Baby Jane had pestered me to read it to her so many times that I finally gave it to her. Ever since, Baby Jane'd taken an interest in hens.

"Even better than Alma Smithy's fortune," she said.

I winced.

"Lots better," she repeated. "Boy, was her ma mad when she hooked up with that troublemaking boy."

"Lordy-jones." I lifted my swear, feeling relieved to put marriage behind us, but not wanting to think about silly Alma. "She should've known to follow the name I'd written for her. Should've known to kiss that redhead instead."

Baby Jane bobbed her head. "That's what I will do—"

"Got to follow the destiny in these folds, Baby Jane. It's important," I whispered, "because it's a one-time thing."

"I'm gonna."

"And don't be in a rush." I tapped the name *Frank*.

"When did it come to you, RubyLyn? Was it like a smoky vision? Did ya—"

I pushed away her questions. The destiny came to me after I let it cure in Mama's pocketbook overnight. Only then did I have a strong urge to write down the boy Frank, who always carried a book, instead of the one who'd been sly-eyeing her down at the Feed. It was like Mama was telling me. Maybe it was because that sly-eyed boy was dumber than well water and had stolen a Necco candy wafer roll from the Feed store. Maybe it was because I wanted her to have someone sweet like her. Just like what I would've wanted for my own baby sister . . .

Baby Jane shook my arm.

My voice thickened with sadness, thinking of Eve and Patsy. "Uh, okay, but remember everyone knows getting my famous fortunes is a lot like getting your decoration with the red roses."

Baby Jane looked puzzled.

"Menstruation." I pinched lightly.

She curled her lip in disgust.

"It's special, but I don't give guarantees whether it'll be peachy or poor." I stretched out on the quilt. Baby Jane sprawled out beside me, playing with her fortune-teller.

"Better than Alma's," she whispered again.

Gunnar'd been furious when the Smithy girl's mama told him about me selling fortunes that hooked her daughter up with a hoodlum. But I couldn't help it if the kids wanted to buy my art inside the fortunes.

Passing it to her in church last month had been my mistake. Gunnar'd caught me and had a dog fit over that and then ripped up my colorful fortune-tellers. He made me give my entire three dollars and twenty-nine cents to the Sunday collection plate, and had given me the bitters to hold every evening for three days straight.

Now I was starting over. I needed to come up with spending money for the State Fair and buy more seed for the Stumps to grow food. Not to mention, getting a book or two would be nice.

I looked over at Baby Jane, who was smiling down at her chicken fortune-teller. I wanted her to have something good here when I was gone. Because I was never coming back to these ugly rows again. I'd hitch my heart to a good man—someone like *Rainey Ford*.

Baby Jane wriggled a finger into a hole in her dress while she peered close at the fortune.

When I won the prize, I'd find the thrift store and trade these dark duds for a purple paisley hippie dress like the one in Rose's magazine. I'd buy me *all* those fancy Days of the Week undies at the big Woolworth's, too, and maybe even get a set of pink baby-doll pajamas.

The very first thing I was going to do was buy me a Honey Girl slip like Mama's. I'd be walking the avenues with her fine snakeskin purse and—

"Why'd ya draw a barn on here? I hate 'backer barns." Baby Jane frowned at one of the opened flaps on her fortune-teller.

"There's lots of barns round here."

"It's pretty and all, and ain't nobody can draw better than you, RubyLyn, but—"

"Lots of women take that first kiss in a tobacco barn," I teased, and lifted another flap exposing a sleek baby-blue automobile, "or here."

"Don't like barns much," she said again, and inspected the sketch of the snazzy automobile.

I wouldn't tell her I'd drawn the barn for just that reason. I'd drawn the automobile to have birth-control bucket seats . . . something I'd snuck and read in one of Rose's tossed excitement books. Details I knew Baby Jane would remember, and would likely cool any eagerness for boys, waiting for an automobile that would never shadow the streets of Nameless.

"Never seen an automobile like this before." She studied the fortune. "Pretty . . . but . . . but ain't none like that in Nameless, just a lot of rusty automobiles and pickup trucks, Ruby-Lyn." She opened back up the flaps and peered at the chickens, then took a whiff of the tobacco paper.

"Never know when a tall-dark-and-handsome might ride through one day." I pulled up a daisy, absently plucked off the petals.

Baby Jane laid the fortune on her lap and reached for a daisy, too. She pinched off the blooms. "Loves me, he loves me not." She dripped words over the falling petals. "Look, Frank loves me, RubyLyn, it's the God-honest-truth!" she announced, holding up the fortune-teller and spent flower.

Smiling, I sprinkled petals over her. *If a field daisy could hold the strongest testament, surely my prayers for Baby Jane could be penned to paper. . . .*

"Your fortunes sure do know a lot about chickens." She admired the drawings again. "Looks like the Millers' Bourbon Reds, even . . . I like the pretty wattle and comb you drew on 'em. And, oh, this pretty automobile is nice, too." She beamed.

I stood up and fluffed my dress. "Better get now. Here comes Rainey."

Baby Jane jumped up and did the same.

I watched him stride up the rows, long, muscular, and dark as the mountain's night shadow. It was always grand when school let out for the summer and I could be out here with him all the time, free from those chalk-winter school walls and dark, shadowy corners of the house. But time was flying, and here it was the second day of August. School and long, cold nights would be back before I knew it. He'd be long gone . . . maybe gone forever once they put him in that jungle.

I'd missed him these last few days more than I ever had. Gunnar'd kept him busy in the barn piddling with that old tractor and then toted him over to Beauty to look at parts for it.

"Ma says it's trouble to keep that coon around," Baby Jane said.

"Hush it, Baby Jane. He doesn't like those ugly names . . . And we hire him every summer. You know that. The Fords have been working for the Royals for over a hundred years. And Rainey Ford's a good man, soon to be a soldier. He's not a coon, he's a black person."

"Black." She washed the word around her mouth, tasting it like I hadn't told her a thousand times. "S-sorry."

"Get those seeds to your mama and you start eating, Baby Jane, you hear?"

"Ain't . . . ain't gonna have them s-selling me." She turned her eyes toward Stump Mountain. "M-ma says there's gonna be some more changes, and it's not gonna be me," Baby Jane puttered.

"*Changes.*" I flicked the word. "Heck, nothing changes around Nameless but the days, and only 'cause they have names." Still, I couldn't help to rub off a shiver after everything that had happened with the baby. I could feel something more festering in this last hot breath of summer.

I turned my attention to Rainey, watching him set down his paper sack and a bucket of soap water on the wobbly gathering table a few feet away. "Hey, Rainey."

"Hi, Roo." He patted the catch bucket for the tobacco worms. "Morning, Baby Jane. Are you picking hornworms for Henny today?"

Rainey was always fretting about the worms, kept a written tally on them even. I knew that they were the death of a tobacco field. Some as big as a man's finger, we were on the lookout for them, knowing they could destroy our entire crop in no time.

Baby Jane wrinkled her nose. "I got me some cleaning over at the Millers'. W-work all the time since Pa traded the Millers my services for eggs. Even gonna work tomorrow. Gotta get." She picked up her egg basket.

"That's real good. Sometimes I don't mind working Sundays either," Rainey said, looking at me, dimples deepening along his jaws. "And Millers' sure has fine laying chickens."

"Sure do. Got them some new hens the other day," Baby Jane said proudly. "And Mr. Miller said I could name the big red one. I'm gonna help with the new coop." She hugged my waist. "Bye now."

"Wait. Is Henny coming down?" I asked, wondering if she would after our argument. I was always sick after we fussed, and would gladly trade her named illness for my heartbreak. Truth was, I needed her more than she did me, her with nine brothers and sisters.

"Sister said tell your uncle she's sick this morning. Don't know what time she'll be down." She turned, smiling, holding up the fortune-teller.

Gunnar strolled through the rows and plucked it right out of her waving hand.

"RubyLyn," he snapped, "what did I tell you about wasting good time and my good paper on your scribbles?"

"*Scribbles.* Scribbles? No, wait, that's my art, Gunnar." I reached for his arm.

"Rubbish," he blew, sidestepping, stopping long enough to shred it and toss it onto the tobacco as he continued on to the back field.

Baby Jane gasped and took a fearful step behind me.

"*Rubbish? What?* Th-that's not what you told the President of the United States," I shot back.

Chapter 9

Gunnar hadn't been able to keep quiet about my art five years ago and had even told the President of the United States different. It was true that my first fortune-teller weren't nothing fancy, or as refined as the ones I made now, but, then, I hadn't planned on it ending up in the White House, either.

It was on a double-sock frosty morning, April 24, 1964, when Gunnar had picked a bunch of Easter flowers in front of our house and drove us over the winding mountain roads to Inez to see the President of the United States and his wife, Lady Bird Johnson.

Gunnar'd worn a freshly pressed shirt and a solemn tie, and had me dress in my best church clothes.

As we bumped along from hollar to hollar in Gunnar's old pickup, hugging the two-lane mountain road, I couldn't help but notice the hills had put on their finest, too. Blooms of pale-purple toothwort cut paths into waking forests, and bluebells and spotted trout lilies greeted us at every switchback. Gunnar slowed to point out that our mild winter had the wild dogwood trees bursting their barked blouse in rosy-pink blossoms. A black cherry spread its arching branches, coaxing the chickadees and titmice with its budding white-clustered lace, while a gray squirrel and her mate scampered down the thick warted trunk into a pile of last year's leaves.

I had never seen Gunnar so excited. He hankered for a finer tie and craved one of those fancy cameras with the newfangled color film.

He went on about President Johnson like he was some sort of famous kin. Being only ten, I didn't understand much of what Gunnar yapped about, but I was thrilled to hear him talking to me instead of at me. Twice I had to look around to make sure that there wasn't actually nobody with us.

Gunnar said the president was a compassionate man and loved to move into the crowd among regular folk and shake hands, telling his Secret Service men to get lost. Several times I watched Gunnar flex his gnarled bark-brown hands over the steering wheel, testing his fingers in case he got to shake hands with the president.

Traffic swelled, and twice we stopped to let plow horses pulling wagons full of families pass. Finally, Gunnar parked his truck and we got out and walked the rest of the way.

The whole world must've come out to see, because Inez, Kentucky, was bursting with busloads of people and pockets full of bystanders. Gunnar pushed us through the crowds. More than once I heard people wondering why the big Texan was coming to the hills. A lot of folks whispered about the president traveling all this way so soon after Kennedy's assassination, murmuring, "It's so sad how he got his job."

We waited for hours. Just when I was starting to think no one was coming, a roar exploded from the crowd, and a loud, metal whirlybird landed nearby, rolling a stinging wind across ducking heads. Another landed beside it, shooting blinding sunspots from the late-afternoon sun. I couldn't believe it. Then the president and his wife stepped out of the second helicopter and walked right onto Tom Fletcher's swayback porch. President Johnson squatted alongside Mr. Fletcher and his eight kids to talk to the family.

Somehow, Gunnar had pushed us through the crowd and up near the hand-hewn porch. The president shook hands and patted backs in front of the small home, and when he said he was declaring his War on Poverty, Kentucky lit up from a million camera flashes.

No one had told us we were poor, and I looked around at the hill folk trying to see something I may have missed before. But nothing had changed, and the people looked the same as me. Still, everyone clapped politely and some hooted.

The president talked about dignity and the Kentucky man. He told about his own grandma being from Kentucky. Then he spoke about the school and the nearby coal mines having the only jobs around. I pulled out the fortune-teller I'd made from inside Mama's purse. I admired my drawings of a Kentucky barn, the White House, and the dollar bills I had sketched onto it, and traced my finger over the words I'd written.

After a few more minutes President Johnson thanked everybody and the crowd gave him a big applause. That's when Gunnar put the flowers into my hand and shoved me toward the First Lady, who was standing elegantly beside her towering husband.

When I handed Lady Bird the wilted daffodils, I dropped my fortune. She stooped over to pick it up, and I caught a look-see of her lily-white slip.

Lady Bird smiled quizzically. "Pretty nifty art," she said, inspecting the folds and looking like royalty in her string of pearls, fancy red coat, and white pillbox hat. "Is this for me?"

I looked up at her pretty face, guzzled a mouthful of her perfumed air, and blew out a stitched "ye-yes, ma'am."

She asked my name and when I told her "RubyLyn Royal Bishop," she rolled the second syllable of RubyLyn under her tongue and pronounced it like "Ruba." I wanted to correct her, but she'd made it sound exotic, and I could feel Gunnar's eyes heating up my backside. I gave a wobbly grin and bobbed my head agreeably.

Lady Bird reached inside her white pocketbook. Smiling, she handed me a shiny half-dollar. I took the coin and gave her the best curtsy I could manage before hightailing it back to Gunnar's side with my heart banging against my bones. Then I dared look at the coin. It had President Kennedy on one side. I'd never seen one of them before, and the look on Gunnar's face said he hadn't either. I tried to give it to him, but he handed me his fresh hankie instead and told me to wrap it up and keep it safe.

As we made to leave, Gunnar pulled us into a small huddle

and shook the president's hand, spilling about my fine art, and then stopped to boast to three strangers, telling them his niece was an artist and her art was *going all the way to the White House in Washington, D.C.!*

I couldn't believe the finest lady in the whole world wanted something I'd made and paid me in silver. Gunnar beamed all the way from Inez to Nameless, the longest I'd ever seen him happy. Normally, he couldn't hold a smile between the porch and the mail post.

I'd shined that silver coin twice a day for a good month thinking about her. And I had folks around here puckering up their syllables for another, to call me *Ruba.*

After the president showed up in Kentucky unannounced, the postmistress said to anyone who would listen it was because of my prediction on the fortune-teller.

Some of the townsfolk insisted I'd chased away the bad luck in Nameless and brought fame and money by sketching the White House and money onto a paper fortune after Kennedy was assassinated. I'd written *Nameless will be rich like the White House* under my drawings. Others laughed and I did, too . . . and greedily ate the free penny candy it earned from Mr. Parker, and pocketed the coins from the kids who'd ask me to make them one.

Still, I couldn't imagine a lady that fine having the need for such charms. Which made me even more determined to seek a fine life for myself in the city where I could become a real lady and earn lots of money from my art.

It made folks feel good, too. Hopeful. *And didn't Gunnar always say that to possess faith was Godly? So how could it be wrong . . . ?*

Fury needled my spine. "It's not rubbish, dammit, it's art and it don't hurt none," I blasted toward Gunnar's backside and took a big breath. It always seemed like I had to take bigger gulps when Gunnar was around. He probably told his God not to give me much because I'd waste *that.*

Baby Jane grabbed her basket and plucked a piece of paper

off a tobacco leaf. One of the sketched chickens rattled in her trembling hand. Clutching it tightly, she hightailed it out of the rows and onto dusty Royal Road.

Rainey shook his head, opened his paper bag, and pulled out a pickle wrapped in newspaper. "Sorry about Baby Jane's fortune-teller. They're making you famous in more ways than you'd like. Come on, Roo, let it go," he said.

I rolled my shoulders, trying to shake off my anger. Gunnar had been thrilled with my fortune-teller back then, but the more he worried over his crop and President Johnson's War on Poverty, the more sour he'd become.

"Hey, girl, missed ya." Rainey tried to cheer, and held up the pickle. "Look what I got you to go with your dinner. Ma made up a batch. The garden's been doing good this year. There's extra cucumbers inside to make your own."

"Thanks, Rainey. Missed ya, too," I said, cooling. "And I made a batch with the last ones you gave me. Really crunchy and sweet, and even the executioner wolfed them down."

"That's 'cause I used my papa's heirloom seeds this year."

"Your papa?" I said, surprised. He hardly talked about Gus.

"Yeah, I found them in a small box of his things this past winter. Ma said he always grew good cukes. I thought I'd plant them and see."

"You must miss him a lot."

"I try to see him from what Ma says about him. But I . . . Well, I miss that I never helped him plant, learned hunting from him, you know, stuff like that," he said, shoving the pickle back into the bag. "Those seeds and my papa's old violin are all I have. Still miss the knowing. Imagine it's the same with your folks . . . losing them like you did."

I never liked to talk about Daddy's death, or Mama and what happened to her. Though Gunnar talked enough for both of us when he was mad at me. And sometimes I wondered if it would've been better to have lost them like Rainey did while he was in his mama's womb—not to know them, because the tiny memories of my folks and what could've been made me miss them more.

I especially missed that I didn't have much of my daddy. The passing of time stole most of him long ago. But a few things I'd snatched back from the thief: Daddy's scent, especially in the thick of summer, wood-soaked with traces of lavender, like the old applewood tree and purple blooming shrub in our yard that he'd planted. The soft gray hat—his favorite, a pork pie—the one that had the smart charcoal-striped band, wide brim, and deep-dish crown that he'd always let me pop up for his preaching and then pass back to me when he was through. His soft whiskers tickling my cheeks as he closed in to drop a kiss on my cheek and plop the felt hat onto my head. Those gentle hands of his that worked the rim just right and cupped my chin before letting go.

Remembering, I whisked light fingers under my chin.

Rainey coughed lightly, pointed to my mouth. "You been taking care of your jaws?" He walked over to a tobacco plant and plucked off the lowest leaf and handed the lug to me. Touching my jaws, he rubbed lightly. "Make yourself a spit poultice," he said.

I pulled myself up from my thoughts, sighing. That was Rainey, always looking out for me. I ground the leaf between my teeth. After a minute I took it out, squeezed it into a wad, and pressed it to my lips. Though the lugs had the least amount of nicotine in them, I could feel the remedy tingling, going to work on the inflammation. "Thanks," I grunted through my lips. I wanted to talk to him about baby Eve, the fair, and everything, but it just didn't feel right.

"You and Gunnar's really been going at it lately," he said, looking down at the littered paper. "Those fortunes and scandalous books keep him pretty riled."

"Not much that doesn't. But since all this baby-buyers business, it's got us locking horns a lot more."

He grimaced and eyed my mouth. "Better?"

"Yeah . . . it's just . . . you—this war—everything."

"*Me?* I'm fine. And we're gonna whip 'em over there, so stop needling it, Roo." He shook his head. "Sorry you had to be up there at the Stumps' like that." He cupped his hand over his eyes and stared toward Stump Mountain. "Sure glad she shooed me off, though. . . ."

"Wish I hadn't been there either. But Mrs. Stump had it in her mind to use my silly fortune Henny shared with her."

"I'm *predicting* you should give Gunnar one of those good fortunes." Rainey made light, side-eyeing me and poking his toe to the torn paper salting the ground.

"He should be so lucky to have one of my fortunes. Then maybe he'd stay away from mine."

"He means well." Rainey turned his gaze back to the mountain.

I shot an eye full of stingers his way. "Tell my jaws that."

He turned to me, raising a brow and crooking his mouth. "You should hook him up with one of those nice ladies from your church; then I won't have to worry on you two when I'm gone."

"*Gone.*" The word crushed.

"Can't wait to see the ocean . . . the city . . . Won't be too long now till I get my ticket." He grinned cheerfully. "Hook him up with that old schoolteacher, maybe."

He was leaving, why wouldn't he be in a great mood? "No one would have him," I huffed. "And you know I don't do the hooking. I let the fortunes do the talking," I teased back.

"Seems like they talk a lot more when you write down a name of the person *you* want them to have," he chuckled, reaching to tickle my ribs.

"Rainey Ford, are you accusing me of stacking the odds? I'm just gifted at giving others their perfect destiny, thank you."

"*Perfect destiny.* Now wonder what you'd see in mine?" he asked, rubbing his chin, sneaking peeks over his back and mine. "Who do you see me having, girl? Huh?" He tried to tickle me again.

I jumped to the side, feeling my cheeks pluck rose red. *Rainey, six, Bur, five.* "Are you asking me to make you one?"

He stared out past the fields, then cut a sly eye back to me. "With this greeting letter from the president, I might be asking for maybe something more. . . ."

"Maybe I'll get started on it," I punched back, wishing he'd tell me that something more.

His eyes twinkled. "Better hurry 'fore the president beats you to it." He turned back to picking. "Let's go, girl. You look out for the snakes and I'll take the suckers off today. And maybe check on some of those flowers, too. Seems like we're feeding too many blooms out there . . ."

Gunnar always had me leave the blooms on a few stalks for next year's seeds, but I could see we might have too many this year. The sweet blossom left the plant weak and spindly, stole the food from the leaves.

"I want to hurry so I can work on my own burley today." *My ticket out of here.*

"Don't worry, we'll find time. I see it's doing real good over there, and it's only the second day of August."

That cheered me up. It was something. *A lot.* And I suddenly felt lucky looking out at the tall plants. It was hard to believe Gunnar'd broke down and told me I could use a patch of my parents' land to grow my own tobacco to try to win the prize. I was sure it was just another plan of his to keep the devil from nipping at my heels this summer—and to keep me away from the Shake King scum he hated. Like him, some folks around here thought hanging out with them would be like tossing your Holy Spirit into a bag of angry church snakes. So I made sure to present a big fuss and all, telling him how much more work it cost me.

Wasn't much to its postage stamp size, but heck, those teensy heirloom seeds I'd found in a jar out in the barn were going to get me to the 1969 Kentucky State Fair and further!

I glanced sideways and caught Rainey looking at me. The wind kicked up a big breeze carrying the growls from Gunnar's tractor, the drone laddering up into the mountain pines.

A torn scrap from Baby Jane's fortune-teller landed near my feet.

I picked up the paper and triumphantly wagged it at Rainey. He smiled as I put the drawing of Baby Jane's egg basket into my pocket.

Overhead, a kaleidoscope of butterflies dipped for the tobacco honey, quivering above the pinkish blooms before flittering away.

Rainey turned on his tiny transistor radio. Sam Cooke crooned "Teenage Sonata." *"My lips, my lips can only kiss you"* softened the long August day.

I grabbed my tobacco knife from the table and cut off a stalk's trumpet blossoms and tossed them into a small heap, leaving them to lie there like sugar-pink tutus.

Rainey wiped his brow, bent over, and pulled off suckers that would weaken the plant, throwing them onto a pile behind him. He stopped to inspect for worms, plucking a big one off and into the bucket of water.

I snapped off a bloom and it landed on his hunched shoulders. Rainey jerked upright, startled, and I couldn't help but giggle. Mischievously, he lurched forward, swatting me with two elephant leaves.

I disappeared into the tobacco rows, topping flowers like some sort of swashbuckler hippie wearing a psychedelic dress over her new black Saturday undies.

Soon, Rainey's laughter climbed onto mine, and the hot Kentucky breezes lifted a child's song to the surrounding hills. For a good five minutes we abandoned our work and chased each other through the tobacco rows, scattering up sugar-pink tutus and lost youth—a tender youth lost to hard work under a hard sun and old people's hard thoughts and prejudices.

Chapter 10

"Hurry it." Gunnar thumped the wood with a hard fist. "Only you. Rainey can't go." Gunnar smacked again. "It's not his shopping day and I need you to run to the Feed and pick me up a quart of oil for my tractor," he yelled from outside the bathroom door that afternoon. "*Now.*"

It was the first Saturday in August—Town Day—and I'd forgot all about it after what he did this morning with Baby Jane's fortune. I had been calling back to him to send Rainey.

"Just a sec, Gunnar, I—I'm tending my . . . menstruation!" I fibbed for a little more time to scrub my hands.

Quickly, he thudded downstairs and shouted from the kitchen. "*Now.*"

When I knew I couldn't make him wait much longer, I went down to the kitchen. Gunnar stood at the sink looking out at the fields.

"Take that fifty cents on the table, RubyLyn," he said, not bothering to look at me.

I grabbed the change and dropped it into my dress pocket.

"Pick up my oil and a loaf of bread. You've been going through loaves quicker than we can get to town . . . Go on and don't tarry." He shot out the back door.

I hurried upstairs and brushed my hair, moving over to my dresser mirror, inspecting. I fiddled with my aunt's old bobby pins and tucked my straggly bangs back with one. Useless, I pulled it out and snatched my purse from the sill. My sketching of Baby Jane's basket fell out. I felt a stab, remembering the pretty fortune scattered over the fields, her face crushed as she held up the torn-off piece of the beautiful hen.

I placed the drawing back into Mama's purse and buried it inside the lining. Then I fished out my kissing fortune and scooped up a loose nickel I'd been saving.

Twenty minutes later I strolled off Royal Road and onto Main Street toward town. I glanced up at Heart Tack Hill, named because my first-grade teacher's, Mrs. Tack's, ticker gave out one day while she chased a truant kid up that very hill. I spotted two young boys at the top throwing down a rain shower of pebbly rocks.

My school, L.B.J. School of Nameless, the name folks gave it after the president came, sat on the little hill, only a few minutes' walk to town. It was a small school with about a hundred kids squeezed into nine small rooms that sometimes doubled up their lower grades.

In a few minutes I spied the Shake King's tall sign. "All part of the 'Happy Pappy' government program—the Shake King is— with its picnic table for the lazy to bird-eye other lazy men across the street, lined up for their free money at the spanking-new courthouse built by a beehive of government workers on draws, too," Gunnar'd said. And then always added, "Humph . . . just another coat rack for the miscreants and hippie folk to hang."

Some thought it made Nameless bigger. Now, the one-street town stretched from the Shake King lording above in a lot by itself at one end, with the Nameless Community Bank on the other end of town—a very different lord every first of the month.

I didn't much like walking past the Shake King, but you had to if you were going into town from Gunnar's place. You never knew what kind of folks were going to be milling around. Whether someone would make fun of you, give a friendly wave or whistle, or even curse you.

Nameless's town whores, Dusty and Dirty Durbin, sat atop the picnic table, smoking, slurping down icy colas and watching the road for their next job. Their mama ran away when they were knee-high, and their daddy died in the mines when they were teens, leaving them to fend for themselves in the company of a blind, ailing grandma.

I dropped my gaze to the ground.

Someone called my name. Once. Twice.

I dared to look up. It was Molly with her baby on her hip. She'd been a grade ahead of me and dropped out to get hitched and have her baby. We always got along because she liked to read, same as me. And sometimes she'd pass me an old book, or I'd loan her one of mine that Rose had given me.

I'd snuck her *Peyton Place*. Rose had thrown it in the trashcan out in the Feed's parking lot after she saw a few of the pages ripped and its cover missing. When no one was looking, I'd dug it out.

After church, me and Molly always tried to whisper about what we'd read. That time we didn't do much talking, only red-faced giggling until Gunnar snatched me back to the truck.

But Molly hadn't been to church since she married her first cousin, Lewis. The church said Lewis and Molly and their baby couldn't attend—said it was sinful because Molly and Lewis were breaking God's law and Kentucky law.

Molly's daddy got hot about that, busted into the church and demanded the preacher marry his daughter and nephew.

The preacher got angry back, and said, "Wilbur, you'll have to take them someplace else where they allow first-cousin marriages—like up north to New York or New Jersey where it's legal."

Molly's daddy lit him up with threats.

Preacher smacked his Bible onto the pulpit, thundering. "No 'tucky kin is a'marrying another 'tucky kin in my church or anywhere else on Kentucky soil!"

One church member stood up, and said, "We ain't gonna keep our race strong with inbreds!"

Another man popped up, "He's right, Wilbur, we ain't letting that happen again."

A woman sassed, "Shut up, Leland, the preacher don't care about you and your dirty night-ridin' Klan brothers."

"He better," Leland snickered back. "We let 'em go a'breeding kin again, we're gonna weaken our race and pollute our church."

"Sinful . . . illegal," others murmured.

Old lady Dottie McCoy joined in. "And don't forget 'bout the feuds 'tween us McCoys and Hatfields—what happened when they tried to breed kinfolk. *Damn inbreds* . . . Sorry, Preacher," she'd laid the apology wide, "would up an' swap loyalties to make their family bigger. Weren't fair."

Preacher tried to calm the congregation. "Wilbur, quiet down. Dottie, we're not here to discuss old family feuds. And Leland and the rest of you, *sit down,* we're not gonna discuss the KKK on the Lord's day!"

Molly's daddy wouldn't listen and puffed up even bigger. The preacher had to send for the sheriff to come by and haul him out of Sunday service.

Later, Molly's daddy found a Virginia preacher to marry the cousins and drove them across the state lines. But our church still wouldn't let them come back, and when their sweet baby girl was born blind and missing two nubs, the church said God had punished them for their incestuous ways.

I waved back at Molly and her little one. Molly grinned and raised the baby's hand, wriggling it real cute.

The baby girl had a sweet face with Lewis's blond curls and an angel's smile just like her mama. It was sad knowing she'd never see it. *What kind of god keeps you from loving . . . ? What kind of god would punish a little girl like that?* That poor baby didn't pick her parents.

I watched them cut across the street to the grounds of the courthouse, jail, and post office.

I thought about Gunnar wanting me to stay in this nothing-doing town. *How could I ever stay in a town that sells and damns its babies?*

I hurried over to the corner of the Feed & Seed. The owner, Mr. Parker, leaned out the door with a small bag. "Do me a favor, RubyLyn, and run this bag down to Apples' for me."

"Yes, sir." I took it and walked past French's next door—a vacant hardware store. A truck rumbled by, shaking storefront windows. Old man Erbie Sipes shifted on the bench in front of the building. He lifted the brim of his faded ball cap to smile, then scratched his pencil across the wooden seat.

Erbie lived above French's in a one-room rental, and you could count on him showing up on the bench bright and early, sure as the sun got its morning fire. He earned his draw by sitting on the town's bench tallying the automobiles and trucks that passed through.

Erbie never went to school, but he knew numbers and things no one else knew. A little man with a big-sky memory. Remembering every detail of everything, a good forty years back even. And a lot of times the *Mountain Sentinel News* asked him things so they could write it in their newspaper and know it was right.

"Hey, Erbie," I said.

"Hey, Miss RubyLyn. Fine weather today. Been out here since 6:03. Yessir, 6:03 . . ." He slapped his knee three times.

I walked on past him and peeked into Althea's, next door, just in case one of the kids from school was getting a haircut. Occasionally I'd drift inside to check out Althea's old hair magazines, sneak peeks at the puffy soft-bonnet hair dryer with the long hose attached that she used for styling females' hair, and her colorful roller collection. No one was there or in Potter's Barber Shop next to it.

I heard the door jingle at Cathy's Diner & Coffee Shop beside Potter's, and an old woman struggled to push it open. I hurried over and held the door for her. Inside, two men sat on stools at the counter, finishing their plate lunches. Old folks sat at a table sipping coffee, smoking, and talking. The other three tables were empty.

The old woman mumbled a thanks and pointed next door at Sue's. I rushed over and opened that door. She hobbled inside Sue's Notions and Repairs, squeezing past an old sewing machine and thread and stuff that was tightly packed into a narrow aisle.

The buzzer sounded on Apples' Apothecary, the last of the

shops that butted up to Sue's. Willow Patton walked out with her weekly bag of tonics and cures for her latest ailment. I went inside and dropped off the bag to the druggist.

Back outside, I nosed sideways in each store again to see if anyone I knew was shopping in the seven businesses.

In front of the Feed again, I looked across the street at the commons. I didn't see anyone there either, just Bur Hancock coming out of his jail and someone going into the post office on the other side of it. Bur took a step toward me like he might come over, but only lifted his hand in a friendly hello.

I waved back and headed into the Feed. The door banged my arrival, rattling its old tin Pepsi advertisement: a cigarette-puffing James Dean told folks the cola promised *more Fun, more bounce to Dance.*

Mr. Parker gave a grateful nod and bent his head back to three other men near the shop window. "*Vietnam . . . Crop . . . War . . . Weather . . .*" The men staggered words into a lazy conversation.

Nearby, a rack of bib overalls hid a group of huddled women, but not their hushed voices ghosting up through their cigarette smoke. It grew quiet when they saw me, and I knew they got word about the new Stump baby and my prediction.

I made my way up to the mail-order catalogs at the register. My home economics and arithmetic teacher broke away from the women. "RubyLyn, I'm looking forward to seeing you back this year." She tugged at the collar of her latest dress she'd sewn—a fine bluebell-print cotton that looked as nice as those in the catalog. "Be here 'fore you know it." She studied me. "You come see me if you need some paper and pencils, okay? Thread, too, though I know you don't have the fancy for that."

"Thank you, ma'am." I figured she was checking to see if I was coming back for my junior year. Some of the kids, even ones younger than me, never bothered, ducking out before their freshman year. They'd say they didn't have transportation, their folks wanted them to work at home, or the girls got knocked up like Molly.

She glanced over her shoulder and then back at me. "Takes a smart brain to stay in school."

"Yes, ma'am."

"I know you have those smarts. Seen it in your drawings."

The old teacher was one of the smartest people I knew and everyone's favorite. On a student's seventeenth birthday, she'd present them with a silver dollar for a taste of a finer life, her reminder that such could be had from getting all your learning. I imagined she had coal buckets full of shiny dollars stashed away in her old house way out on Briar Road, to have given out all that money over the years.

I wanted to say something exact and smart for her and then I messed up by looking down and seeing the *Sears Summer* mail-order catalog with the pretty blond woman standing on some faraway beach in her brown and white skirted bathing suit.

I spouted stupidly, "I saw an advertisement for paper dresses, ma'am, in one of Rose Law's old magazines. I wonder if we can make some this year? They said they're real economical, too."

"I believe I heard a woman's paper gown caught on fire . . . Yes, I believe her husband got too close with his cigarette and that pretty paper dress lit up lickety-split," she said, and nodded toward the customers. "That wouldn't do in Nameless, now would it, RubyLyn?"

I looked over her shoulder and saw most of the folks had cigarettes. "No, ma'am. But it sure would help with my laundry chores."

Her eyes softened. "Take that imagination and get your smarts, Miss Bishop." She lightly tapped my head before going out the door.

Better to take my art and get out of Nameless, I thought.

I picked up a small shopping basket and strolled through the Feed's two aisles. I studied a row of bins, half pretending to look at the wooden one filled with toys: yo-yos, a few spinning tops, small colorful knapsacks filled with ball 'n' jacks, and the latest: clacker balls. Carter Crockett had a set of the knockers. He'd hold them by a ring in the center, click-clacking, banging the red plastic balls held together at each end of the rope till it burnt up your nerves. Carter liked to knock them especially hard, up high, on the side, and one day the balls shattered and hit his mouth, loosening a front tooth. He didn't see a dentist, so he lost it. Henny declared him "cuter."

Slowly I made my way down the other aisle, past a bin full of wool socks, shelves packed with canned meat, pickles, corn, and mouse traps piled next to candied fruitcakes. Over by the wall where they stacked the bread, I squeezed several loaves and grabbed the freshest. Then I walked up to the long, narrow cooler full of bologna and other cold cuts, cartons of Millers' brown eggs, and Styrofoam cups filled with night crawlers. *Nothing new.* The cooler's soft motor kicked on and I stood there soaking up the coldness, nipping the morning's memories.

Paula, one of the Shake King hippies, squeezed past me with a bag. She gave me a shy smile. I tossed one back, grateful she'd given me a ride home that day when a bad storm blew in as I was leaving the Feed. *Saved me,* I thought. *Damned you, and better to have been struck by lightning,* Gunnar'd preached.

From behind, Mr. Parker cleared his throat as I looked above to the long wooden shelf lined with the artificial flowered funeral pots, spices, and sardine tins. I studied a box of Corn Flakes that cost twenty-nine cents, and looked at quart Mason jars filled with carrot, mustard spinach, beet, and other precious seed. Picking up a jar of cress seed, I opened the lid and sniffed.

Mr. Parker said, "Can't live without cress on my eggs and meat. Also helps with the gout."

I set down the jar. "I'm needing a nickel's worth of seeds, Mr. Parker." I pulled out the nickel I'd brought along to buy the Stumps some seeds.

"Sure thing, RubyLyn. For fall planting?"

"Yessir. Some cabbage and lettuce and maybe some of those snap peas, please." I knew Baby Jane loved them and ate them straight off the vine.

Mr. Parker opened lids and began sprinkling the seeds onto squares of the wax paper beside them. "You sure buy a bunch of seeds—enough for three families," Mr. Parker commented.

"Yessir," I said, picking up a spool of ribbon from the shelf.

"That just came in," he said, noting my interest. "It's called Hens-and-Biddies."

It would be perfect for Baby Jane. I studied the tight little green rosette leaves running on the creamy silk ribbon, thinking how beautiful it would look in Baby Jane's hair.

"I can let you have a snip for, lessee . . . I suppose two cents would be fair."

"Pretty," I said, admiring it.

"You can get that and the seeds for a nickel."

"Thank you, Mr. Parker. I'll take it and put back the lettuce seeds," I said, deciding, and not wanting to be greedy.

"Sure thing, RubyLyn," he said, unrolling the ribbon. "It'll look nice in your hair."

"It's for Baby Jane. She's gonna look real pretty with it in church."

Mr. Parker wrinkled his brow. I was thrilled to have it for her. Out of the corner of my eye, I spied the skin balm. I stared hard at the tin of Handmaiden's Salve, longing to rub the ointment across my rough, cracked hands. If Mr. Parker wasn't here hanging over my shoulder, I might've. What I wouldn't give for a tin full of that instead of the lard I rubbed into my ugly hands. Gunnar sure liked things clean, but he let you know he wouldn't waste his money on female pretties.

I rolled the nickel between my fingers, looked over at the gumball machine. Mr. Parker always spiked the machine with his *pot o' gold balls:* a bright yellow wooden ball about the same size as the colorful gumballs only with a black stripe circling it. For a penny you could get a piece of gum. But if you got a pot o' gold ball, it could be redeemed for a nickel's worth of merchandise. I knew folks who'd gotten as many as three of the lucky balls with just a nickel's try. But I'd never had the nerve to gamble.

"Fourteen cents," Mr. Parker tempted, lifting the small can of salve. "The missus swears it makes her skin feel like rose petals." He raised the lid and put it under my nose.

I got a whiff of roses and honeysuckle and could almost feel the ointment seeping into my chafed hands, silky, soft. I eyed the gumballs and then the ribbon and seeds. Giving a wiggle to my head, I picked up the can of oil that Gunnar wanted.

Mr. Parker capped the tin, took a pen out of his shirt pocket, and marked the seed packets. Then he dug inside his apron pouch and pulled out tape to seal them.

"Gunnar's tractor again?" he asked, side-eyeing the oil I'd put in my basket. "Let me just take these up to the cash register for you, RubyLyn."

I wanted to tell him it wasn't necessary—I'd like to wait around and cool off—but he took the basket from my grip, making me follow him.

At the register, Mr. Parker bagged my stuff, dropped in a sheet of S&H Green Stamps, then leaned over the counter. "Mighty fine casting you gave the Stumps, RubyLyn." Grinning, he reached past the box of Pall Mall candy cigarettes and tossed in a Clark candy bar. He pushed the bag toward me. "Yes, ma'am, fine Granny Magic for that new Stump baby."

Behind, murmurs of affirmations and a few snickers drifted my way.

I wondered how much they knew. My face felt hotter than the Red Hots he kept in the candy jar. I gave him change, and whispered, "I don't have the extra money to pay for the candy, Mr. Parker—"

He fanned away my words and took the money. "Just filled the cola tub." Mr. Parker nodded, letting me know I could take one.

I bobbed my head, then spied the latest *Sears Fall and Winter* issue on the counter beside a stack of others. I studied the girl on the cover with her short knit dress, gold jewelry, and perfectly bobbed flipped-up hairdo. I inched my fingers toward it, dying to open the thick pages and see the new slips inside.

"Anything else for you today, RubyLyn?"

"No, sir." I ran my hands through my unruly hair and murmured thanks.

He reached under the counter and pulled out a box of

laundry detergent. "Mind dropping this off at the Laundromat for me?"

I took the box of soap and my bag and exited the back door to the store's porch and lot.

Rose's traveling trader was parked in the gravel, a few folks milling about. For a minute I watched the people rummaging through her stuffed boxes stacked neatly in the back of the covered truck bed and the cartons on the ground piled around it.

Crawling around inside the back of the Canopy, Rose looked up and blew me a kiss out the side opening.

I tossed one back, then headed over to Mr. Parker's Laundromat in the lot behind the Feed's. I stared past the stenciled letters on the glass door: WHITES ONLY—MAIDS IN UNIFORM *Allowed.* Mrs. Parker waved me in. "Hi there, RubyLyn," she said, busy with a stack of laundry. "Set it there, hon. Thanks." She pointed to the table.

I traipsed back out to the Feed's lot and plopped down on the shaded bench snugged against the concrete wall and waited for Rose to take a break.

Mr. Parker's black worker, David Young, came by, picking up litter and emptying the ashcan. "RubyLyn," he said, smiling. "Goldie was jus' speaking of you and Mr. Royal the other day. How's you and Mr. Royal doing out there? He still using that salve Goldie made for his arthritis?"

I missed David's wife, Goldie. Long ago, when I first came to live with Gunnar, she'd kept his house four days a week, cooking and cleaning. Then he couldn't pay her anymore and had to let her go. Goldie taught me how to do chores and cook before she left. She still dropped by on occasion to bring a special menthol balm she'd concocted to help Gunnar's old bones.

"Hey, Mr. Young." I smiled back. "Gunnar's almost out of it."

"Goldie just made a fresh batch. Best ever." He rubbed his bad shoulder and grinned. "Tell him to stop by for a refill."

"I will. I'm sure he'll stop next time he's in town." I would've loved to go get it myself and say hi to Goldie, but the Youngs lived on Color Row, an old busted sidewalk section with six shacks located in back of the courthouse commons that was for four black families—the only ones in Nameless besides Rainey and Abby. And no white female would be caught dead walking it unless she wanted a whipping for herself or the colored she was visiting. *Folks didn't dare.*

I was barely six years old when the preacher took his wife over his lap on the town bench after she'd gone looking for her maid, Hallie, on Color Row. Folks still whispered how the preacher'd pulled up his wife's skirts and smacked her on her baby-blue satin undies. The jeers and cheers from bystanders were worse than a Bible stoning. Hallie got the same, but weren't no fancy undies under her skirts to take the bite off the skin slapping, just a pair of raggedy white knickers. And the preacher's wife never went looking for maid Hallie again, unless her mister went with her.

My stomach growled and I poked inside the bag. Just as quick, I rolled it shut. I'd wait to share the candy fair and square with Rainey.

I reached over to the large metal washtub, brimming with tiny bricks of ice and cold drinks, and pulled out a Barq's cream soda. I popped off the top with the wall-mounted bottle opener and swigged down a big gulp, and another, letting the icy red liquid sugar numb my tongue, bite my throat. I closed my eyes, savoring. It had been at least a year since I tasted a cola. Maybe this was reward for a troublesome time working the charms. After all, baby Eve would probably grow up and have cream soda and Clark bars . . . maybe every day.

I sat my bottle down, smoothed my hair, trying to hand-curl myself a bottom flip like the girl on the catalog page.

Rose walked up to the bench. "I could cut it in a city style," she offered.

"Gunnar'd have my head if I ever did." I blushed and pulled out my fortune.

She chuckled and laid a pad of paper beside me. My eyes lit. "Another sketch book . . . Rose, this is great. I've nearly filled up the other."

"Just got back in town from picking up Mr. Parker's order up in the city and getting my stuff. Figured ya might need some more of your own paper. Maybe make yourself some pretty pictures or something fancy like what's on them book covers even."

"That'd be swell. Forty whole pages—clean, too," I said appreciatively, fluttering the thick art pad.

"Well, it's got a couple of pages missing, so I couldn't sell it."

"Are you sure, Rose . . . it looks brand new?"

"It's yours, honey."

"Thank you, Rose," I said again, stuffing it down into my bag and pecking her cheek.

"Welcome, kid. Three more weeks till the State Fair."

I picked up my fortune. "I can't wait to be gone."

"Just be ready to leave out about three a.m. on the eighteenth."

"Sure will."

"That's a pretty one, kid." She tossed back her long, flowing neck scarf, bent over to get a closer look at my fortune-teller. "You sure can draw." She pointed to the flap with the picture of the barn. "City folks pay a lot for this folk art. Once, I even saw a painting of an outhouse for sale in a city store window."

"Outhouses." I wrinkled my nose. "Folk art?"

"That's when artist folk like yourself and me make beautiful stuff out of simple things . . . like this pretty fortune ya made out of ordinary tobacco paper—like my daddy's barn you painted for me on the old plank of his barn wood."

I remembered how much of a fuss she'd kicked up showing it off to everyone. How she shocked me by hanging it above her mantel.

"And like the musical spoons you carve from wood," I said. Rose had been making music spoons since before I was born. Something she taught herself long ago. She'd make her instruments from blocks of Kentucky Coffeetree wood, carving out two long, joined handles for the bottom, fashioning smooth heads for the tiny split wooden cups at the top—pretty spoons for slapping against the hand or leg. Folks swore that Rose's Kentucky bones were the best for clapping and snapping out a fine tune.

"Uh-huh."

"Folk artist." I liked those words, and I liked that we shared them.

"And"—Rose raised a finger—"folk artists like yourself need good paper. Lots of new places to visit, too, so you can be inspired." She lingered over the fortune-teller and licked at gossip. "Heard tell about the new Stump baby. You claiming it would be a girl and grow up rich, folks been a'saying."

Shrugging, I flicked at lint growing on my dress. "Never claimed *nothing*. And I wish folks would forget about Lady Bird Johnson and all that. Need to claim my own destiny out of here."

"Now, honey, ya know small towns don't ever forget. Folks like to think of you as the next Granny. You get your small-town tag when you're young."

"One day I'll get a proper one in the city," I grumbled, "and not from a town that can't even tag itself a name."

"That you will, kid. Just don't stray too far." She brushed a fallen bang off my forehead. "Speaking of stray . . . stop by the Canopy. I have a coloring book with chickens. You might want it for that little one that's always following you."

Remembering, I dug inside my bag and pulled out the ribbon. "Done spent my money on this, Rose. It's going to be so *beautiful* in her hair!"

"Ah, a print of a Hens-and-Biddies plant. Perfect for lil' Baby Jane." She admired it a minute.

Nameless's deputy sheriff came out of the back door of the Feed & Seed and scanned the lot. Frowning, he rubbed his thick mustache and took hold of Rose's sleeve, and said, "Have you seen the Crocketts?"

Rose handed me the ribbon, and I placed it carefully back into the bag. "No, Deputy," she said, somewhat startled. "Is something wrong?"

Deputy looked at me sitting on the bench and stepped in front of me. "Crocketts is wrong," he whispered to Rose. "Sheriff saw Carter Crockett assault his girlfriend."

"Again?" Rose grimaced. "Is she okay?"

"Yeah," Deputy said. "Got a warrant for his arrest, but he's missing and so is his rifle. He's a dangerous cuss. Soon as I nab him, I'm hauling him into the can for a long sitting spell."

Chapter 11

Fearful for Henny, I hurried off to go find her.

In front of the Feed, folks were already gathering, buzzing about how Carter Crockett was missing and wanted.

I walked home in a cloud of dread. Three times I came to a full stop when I thought I heard something in a passing cornfield, and again at the fork in Royal Road, and then again over in Devils Bone, the creek on the other side of the road that circled and snaked around our property and out past town.

When I came to the tobaccos, Ada Stump popped out of a tall row, munching on a tomato. Seeing her red, wet face like that, almost jumped the bumps clean off my flesh. I knew she'd stolen it from Gunnar's vegetable garden. I scowled at her as she brushed bits of tomato off her cheek and ran off before I could ask after Henny.

Almost home, Rainey rounded the bend startling me again.

"There you are, girl. Gunnar sent me after you," he said, black brows knitted tight, taking my bag. "Did you hear— they're looking for Carter? The sheriff was just here asking if we'd seen him—"

"Henny . . . Where's Henny?" I burst.

Rainey snuck peeks behind us before moving in close to pat my back. "Just a broken nose, Roo. She'll be fine."

I sagged against him, relieved she'd be okay. "The sheriff said he had his gun."

"Probably gone off to drink with the raccoons till it dies

down. Let's go. Gunnar asked me to collect you and see you safely home."

Lightning rumbled in the distance. He looked behind us first, then hugged my shoulder. "Come on, girl. It's going to storm."

It did. For the next four days a hard, whipping rain soaked Nameless, leaving me with little to do other than to watch the tobacco grow in between taking care of Gunnar and the house. Gunnar paced the porch with his old Stevens 12 gauge double-barrel shotgun, on the lookout for Crockett or any of his kin.

Days of rain left the paint blistered on the old clapboard and then the downpour gave way to a drizzle. I couldn't see Henny, and worse, I missed Rainey.

On Thursday evening, Rainey came by with a bag full of cucumbers and a newspaper rolled underneath his damp shirt. Gunnar was up in his room, tucked in with the Bible, when I spotted Rainey crossing the field. I grabbed my quilt jacket and hurried out the front door and met him on the porch.

"Ma wanted me to bring these by," he said, setting down a soaked bag. Cucumbers burst through and rolled out onto the wooden boards.

"I'm glad you made it over. Seen Henny or anyone?" I lit one of the hanging kerosene lanterns. Rainey took off his hat and shook the wide brim. He slipped out of his oilskin jacket and dropped it on the rocker.

"Nuh-uh. Take this, Roo." He pulled out a newspaper tucked under his shirt and handed it to me.

"Gunnar's been missing his news. Thanks," I said, holding it up to the light of the lantern, peeking at the latest edition of the *Mountain Sentinel News*. "Me too." I thumbed through its six pages and stopped at an article. "Says we might finally be getting a mobile library to visit Nameless." I perked.

"They'll need a good working bus to tote anything up and down these hills," Rainey said.

"Here's the almanac for today, says so here, *Thursday, August 7*." I pointed it out to Rainey. *Fair fishing, Castrate farm animals, Cut firewood, Set out potatoes and turnips,* it read. "You know Gunnar's really taken to those cukes of yours."

"Ma said my papa ate the pickles for breakfast." Rainey laughed low.

"Caught Gunnar just the other day having one with his morning coffee."

Rainey put back on his hat, stooped to pick up the cucumbers, and stuffed them into my laundry basket on the porch. "Ma said to tell you she'll be by with her sewing stuff soon as she can. She's still working on the Parkers' drapes."

I folded the paper and placed it atop the cucumbers, and said, "That'll be great. I haven't seen a soul. Sure wish I could see Henny."

"Henny'll be okay," he said.

"Are they still looking for Carter?"

Rainey scratched his chin. "I haven't heard or seen any of the other Crocketts around here lately . . . Land's quiet, except for one of the little Stump girls, soaked, playing along the creek line, looney kid. But Sheriff'll catch him. Don't you worry, Roo."

It was hard to hold anything but worry in this gray weather. Henny, him, and now my winning crop could die.

As if hearing my thoughts, he looked up at the low, leaky clouds, and said, "Look at this soaking . . . Good thing July was dry. Listen, Roo, tell Gunnar I have to leave earlier than I thought. Got word I have my army physical up in Louisville on the eighth."

"What—But . . . but that's tomorrow."

"Yeah, I'm hitching a ride with Mr. Parker. Wanted to tell you good night 'cause he's heading out before daybreak and said he doesn't mind dropping me off on his way. I'll find a ride back the next day."

"Sleep there? Where will you stay?"

"I'll check with the army doctors and see if they have a resting spot for folks like me."

"*Louisville.*" For a second I thought about laying my head

under all that city bustling and what it would feel like. I imagined those twinkly city lights would be beautiful, just like a star-packed night sparking over Nameless.

"Maybe you'll see Eve," I said.

"Who?"

"Eve. That's the name the city couple gave to Lena's baby."

"Ah, maybe so." He frowned slightly, stuffed his hands into his pants pockets. "I saw Lena heading down to the Shake King . . . she looked pretty sad."

"I haven't seen her." I shuddered, pushing back the thoughts of the birthing. Instead, I said, "Wonder how big the city Shake Kings are?"

"Might be a lot bigger, maybe as big as the Feed."

"Oh"—I raised a finger—"the store. Wait here, Rainey." I slipped inside, hurrying upstairs. Across from my room, I could hear Gunnar softly snoring, see the light spilling under his door. Quietly, I went into my room and found what I was looking for.

I returned about a minute later and handed Rainey the Clark candy bar. "In case you get hungry," I said, flushed.

"You sure?" He pulled his coat on. "I know how much you like them."

His eyes lingered on mine. Scents of soaking earth, leaves, and warm jasmine pulled into the soft rain, sweetening the porch.

Rainey tilted his head, his face shadowed by the brim of his hat, eyes narrowing. It weren't no more than a few seconds, but long enough for me to bend into him and want more. *Rainey, six, Bur, five,* my fingers had played the paper folds. I hadn't reached my favorite number. Now, more than ever, I wanted that seven—his kiss—and question.

Rainey leaned closer, smelling like morning rain.

The wind lifted, swirling the hem of my dress, baring my legs. *Five.*

His pant leg brushed against my skin.

Six.

A milk moth circled above the lantern, bumping shadows against porch walls, dipping close to the licking flame. Our hands met and I pressed my palm to his and felt the heat in his touch. Silence swelled and spilled into the patter of rooftop rain.

Seven. . . .

Inside, a clatter of dishes snared the unfolding, magpied the wanting. Gunnar was up and rambling around the kitchen.

Rainey startled and tipped back his hat. He sighed my name, and whispered, "When I get back I have an important question to ask you." Gently, he pinched my pinky finger. "Good night, Roo. Take care of that prize crop and I'll be back in two days. *Two.*"

He stepped back and broke the candy bar, giving me part of it. He was halfway down the steps before I could collect my dizzy mind and beg the answer.

From the darkened porch I watched him cross through the tobacco rows until the fog folded in and claimed him.

A few minutes later Rainey's violin cried across the rain-soaked field into the night as he played "The Wayfaring Stranger." "*. . . I'm just a poor wayfaring stranger . . . travelin' through this world of woe . . . no sickness, toil nor danger . . . in that bright land to which I go . . . I'm going there to see my father . . . going there to see my father . . . no more to roam . . .*" His raw words climbed out of the horsehair bow and melded into the Kentucky skies.

Chapter 12

A muddy rain splashed into Friday afternoon, washing out the crumbly road up to Stump Mountain as it usually did, and with Henny trapped at home and Rainey gone, I needed a distraction.

Thinking about Rose, I snuck out the artist pad and began sketching spoons, stopping in between each picture to soak up a new thought. On each handle of the spoon, I drew a dollar bill. On the next fold I put Rose's old traveler, its dings and rust, and on the next, more spoons and a smiling Rose. When I was through, I tore it out of the pad, folded it, and then took the fortune-teller upstairs and put it into Mama's purse for the cure. It would be a good way to thank Rose for toting me to the fair.

Then I turned to the porch, squeaking the boards, cocking my ear for Rainey's homecoming—his violin.

When I saw something move behind the willow oak, I leaned over the rail, hoping. Soaked, Baby Jane rushed over with her basket of eggs. She stood at the bottom, shifting her weight from one leg to the other, chewing on her nails.

I was thrilled when Gunnar popped out the screen door and motioned her up onto the porch. Taking a seat, he rocked, and asked, "Miss Stump, are you selling those eggs or toting them home?" He crooked his finger.

"I-I'm s-sellin', sir—"

"Get your fingers out of your mouth and speak up," Gunnar bristled, "and get on up here and let me see."

Wary, Baby Jane climbed the steps. She lifted the cloth and took out an egg. "Sellin'. Be a nickel for four of 'em if you want 'em, sir. One nickel." She bit on another nail.

Gunnar thrust three wiggling fingers in front of her face. "Three cents."

Paling, Baby Jane looked down at the boards and brushed her toes across a plank, pulling fingers back to her mouth. The egg trembled in her other hand and rocked softly against her wet skirts.

I lit into Gunnar. "Eggs cost forty cents for a dozen at the Feed, Gunnar. Give her five cents," I scolded.

"Highway robbery," he growled, then raised his chin and flashed three fingers back to Baby Jane.

"Five." I waved five fingers at him.

"Three."

"Five," I pushed harder.

Baby Jane's hands shook so bad, she dropped an egg at Gunnar's feet.

"Baby Jane's worked all week for those eggs," I snapped.

"Working at cheating honest folks," he clipped low.

A tear caught on Baby Jane's bottom lash.

"How could you?" I shot.

Me and Gunnar continued the argument until he went inside to get the bitters. When he smacked the jar down on the rail, Baby Jane startled and took off. For most of the afternoon we bickered.

Since the long rain, I'd already suffered the taste of Gunnar's bitter herbs twice for back talking, and it would've been a third if Abby hadn't interrupted and saved us both by stopping in to drop off a pile of socks she'd darned for us.

"Lord o' mercy," she clucked, stepping onto the porch, "if this weather ain't making even the birds fussy. I can hear the barn swallows from my porch even." She snuck us meaningful glances.

I dropped my sass. Gunnar grimaced. It was rare for Abby to come by without Rainey, and I was sorely disappointed to see her alone. Gunnar rose from the rocker, greeted her kindly, then cut me a warning look. I hung back watching.

"Abby, it's always a pleasure to have your company, but it's not a good evening to be out. Is everything okay? Rainey—"

She wagged her hand. "Fine, I reckon, but he's still not home, Gunnar. I wanted to get these socks back to you before I needed to build an ark to tote them across the field." She set down her covered basket and slipped out of her wet overcoat.

Gunnar took her coat and hung it on the hook beside the screen door. "RubyLyn, where's your manners?" He turned and tutted. "Go get a towel—one of those pink towels for Abby, and clean up this egg mess."

Had the rain drowned his brain? Gunnar never liked anyone to use Claire's fancy guest towels in the downstairs bathroom. "You mean the company's-coming towels—Aunt Claire's?"

Abby pressed her lips together. Gunnar glared back his answer, shooing me away. "Abby, let's get you dry. Have a seat in the rocker and I'll go fetch us a cup of coffee," he said.

"No need to fuss," Abby said.

I went back inside, grabbed Aunt Claire's towel and took it out to the porch for Abby, and then cleaned up the egg with soap and water.

While Gunnar went in for coffee, Abby sat with me on the porch and tried to teach me about the crisscrossing and stitching, like so many times before. More than once I tangled it up, and when I dropped her wooden darning egg that Rainey had carved for her long ago, she calmly said, "Maybe another lesson, another day, chil'."

Likely never. I was all thumbs when it came to sewing.

Gunnar came out with the cups, and said to Abby, "Don't know what they're teaching her in school. Fifteen-year-old girl can't even darn a sock." He set down the coffee and went back inside for napkins.

"Almost sixteen." I fussed after him.

Abby chuckled. "I'm sure your talents are waiting for bigger things." She patted my arm. "How's the tobacco, RubyLyn? Rainey thinks it won't be long till harvesting. Hard to believe this season is almost done."

"It can't get done quick enough, ma'am." I flexed my hands.

"Rainey says your prize crop has shot up real fine. I've never been to the State Fair. Bet you win all the pretty ribbons."

I held up crossed fingers.

Despite Abby's polite refusals, Gunnar insisted she stay for a late supper and sent me scampering to fix it. When we joined hands for Gunnar to bless the sinner who prepared the dinner—me—Abby scolded him with her eyes. Gunnar cleared his throat and mumbled an added blessing for our visitor. Abby squeezed my hand, and a satisfied smile rolled across her lips.

After the meal, they took their coffee and blackberry cobbler out to the front porch. Then Gunnar had me light the two lanterns hanging at each end of the boards.

A small woman with earth-darkened skin, Abby's soft brown eyes and easy smile somehow softened him, too, and many times I'd wondered why, since Gunnar tolerated very few people. I hurried to wash the dishes, then slipped back outside to watch them from the other end of the porch. Lazy, I rested against a beam.

They set their empty cobbler plates on the floor boards and settled into their porch rockers, watching the rain mist over Nameless.

Sierra, the orange barn cat, jumped onto the porch, mewing a greeting, brushing against Gunnar with her whiskers before settling at his boots. He'd never had a fancy for dogs, saying his cat worked more than three dogs and kept the critters out of his house, barn, and the vegetable patches. Sierra followed him everywhere, too, and you'd see her trailing behind his tractor even. Sometimes, Gunnar'd stop the tractor, get out and inspect one thing or another, sneak his eyes around to make sure no one was looking, then lift that old cat up onto the seat and let her ride home beside him. *Sometimes, I wished I was that old barn cat.*

"You make the best cobbler, RubyLyn," Abby said, sipping her coffee. "Wasn't it delicious, Gunnar? Sure does have the skillet smarts, don't she, Gunnar?"

Gunnar grunted into his mug.

I took a seat on the floor, watching the rain, too.

"I pray Rainey didn't meet trouble," Abby fretted. "He should've been home by now."

"I'm sure he's fine," Gunnar said. "Did he take that brown tie?"

"Yessir, he sure did," she beamed, "and practiced that Windsor knot you taught him."

Tie. I'd never seen Rainey in anything but his old jeans and a soft blue chambray shirt, even when him and his mama set out for the colored church on Sundays. Maybe he was walking the avenues now. . . .

"I packed it in the satchel you lent him," she continued. "Sure appreciate you getting it for him. I hope he found himself a safe room . . . Oh, Gunnar, do you think he found himself a safe place to sleep up there in Louisville?"

He rubbed his whiskered chin. "I imagine Rainey'll be fine as long as he keeps his mind on the business of the real war."

"His mind." Abby sighed heavily. "Just don't know what that boy's thinking, Gunnar. A fool mind he has sometimes. Going to the fighting like that in Vietnam when he could've been a smart boy and joined the navy before he got drafted." She rocked a little, then asked him, "How many miles did you say it was to Louisville?"

"I reckon about two hundred fifty, maybe a bit more," he said.

She took another deep breath. "Sure wish his papa was around to talk to him. The fool things Rainey takes a mind to. Wanting to be in the jungle like that instead of on a big boat."

Gunnar shifted in his rocker, bent over, and scratched Sierra's ear. "Now, Abby, it's a wise man that knows to be shooting at what he can see."

Even from my end of the porch I could feel her slapping his words with a glare.

I expected Gunnar to lay his executioner's stare on her, but he didn't—only lifted his mug, and said, "More coffee, Abby?"

Abby puffed up. "Should've given him a bus ticket to Canada instead."

Gunnar chimed in about a Kentucky boxer named Muhammad Ali, who'd been arrested a few years back for evading the draft.

"Why folks call him the Louisville Lip," Abby muttered.

Gunnar spoke a little about the brave troops in Vietnam and an ugly battle called Hamburger Hill until Abby shushed the talk.

He moved on and told about a prison execution that went wrong in another state, and one here in Kentucky until Abby shook her finger and took the subject to the weather. "Gunnar"—she lowered her voice—"let's not talk 'bout that. It makes you upset. Lighting on bad things is the devil's doings. You took the job to save your family's homestead, and when you saw the meanness in it, you tried to fix it."

She fluffed up the soft collar on her plain brown dress, straightened her skirts, and shifted in the rocker. "Now when do you think this rain's gonna let up?"

Gunnar wouldn't let it rest until he laid the last word. "*Only* government job around at the time," he grumbled. "But then I saw how bad things were with the condemned men—the rotten treatment of those poor lost souls. There's a right way and a wrong way to punish, and you start with the teachings of the Bible—"

"*Gunnar.*" Abby raised a brow.

I rubbed my jaw. I could picture Gunnar brewing up his bitters and dumping the potion into prisoners' mouths.

Gunnar nodded like a scolded child, rubbed his hands. "This rain takes a toll on the bones."

"And soul," Abby said quietly.

They went on to speculate about the weather some more and then chatted about the man named Neil Armstrong, marveling how he'd walked on the moon two weeks ago.

Abby said someone had seen it on the television, and she thought America had come a long way since the old days when they'd send monkeys and mice up there, and wouldn't she just love to have herself a television set one day so she could watch

The Johnny Cash Show? The postmistress told her all about the show, saying she'd heard of it when visiting her kin in Ohio— and "wouldn't that be something to see a talking picture right in your sitting room? . . . Oh, and a telephone! I'd get me a pink telephone," Abby added. "Talk to my Rainey anywhere. Now that'd be something grand!"

Gunnar actually chuckled and agreed it might, though he'd never seen the need for a house telephone.

"Love the sound of rain, but not every day. Gunnar," she said, restless. "Why don't you go get your harmonica."

He cleared his throat.

"Go on," she poked, "play us a song. I remember when you and my Gus used to play together. Him with that old violin and you with the harmonica made some sweet music."

"Afraid I haven't played in years and would only kick up the coyotes," he said.

"Humph, you used to make them wild dogs sit up and howl. Especially when you played 'Kentucky Babe.' Remember that?" Abby hummed a verse, motioned for me to join her.

Smiling, I shook my head no, the cut of missing Rainey digging deeper, his other song "Kentucky Lady" first in my heart.

"Rainey sings it just like his pa did." She rocked and sang the song soft and sweet. "*'Close your eyes, close your eyes and sleep. Skeeters are a-humming on the honeysuckle vine. Sleep, Kentucky babe. Sandman is a-coming to this little babe of mine. Sleep, Kentucky babe . . . You are mighty lucky, Babe of old Kentucky.'*"

I found myself humming along to the old Kentucky lullaby.

Abby watered the last verse and suddenly remembered something else. "I hope Rainey doesn't lose his change for the pay telephone. Do you think the city will have—"

"Likely one telephone on every block." Gunnar read her mind.

"Speaking of calling. Have you called on Mrs. Wise?" Abby asked.

"Maybe after housing," Gunnar answered.

"That's what you said last year," Abby reminded him. "She's

a good Christian woman . . . could keep a good Christian house for you."

Widow Wise lived on a mountain two hills over. Whenever she visited town, I could see she favored Gunnar. She'd stop him to talk about this or that, then let him know how lonely she was up on Wise Mountain. How maybe him and his niece could stop by for supper sometime? Once, she had him come over to kill a rabid fox on her land and she made him a covered dish to bring back home. She was sweet on him and I could see Gunnar was giving it some thought, too.

While Abby and Gunnar talked, I visited my mind on Rainey and missing my "seven." Maybe he's not too hot to get home after seeing those city girls. Them in their stylish Sears and Roebuck dresses covering Honey Girl slips of every color of the rainbow—and their twisted up sprayed hairdos. *What a grand important life!*

I tried to flip the ends of my hair upward, tugging. Again, and again, trying to tame my long, tangled curls into a spiffy city hairstyle.

Maybe I should make my own fortune come true, take that first step. *Rainey, six, Bur, five.*

I'd only been kissed by one boy in my life and that didn't count since it was Henny's eighteen-year-old brute cousin who'd paddlefished his tongue inside my mouth. A kiss that was pried, not privileged. One that he'd tackled me for when I was eleven. He'd pushed me to the ground in back of the Stumps' cabin when he thought no one was looking. Rolled atop me, pinning my arms down with his knees, bruising bones. Mrs. Stump caught him and took her broom to his head, batting him all the way down Stump Mountain. Henny, too, hot on his tail with a thorny locust branch. And when Rainey got wind of it from Henny, he sharpened his pocketknife and searched the hills for him for two days.

A thousand years I'd been practicing for that important kiss, waiting to be kissed properly . . . at least since I was ten, I reckoned.

I'd often steal into the barn when no one was around and

take the sheet off the tall gold-painted floor mirror that had been stored in the dusty corner. Being extra careful not to disturb the corn spider who'd caught my hopes and dreams in her arching web above it. When I asked about the mirror long ago, Gunnar only said it belonged to my aunt. And that it was vain to have it in the foyer of our house. I didn't think it was any more vain than his other stuff, though.

There in front of the six-foot mirror I'd stand on dried corn husks, practicing and planting my perfect pucker, the slant of sun slipping through the slatted dark oak boards. Hidden behind the mirror was a tiny jar of shortening that I'd put there. I'd unlatch the jar, paint the cooking oil across my lips. Then I'd fix kiss after kiss on that ol' barn mirror, my prints sawtoothed across the looking glass like spreading dandelion heads.

I couldn't help wondering if Mama had practiced her kisses this way. I tried not to think about the latest dreams I'd been having of her—the hissing snakes in those sleeping hours, about drawing the broken heart on Mama's fortune-teller—and what everything meant.

Over the years, I'd tried to talk to Gunnar about my folks, but he'd shoot down any more talk about them, saying he was *too busy for chat, done with useless things that can't be done over,* and that I needed to stop wasting my time on the dead. Then he'd send me out to the porch with a bucket of water and a scrub brush or back to the fields to appreciate the *living bones* in my knees.

Why it was so hard to believe he was talking so nice to Abby now. It didn't matter that they had known each other since they were kids. He'd known lots of folks forever and he hadn't shared a long, quiet porch-talking with any of them lately—heck, in forever.

Growing drowsy, I scooted closer to the wall, pulled up my knees, and rested my head on them. Sierra came over to bunt her head against my legs.

Abby shifted suddenly in her seat and clucked softly. "Trouble's coming, I can feel it." A firefly brushed a glow past her cheek.

I shuddered. Abby could smell trouble, same as a rain crow could bad weather.

A coyote called from the hills. The lanterns burned low. Gunnar went inside and poured them each a bourbon. In a few minutes, their hands slipped into the shadows, talking.

Where is he? My Rainey seven.

Chapter 13

The rain stopped, and sinners' prayers were answered till God snuck out from the slippery shadows beckoning for more.

Gunnar yelled up the stairs while I tried to safety-pin a button to my church dress. "Time to get, RubyLyn. *Now!*"

"In a second," I called back, same as I did not two seconds ago.

I hated Sundays. It seemed useless going. Here my daddy was a preacher and drank himself to death. What kind of God-fearing man does that? And for all Gunnar's fine talk about good and evil, he drank, too. *Hypocrite!* It was no wonder I had to spend every service praying for God to make him less ornery. But God didn't listen and I found myself drifting during sermons, praying for a way out of this town in the folds of my *sinful* fortunes.

Sunday was supposed to be my day to rest, *He'd* said, but I had to get up even earlier to cook a hot breakfast for *him* and get myself neat for church. Still, once I got there I felt a little better seeing all those folks. With only the Fords and Stumps as my neighbors, and the visits to the Feed, it got pretty lonely during the summers, unless you could drive to other hills to visit. Which Gunnar'd made sure to let me know long ago: *not happening.* And except for the few times the church held a picnic and a swim in its creek, it was rare to visit other kids. And that was only when one of the mamas or a schoolteacher wore Gunnar down with their pleas to let me stay.

I stuck myself with the pin, bit back a curse, and threw the button onto the bed, wishing I had the good sewing fingers like Abby and Rose—wishing I had a prettier dress. I threw on my quilt jacket to cover the missing button and stuffed my hairbrush into my pocket.

I rushed down the stairs and pulled the pie out of the oven that I'd made for Sunday supper. Grabbing a peach off the kitchen table, I dashed outside to the truck. Gunnar snapped for me to get in.

"Baby Jane should be here any second," I said, pulling out the brush, tapping it against my leg.

"Time to get," he warned.

"Not yet." Patting the peach inside my other pocket, I watched the road, stealing looks at Stump Mountain behind me.

He shook his head and got into the truck.

"*Gunnar.* Just a few more seconds. She's working Sundays at the Millers'." Baby Jane hadn't missed a Sunday ever since I'd invited her to the Easter Sunrise Service and Egg Hunt last year.

Gunnar'd fussed about her stinking, fussed about her being barefoot, fussed about her being a Stump. So I'd snuck her a pair of my old sneakers, even though they were two sizes too big, and gave her a bar of soap, telling her to wash her dress on weekends and to be sure to take a creek bath on Saturdays. I'd bought an old Bible from Rose for ten cents and Baby Jane kept it buried inside her metal box she had hidden in the woods. Every Sunday morning she'd come flying down the mountain, drippin' and a'squeakin', waving her Bible. Always on time, Gunnar'd let her crawl into the back of the truck to hitch a ride.

Today, Gunnar wasn't having none of it. He slipped his arm out the window and thumped the door twice.

I climbed inside, smacked the hairbrush down between us. He turned the motor over and took off down Royal Road. Then I saw her tearing through the tobaccos. Tiny shouts lifting, her Bible held high.

Gunnar kept driving.

"Pull over . . . pull over . . . *Please.*"

Gunnar pushed down on the gas pedal.

"Stop!" I cried.

Leaning out the window, I shouted, "*Hurry!* Hurry, Baby Jane." I turned to Gunnar and shook his arm. "She's almost here. Wait up."

Gunnar elbowed me off and puffed. " 'Most men will proclaim every one his goodness: but a *faithful* man who can find?' Proverbs 20:6."

I looked over my shoulder and saw Baby Jane running in the road behind us, flailing her arms, face bright red and dirt-streaked. "And, Mark 12 says to 'love thy neighbor as thyself.' There is no greater Commandment!"

"Silence," he nipped.

"God don't climb into mean bones . . . No *GodPretty* in that, Gunnar. Can't we hold up long enough for her to jump into the bed?"

Hard jawed, he pressed forward, the truck snaking in and out of dying fog as we made our way up the narrow hill to Nameless First Baptist Church.

Gunnar parked in the church lot, pulled his Bible off the dash, and strode inside, leaving me in the truck. Grabbing my brush, I started down the hill for Baby Jane.

I met her at the first bend, limping and sobbing.

"S-sorry for being late. D-d-dropped some of Miller's eggs this morning and . . . and he got real mad. He wouldn't let me leave till I cleaned the coop," Baby Jane cried. "Th-th-then his best chicken, Earlene, took off . . . Found her, though."

"You eat breakfast?" I asked.

"Ain't hungry—"

I pulled out the peach and stuffed it into Baby Jane's dress pocket. "Maybe after church then."

Hurried, I turned her around and brushed her hair, patted my pockets. I'd forgotten the Hens-and-Biddies ribbon.

Baby Jane fished inside her own pocket and held up a rubber band, small mews whisking through her lips.

"It's okay, Baby Jane. Shhh, shh . . . Hey, how's Henny?"

"Sister don't like her crooked nose. Won't come out . . . outta the house, or help with chores." She hiccupped.

"Tell her I miss her . . . and it's real good you found Earlene," I added softly, stretching, winding the tight band around her ponytail.

"Earlene don't like Mr. Miller much, but she always comes for me."

"Where's your other shoe," I said, spinning her back around, noting one of them gone.

"M-m-mean dog came after me back there . . . I threw it at him."

"Okay, maybe we can find it on the way home."

"Dog ran off with it."

"Don't worry none," I said, brimming with enough for both of us. She could slip in maybe once, but sharp-eyed Gunnar wouldn't let her the next time.

I took the hem of my dress and wiped off her dirty face, wishing I had a bottle of Rose's perfume to help with the chicken poop smell that stuck to her.

Baby Jane sniffled loudly. "Saved me . . . that the dog grabbed and worried my shoe real good and not me."

"Sure did . . . Take off that other shoe."

She pulled it off, handed it to me, and I threw it into a bush.

Another sob escaped her trembling mouth. "Gunnar'll get me real good, RubyLyn."

The church organ puffed out soft notes.

"Hush it now," I gently warned. "Nobody will pay a mind to your feet, unless you're making 'em by limping into church."

I plucked a thin stem of yellow-blossomed beggar-tick from the side of the road and tucked it into her ponytail. "*There.*" I kissed the top of her forehead. "You look real pretty. Let's go in." We set up the hill.

She groped for my hand, latched on tight. I looked down and saw that her nails were bitten to the quick, blood-specked from the worries again.

I pulled her over to Gunnar's truck, and leaning against it, I took a toe to my heel, pried off one shoe, then the other, kicking off the tight, dingy pair of cream patent leathers.

"We'll be sisters." I winked and dumped them into the truck's bed.

"*Sisters.*" Baby Jane widened her eyes and broke a slow grin. Barefoot, we walked into church together, up to the third row and squeezed in beside Gunnar.

Relieved to see folks coming in behind us and no one noticing, I plopped down, tucked my bare feet under the bench, tugged at my long skirts, and nudged Baby Jane to do the same.

Except to toss Baby Jane a frown, Gunnar kept his nose in his Bible. He didn't want her here, but yet he complained that Henny, or *Henny and the Heathens,* as he said most Sundays, *didn't practice His Word.* Same as he said about the Crocketts, but a bit gruffer.

Talk was, the fifth row had once belonged to the Crocketts, but Mr. Parker and his wife had claimed it long ago 'cause theirs was splintered and creaky. Folks said that the Crocketts stopped coming after their missus passed. Most hill folk had their own prayer benches made for church. But the tiny building couldn't fit more than ten small benches inside, five on each side, so Brother Jeremiah suggested Mr. Parker use the Crocketts' and give a nice church donation instead.

On the bench across from us sat two girls about my age, Margaret and Millie Vetter. They were from the mountain over and sat behind Bur Hancock and his mama. Bur was a looker and one to hook, most girls and their mamas said.

Gunnar must've thought so, too, because once in a while he'd stop long enough to chat with him about weather, and even had me bake his ailing mama a pie a month ago.

Erbie Sipes sat a row behind us counting the congregation by clicking his teeth. When he chopped off the last of his snaps, I knew everyone was seated. Brother Jeremiah would start the worship after the hymn. Beside the pulpit, my favorite teacher pumped the old Estey and sang "The Church in the Wildwood."

Today's sermon was about forgiveness, enemies, and trespasses—one of Brother Jeremiah's favorite topics, and one that he delivered with a mighty wrath.

When church was done, Gunnar headed straight to the parking lot, barely nodding a greeting to anyone. I lagged behind with Baby Jane clutched to my side.

Millie Vetter grabbed my sleeve. "Hi, RubyLyn," she said, sneaking glances at my feet. "We heard they're looking for Carter. Do you think they'll find him?"

"Sheriff thinks so," I answered.

"We saw him and his old girlfriend hanging out down in front of the Laundromat a few weeks ago. It looked like his girl had been crying . . . Didn't it, Mags?" Millie looked at her sister.

"Uh-huh," Margaret replied. "And I even waved, but he acted like he didn't see me. Heard they were arguing about one of them Stump girls, too." She pursed her lips at Baby Jane.

"Baby Jane, go wait in the truck so Gunnar doesn't see your feet," I whispered to her. Reluctantly, Baby Jane let go of my hand.

Brother Jeremiah strolled by with a greeting. "Ladies, mighty fine day the Lord's given us. Enjoy His Sunday." He tipped his head. We quieted for a second.

"Hey, you wanna come over to our house today?" Millie asked. "Mama's going to fry up chicken for a picnic."

I looked over my shoulder to Gunnar, then back at her. "You ask me that every Sunday, Millie. You know I can't."

"Thought maybe you could ask him again," she said, friendly-like.

"Ask him," Margaret pushed. "We're going swimming in the pond, and Bur said he might come by and bring his cousin. Heard he's just as cute as Bur."

"Go ask," Millie urged. "Daddy's put up a new tire swing, and it'll be buckets of fun."

Fried chicken and a cool swimming hole sounded a whole lot better than going back to my stuffy house and the fields. It would be good to get away from my troublesome thoughts, Rainey, the baby-buyers—everything and everyone.

"He's gotta let you . . . summer ain't gonna last *forever,*" Millie pressed.

I stole a sidelong peek at Gunnar. Baby Jane was sitting in the bed of the truck. *To feel free for a few hours—free and fifteen would be divine. . . .*

"Go ask"—Millie tugged on my arm—"I have me seventy-five cents saved. I'm just dying to see what one of your fortunes will say about me kissing Bur."

"Not unless I pucker first," Margaret teased.

"A lot of good puckering there," I joked, but perking at the thought of money for the fair.

The girls giggled, and I couldn't help joining them.

I glanced over at Bur, him standing there a little bowlegged, all clean-jawed, in a starched shirt, pressed trousers, talking with Brother Jeremiah, watching everyone out of the corner of his eye. He was a good man who still had that sweet look, the one boys have before manhood and the hills and hardness grab hold. And the handsome looks to boot.

Bur caught me peeking and pulled himself up taller, lit a soft smile.

"Sounds fun," I said to the girls. "Reckon I can try again."

I went over to the truck where Gunnar was talking to Erbie. Baby Jane was stretched out in the bed, dozing.

"Uh-huh . . . yessir, fine boots, and nary a pinch walking up the hills, Mr. Royal," Erbie was saying with a grin.

I looked down at Erbie's boots and back up at his happy face. Erbie had never learned to drive. He'd wandered all over these hollars and hills mostly barefoot until about seven years ago when me and Gunnar saw him sitting on French's bench. It was a cold day when we spotted Erbie's feet hardening to white wax. Gunnar stopped and helped Erbie up. He walked him into the Feed store and sat him in a chair next to Mr. Parker's potbelly stove.

Then Gunnar went straight out to the back lot and bought Erbie a pair of boots and some thick socks from Rose. Every year since, when the tobacco money came in, Gunnar'd made sure ol' Erbie would get a new pair.

"Thank you, Mr. Royal," Erbie said, waving good-bye. Him, thanking him each and every Sunday for seven years.

Gunnar gave him a nod and then turned to me. "RubyLyn, it's not time to take off your shoes, get 'em back on; we haven't left His Gathering . . . And are you forgetting your manners again?"

"Yessir, nosir . . . Hey, Erbie." I waved back.

"Hey, Miss RubyLyn." He lifted a leg, showed off his boot. "Two thousand five hundred twenty-one stitches in these."

"That many?" I asked, stepping forward to get a better look. "Those are real nice boots, Erbie. I like the color, too."

Erbie bobbed his head proudly and waved good-bye one last time.

I turned to Gunnar. "Can I go over to Millie and Margaret's today? Their mama's gonna cook a chicken and—"

He grabbed my arm, shoved me to the passenger side. "And you have Sunday supper to fix."

"There's ham 'n' biscuits from last night and some potato salad. The buttermilk pie's cooling on the counter. Wouldn't be much to fix yourself a sandwich, Gunnar. You can drop Baby Jane off in the field."

He looked at me like I'd sprouted an extra nose, then jumped into his truck.

I leaned into the window. "For just a little while," I pleaded. "Summer's almost done—"

"I'm done." He hit the horn, making me jump.

Alarmed, Baby Jane popped up in the back.

I held the curse thickening on my tongue, looked over my shoulder to Margaret and Millie, and shook my head.

Chapter 14

Monday morning roused Sunday's sinners with sharp raps to the door.

Abby knocked first, troubling for news on Rainey. She told us she was going to the Feed to work on the curtain material for Mrs. Parker. She'd be sewing there all day and would we tell Rainey if he came home? Before Abby left, she asked Gunnar to write down the name of the hospital Rainey went to, and the number for the State Police.

A few minutes later, I watched the sheriff drive by, heading toward the Crocketts'. Twenty minutes passed and Sheriff pulled up to our house. I was halfway out the door when Gunnar snatched me back inside. Worried about Rainey, I stayed shadowed behind the screen and listened to the men.

Sheriff got out of his automobile, rested his foot on the porch step, and told Gunnar, "Thought we'd let ya know, we found Carter Crockett late last night. He'd set up camp in the brush alongside Devils Bone, and 'bout a quarter mile downstream we found him."

Sheriff hitched a thumb over his shoulder. "Tucked away back there behind your line on the other side of Devils Bone, he was. Seems he was holing up in an old pup tent. And somehow the boy set it afire . . . I guess he was trying to keep himself dry from all this rain we've had." He shook his head. "That damn tent went up like tissue paper. Hardly nothing left but the metal snaps."

Relieved Rainey didn't meet trouble, my thoughts turned to Carter.

Sheriff went on to say, "Me and Deputy figured during it all, he was trying to escape the tent and fell down the bank and busted his head on rock—drowned in them rushing waters."

Carter . . . drowned. I pressed a hand over my dropped jaw.

The deputy broke in. "We found more than one set of muddy footprints around that camp. Looks like his kin was helping him hide out from the warrant, probably giving him food and all, though Beau Crockett—all of 'em—is keeping it zipped."

Gunnar shook his head, uttered, "*Good Lord.*"

"Uh-huh. Crockett buried his boy this morning." Sheriff grimaced.

Surprised, a tear escaped from the corner of my eye. When I was seven and Carter was eleven, I'd fallen, scraping my knee on a sharp rock in the backfield along Devils Bone Creek. Hearing my screams across the fields, Carter came running. He tore a strip off the bottom of his shirt and used it to make a bandage for me. Then he walked me back to my house, careful to go real slow. Instead of thanking Carter, Gunnar'd just lopped off one of his killing looks and scolded him for trespassing.

I hoped Gunnar would show some sort of forgiveness for Carter's passing, especially after yesterday's sermon. But he just rolled his shoulders and mumbled something that sounded mean and cursing.

I wondered about my daddy, what he would've said, him with those kind eyes in the photograph.

I wished Rainey was home, and I missed Henny, too. I patted the new seeds saved in my dress pocket that I was waiting to give her. I could never stay mad at her too long, easily forgiving her, and frankly I knew she was going to need me after Carter's death.

Forgiveness. Carter. Carter before the devil took away the good soul he was born with.

When Gunnar came into the kitchen and took his seat, I toasted his bread, and asked quietly, "Should I make a pie for the Crocketts?"

"No." He snapped up his newspaper, flicked open a page.

"But—"

"No." He whacked the paper down on the table.

"A dish maybe?"

"Dammit," he boomed, "you stay clear of biting snakes."

I slapped the plate of toast down in front of him, muttering I wished I could.

Gunnar ate and read his newspaper. I tried to nibble on my toast, but let it grow cold, my appetite lost on Carter and his family. And I was trying to think up a million reasons to talk to Henny—to find an excuse to go up to Stump Mountain, when Gunnar said, "Since Rainey's still gone, go get Henny and bring her up to the tobacco to work. Need to dust those plants."

I jumped up from the table and Gunnar latched on to my arm and pulled me back down to finish my breakfast. When I was done, he pointed to the broom for me to sweep the floor. After I started to pour him a third cup of coffee, he shoved me off to go.

I ran out the door not bothering to grab my shoes, even though Gunnar would have a fit if he saw me running around barefoot. More than anything I needed to feel this last lingering of summer—life—alive—and the living slapping at my feet, pounding up to a beating heart.

The damp grass was cool and sweetly scented. Under a bright blue sky, I spotted blooms and stopped to pick a bouquet of field daisies, bishop weed, and foxglove. When I had a handful, I cut over to the Crocketts', following the creek, inhaling the breeze-soaked wind, lighting through the switchgrass and green-legged Sweet William.

Sneaking behind the cabin to their small family cemetery, I stopped under dark pines to catch my breath. I spied the fresh dirt amongst the half-dozen scattered graves buried in hollow earth, and stepped carefully over to Carter's burial spot and placed the flowers atop the loose grave dirt.

Looking over my shoulder, shaking, I tried to collect a prayer. If Gunnar caught me, he'd kill me; if the Crocketts caught me, I'd be deader.

I kneeled down, and breathed out, "God, if You're in Name-less, please bring Carter to Your home. Let him be with his mama and . . . not be mean anymore." I stumbled through strings of Psalm 23, scattering the words upward. I couldn't help adding a plea to Him for my swift leave of Nameless.

Overhead, a crow barked a warning. I rearranged the color-ful blooms, dragged my fingers through the raw dirt, and patted softly. "For all your dreams—secrets—and prayers, Carter. I hope you have them now."

I dusted the clay off my dress and dashed back across the field to the foot of Stump Mountain.

Breathless, I trudged up the hill, keeping on the narrow, balded trail and jumping across the ruts.

At the first switchback, Ada Stump marched by, her blond hair blowing over a pale face, feet pounding the mud trail. I looked over my shoulder, and Ada peered back over hers. Stop-ping on the path, she struck one of her matches and flicked it my way. I stumbled over a stone, stubbing my toe, and cursed her heartily.

"Ada Stump . . . *Dammit, Ada.*" I caught back up with her. "Give 'em here, or I'm going to light your tail real good." I held out my hand.

Ada clutched the matches to her chest. I grabbed her by the wrist and pried the matches away. "You're gonna hurt your-self."

She tried to snatch them back. Then I noticed her swollen lip and black eye. A front tooth was cracked.

I jerked her wrist and held on to her. "Who did this, Ada?"

Ada screwed up her tiny face. "My matches . . . *Mine* . . . Gimme my matches," she hissed.

"Does it hurt? C'mon, I'm taking you home to your mama." I tugged on her.

"No." She shrank. "I ain't going back in there. *I ain't.*"

"I'm taking you home, Ada Stump."

"I want MY matches." She slapped at my arm.

"Stop—"

"No! It's . . . it's too dark."

"Dark? What are you talking about, Ada?"

"Matches . . . give 'em here." She clawed while trying to wiggle out of my grip.

"Stop it, you need to go home."

"The shed!" she spit. "*Shed* . . ."

"Let's go."

"Pa . . . he-he locks me in there—in the shed!"

"*Shed* . . . You're lying," I said, refusing to believe, but narrowing my eyes, remembering Baby Jane's lost words "lock me away up there . . . like Sis."

"Ain't a'lying . . . *ain't.*" Angry tears leaked out of her dark eyes. Then she lowered her mouth to my hand and clamped down.

I shrieked and jerked away, shaking my wound. I dropped the matches.

Ada scrambled to snatch them up and then lit off into the woods.

Damn kid. "Ada Stump, you're gonna burn down the mountain, you don't stop," I hollered after her, blowing on my injury.

Chapter 15

Little Charles sat on the porch teething on a stick, smacking his swollen gums. I climbed the steps and picked him up. Rocking him on my hip, I called out for Henny.

Charles crinkled his smiling eyes, drooled as I held him. "Hey, you handsome devil. Yes, you." I gently poked the baby's chest and kissed his cheek.

Henny walked out from around the back of the house, sullen and eyes red, nose big and crooked.

"What are *you* doing up here?" she said, setting her feet onto the downward trail.

"You okay? I've been worried."

She tossed me an icy look.

"Gunnar sent me to tell you, you're working the field with me today. We're going to dust 'em." I set Charles down and stepped off the porch.

She shrugged.

"I just tangled with Ada. She bit me—"

Henny brushed past me.

"Wait up, Henny . . . Stop . . . Ada's hurt—"

"I'm hurt, *dammit!* She pointed to her fat nose. "And she's okay . . . just . . . just fell, is all," she snipped.

"Sorry, does it hurt bad?"

"Going to all my life."

"Hey, are you sure about Ada, she looks—Hey, wait . . ." I reached out.

"They found Carter." Seeing the sight of her sad eyes, I reckoned the news about his death had reached the mountain. "I'm sorry. Guess you heard."

She wiped away a tear. "More than enough. Sheriff came up and told Pa he found a note beside Carter's camp. Two hearts, and that fancy penmanship like we learnt in second grade . . . Pa lied to him and said it weren't mine even though he knew it was 'cause he makes me write to them damn government men for him all the time."

"You wrote to Carter?"

"Yeah, twice. I tacked one of 'em to the cedar post alongside your property. Wanted to tell him I was sorry I made him mad, arguing with him about seeing another girl like that . . . My fault."

"Oh, Henny, no—"

"It is . . . After the sheriff left, I had me a cry. But Pa weren't through—he whipped me for bringing the law up here snooping. Then Lena caught me wearing the pecker bone that Carter'd gave me . . . She told Pa, and he got ahold of it and I got the switch for that, too . . . 'Spect Sister was mad about her own beau not giving her one, why she told like that. See?"

Henny slipped off the shoulder of her dress and showed me angry red slashes, then jerked the sleeve back up. "Whipped me good this time, Roo. He's gonna kill me one day."

I inspected the marks, rested my head next to hers. "We need to get you some salve." I clenched my hand and felt it throb a little. "Me too."

She rubbed her damp eyes. "Just wished Carter'd gotten my second apology that I'd snuck down to the fencepost . . . I wrote it real pretty, too."

"C'mon, Henny, I'll run into my house and get you some medicine." I hated the thought of her being whipped. Her daddy taking his "talking stick" to her. Last month was little Charles. And though I'd had my own share of "talking" from Gunnar with his bitters, at least he never beat me.

"He was the only boy around here who was nice to me. Didn't hit much . . ." Henny sniffled. "He had himself dreams for us, he sure did . . . Was my best chance of a marriage bed . . . Ya know'd he was nice, Roo . . . remember when ya cut up your knee?"

"Yeah." I patted her hand, feeling sorry that was the only good she'd clung to and would always remind me of. Sorry that it was mine now, too.

"I know'd folks think he got his due"—her jaw twitched—"but whoever lit his camp afire will get theirs."

"Probably fell asleep with one of those cigarettes he was always puffing on."

"Humph . . . The hills got its own law round here," she said stiffly.

I stared at her, not knowing what else to say.

She looked behind her. "Lots of accidents round here . . . Them graves up there?"

I glanced back. "The babies that didn't make it," I said matter-of-factly.

"The big, fresh one."

I raised a hushing hand, not sure if I wanted to hear.

Henny snatched it. "My cousin, Lloyd . . . 'member him?"

"Mister Icky Sticky Lips?"

"Uh-huh, 'member when he"—she pointed to my mouth—"tried to have his way—"

"Weasel!"

Her eyes flashed. "Swear to secret."

With a shaky finger, I laid an X across my heart once and open palm twice, locking in our secret swear.

She swiped hers across the chest and hand, too, then quickly pressed her hand to mine, and whispered, "Ma caught him with one of Sisters last fall."

"What? He came back to the mountain? . . . Oh, hell."

"It's true . . . *Ada*. He'd done it to her, too."

"Lordy-jones—Ada? But she's only ten—"

"She was nine and ain't sayin' much more, but he got his trial of sorts this spring when someone spotted him near town . . . Law of the hills runs hard here in Nameless."

"I know." I whistled low, knowing more than I wanted, the thought of him buried up there weakening my knees.

"Got his due." She tightened her jaw.

"I sure hope Ada's okay, she looked pretty busted up."

"Humph. Pa's gonna bust her good if she don't stop bed-wettin' everything."

"Huh?"

"Started it this past winter. We'd wake up with our pallets soaked. Sit down in a chair filled with her puddles . . . A few months back Pa took to locking her in the woodshed every night. Now she's stealin' matches and stuff. *Brat*."

"Poor Ada."

Henny rolled her eyes. "*Dead Ada* if she don't stop . . . Pa's gonna kill her if Ma don't do it first."

"Your daddy's beating her, locking her in that dark shed every night . . . Ain't right, Henny." I shivered.

"Better than sleeping in her piss," she nipped. "And me or Ma always let her out in the mornings."

"Damn Lloyd." I thought of little Ada suffering, clenched a fist.

"Ain't sayin' no more," Henny said again, and buttoned her lip. "And you better not either." Her eyes warned.

Who would I tell? Gunnar, who hated the Stumps? Rose, who couldn't stop Gunnar from giving me the bitters? Or Rainey, who couldn't stop the townsfolk hating his skin? Deep down I knew this land claimed its sinners and held tight its secrets.

I answered with an extra X across my chest and trembling palm.

We walked a few minutes in thought, my curses to the town hanging like low, leaky clouds. I kept looking over my shoulder expecting the ghost of Lloyd to appear, expecting Carter to come flying out of the woods. Then, wanting to burn the thoughts from my mind, turn the talk around the bend, three wide bends, I said, "I'll let you pick up any torn leaves today while I take the tobacco to Paris."

"Really? I hate going to Paris."

"Huh-uh, sure will." Henny'd break out in hives every time

we had to "go to Paris"—dust the rows with the Paris green poison. Gunnar would have us mix up the green powdery insecticide with some road dust or flour and pour it into a coffee can that had been punctured on the bottom. We'd shake the poison out over the tobacco to get rid of the worms, flea beetles, and other tiny critters that were hurting the crop. By the time we'd finish, we looked like green leprechauns—our hair, eyebrows, everything coated.

"Sure ya don't mind going to Paris?" she asked.

"Nah, the rain's dropped some leaves and you can clean 'em up. I know how much Paris makes you sick. And Rainey took the ice pick to the coffee cans before he left for the city, but maybe he'll get back soon and help. Least everything's ready." Anything to make Henny perk up. "Maybe we won't find any hornworms. . . ."

She snorted at that, knowing how much I feared them and how I'd holler for Rainey to get them.

"Ya miss him," she said.

My face heated. "He's been gone five days . . . I'm worried that he found trouble. Same as his mama. That's all."

"Knows better. Your eyes say different. Says ya got the woman worry in 'em. Has he kissed ya yet? Ya know, the real kissing, not the clowning around kid kissing."

"You should do Granny Magic. . . . And, yeah, five whole days is a long time missing him—we're practically family."

Her mood lightened. "I ain't never kissed a darkie." She wiggled her brow and bumped my shoulder. "I bet it's like kissing the night air, sweet and dark."

"Black, Henny," I scolded. "You know he doesn't like being called those other names. And, yeah, that boy's been nibbling at my feelings a lot lately," I admitted.

"*You* better latch your lips on to his 'fore it's too late, Roo, and he's gone for good. Just don't let anyone catch ya"—she snapped her head toward the hill—"or it could get bad . . . real bad. You're gonna have to be really careful, Roo."

"Let's get down to the rows." I picked up my pace, wanting to get off the mountain.

We let the uneasy silence take hold to the bottom and for most of the day, leaving the mountain's sins scattered on the mud-caked path.

Gunnar let me and Henny take a longer dinner break to clean up. I spent most of it over by the well scrubbing the Paris poison off me with Lava soap, while Henny ate the cheese sandwich I'd made her. After I washed, I ate mine, then slipped into the house and put on a fresh dress to wear back to the rows. I helped Henny look for more tattered leaves to pluck. We tossed those into the trash with the ones the rain beat off. Every so often I would stare off toward Rainey's place.

Nearing suppertime, I saw him, and tapped Henny's shoulder, telling her to go on home.

She snapped up her head, followed my gaze. "Wouldn't mind going *home* to that."

I took off, feet pounding Royal land to Ford's cabin, my dress pasted to my thighs. My heart hammering out promises, forgetting and forgiving the darkness of recent days.

Rainey leaned against a pretty teal-colored automobile that had somewhere, sometime, and somehow lost its whole entire lid.

I slowed a second to gape. Rainey opened his arms and before I could stop myself, I fell into them like when we were littler and hadn't seen each other in a day, knocking off his hat, laughing as he spun us around. When he put me down, I noticed the Oertels '92 beer bottle in his fist, and in each of the hands of the two folks sitting in the front seat of the car behind him.

"RubyLyn," he said, picking up his hat, smiling broadly, "this is Dena and Donny Justice from over in Harlan." He patted his brown tie Gunnar had sent with him. "Their daddy leases out land to the big coal company down there."

Rainey put his arm around me and pulled me closer to him and the automobile. "Gave me a fine ride in this here fine Pontiac . . . convertible! I missed you, Roo," he breathed into my ear.

I got hold of my senses. Alarmed, I tried to push him off, but he had a strong grip on me. "*Careful,*" I said quietly over his shoulder.

"S'ok, they told me they're friendly with niggers," he whispered back.

Nigger? I raised a brow at his slip of a word I knew he hated.

"Hi, RubyLyn," the Justices chimed, and raised their beers in one hand and wiggled a wave in the other. On a creamy white bench in the backseat lay a half-dozen empty beer bottles.

"I met him at the big hospital." Rainey pointed his beer to the driver, a smart dressed man sporting a blue striped white vest and long bushed sideburns. "Donny, here, was getting his army physical, too, and his sister tagged along to shop in Louisville."

Donny opened the car door and climbed out clutching a beer. Rainey jutted out his chin, squeezed me, and said to him, "Call her Roo."

Donny tugged at his knee-high britches and reached for my hand. "*Roo.*" He shook while his red-mapped eyes snaked the length of me.

Words buttered on my tongue and all I could do was look away. From the passenger side, Dena cracked one of those catalog smiles and adjusted a silky scarf on her head, tucking in wisps of blond hair.

I ran my hand over my stained dress, folded my arms across my chest, and tucked one of my mud-caked shoes behind the other.

Dena slid out of the passenger seat, her in a bright busty pink sweater with pearl buttons—and I couldn't miss it if I tried—no slip under that short white skirt skinnied over her print-flowered undies.

I lifted my eyes and met her cool gaze. She reminded me of Daisy in *The Great Gatsby*.

"We had a swell time," Rainey chirped, clasping me tighter to his side. "Swell and they offered me their hospitality—their uncle's sleeping porch while they stuck around to rest and visit relatives. Gave me a ride home in this sweet GTO . . . a great goat!" He took a gulp of beer, then let his hand fall casually to my rear.

I shifted my feet, looked up at Rainey, and knitted my brow.

Roo, he mouthed back. *I missed you.*

I slipped out of his hold.

Donny laughed. "Yessir, anytime, pal. You never know when I'm gonna need you to cover my freckled hide over there . . ." He looked at me, winked. "Roo, them officials at the army hospital said Rainey here was such a big, strong, country nigger, all he had to do was show up and them gooks would run." He slapped Rainey's back and swizzled the rest of his beer before tossing the bottle into the backseat. Then he lifted out Rainey's brown satchel and dropped it on the grass.

I figured Rainey must've left his brain on that sleeping porch to ride in an automobile with no roof and get boozed up with strangers, and being real friendly to me in front of white folks.

I looked past those flapping folks, not sure what my eye just caught. At the edge of our property, one of the Crocketts stood beside a tree watching Ada and her brother walk down the property line. Crockett wasn't trying to hide, but he didn't want to be seen either. Then he caught me looking and stepped into the woods.

I scooted farther away from Rainey and mumbled something about getting him back to the fields and picked up his traveling bag.

Dena sidled up to Rainey, put her hand on his shirt, then puckered up her painted lips and I watched his whole mouth disappear behind her kiss. Until this second I'd never really seen the hardness of Rainey's long arms and lean chest, the deepness of his laurel-green eyes in his coffee-brown face, his welcoming smile. Never seen anyone else notice either.

Dena slowly leaned back, trailed a nail across his cheek, then waggled her slipless behind all the way back to the automobile.

Rainey licked his limp lips, rubbed his chest.

Dena settled inside the Pontiac, pulled down the visor, and dabbed a pinky at the corners of her mouth. Donny climbed in behind the wheel and they sped off, collecting mud, spraying rock and warbly yee-haws down Royal Road.

Rainey stuffed his hands into his pants pockets, rocked on his heels, and tipped back his hat. He grinned down at me with his shiny, plum-colored, beer-soaked lips.

Chapter 16

I tightened my grip on Rainey's satchel, then swung it and hit him square on the shoulder. Twice, then another on his back before he fell to the ground laughing, arms crossed as he shielded himself.

"Here you are, Rainey Ford, all liquored up with those flyby floozies when everybody's been fretting about you!"

"Roo, stop it now . . . no . . . c'mon—stop . . ." He pulled himself up unsteadily onto his knees, leaned back on his heels, and spread his hands.

"Five long days you've been gone," I preached.

"You missed me?"

I shook the suitcase at him.

"What was I supposed to do, girl? Hitch when I've got a good ride?" He pouted, his lips bruised with paint by another.

"Humph, good ride my eye. What if those white folks would've turned on you? What if they're doing it now—gone to town *right now* and said you hugged me and—"

"What . . . ? *No.* Now, Roo, me and Donny made us a pact . . . uh-huh, to save each other in Vietnam. Hell, I'd likely be gone forever if the wrong white folks picked up my black hide hitchhiking—"

"Five." I raised my fingers. "Five days, Rainey. You ain't never been out of this hollar more than five minutes and now I see why. No sense! Your mama's been worried sick. You could've called and left word with the postmistress. You—"

"Now, Roo, those were friendly folks."

"Too friendly and up to no good."

"Huh?" He rubbed his mouth. "You don't think *that* meant anything?"

"It meant a lot to me, Rainey Ford."

"Hey . . . hey, c'mon, Roo. You know I missed you. You're my girl. Hell"—he plopped back on his heels, spread his arms wide—"wait, come here . . . I'll get my violin . . . here, Roo, take a dance with me in the fields. I missed you. C'mon, girl . . . c'mon *'Sw-Sweet Ken-tuck-eee Lady'* . . ." he crooned. " *'Now that I'm home again, deee-ry . . .'* " Swaying on his knees, he pressed a hand over his heart and sang.

I raised the small suitcase.

He twisted sideways, dodging as I swung the bag again. Missing, I threw the leather satchel onto the porch, busting the lock, scattering out the tightly packed clothes and newspaper inside.

He fell back onto the grass, lost in a fit of giggles. I stomped across the field toward home to his caterwauling tunes.

Gunnar stopped me in the rows, took off his straw hat, and wiped his brow. "Did I hear Rainey?"

"Oh." I looked over my shoulder. "Yessir, you did. Going to fix us meatloaf sandwiches for supper, then go to my room for the evening . . . I . . . well"—I dropped my voice—"I got my you-know-what . . . er, it hasn't stopped. I feel . . . and I—"

He ran a hand over his reddening face, stretching skin, wagging his head for me to hush it.

When I was about a good fifteen feet away Gunnar called out, "RubyLyn, fix up one of your fancy pies or nice cobblers." He stared off toward Rainey's house. "Think I'd like to call on him in a bit, see if he picked up my *Louisville Times* newspaper I wanted."

Fancy. I stopped dead in my tracks and turned to him. He'd never said anything good about anything I did. And except for the rare church socials, an ill neighbor, he'd never asked for one of my dishes to go calling on him.

I said, "Yessir." I thought about the kiss, my daddy and Mr. Stump, the empty beer bottles strewn across the backseat. Fury railed my senses. "I'll see if I have any peaches left, but I reckon a pie won't go with what he's been drinking. You may need some coffee for that."

Gunnar narrowed his eyes and locked them to the fields.

I headed for the house. In the cellar I found a few peaches for the pie. I prepared the dough, not bothering to take extra care to knead it lightly so I wouldn't toughen it. I punched the dough, calling out "Dena" after each blow . . . When the pie came out of the oven, I set it on the windowsill to cool.

I knew Gunnar wouldn't bother asking me to go with him now that we had my unmentionable menstruation to keep us at his comfortable distance for the next few days, or until he forgot about it again. Weren't no time after I'd set the pie out to cool when he took it over to Rainey's porch.

I sat on my bed staring at Mama's Rattle-My-Tattle lipstick, rolling the gold tube across a palm. I pulled off its top and glided the soft creamy bullet across my lips, smearing, tasting. I wondered what color Dena was wearing and how many of those hussy kisses she'd given to Rainey. Surprised, an ache took hold of my heart. I couldn't bear losing him.

I heard the screen door bang twice and then Gunnar's heavy footsteps on the stairs. Quickly, I wiped my mouth on the back of a hand.

"Gunnar?" I poked my head out the bedroom door. "You're back early. I left your sandwich on the stove . . . How'd they like the pie? Did—"

He had his jaw set tough and fists clenched.

"What is it? Gunnar?" I followed him to his room and stood in the doorway. "Is it the Crocketts?"

He went straight to his closet and rummaged inside, then turned around and scanned the bedroom. In two long steps, Gunnar reached his tallboy sitting across the room, ran his hands over a stack of clean shirts, spilling clothes onto the floor. Then he peered behind the dresser. Bending over, he snatched up his thick leather belt.

"Gunnar?"

He shoved me aside, plodded down the stairs, and elbowed himself out the door.

I made it outside the screen before its clap could cry the warning.

Gunnar was heading back to Rainey's, his belt coiled tight around a fisted knuckle.

I grabbed my shoes off the porch and put them on.

When I got near Rainey's place, I saw him and Gunnar in the side yard. Abby stood on her porch, braced against the rail. I stepped behind the Fords' thick old cherry tree and peeked out.

Gunnar dragged Rainey by the shirt over to a waist-high rotted stump in the yard.

Rainey jerked his arm away once, and Gunnar snatched it back and shoved him forward onto the splintered stub. Rainey looked like he might try to light into Gunnar, but my uncle had a power and size I'd not seen.

"Going to get a whipping for upsetting your mother," Gunnar bit.

Rainey looked back at Abby.

"Never once thinking of home." Gunnar snapped the leather against the ground.

"Sorry, Ma, I never meant to," Rainey called to her quietly.

Abby moaned and buried her head in her hands.

"Letting our women see you like that . . ." Gunnar's voice shook. "Tearing up my satchel."

I pressed my mouth to the bark, groaned. *If only I hadn't told on him . . . if only I'd sent Rainey off somewhere till he sobered.*

"You will learn to keep your manners here and all of those sins in the city," Gunnar hissed. "You not bothering to call, coming home with your boots soaked and smelling of whore. Why, you worried this family for days, son."

Rainey gripped the stump and peered up at Gunnar. "You're not my pa."

"I am today," Gunnar growled, and let the belt fly ten times.

Chapter 17

Shaking, I moved back into the tree's shadow, sucking air through my teeth between each slap on skin. Rainey never so much as whimpered. I shouldn't have told knowing how Gunnar felt about the alcohol—my daddy. I couldn't help feeling some of those lashes were meant for me.

From the porch, Abby cradled her face and wept quietly.

When Gunnar was through, he tossed his belt to the ground. "Rainey, get to the creek and clean yourself up. Don't be going in the house like that."

Rainey pushed himself up and staggered away.

Gunnar stepped onto the porch, put a hand on Abby's arm, and said, "We're not careful Rainey's gonna end up same as his namesake. Our Rainey in his life's got to honor Bethea, not end up like him—"

"Don't say that, Gunnar!" she gnashed. "My boy's not gonna end up like Rainey Bethea—he's gonna be a fine soldier."

I gasped. The colored boy, Rainey Bethea, had lived over on the banks of the Ohio River in Owensboro. He was the last one publicly hanged in Kentucky—even the whole country. During the Depression, Gunnar had gone to the spectacle, and for years now I'd overheard him talk about Bethea, comparing his own prison executions to this last hanging. Many times Gunnar'd told Abby the picnic hanging made him become an executioner so that he could bring dignity to the condemned man.

Gunnar said folks accused Bethea of robbing and killing an

old white woman, but most weren't satisfied. "Those type of crimes meant Bethea would get a private electrocution in prison," he'd said. So they'd convicted him only of rape—a crime that called for a sure Kentucky hanging.

Gunnar said things went sideways when the new female sheriff, who was also a mama, and other officials botched the hanging. The sheriff didn't want to pull the trip lever, so she hired a man from Louisville to do it while she watched from afar in an automobile.

Gunnar'd told about the thousands and thousands of people who'd swelled the small Kentucky town on that hot day in August 1936, saying most came from far and wide, with lots of reporters coming from big city places. But the hangman, Hash, showed up drunk, fumbled on releasing the trap, and later had the gall to bill the town $6.19 for his travel expenses. A few of Gunnar's old newspaper clippings likened the whole affair to a "carnival," saying as soon as the lever finally got pulled, some rowdy folks clawed and ripped at Bethea's hood cloak to steal a keepsake. Other witness accounts said it wasn't true; it was calm, hushed amongst them 20,000 folks, and they gave the Negro a dignified hanging.

"Just another colored boy gone fishin' in a pond where he wasn't supposed to be," Gunnar would always say.

"You should've never come home telling 'bout Bethea," Abby accused. "Getting my Gus so stirred up that he even swore the name on his firstborn . . . made me swear, too."

Gunnar hardened his jaw, tipped his face to the sky. "A tribute—"

"*A stain,*" Abby wheezed.

I sped back home, letting the wind dry my wet face. Racked with guilt, I paced across the kitchen floor. When Gunnar didn't show up in a few minutes, I went up to my room. Hours later I heard the front door ease shut.

I tiptoed halfway down and leaned over the banister. Gunnar was in the sitting room, elbow on the mantel, worrying his fingers alongside the carved box, talking to Claire again. He dabbed at his eyes and looked upward several times. Then I watched him wring his hands, not sure if his ailing arthritis had gotten the best of him or something more.

I tucked my head and stole back up the steps. Leaning out the bedroom window, I listened for Rainey's violin. Silent, except for a chorus of night musicians trilling their insect song of rattles, chirps, and lisps.

Quietly, I climbed into bed ticking through thoughts. Gunnar had only whipped Rainey twice, and he'd never hit me. What had brought on the change? I thought about my drunk daddy and buried my moans into the pillow with a knowing that I was the change.

For the next few days Rainey didn't show up in the rows. Gunnar didn't seem to care none. He went straight to work and ordered Henny back to her daddy's field, planting, while he bush-hogged the property lines, inspected one thing or another.

I suckered the tobacco and worked the burley as much as I could, worrying for Rainey, wondering when I'd have him back at my side.

On Saturday morning I found myself alone again, facing two hornworms hitched to my prize tobacco. I got a stick and poked at the leaves. The stubborn 'bacco-thieving worms clung to the plant. Furious, I tried to curse them off. Then I raised my stick to slap the ugly things off only to have it snatched from behind.

I whirled around to find Rainey. "Hear, now. You're bruising the tobacco, girl." He plunked down a bag and five-gallon Pepsi Cola drum, reached around me, and snatched off the worms.

"Rainey, I . . . what are you doing?"

"Working," he said matter-of-factly, as he tossed the ugly creatures into the catch bucket beside the drum.

"You feel okay?" I wanted to hold him and make all that hurt go away. I wanted to curse him, too, but I couldn't do neither with all that sadness in his eyes.

He straightened, grabbed his side. "A little tight in the back." He stared off and his eyes took on a distance.

I let the silence land at my feet, not wanting him to know I had seen what brought on the "tightening." I turned to the tobacco.

In a minute he said, "Ma told me the news about Crockett."

"Drowned." I looked back at him, rubbed a chill off my arms that prickled like slapped skin.

"Pretty bad thing," he murmured.

"Henny was really broke up about it."

"Shame that boy never learned how to swim." He grimaced.

"Shame," I repeated.

"Oh . . . hey, I have something for you." He pointed to the Pepsi drum, then pulled out a folded paper from his back pocket and handed it to me.

It was a flyer for the Kentucky State Fair.

"See there?" Rainey pointed to the dates *August 18–23.* "Picked this up while in the city. Just two days away . . . and on the way home I passed the big exposition center—that's where they're having it—and I saw them raising tents and putting up a huge contraption called a Ferris wheel. A big thing folks pay to ride on."

"A Ferris wheel?"

"Yeah, it's a big metal circle with tiny buckets sticking out all around it." He drew a big ring in the air, looping round and round. "They say folks sit in the buckets high up there and spin about."

"Why?" Just the thought made me woozy.

"Fun, I reckon." Rainey shrugged.

I stared at the flyer and then to the tobacco. "Can't believe it's happening. I'm still not sure how I want to exhibit."

"I do. Got this for you when I was in town on my shopping day." He kicked the empty cola drum. "Now pick your best plant, girl, and we'll pot it for your exhibit."

"My exhibit," I said, growing excited.

"Uh-huh." He smiled and began cleaning the drum and shining it with some turpentine and beeswax he'd brought.

"Two more days," I moaned, busting to get to the city.

I helped him buff the container until the red and white advertisement markings on the heavy tin gleamed. Then I pointed out my fattest plant, and carefully he dug up the tobacco and the rich soil and potted it.

That I was really going to finally go to the city sent my nerves flapping.

Excited, I turned around to thank him, but he had this tied-up look on his face again. "What is it, Rainey?"

"Well, Roo"—he pulled out an envelope from his back pocket—"I got my induction papers. This letter beat me back from Louisville."

"What's that mean?" I asked, fearing the answer.

"Travelin' time for Rainey boy."

I shook my head. "Thought you'd be helping me show at the State Fair. I need you—"

"Thought so, too, but there's no time. Ma will keep me close, and Gunnar"—he spread his hands together—"even closer. He needs me here. Time for the cuttin' and stackin'—get this crop up and hanged in the barn before I leave."

"I thought maybe the first week of September, but I reckon it's time for the barn. How soon will you be leaving?"

"Paper says I'm due back in Louisville at the end of the month—the thirty-first. Betting they'll pack me off for good then."

"Not coming back?" It was hard to believe I'd be in the city one day and he'd be there on another. That we were really losing each other.

"Me and Donny heard one of the officials talking when he thought we couldn't hear. He said us guys wouldn't have a clue when we're told to board the bus after the final testing. Said that old army bus carries those boys off into the lonesome night real quiet-like."

"Oh." Sorrow stabbed at my heart.

"Guessing that's gonna be me when I go back, Roo . . . The Parkers will be traveling there to stock their wares on the Friday before, and said that they'd tote me up in the back of their truck."

"No convertible?" I couldn't help whispering.

He grinned a little sheepishly and lifted my hand, tapped my fingers. "Not unless you sketch it on one of your nice fortune-tellers for me."

"Your fortune?"

"I 'spect I'm gonna need one of them now. Man shouldn't have to face the world without some sort of good-luck charm and a good woman's promise." Devilment shone in his somber eyes. "*Your* promise."

"'Spect so," I said, knowing there wasn't enough tobacco paper in Turner's barn, nor enough woo-woo magic in all the hollars of Kentucky to describe the promise I was itching to give him.

Rainey hoisted the potted plant onto the gathering table. "And this fine-looking tobacco here"—he patted the shiny container—"is a sure *promise* to take the State Fair prize."

Chapter 18

At four in the morning on Monday, Rose Law sped down State Road 1822 in black feathered satin high-heel slippers, a rustling waitress-red skirt, truck windows cranked wide, talking about undies and other unmentionables. The radio's staticky announcer called out the hour and his latest diddly.

Rose paused to swat at a cigarette ash landing on the Isadora Duncan scarf that teepee'd her neck and trailed down behind her small frame. Angling her face to the window, the wind dented Rose's big hair, ballooning her red polka-dot scarf while she took one last puff. Lazy blue smoke dimmed the dashboard lights, wrapped around the crashing lyrics of "Piece of My Heart" and Rose's flying words.

"And them Durbins . . ." Rose flicked her cigarette outside. "That Dirty Durbin—you seen her lately—haven't ya, kid?— *Lord!* Her always complaining about the sizes I carry. I told Dirty she may as well not buy any more panties, seeing she's hissy fittin' to squeeze her big twat into three sizes smaller. Shake King dirt, her and them hippies is! *Lord!*"

"*I want you to come on, come on, come on, come on . . . and take it,*" Janis Joplin screamed.

"Lordy-jones," I bounced back, red-faced and grateful for the blackness of the rolling countryside and the dimness of her old Dodge Canopy Express automobile.

My mind spun with Rose's stories and here we'd only been

on the road for thirty minutes and had this chatter, all before daybreak.

I pressed a hand to Mama's snakeskin purse resting on my lap and rubbed the skin, oiling it with my fingers to quiet my thoughts. Still fidgety, I brought my hand up to my chest and patted the paper pinned to my dress.

Gunnar had insisted I write my name on the tobacco paper and pin it to me, saying, "Do not lose it!" By the time he'd made me call back all his instructions to him, I couldn't remember my own name much less worrying about losing it for the folks I'd yet to meet. I plucked off the paper, folded it into tiny squares, and slipped it into Mama's purse.

Rose chuckled. "That Gunnar is something else, ain't he, kid? In my forty-four years on this ol' earth, ain't never met another the likes of him. I remember after your grandma, Mrs. Royal, died, Gunnar took on his baby sister. He used to do the same with her—wouldn't let your mama out of his sight unless he marked her up like a sign. Then she grew up . . ."

"Did you know my mama well?" I asked.

"Nah, honey, Gunnar kept his little sister busy on his farm till she was good and growed up. Quite the big brother to your mama. There was a big age difference 'tween 'em, too, something like twenty years. Your mama sure was a pretty thing, though. I do remember when your pa came a'courtin' they didn't waste any time getting hitched. Remember that purse, too. She always carried it. They married and moved over to Dearsome County."

"Did you know him?" I remembered so little of them. Rose seemed a little surprised that I did, because I'd never talked to her about them. I'd never had this type of opportunity.

"Not too well. Only that he came from Laurel County, she was crazy about him, and that folks said he could sure preach some pretty words—said he could make snakes walk backward. Followed a strict Gospel . . . A fine handler. Talk was, he had himself a nice-sized following, too."

Rose dug into her purse and pulled out a gold tube of Tangee lipstick. Swiveling the base, she brushed the red color across her mouth, smacked the paint into her lips, then leaned over and offered me a swipe.

Politely I shook my head.

Silence settled for a bit. We stretched it out with the radio and soon the bumpy mountain roads and whirr of passing pines lulled me to sleep.

Sometime later, Rose poked me and I jerked awake. "You've been squirming in your sleep. You okay?"

"Uh-huh." It had been a fitful sleep about snakes stretched over a telephone cord, but I couldn't remember the rest.

"We'll be in Louisville soon," she said. "Reach around there, kid, and grab that brown sack inside the back."

I rubbed my face and sat up straight. Morning clambered over the hillside, kindling an ashy gold sky. Scents of hay and grass filled the air.

Yawning, I twisted around, parted the curtain behind me. I checked on my plant stretched out longways, propped up by a half-deflated spare tire. It took up most of the wagon's rear, leaving Rose's boxes stacked down the other side. I pulled out the bag and set it beside her.

With one hand on the steering wheel, Rose pushed it back across the wide bench seat toward me, and said, "Thought it'd look pretty on you. Have a gander . . . Go ahead and open it."

I pulled out a soft cotton dress with a swirling print of tiny delicate strawberries running on leafy vines on a crisp white background. Below the sleeveless bodice a soft red belt fitted the waist and a full skirt gathered—it was a splendid flared bottom that looked like it could twirl the night away on big-city avenues.

"*Ohh*. Oh, Rose—it's so pretty . . ." I traced a finger over the berries. I hadn't seen anything this lovely, not even in the catalogs. "Pretty, but I . . . no, I couldn't." Quickly, I stuffed the dress back into the bag and placed it between us. I pinched open the clasp on my pocketbook, dug inside. I touched the Kennedy coin from the First Lady. *Wasn't near enough. And I couldn't bear to part with it for something as vain as a prettier dress. . . .*

"Try it on, kid. Don't want to end up using it for rags."

"Using anything this fine for a rag would be sinful." My old dress was faded, patched, and near busting at the seams from wash and wear. The clean tube socks I wore were stained from the fields, and the GodUgly patent leathers that Gunnar had picked up almost two years ago were scuffed and yellowed, even though I'd tried to clean them.

"Go on, honey," she urged. "Gotta have you some fancy on when them judges award you a blue ribbon and take your picture."

When I win the ribbon I can pay her back. A smile burst on my lips. "Only if I can pay you when I get my prize money."

"A birthday present, now put it on."

"Birthday . . ."

"Sixteen soon," Rose reminded.

I loved how Rose never forgot my birthday. Her and Abby were about the only ones . . . It weren't no big deal to Gunnar, he never celebrated his or anyone else's. Still, on mine, Abby would drop by plump cherries she'd picked from her tree, and I'd make my favorite pie with them: a cherry one with buttery latticed-top crusts, brown and bubbling full of sweet juicy cherries with just the right smack of tartness. In October, for Gunnar's, I'd bake his favorite, too, a cinnamon-dusted apple. On those two days each year, we'd share slices and an easy silence— the quiet, our gifts to each other.

"Thank you . . . it sure is a grand present, Rose."

"Go on. Try it on."

"Here? Oh no, not here—"

"Don't see any fancy dressing room out here, do ya? See that berm up ahead, kid? Hold on and I'll pull over, and you can change behind them bushes." She laughed.

When she parked, I climbed out of her old green automobile and rushed over behind the thick brush. I pulled the dress out of the bag and held it in front of me. It only came down to my knees instead of, like mine, to the ankle. Alarmed, I held it up to the thin light of morning and could see through the white fabric.

With my fingers, I pinned Rose's dress to my shoulders. It felt short. I ran my hand inside the dress and stretched fingertips against the fabric, peering closely. What would Gunnar say about me wearing a daringly short see-through dress? I thought about him whipping Rainey for his sins—about the town whores, Dusty and Dirty, and that kissing fool, Dena . . .

"Okay, kid?" Rose hollered out the window.

Shaking my head, I walked back to the automobile and got in. "Rose"—I handed her the bag—"I can't . . . you can see through it. Folks could see my—well, and there's—"

"Huh? Here, let me see." Rose took the dress back out of the bag and lifted it up to the windshield, then pushed a fist inside and ran it along the cotton. Shoving the dress onto my lap, she turned and climbed through the curtain, squeezing her wide hips into the back, muttering.

She slithered back up front and plopped down onto the driver's seat. I gasped.

In her hand was a Honey Girl slip the color of powdery roses—a blushing hint of the wild ones that grew in our fields. So beautiful that the thought of wearing it heated my face. The bodice gathered in the front, sheathed with delicate white lace, and the hem was trimmed in a pink satin ribbon. Never had I been this close to anything so pretty. Not even with Lady Bird in her fine fancy coat and gloves.

I got a fierce homesickness for Mama, for that long-ago day when she'd held me close to her own slip, and my eyes filled. "My mama had one of these fine slips . . . she did."

"I imagine so, being the wife of an important preacher, she was." Rose sniffled and tapped the dashboard clock. "Gotta scoot, kid, if we're gonna set up all my stuff and get your exhibit in."

I nodded, wiped my eyes, and jumped out of the wagon. Undoing my buttons, I hurried over to the thicket. I laid my old dress on a twig and wiggled into the slip, its softness, cool and cradling like the morning breeze. Under the open sky, I took a deep breath and felt skin shiver against the satin. *Important things could happen in a slip like this.*

Rose yelled out, "RubyLyn?"

"Almost through," I called back, running my hands over the lace. "*Oh my.*"

Carefully, I slipped the strawberry dress on. A near-perfect fit and grand enough for a marrying day even.

I studied my Sunday church shoes, rolling a foot onto its side. One day I'd have me a pair of those heels that women always complained of hurting their feet. The prettiest pinchers in the world. I'd go dancing in the city with Rainey until my feet burned and I wore off the polish on my painted little piggies. I wiggled my toes inside at the thought.

I took off the tube socks. The shoes didn't seem as bad without them. I grabbed my old dress off the bush and ran back to the Canopy.

Rose whistled her approval, and I blushed and gave a tight twirl before climbing inside.

"Have you ever, Rose?" I breathed, fluffing up the skirt, smoothing, tracing the tiny strawberries. "Couldn't find a prettier dress in the Feed's catalogs, anywhere, I bet. It's so beautiful, thank you!" I dropped the socks onto the floorboard.

Rose grinned, then turned on the ignition and pulled onto the road. I saw her dab at her lashes. A minute later she reached over and nabbed my old dress and tossed it out the window.

"Rose, no . . . *no!* Gunnar will preach me a sinner's funeral—"

She cackled. "Tell Gunnar it is a *sin* to wear a rag when there's beauty to be had."

The dress parachuted up and scalloped the blue Kentucky sky. I laid a hand down on my new dress baring my crossed legs, the silk-soft blush slip peeking out.

Leaning out the window, I looked up. The dress sailed farther away, taking Gunnar's *GodPretty* worries with it.

Chapter 19

The city flagged the day with automobile rumblings and horn blasts and a busy crawl in its air as Rose drove us through downtown Louisville. I hurried to choke down the last bite of one of my cheese sandwiches I'd brought from home. Craning this way and that, I gaped at the long block of tall buildings.

"There's even a store that sells books, Rose!" W. K. STEWART CO.—BOOKS—STATIONERY—OFFICE SUPPLIES, the sign read.

"Look, it's as big as the Feed & Seed! Imagine! A whole store for books . . . just books? and looka there at that big one. Rose! Over there." I jabbed my finger at another building. "All that for clothes?"

Rose laughed and slowed. "Look there, kid"—she pointed across me—"remember me telling ya 'bout the folk art they sell. . . . There ya go." I followed her finger and sucked in a breath. *Leon's Art Studio and Fine Art.* It was a skinny building tucked in between the bigger ones, with a bright yellow awning hanging with the shop's name. In the window were pictures of landscapes, portraits, and there on an easel sat a large charcoal drawing of an outhouse in the weeds.

Giddy, I clapped my hands in astonishment.

"Lots of big doings round a big-doing city." Rose perked. "Lots."

"Ain't never been out of Nameless, unless you count going to see the president in Inez, and once when Gunnar took me with him to Loyall to look at a used tractor." I whistled low.

Dressed in fancy clothes and looking important, people strolled into buildings. I smoothed down my new dress and hugged Mama's snakeskin purse closer. Why, wasn't that much fancy in all of Nameless's packed Sunday churches—or a courthouse meeting. Here it was almost eight on a Monday morning and folks weren't in the mines, out in the fields, or in the barn milking. They were at book and clothing stores doing important things.

Despite little sleep, I felt full of energy, like I'd drank a cup of Gunnar's black coffee.

A few minutes later we drove under a WELCOME TO THE KEN-TUCKY STATE FAIR sign and stopped by a tiny shed. A sweaty man popped his head out the window, gave Rose a ticket, and pointed to a parking lot.

Rose pulled into a big grassy field and snugged her Canopy alongside other automobiles and trucks.

"Never seen so many automobiles." I turned to Rose. "Reckon they're all here for the fair?"

"Uh-huh. Most folks in this permit lot got here on Saturday to unload, but they'll be a few stragglers like us coming in today. Let me fix myself up right quick," she said, reaching around to the back and pulling out a bag with a canary-colored satiny blouse and matching heels inside. She hopped out of the automobile. I followed.

In a jiff she'd scrunched down behind the tailgate, wiggled out of her traveling blouse and into the clean one. Then she pulled out a pair of nylons from her pocketbook. Balancing against the tailgate, she stuffed her feet inside them, walking the hosiery tightly up her legs, wriggling, snapping her garter straps to them.

I handed her the heels.

"C'mon, kid, let's get your 'bacco signed in"—she put on her snazzy yellow shoes—"and then ya can help me set up my stuff. It's getting late." She opened the tailgate, rearranging her boxes, and slid out a skinny wagon.

I gripped my Three States tobacco pail where I had my other cheese sandwich stowed for supper, and clutched Mama's purse.

I took deep breaths of a world that smelled a lot like a Sunday dinner. Onions and scents of pie exploded, perfuming the grassy field.

Nearby, I glimpsed folks with their own carts, some dragging stuffed bags and boxes, others leading goats on rope and carrying caged chickens and other critters I couldn't get sight of.

Then, against the fresh morning light, I saw it way across the field, glinting against the morning sky. I stood loose-jawed and pointed.

Rose followed my finger. "That's the Ferris wheel," she said. "Never seen one, huh?"

"Never," I said, wishing Rainey was here to see it with me. It was like a big shooting star speckling over a summer day.

I watched the big wheel spin around once, twice, then nailed my stare to the ground to keep from dizzying my mind.

Folks walked past not even noticing the big metal contraption.

Rose must've sensed my stupor, because she patted my arm. "Let's go, kid, or they'll close your entry out."

A couple in dapper clothes strolled past, laughing and chatting. The red-haired woman stopped and turned back. "Why, is that you, Rosie gal?" she called out musically, thrusting her shapely body our way.

Rose turned around. "Well, now, if it ain't Bonnie Kate!"

The woman hurried back to Rose and dotted her in small smacking kisses, then turned to me.

"This is RubyLyn," Rose told the couple. "She's going to exhibit today."

From behind her, the man mumbled a howdy while the woman looked me over, and said, "Hi, RubyLyn."

"Hi," I said.

"Now, ain't you something. . . . Looky here, Samuel, this is Rosie's little girl. The artist she's always telling us about," the woman said.

The man tipped his straw hat my way. "*Rosie's little girl,*" he said warmly.

I set my Three States tobacco pail down, tucked my purse behind my back, and nodded, then half-curtsied, not knowing
what to do, my face scalding with embarrassment. I wanted to
correct them, but it felt good hearing them call me an artist and,
even better, someone's little girl.

"Rosie showed us some of your drawings over the years," the
woman chatted on. "Masterpieces if I ever saw one. And, Rosie,
I see you finally finished yours." She poked her slender finger toward my dress.

Rose picked up my pail and set it on her tailgate. "Sure did."

The woman said, "RubyLyn, we have us a little novelty store,
Zachery's Novelty and Fireworks, in Tennessee. Maybe you'd
like to put some of your artwork in there to sell? Come by the
booth and I'll give you our address."

Flattered, I managed to bob my head.

Rose shook hers. "Can't promise we'll have time 'cause we'll
be leaving to go back to Nameless tonight. But I'll be sure and
write it down for her, see if I can't drop ya off something the
next time I'm in Tennessee."

"Oh, Rosie, do try and stop by the booth for a drink at
least," the woman pouted. "Samuel brought along one of his
fine bottles of Van Winkle. And you know ain't nothing better
than visiting our Kentucky cousin, Old Rip." She latched on to
her husband's arm and flicked a wave over her shoulder as they
strolled away.

Rose chuckled. "The Zacherys are good people. Bonnie
Kate's a belle from the Tennessee sticks. Owns the biggest novelty store three states deep. Sells fireworks, Elvis rugs and mugs;
you name it, they trade it. She gave me the material you're wearing."

"You made this dress?"

"Sure did. Worked on it last year in the exhibit room on a
friend's old Singer and finished putting on the buttons just two
weeks ago. Knew it would fit ya, too." She smiled sheepishly.

Warmed, I leaned over and pecked her cheek. "Ain't never
owned something this beautiful. A grand birthday gift . . . I'm

going to wear it every time I come back here so I can remember this first time," I declared, suddenly feeling proud and stylish. "Thank you, Rose."

"Work to do." She fanned a hand in front of her flushed face, shooing me away.

I ran my hand down the front, admiring the perfect tight stitches I'd missed earlier. What a grand thing to wear this fine dress that was made right here at the Kentucky State Fair. Surely that was a good omen.

Together we lifted out my tobacco plant and put it on the wagon. I put on a pair of Rose's old work gloves, scooped up fallen dirt, and placed it back into the bucket. Rose guided the wagon through the rows of automobiles. I tucked my purse underneath my arm and rested my other hand on the Pepsi drum, steadying the tall plant.

When we passed by a big wooden platform up near the front of the exposition building, I stopped to gander. Rose stopped, too, and hitched a hand to her hip.

Sitting atop the stage were eight men and one woman in folding chairs. Another man wearing a white straw hat and yellow bowtie stood in front of them with a microphone, dandying himself back and forth in front of a crowd of onlookers.

The man motioned to one of the seated men on the stage. The tall man in bib overalls stood and took the microphone. The crowd hushed and the man let out a string of squeals, then another. Folks hooted and clapped.

Puzzled, I looked at Rose. She caught my eye, and explained, "A hog calling contest."

After the caller was finished, another man in a blue cap stood and did the same, belting out screeches.

Then the announcer called for the lady named Emma.

Emma stood up, straightened her flowery dress, and stepped up to the microphone. The white-haired woman curtsied to the audience. She took a breath, tucked her arms behind her back, and let out a long string of quivering *soo-ee, soo-ee, soo-ee*'s, followed by a trail of quick musical yelps. The crowd cheered. The announcer came forward, took her hand in his, and raised them to the sky. He bowed to Emma, then pinned a blue ribbon onto her lapel. "Winner!"

Someone stepped forward and took a photograph.

Rose nudged me to move on. We pulled the wagon out of the crowd. I peeked back over my shoulder and saw Emma bowing to the audience, face lit up like a candle, a silky white slip hung inches below her colorful dress. She caught my eye and smiled kindly.

Blushing, I smiled back.

"Come on, kid, I want you to meet Freddy." Rose led the wagon to the front of the exposition center.

I laughed when she pointed to Freddy, a huge wooden doll almost as tall as the building, wearing jeans and a denim shirt, sitting on a big haystack. A white picket fence surrounded him. Freddy had his hand half raised in a friendly wave.

Rose pointed, and said, "Now, if you get lost, RubyLyn, ya come wait here by Freddy till I can find ya, okay? He helps folks find each other. And be sure and check in here at suppertime to see if I'm around if ya can't make it back to the booths."

Then all the sudden, Freddy said in a deep, smooth voice, "That's right, RubyLyn, lots of folks come to me when they're lost. If you're lost, just give a whistle. I like to get folks together."

Stunned, I finally found my tongue. "Yes. *Yessir*." I stepped forward and leaned over the fence, studying him. "*A talking doll . . .*"

Rose laughed. "That Freddy's a smart one, all eighteen feet of him."

Someone rubbed my arm. I turned my head sharply. A tall man with dirty hair, wearing an oil-stained plaid shirt, pushed against me. "Hello, good lookin'," he said, his eyes traveling the length of me. His whiskey breath blew hot and ugly in my face.

Rose batted him out of the way with her elbows, squeezed herself next to me. "Don't mind the likes of him, he's carny trash."

"Carny?"

"Works for the carnival rides. He bothers ya again, I'll sic security on him." Then louder and to him. "Stay away from my girl." She cut a mean eye toward the man, elbowing him farther away.

Out of the corner of my eye I saw another man slip in on my other side. I scooted closer to Rose as he gave a low whistle.

He tapped the fence, wagging a missing nub on his left hand. I couldn't believe it. Of all the people in Kentucky, I'd never thought I'd be seeing him again. Leaning against the picket fence, he stared at me. He had smiling blue eyes and wore tight-fitting jeans and a gray T-shirt that stretched across a broad chest and slim waist.

"Now ain't you a pretty sight for lonesome eyes," he said with a lazy grin, rubbing his morning whiskers.

I looked closely at him, his slicked-back locks and easy smile. He sure had changed in two years.

Beside me, Rose loudly cleared her throat.

"Why, if it ain't Miz Rose . . . Rose Law," he said, surprised, stretching his neck her way. "Thought I'd see you here yesterday. Hey, hope you brought a lot of musical spoons. I have a fella here that wants to buy a set."

"Yup," Rose said, "I'll be setting them up as soon as I take my charge into her exhibit." She hooked my arm, in a hurry to leave. "Let's go, RubyLyn."

"Exhibit ya say?" he said, looking at his watch and then back at me. "Why, Miz Rose, I'm working in the exhibits and I can escort her in." He shot me a smile.

She squeezed between us and blocked him. "Time to go, RubyLyn." She shook her head at the man. "No thanks, Mr. Crockett."

Chapter 20

"What's Cash Crockett doing here?" I said as Rose steered us inside the big doors.

"Don't fret none, honey," Rose said, catching just that in my voice. "He ain't got no business with us."

The Crocketts had made me and Gunnar their business. I worried if he was holding a grudge against me for what my uncle did to him. I hadn't heard or seen if he'd been home for his brother's burial. Still, he seemed awful friendly.

Rose wagged her hand. "Over here." She directed me to a long table where a woman was seated, and four people about my age stood in line. "You did mail in your entry form?" Rose asked.

"Uh-huh, I posted it a long time ago."

Two girls had quilts draped across their arms, and one boy carried a big melon, another a droopy tomato plant. The girls chatted with each other about fabric, while the boys talked about crops. Each one handed in a badge and the lady made marks in her book. Two of the kids held up red and blue ribbons to show the woman.

"Must've had their judging already," Rose whispered over my shoulder.

"Name?" the woman said, looking down at a big book with pages.

Rose pushed me forward and I quickly forgot about Cash.

"RubyLyn Royal Bishop," I said, feeling my arms grow sticky and my neck sweaty.

The woman looked up my name, glanced down at her wristwatch, and shook her head. "Where are you from?"

"Nameless," I barely breathed.

"Hmm . . . on the eastern side?" She studied her map, shook her head again, and then wrote a checkmark and some words beside my name. Then the lady picked up a paper badge with a stickpin that had AG EXHIBITOR SUN 1004 on it, and just as quick set it back down. She lifted another that had AG EX- HIBITOR MON 1004 written on it. She tapped her pen on the table. "Wonder what your judges will say about your timing, young lady?"

I stared at her not knowing what they would say, or what I needed to say.

"Pin it on, miss," she said, giving it to me, "the judging will be at three sharp." She handed me another card with tape. "Place this on your container." Then she pointed across the room, showing me where I could put my plant. "Hurry up! Next," she called out to the people waiting in line behind me.

With trembling hands, I pinned the badge onto my chest.

Rose clapped my back lightly. "Exhibitor 1004! Now them's good words to wear, huh?"

"The best I've ever heard."

We rolled the tobacco plant over to a far wall and placed it in between seven others, with me fretting and moving it twice.

"It's a fine exhibit, kid," Rose declared.

Its leaves were plump and deep green, the plant perky compared to the other straggly ones around it.

"Let's go freshen up." Rose pulled me away and showed me the ladies' restroom. I was shocked when I counted four inside toilets behind four wooden doors. All for females! Hanging from the wall were two sparkly white sinks.

We set our purses on a nearby folding chair. Turning on the water, I splashed it over my face, neck, savoring the coolness. Rose handed me soft paper from a box dispenser and I dried my face.

A girl about my age with bouncy golden curls swept up in silky ribbon came in. She wore a powder-blue eyelet dress with a full skirt, and soft pink lipstick and eye paint the color of blue sky. She flashed me a smile, and said, "Hey."

"Hey," I mumbled back a little shyly.

The girl went through one of the toilet doors and disappeared. Rose stepped up to the sinks.

After Rose freshened her face, she put on rouge and more lipstick.

I turned my back to Rose, reached inside my purse, and pulled out Mama's Rattle-My-Tattle. I swirled the lipstick up and compared the red to the strawberry print.

The girl came back out of the stall. Cheerfully, she leaned toward me. "That color sure is pretty."

"Oh, this?" I lifted the tube. No one had ever seen me with lipstick. Here I was inside the State Fair's women's restroom getting ready to publicly paint my lips.

"Uh-huh, sure is and it'll be perfect with your pretty dress. Did your mama make it?" She glanced at Rose.

"Uh . . . No, I mean yes, she—" I nudged my chin to Rose.

"Pretty. Name's Ellen Smith," she said, moving to the sink. "I'm showing my knitting."

"RubyLyn . . . RubyLyn Royal Bishop," I told her. "I brought up my tobacco."

"Hope you win. I'm from Whitesburg. Long trip and we barely made it in. Late, but they let me squeeze in my knitting. Where you from?" she asked.

"Nameless. And I sure hope you win, too."

A woman poked her head in. "Ellen, it's time to go."

"Coming, Mama," she answered. "See you around, Ruby-Lyn."

Ellen's mama walked over to her daughter, brushed a curl from her face, and prettied her bow.

"Sure is a beautiful dress you made your daughter, ma'am," Ellen said to Rose, then lopped off another sunny smile and left with her mama.

Silence thickened for a second, then Rose peeked over my

shoulder, and said, "She's right, honey. That red sure would brighten your face and go real nice with your new dress."

I nodded, feeling my face heating while Rose waited. Quickly, I swept the lipstick across my lips and stuffed it back into my purse.

Rose took a tissue out of her pocketbook and dabbed lightly at my mouth. "There," she said, "don't want it to bleed, honey. Here, let's fix this, too." She turned me around, pulled back my long hair, and plaited two pretty cornrows.

It had been a decade since anyone touched my hair like that. She did it just like I imagined a mama would, and for a second it stole my breath and I could see my own standing in front of me.

Silently, we lugged the wagon all the way back to Rose's automobile. We ended up stacking six boxes onto it. They looked a bit wobbly, and I wondered if we should make two trips.

Rose opened one box and pulled out a set of her music spoons, their warm dark honey tones gleaming on the wood. She slapped the spoons onto the cup of her hand and then against a leg, back and forth, picking up a rhythm, playing a catchy tune.

"Hear that, kid?"

I laughed.

"That's the sound of a full belly, stacks of wood, and warm woolen clothes."

"Oh"—I held up my finger, then rummaged through my purse—"almost forgot."

"What's this?" she asked, setting down her spoons and shyly inspecting the folds on the fortune-teller I gave her. She ran a chipped nail over my sketches. "It's your best."

"For you."

She whistled. "Some of your *very* best work, kid . . . Ya sure are your uncle's kin."

I looked at her quizzically.

"Same as Gunnar . . . Thought you knew he'd had the same art fancy as you." She raised a puzzled brow. "A decent artist.

But then he got called home from his schoolin' and got himself a job with the state. He never told ya?"

Shocked, I mumbled, "Not a word."

"Can't believe he ain't never showed you his stuff?"

"No, he hates anything to do with art."

"He don't hate art, honey, he hates *missing* his art. That man was a fine portrait artist. . . ." She peered closely at her likeness on the paper. "That was so long ago, I'd almost forgot that he used to ask me to get his art supplies. Gunnar always grinned like a schoolboy when I'd give 'em to him . . ." She screwed up her mouth. "When he retired from his state job, he stopped asking."

It was puzzling and hard to believe he'd ever done art, him preaching for me to stop all the time. Still, it made me feel a little proud to know we both shared it in our bones.

Rose stuffed her fingers inside the paper pockets and opened and shut the fortune. Then she peeled back another corner and squealed. She plopped a loud kiss on the sketch of spoons with the money and smacked my forehead with a grateful smooch. "From your pen to His ear!"

"Wanted to wish you good luck selling, and make you a pretty picture." I blushed.

She laughed and put her arm around me. "I'll be the luckiest pitchman at the fair."

Happy, I leaned my head to hers, and said, "You're the *best* folk artist in Kentucky—maybe the whole world."

" 'Nuff of lollygagging." She sniffled and shooed. "Let's go get our luck, kid! Gots me four hundred dollars to collect. Yup, *four hundred* smack-a-roos," she crowed, then placed the fortune carefully into her purse, picked up the wooden spoons, and hummed "Black Jack Davey."

Four hundred. That was more money than I'd seen in my life, than most folks in Nameless would see in a year. When business in Nameless slowed during the dark months, and folks' money ran low and food was scarce, Rose depended on her spoons to see her through. Worked all year on them so she could sell to the fairgoers and make enough money to live during the winter.

Other folks like widows and bench sitter Erbie depended on the spoons, too—Rose's charity. She would see that those folks stayed warm and had full bellies this winter.

I turned my thoughts to the two hundred dollar prize money. Two hundred dollars would mean an art studio and a new life closer to Rainey.

Rose broke through my thoughts, and chirped, "Sing along, RubyLyn . . . '*Black Jack Davey come a'running through the woods . . .*'"

I joined in and sang the old ballad with her. "'*How old are you, my pretty miss. How old are you, my honey. Answered him with a silly smile. I'll be sixteen next Sunday, be sixteen next Sunday . . .*'"

I felt someone's breath on the back of my neck, humming along with me. Whirling around, I found Cash standing there, grinning and tapping his foot.

"Now that was a pretty song," he said. "Can you play 'Plant a Watermelon on My Grave and Let the Juice Soak Through' . . . '*Just plant a watermelon on my grave and let the juice seep through.*'" He made a slurping sound.

"Got business to do, Mr. Crockett," Rose puffed. "What are *you* doing here? Thought you'd be back home with your kin after what happened to your brother. *God rest his soul.*"

"God rest," I said sincerely. "Sorry about your brother, Cash."

Cash looked miserably down at the boxes, and said, "I had to slip in and out of Nameless real quick because of my job here."

"Real sorry," I said again. And then mumbled stupidly, "He helped me with a bad fall I had."

Cash eyed me closely, then brushed off the condolence, and said, "Shame nobody was there for his." His eyes flickered between anger and grief, then just as quick changed to something else. "Enough about Carter," he said. "This is a fair, not a funeral, and I have work to do. Here, let me start with these."

"Me and RubyLyn's got it just fine." Rose anchored her hand on the stack of boxes.

"Now, Miz Law, I wouldn't want you to ruin your nice outfit." He flashed a smile at me. "Or have RubyLyn's pretty dress getting all dirty with these dusty boxes. Might drop 'em and tear up your nice spoons, too. There'd go your money." He bent over and pulled up two boxes, lifted them up into his muscular arms.

We had no choice but to follow him back through the lines of automobiles, across the lot, and into another building beside the exhibits. Him singing, fox-trotting "Ole Kaintuck" until he reached the doors.

We passed rows and rows of tables full of stuffed toys, signs, colorful pinwheels, candy, and quilts and more. People moved this way and that way, passing, coming. My thoughts picked up speed.

Cash seemed like an okay fella, different from the rest of his kin, and a few folks gave him a friendly wave and smile when passing. I stole another glance at him while we walked.

A pretty woman wearing a red satin ruffled blouse and pair of man's white britches painted onto mile-high legs tapped Cash's shoulder. "Hi, Cashy," she breathed, "get a chance I could use some help over at my booth hanging up rope." She batted her lashes and sashayed away. Cash nodded and kept pushing us through the pockets of people.

One man in a white suit reached right over his booth, tapped my arm, and gave me a shiny red sharpened pencil. He grinned and tipped the straw hat he was wearing. Another woman smiled, leaned over her table, and handed me a small rope of taffy candy. I stopped and tried to give it back, but she waved my hand away.

Cash turned around and must've seen because he dug into his pocket and pulled out a nickel and reached past me to give it to the woman. "Thank you, ma'am," he said.

Rose shot out a protest, stopped in the aisle, blocking folks, then reached inside her pocketbook and pulled out a nickel. She stuffed it into Cash's shirt as he tried to wriggle away.

I heard her grumble to him, "My girl's not gonna be beholdin' to you or any man."

Cash nodded politely and tucked his head down. Me too.

I wondered if Cash was different because he'd been living here in the city. Maybe the city made folks nicer. . . .

Still, when we got to Rose's booth, she pushed him back, grumbling, "He's a pest, and I don't trust a Crockett."

When Cash gave me a lopsided grin, I couldn't help returning it with a small smile. Then a woman came by and linked her arm into his. "*Caashh*," she sang out, "got time to help a gal arrange her booth?" She led him away.

It took us two hours to set up Rose's spoons in a tiny spot where you could hardly turn around. We strung rope up high from her booth to the poles on both sides, hanging the spoons by their slotted middles.

Twice while we were working, Rose sold spoons, and folks paid her each time with a whole six dollars. Rose said she only had sixty-eight sets left to sell.

When we ran out of rope, Cash was there with more. He insisted on helping me hang it, lingering his hand on mine as he took the rope from me. "Can't have you standing on that stool, getting your makeup all sweaty now," he said.

Embarrassed, I mumbled thanks, more than happy to let him climb up the rickety stool and hang the rope.

Rose, itching to be rid of him, snatched the rope out of his hand, saying she'd do it her way.

"I won't hear of it, Miz Rose," he insisted.

"Pesky boy, he should've been called Sprocket, him latching and attaching himself where he don't belong," she grumbled. "Sprocket—all those damn Crocketts."

"Rose," I hushed, and served him an apologetic smile.

Cash just grinned, took out a red-checked hankie, and dusted the counter.

We finished around noon. Rose asked the couple in the booth beside her, Ann and her husband, Dan the candle man, to watch her wares while she fetched dinner.

Dan the candle man must've had a hundred beeswax candles in his booth. Some, the shape of hearts, bunnies, and bears, and even two tiny villages with little houses and pine trees. I admired his many hand carvings of Bibles and crosses, wishing Gunnar could see them, wishing I could buy him one to sit on the mantel next to Claire. They were so beautiful I couldn't help softly tracing a fingertip over one of the sweet crosses.

Dan picked up the cross that was a little taller than my finger and held it up. "Take it so you'll always walk in His light," he said.

Stunned, I stepped back. I couldn't accept it, not without payment, it would be wrong. Rose leaned forward, took it from Dan, and passed it to me, whispering, "Can't say no to having Jesus, honey."

Dan the candle man smiled.

Fumbling with words, I thanked him, still wishing I had something to trade for it. I held the pretty candle, the ivory beeswax smooth and lightly scented, a miniature carving of a perfect crucifix Jesus formed over its center. This was a fine thing. As fine a thing that Gunnar would ever have, I was sure. I pictured Gunnar holding it, him smiling like he did long ago when Rose gave him art supplies. Smiling like he did the day the president came to Kentucky.

Quickly, I dug into my purse and handed him the first lady's coin before I could change my mind.

Dan turned it over, then pressed it back into my hand. "Looks like someone knows her *Good Word*," he said.

Chapter 21

Busy words from bustling people spilled into the big hall, bouncing off tall concrete walls. *This has to be the happiest place in the world.* If only Rainey were here to see it with me. Gunnar and Baby Jane and Henny, too.

I studied the candle again before slipping it and the first lady's coin back into my purse. Happy, I watched Rose eat a corn dog and drink a Coke. Twice she offered to buy me the fried stick dog dipped in cornmeal batter, and twice I wrinkled my nose and told her I had a hankering for the cheese sandwich back in my tin. Rose made me promise to go straight to the automobile for it and hurry back to my exhibit while she worked.

As soon as she disappeared into a row of booths, I went over to a water fountain and drank heavily. The smell of the corn dog smeared in mustard tempted my rumbling belly. I dug out the small piece of rope taffy the candy lady had given me and stuffed it down. Feeling somewhat better, I watched the passersby for a minute before slowly making my way outside.

I stopped to stare up at Freddy, marveling how a doll talked like that, wondering how he hooked up lost people.

Behind him a big clock showed it was almost one thirty.

I gave a small wave. Freddy called back a friendly "Howdy," making me turn as beet red as the kerchief that hung out his shirt pocket. Then I caught a glimpse of a shiny tractor beyond him. Curious, I went over and inspected the two green machines. One man kicked at the big yellow tire and said he would feel like a king riding it. Another snorted and said it would take a king's ransom to own one at the ten thousand dollar price.

I moved on to the grassy parking lot, a quiet pocket now. It was full of automobiles, but empty of people except for a few folks making their way up to the big building.

Once I'd made it to Rose's automobile, I lowered the tailgate and pulled out my pail. I relaxed and took a breath. It felt like I had to take deeper ones to think in this big place. Still, I would give up a thousand more to live here.

Plopping down on the gate, I munched on my cheese sandwich. The cheese had melted and was runny from sitting in the hot automobile. It tasted good. Almost as good as the fair smelled. I debated on whether or not to save half for my supper. Thinking about the prize money, I decided I'd buy myself a corn dog, and one for Rose, too, and happily wolfed down the rest.

With my feet dangling, I hummed "Black Jack Davey" and watched the big Ferris wheel go around and around. I was so caught up in the big happenings I didn't hear his catlike steps slip up alongside Rose's automobile.

Startled, I cried out. The whiskey-breath carny man took hold of my knees, pressed them against his red-plaid shirt. "There you are, dollbaby. Maybe you'd like to ride the bumper cars with ol' Luke—"

"Get!" I tried to jerk away, but his fingers dug in through the fabric.

"Would be nice to take a ride on a fine split-tail like yourself." He pinched my right thigh.

"Get your dirty hands off me!" I tried to kick and he gripped tighter. Grabbing my pail, I battered the side of his arm and head.

Wriggling, I got a foot loose, kicked and kneed him into tomorrow. He let out a sharp grunt, bent over swaying, and dropped to his knees.

Then, bigger than two Mondays, Cash Crockett appeared. He gave the carny a hard kick to the rear, plowing him into the dirt.

"Luke Hughs," Cash hollered, "better not catch your drunk ass around here again, or I'll have ya canned! Get outta here!" he ordered with another boot. The carny man moaned, pulled himself up in a stoop, and staggered off.

Cash brushed a lock of hair out of his eyes, straightened his shoulders. "Sorry 'bout that. He don't mean any real harm, just a drunk, but lately he's been getting too fresh with the ladies. Are you okay, RubyLyn?"

Breathless, I found my voice, and squeaked, "Yeah, thanks." I inspected my dress, flicked away the man's grimy air.

Cash pointed to the tailgate. "Mind if I have a seat?" He plunked himself down right beside me before I could answer.

"I . . . I better go," I said, shifting, smoothing my skirts and still shaken from the man's attack.

"I'll see you back safe." He smiled.

"Thanks," I said, relieved, craning my neck looking to make sure he was gone.

"He won't pester you again," Cash promised. Then he pointed to the Ferris wheel. "Have ya ridden it yet?"

I firmly shook my head, scooted farther away.

"I've ridden it 'bout a hundred times," he said.

Amazed, I said, "A hundred times . . . Don't think I'd have a single breath left in me if I rode it once."

Cash chuckled. "You can't come to the fair without riding it. That'd be like, well, like looking at a flower without sniffing it, RubyLyn."

I couldn't help but laugh.

"Oh, come on"—he jumped off the tailgate and held out his hand—"my friend runs it and he'll give us a spin."

"I—I don't know . . ." I met his bright blue eyes, playful and warming, then eyed the big metal contraption wheeling around in the sky. "I better get back to my exhibit."

"It's safe and I'll be right there." He stretched his hand and jiggled. "A lot of fun up there looking out at the city."

City. I was finally here and what better way to see it all than from on top . . . I could tell Rainey all about it.

Scooting off the tailgate, I jumped down and smoothed out

the crinkles in my dress. I pressed my purse under my arm. "Maybe I have time for one spin."

He tapped his watch and grinned. "Maybe two." He helped me close up Rose's wagon.

As we walked across the field toward the Ferris wheel, Cash said, "Been working with the State Fair now for over a year doing important jobs." He dipped his head to a passerby. "Love this fast city."

I wondered what it was he did. He seemed like he was moving everywhere. Plumb full of buzz. I thought it was grand to be able to work in such a happy place with so many happy folks. Even the loss of his brother didn't seem to ruffle him much in this place.

Cash broke the quiet with his own thoughts. "Sorry I didn't see you in Nameless when I came back for Carter's burial."

"I left him some pretty flowers on his grave," I said softly.

Cash studied me. "You must've really liked him?"

"You mean . . . ? No. Well, I—"

He held up his hand. "Never mind. I know all the girls liked him."

I looked away, not wanting to hurt his feelings.

"Anything else going on back home?" He changed the subject.

"Tobacco will be housed soon. Town's quiet."

He grinned. "I bet it is now that I'm not scratching at your door and Gunnar ain't firing his shotgun."

Awkwardly, I said, "Gunnar gets riled up easy. I'm sorry about that, I—"

"Ain't your fault. 'Sides, he pretty much missed except for a place here. It still pains me once in a while." He pointed to his hiney.

I looked down.

Good-naturedly, he laughed.

I laughed lightly with him and pointed to the merry-go-round ride. "Those are about the prettiest carvings I've ever seen. Remember Mr. Cox back home? They remind me of those little stick horses he makes."

"Yup, when Governor Nunn visits, he stops by this carousel first. It's his favorite."

"Oh . . . You've seen the governor?"

"Sure have. Last year. Even shook his hand once."

Cash didn't seem at all like his kin back home, and I couldn't help but wonder what Gunnar would say about this city Crockett now, him being all smart and with a fancy city job. I began to relax.

"Now let's hurry, I want to show ya his other favorite ride."

"Lordy-jones," I prayed, my eyes growing big.

When Cash stepped into the red metal bucket and held out his hand, I wanted to hotfoot it back to the automobile, my exhibit, anywhere but here with these colorful swinging buckets.

He finally latched on to my wrist and pulled me down onto the bench seat beside him. I wiggled as far away as I could. Gently he pried my purse from my grasp and set it next to me.

I couldn't do anything but shut my eyes, even when I heard the latch gate click and the motor thrum, and even when Cash rested his hand a little too close to my knee. I was so scared.

Cash said, "Open them pretty eyes and see what's out there."

I squeezed them tighter when the metal cage began to rock slowly, clawed my nails against the slick bench seat. I fumbled around, reached down, and rubbed my hand over the snakeskin purse. *Help me, Mama,* I prayed silently.

On the second spin around, I risked one squinting eye, then slowly peeled open the other. Near the top, I could see for miles and miles, a big daring world, a busy world with busy buildings and busy automobiles with busy folks inside. It made me feel hopeful. *Bold.*

On the third spin, I hardly noticed when Cash pulled my hand into his.

On the fourth, the brakes hissed, rocking, landing our bucket at the top.

Scents of candy and pies swirled through the breeze.

Cash gave a hard jiggle and the bucket rocked again.

Laughingly, I squealed, then Cash leaned into me, pressed his lips to mine. A burning, busy, bold kiss.

The motor roared, the bucket shook, and I turned quickly away, dropping his kiss to the earth, ballooning my thoughts with worriment.

What has this city air done to my brains? Here I am with a city Crockett latching hands and lips to mine.

Cash squeezed my hand.

Shamed, I snatched it away, picked up my purse, and put it in my lap and folded my hands over it. *If only Rainey were here.*

Mistaking my disgrace for shyness, he said, "Hey now, I know a place where we can be alone."

Before I could answer, he bent over the bucket, rocking it wildly, whistling down to the operator. He pulled a whiskey flask out of his back pocket, took a nip, then offered it to me.

"Stop!" I plowed my foot hard against the metal floor, gripped the latch, and shook my head. "Get me down, *now!*"

He leaned over the bucket's lip and waved to his friend, then took another sip and put it back before resting his hand on my knee.

I brushed it off and felt my temper warm as we slowly spun to the bottom. Grinning at Cash, the operator popped open our gate. Cash gave him a friendly slap on the back as he hopped out.

I stepped off the platform, and said, "I have to get. My judging is soon."

He glanced down at his watch, then back up at me, smiling. "Got some time still. There's a lot more fun—"

"No, Cash. I have . . . I have myself a man back home now," I said, wishing it were true and knowing Rainey wasn't gonna be nobody's man once the army got hold of him.

Something dark passed over his eyes; then he gave one of his pearly smiles. "Ain't back home now, are we?" He raised a brow, lifted his arm to the sky. "City doings is different from hill doings, let me show ya."

"Thanks for the ride, but I best go now."

Hurt, then a hard look gathered in his eyes. He dug his hand into his back pocket and pulled out a fair badge of sorts, waving. "You wanna win your exhibit, I could make it happen."

"I have to go."

"Make it happen for ya," he said evenly, and again, "and a whole lotta other things if you wanna take a walk with me over there behind that building and find out." He put the badge back in his pocket and gave a pat.

Stunned, I felt my cheeks burn. Taking a step back, I stabbed him with an icy look.

He sidled up closer and gripped my arm.

I jerked loose. "I *said* I need to go, Cash."

He fished inside his front pocket, dug out a key, and whispered, "There's a nice dark storage room with some fresh hay that was just delivered for the show horses . . . Make a mighty fine bed for a hot hillfilly like yourself."

He flashed a dark smile and dangled his key in front of my face. Leaning closer to my ear, he breathed, "Whachya say, gal, small favor for a big favor?"

He stood sour in my air, claiming and churning it. For a second I couldn't speak. Disgusted, I shoved him back, and said, "Me and my tobacco don't need any of your damn ugly favors, Cash Crockett!"

A coldness claimed his twitching jaw.

"That's just like you *damn Royals,* thinking you're better than the rest of us," he spit.

I spun around and ran. I didn't stop until I was leaning over Freddy's picket fence, trying to collect my wind and wits.

I'd been foolish to think I could ever be friends with a Crockett. *Damn foolish.*

"Howdy, howdy," Freddy the doll cheerfully chirped between each of my breaths. After a few seconds, I lifted my head.

On the building's wall behind Freddy, the clock showed twenty minutes until the judging. Twenty minutes, only twenty minutes left until my life would change. I'd never have to see another hill Crockett, Nameless . . . I'd be on the avenues in my art shop . . . meeting Rainey and having our own ride on the big wheel.

Emma, the hog caller, walked up to the picket fence with three blue ribbons pinned to her pretty dress, carrying roses and a happy tune. She stopped beside me, merrily shouted a "howdy" to Freddy. Turning to me, she said, "Howdy! Lovely dress you have there. Where you from, sweetheart?"

"Nameless, ma'am. Thank you."

"Paintsville. We're practically neighbors." She lit up.

"Paintsville? But I thought maybe you was a city lady and all—"

"Mountain woman," she said proudly, bending slightly, moving a hand down her knee, fluffing the dress fabric over the small hitch of her pretty peeking slip, "and educated at Centre College."

"*Centre*." I looked up at her old face, crinkly eyes remembering teachers' talk of the fine college. I peeked back at her winning ribbons. "That's sure a lot of prizes, ma'am," I whispered in awe.

"A lot of faith, practice, and patience, sweetheart," she said. "You showing something?"

"Yes, ma'am, my tobacco. I can't wait till I get one of those ribbons."

She plucked a rose from her bunch and gave it to me. "Faith, practice, patience, sweetheart," she chimed sweetly before moving on.

I looked at the delicate rose with tiny, sharp thorns, then back at her speck of flashing slip hanging below. It reminded me of Emma, meadow soft and mountain strong.

Straightening my shoulders, I called upon faith, letting it steady my bones and claim some surety. A minute later I walked into the exhibit building.

Next to the eight tobacco plants, seven boys of different ages waited.

Two important-looking men stood chin-to-chin talking. I peered at the judge badges pinned to the breasts of their white jackets.

The boys huddled together in a circle, stretching their necks to peek at the judges in bowties.

The slap of my shoes smacked, echoed throughout the quiet hall. The judges glanced up, then turned back to their clipboards. The boys gave a curious look, before taking back up their conversations.

Relieved that Cash hadn't followed me, I took a spot nearest the plants. My tobacco looked fresh, strong, and promising.

In my mind, I practiced my thank you, mouthed a prayer, and waited for the announcement.

Faith, practice, and patience. I twirled the rose in my hand.

One of the judges called loudly, "1004."

I looked over to the boys and scanned their pinned-on numbers.

The boys looked at their own tags, each other, and all around to see who the judges were calling.

"1004," the judge said again. "Bishop?"

"Right there," Cash said as he swept past me, hiking his thumb my way before taking a spot beside the other judges.

Chapter 22

Faith, practice, and patience, the words juggled into air, squeezing.

The old judge looked at Cash, then back to me, nodded and scribbled something down on his paper. He lifted his pen and pointed. "1004. Step up here, 1004 . . . Yes, you, Miss Bishop."

I blinked and climbed out of the cloud of Emma's words.

"Miss Bishop," the older judge with a white bow tie said, "is this your plant in the Pepsi container?"

"Yessir."

"A fine plant you got here, ain't it, Tom?"

Tom, the judge with a long droopy mustache, wearing a green bow tie, murmured a soft "yessir."

A sappy smile weighted my cheekbones. *Faith . . .*

Cash shifted and pinned angry eyes to mine.

I set my mouth tight and looked away.

"Yessiree," the judge in the white bow tie said, "you got yourself a fine plant there, miss. Must've taken a lot of work and years to learn this fine a'planting."

Practice. I drew myself up taller, mumbled a shy thank you.

"Yessiree," he said again, "lotta patience to grow burley this good . . . Admirable, young lady. . . ."

Patience. Patience. Patience. I felt myself bursting—my toes wiggling, stretching—my fingers tap, tap, tapping the rose.

"I say the blue goes to Miss Bishop, this year." He grinned. "Whatta ya say, boys?"

Judge Tom nodded. "I say that's exactly right, sir!"

I couldn't help but nod, too.

Then Cash slowly wagged his head, stepped forward with a tiny book, and laid it on the judge's clipboard. "Page three," he said, cutting me a sharp look and taking a badge from his back pocket.

His eyes never left mine as he pinned it onto his shirt.

C. CROCKETT—AG JUDGE, it read.

Judge. A breath caught in my throat. *Oh . . . he's an Ag judge . . .*

"Page three? What's this, Crockett?" the judge asked.

"The deadline, Judge." Cash thumped the book. "Girl done missed her exhibit deadline."

"Hmm?" the two judges grunted.

"Page three states that all exhibits must be on the fairgrounds and tagged by six a.m. August eighteenth, to be eligible to show for judging and any awarding of a ribbon and cash prize . . . She didn't get it in till midmorning," Crockett rattled. "Late."

Sweat circled my neck, dampened my chest. "Wonder what your judges will say about your timing, young lady . . ." the lady at the entry table had said.

The crowd of boys scooted over to the judges, murmuring, craning to glimpse the handbook.

"See here, Crockett," the older judge said, pointing to my plant, "this is the best burley I've seen in years. Right, Tom?" He slipped a finger under his bow tie, stretching the collar, angling his reddening neck toward the ceiling.

"Indeed it is," Judge Tom affirmed, adjusting his spectacles. "In my twenty years, ain't never had the rule invoked." Big-eyed, he glanced at Cash. "Yessir, best burley this building's seen in quite a while."

"Says right there in them rules, it *ain't,*" Crockett spat. "Unless you want me to go get Mr. Harlinger to explain his official rules . . ."

From behind me, a boy said, "Had my entry in 'fore first light. Don't seem t'all fair."

Another grumbled, "Mine's been rotting in this stuffy building since Saturday morning."

And another, "Two long days without sunlight for my plant. Made two trips for it, too. Tain't a bit right."

I looked down at my rose, its crimson head shaking, tapping faster and faster against my side, petals falling.

"Here now, boys!" the older judge hushed. "I'll be the judge of what's fair! *Pauline!* Pauline, over here," the judge barked, motioning across the room to the woman at the entry table.

Pauline jumped up from her seat, straightened her skirt, and hurried over to the judge. "Yes, Judge?"

"What time did you sign this gal in? 1004 here?"

My knees banged along with my heart so loudly that I thought folks might hear the clanging.

She pinched her lips, looked at me kind of pitifully, and that's when I knew she would remember the exact second.

"It was 10:04, sir . . . today, Judge . . . *four hours and four minutes late,*" she said, darting her eyes at my tag before dropping her lids.

Ten o four. Mon 1004. I sucked in a breath, pressed my hand over the badge. She'd assigned the time to reflect my late arrival.

"Ten o four?" he called back.

Pauline touched his sleeve. "You know how it is, sir . . . some of these . . . these hill people can't even read or write, so I, well—"

Drifts of boyish snickers punched the canned air.

Shame filled up and rumbled inside me. I lowered my head.

"Very well, Pauline, that's all," the judge grimaced.

Pauline gave a curt nod and left.

Cash tucked teeth over a tight grin, crossed his arms.

The older judge huddled close to whisper to Judge Tom.

After a few seconds the two men parted.

Judge Tom took out a white hankie from his back pocket and wiped his forehead. Then he stuffed it back, pulled out a blue ribbon from the stack fastened to his clipboard, and cleared his throat. "First Place. 2322. Franklin."

Faith withered.

Cash raised a smug brow.

"1805. Leakman. Second Place," Judge Tom announced, and held up a red ribbon.

I pulled off my badge, then crumpled and tossed it to the floor.

"And it's 1123, Tim Dooley, for Third Place." The judge dangled the yellow ribbon.

The room tilted a little, my ears roared. Stepping away, I felt Cash's hand land on my shoulder. "Ain't so royal now," he whispered thickly.

"Sprocket mouth," I shot back, knocking his hand off, blindly making my way to the ladies' room.

I don't know how long I stood there in the tiny stall, my breakfast and dinner swirling, disappearing down the toilet. Cussin' and a'fussin' the Crocketts. Spent, I sagged against the door, wiped my face with tissue, gulping down dry air.

A light knock startled me.

"RubyLyn," a soft voice called. "It's me, Ellen. Saw you come in, but when I didn't see you come out, I got worried. You okay?"

I found my tongue and gave a wobbly "fine," then opened the door and stepped out.

"That's good," she said, looking me over. "Saw you passing me, looking peaked."

"My dinner," I fibbed, "didn't set right." I touched my clammy forehead.

"Want me to go find your mama for you?"

"Mama . . . ? No, no. I'm okay." I tried to smile.

"Okay, if you're sure." She patted my shoulder. "Sure is a pretty rose," she said, noting the flower in my hand.

"Yeah, and thanks, I'll be better in a bit." I set the rose and my purse down on the seat beside the sinks, straightened the collar on my dress.

"Hey, won me a blue ribbon with my knitting." She pointed to her chest. "How'd your tobacco do?"

She'd been late like me, but I was glad she won. Shaky, I said, "That's real nice, Ellen. I—"

"Ellen, Ellen," a woman's voice floated in, hovering. "There you are, sweetie! Say good-bye to your friend, we're leaving for supper."

"Well, hope you feel better. Bye, RubyLyn," she said, smiling. "Maybe I'll see you around before we go home."

I nodded and offered another wobbly smile.

At the door, her mama straightened her pinned ribbon. Then the woman bent down to kiss her daughter's cheek. Beaming, they locked arms together and left.

Wasn't a day that went by that I didn't miss her. But standing here alone in this big echo-slapping building, I missed Mama worse than ever. I closed my eyes and felt the tears pressing, piling on the years of loss and loneliness.

Clutching a fist to my chest, I pounded back the low chirp of Patsy's song, striking once urgently, twice, and a third more fiercely.

A black cleaning woman wearing a starched gray dress and heavy black shoes walked in with a stack of paper towels, pulling me out of my misery. Silently, she offered me one before stuffing them inside the hanging box. Grateful, I took it and wiped my nose. I noticed she had the same coloring as Rainey. Pinching another glance at me, she toweled the water off the sinks and left.

Thoughts of Rainey leaving me alone in Nameless pushed in, crowding. I picked up the rose, clenched it in a fist. Wincing, I flexed my fingers, loosened, tightened.

The petals and stem fell, littered the floor. My fever'd palm smarted, scratched, and blood-specked from the thorns—my chest aching from the thrashing.

Chapter 23

"**D**amn all Crocketts," I scratched out, bent over the ladies' room sink and washed my face. *Rose had been right.* I wondered what she would say when she found out I'd been disqualified because I hadn't even bothered to read the rule book. Here she'd made me this nice dress and toted me all the way up here.

I left the restroom and crossed the big hall over to the plant exhibits. I stood there a long while staring at my tobacco, the Pepsi drum Rainey had shined and filled so carefully, now nicked and dented. Dirt spilled out beside it. Leaves scattered about. Then I spied it, and hot anger crawled up my neck, warming my cheeks. Peeking out from under the drum was Cash's hankie. I pushed the tobacco over to the trash can and left it to be put out with the garbage.

A minute later, I opened the metal doors and escaped outside, a blast of candy and onion scents almost sending me back.

I huddled inside my thoughts alongside Freddy. After a few minutes, Freddy called out, asking if I was lost. I shook my head and decided to head toward Rose's booth, stopping to glance at the different wares and listening to the barking pitches. Anything to distract me from my gloom.

I passed the booth of Rose's Tennessee friends. Bonnie Kate sat perched on a metal stool wearing a glittery tiara on her head, smoking a long filtered cigarette while her husband sold their wares: stiff aluminum crowns with sparkly plastic stones, little boxes of sparklers, and pictures of Elvis Presley. "Be a State Fair

Princess—A Crooning King—Get your best sparkle from Zach-ery's Novelties and Fireworks," he barked at the passersby. Bon-nie Kate caught my eye and smiled.

I lifted a polite one back and moved on to the next booth. One man in overalls sold spices at his stand. Next to that booth, a gray-haired woman with a lodestone hanging from her neck sold jellies and jams. I lingered at her counter, studying a jar of pawpaw jelly. A small basket holding two rocks cozied up to the stacks of jars. She picked up one of the reddish brown stones and placed it in my hurt hand.

"Here you go, child," she said, sneaking her old eyes to my scratched hand. "Take you a madstone back home. Cures the fevers, mad bites, stings, and more. Special 'cause it comes from the belly of the ghost deer, it does."

"Thank you, ma'am, but I don't have the money." I held it back up to her.

"Bad luck to sell a madstone." She pushed my hand away. "Can only be given. Got that special one from down round east-ern Kentucky," she said. "Nameless."

Surprised, I said, "I'm from Nameless, Kentucky, ma'am. But I ain't never seen an albino deer before." I flipped it over. "My uncle said he saw one when he was a boy, though."

"Well, there you go. The stone knows its way home. And Lord-love-Betsy-and-her-babies, Nameless sure is a pretty place!" She peeled back a toothy grin.

I rubbed the stone, and told her, "Back home, Mr. Turner has a rock he found in a catfish head, and he said it cured sore eyes and got rid of dust gathering in them. Keeps it sitting close to his tobacco paper press. And Oretta, that's our midwife, always wears a cock-stone around her neck. Says it will protect the ba-bies she delivers."

"Sure will," the old woman said.

I examined the madstone, turning it over several times before I thanked her and tucked it into my purse.

Ellen and her mama passed by me, chatting in smile-filled song.

I wondered if there was a stone for the things I'd been afflicted with. I was feverish with the sadness, a longing for my parents, Rainey, and a longing to live here in the city.

I passed a few more booths, stopping beside a smiling couple in front of a covered stand. They pointed and peered at strips of tiny photographs. Curious, I looked up at the Strike a Pose Photomatic! 3 Instant Photographs! booth. Behind the red half curtain, I heard a woman's giggles and looked down and saw her sitting on a man's lap. They spilled out laughing, the black man's shoulder pressed close to the white woman's arm.

I watched as they strolled away. Except for a few old farmers and their wives, folks hurried past the couple without so much as a blink and nary a stink—and not a soul came forward to give a whipping.

I stood there gawking a good while until an applause jolted me out of my thoughts. I edged toward the noise. In front of a large booth, a group of kids about my age lowered their clapping hands and listened to the pitchman who ran it. Some of the boys in the group wore navy-blue corduroy jackets with a gold eagle emblem on the back.

A FUTURE FARMERS OF AMERICA banner hung across the booth. The man behind the stand also wore the nifty blue jacket. A corn-yellow tie hung neatly over his pressed white shirt. I stood back and watched. Three girls wearing green pin-striped dresses with four-leaf clovers on breast pockets came up behind me. The man talked about agriculture education being important, about being a good citizen, and how important a job it was to feed so many. How to grow better crops and different crops. Then he recited a creed that told what things the farmers' club believed in.

" '. . . I *believe in less dependence on begging and more power in bargaining; in the life abundant and enough honest wealth to help make it so—for others as well as myself; in less need for charity and more of it when needed; in being happy myself and playing square with those whose happiness depends upon me . . .*' "

The Future Farmers of America spokesman told everyone the important creed was written by an author named E. M. Tiffany, 'specially for his club, and then went on to say that for the first time ever, females could have membership. "Including 4-H females," he pointed and said to the girls behind me. The girls in the neat pinstripes giggled, and he waved his hand at them, and also to me, to come forward.

The boys spread a path, clapping politely. I accepted the spokesman's pamphlet and a packet of fat sunflower seeds.

Somewhere behind me I heard a baby's squall trailed by familiar voices.

Turning, I saw them beside a toy booth. Mr. and Mrs. Emery bent over a baby buggy, tending to Eve.

Half-hidden behind fairgoers who were milling around the table, I watched the family.

"There there, sweet Eve," they prattled to the baby. Mr. Emery's arms were filled with stuffed toys. The bottom of Eve's periwinkle-blue buggy burst with more playthings. Mrs. Emery picked up the baby and gently rocked her.

"Is she okay?" Mr. Emery asked. "She's not sick, is she?"

Alarmed, I took a step toward them.

"She's fine, darling," Mrs. Emery assured, lifting the baby higher for a better glimpse. "Just a busy day for our daughter's first State Fair . . . Come on, little one." She smiled. "We better get you home. Tomorrow's another busy day. There'll be more fairs."

I breathed a sigh of relief.

Mr. Emery cooed and wiggled a stuffed doll in front of Eve. "Lots more fairs for our fair princess," he said, kissing the baby's forehead. "Let's go home, Eve." He tickled Eve's belly. "We've got the dressmaker coming bright and early so she can make our girl the most beautiful baptismal gown in the world. Yes, the most beautiful for the most beautiful."

Eve whimpered a little.

"You're my princess, and Daddy's here to protect you," he comforted.

Eve quieted and smiled at her daddy. I smiled, too.

Mr. Emery babbled on.

I opened my purse and pulled out the madstone. Maybe if

Eve had this special stone it would protect her like Oretta's cock-stone that had been taken from the knee of an old fighting rooster.

I raised my hand, waving. "Mr. and Mrs. Emery," I called.

Mrs. Emery spied me. Surprise flashed in her eyes. Then just as quick, deep worriment took hold and disgust pinched her mouth.

I waved again. "Ma'am, it's me, RubyLyn."

Quickly she turned and tucked the baby back into the carriage. "Time to go, darlings," she said, skittering away. Mr. Emery followed her, a tied-on balloon tailing behind them.

I waved once more, wanting to see Lena's baby one last time. To give Eve this madstone for protection. To leave a part of me and Nameless and her family back home with her . . . But Mrs. Emery looked at me like I was dirty. I looked down at my dress. *How could she not speak when I was wearing this fine dress with a fine lady's slip like her . . . ?*

Mrs. Emery gave one last nervous look over her shoulder, leaving me to lower my hand, tuck it close to my side. Blinking back the stinging dampness, I turned my gaze and saw Cash push beside the couple, heading straight my way. I meant to grab him and give him a piece of my mind, but he didn't even notice as he whizzed past me, him so full of his fire to follow a girl in a white blouse, navy skirt, and fast wiggle.

I glared after him until a whistle turned my attention. A balding man in a bright green Paramount Pickle T-shirt with a pickle-shaped whistle around his neck motioned me up to his booth. Grinning, he passed around a plate of free pickles to me and a few others. Hungry and knowing it would be a long time till my next meal, I grabbed one.

I took a small bite. It was crunchy and delicious—and almost as good as Rainey's. The Paramount Pickle man talked about his company in Louisville and how lots of folks liked pickles. He told us that people with land could work with his company and produce great tasty pickles—*the country's best.* He ticked off big numbers—the money that hardworking pickle farmers could make.

Then the friendly pickle man passed out a packet of cucumber seeds and a flyer with his company name and information. I studied the green paper with its border of pickles and line touting, "Be a Sweet Pickle and Grow Paramount" before stuffing it and the seeds into my purse with my other things.

I walked out of the rows of vendors. Leaning against the wall, I munched on the rest of my pickle and watched the fair people.

Everyone laughed or packed a smile. Some talked with hawkers, tried the games, and bought the goodies. Others rushed to the next fun thing with that once-a-year excitement only a fair could bring.

I didn't belong in this place, but somewhere else, a darker place where troubled folks had no laughter for this day or tomorrow.

Chapter 24

We pulled out of the Kentucky State Fair's parking lot shortly before nine p.m., the flickering lights of the Ferris wheel and the city fading as Rose drove away. The shine I'd trumpeted some twenty hours earlier had waned, the glum of going back home empty-handed hovered. I turned back once more to catch the pretty sparkly lights, wishing I could never leave.

So far, Rose had been great about not asking why my tobacco didn't win, or why I hadn't met her earlier. She was pleased about all of her spoons selling, and chatted about this hawker and that hawker, a drunk pitchman and a sober one, the folks who spent and those who didn't.

An hour later Rose stopped at a filling station. She had the attendant fill up the tank, then went inside. She returned with Zero candy bars and two Cokes. "Helps with the belly ache." She guessed at my quietness and shoved one of each into my hand, then swigged her Coke and unwrapped her own candy.

My mouth watered. I guzzled down a big drink of Coke and bit into the candy bar, savoring the white fudge, caramel, and peanut concoction.

When we'd finished, she said, "Sorry ya didn't win, honey."

I mumbled, "It's okay."

"I waited for you to come by the booth after the awards . . . ."

"I'm sorry, Rose, I—I, well, uh, I met Ellen—the girl from Whitesburg and we got to talking—" I half-fudged.

"Nice gal." She patted my arm. "I had myself a talk with one of the judges. Heard Crockett invoked the time rule."

"Sure did," I admitted, red-faced.

"Judge went on to say you grew some mighty fine burley, and you'd surely win next summer. Know what? Next year you might want to enter your drawings, too."

"They have a spot for art?" I perked.

"Yup, and so do the Zacherys if you want to sell 'em." She reached over and smoothed down a pucker on my dress.

"It's a fine dress, Rose."

"Like the Cinderella slipper. Meant only for you."

Grateful to have her soft cheer, I sank back into the seat and let the day dissolve. As the automobile sped down the road, I felt myself peeling off the day's losses.

Rose turned on the radio and lit herself a cigarette. "Keep drawing, kid. There's money in your art," she exhaled the affirmation into the smoky air.

Loretta Lynn crooned "Blue Kentucky Girl." I leaned my face to the window, inhaling the cool breeze. Tuckered, it weren't no time till the sweet melody and the hum of tires pulled my shoulders in, drooped my head.

When the bouncy mountain road jarred me awake, the big clock on the dash showed it was two in the morning. Ten minutes later Rose pulled into town and braked at the stop sign beside the Shake King.

Surprised, I popped my eyes. Lena Stump loitered in the parking lot wearing a short skirt and an even shorter top, leaning into a man's automobile window.

Rose gave a disgusted *humph* and sped off toward Gunnar's. When she pulled up to the house, she said softly, "Honey, I sure am sorry you're coming home without that blue ribbon."

"Had a great time seeing the city, though."

"I better get, kid. A woman in a booth down from mine ordered eight spoons. I was saving them to have on my wagon this fall, but that's a lot of cash now. Need to take me a quick nap and then head back to the city."

I climbed out of the truck and circled to her side and poked my head into the window. "That's great, Rose, and thanks for taking me and all." I felt like I'd let her down. I had to fix it.

"See ya soon, honey. Next year your tobacco *will* win, you'll see. And your art will, too." She lightly cupped my chin, before backing up her big automobile. I watched the headlights cut through the fog as she pulled away.

I looked over to the Fords'. Rainey must have heard the automobile, because his porch lit up.

Thoughts of him leaving surfaced and I struggled to push them back.

Weary, I stepped onto my porch. I was surprised to see him waiting up. Gunnar sat in the rocker, sipping a drink. A lantern cast soft yellow bands across him, slipping into slats, licking the porch boards.

"Hey, Gunnar." I hadn't realized I'd missed him a little till now. I fumbled with my purse, digging for his present.

Slowly, he stood. "You wore *that* in Louisville? Baring your knees to menfolk?"

"I did. Nothing wrong with it, Gunnar," I said, my heart dipping. "Ladies in the city wear these kind of summer dresses. Shorter ones even—"

"*Ladies?* Throw it in the woodpile," he spat, "I'm burning it."

"City folks wear the latest style and—"

"And you don't live in the city. Get in the tub and soak off those sins before bed." He plopped back down into the rocker and pulled the glass of bourbon to his lips, dismissing me.

"You're right 'bout that. I live in Hell," I muttered under my breath. Defeated, I let his candle cross fall back into my purse.

Upstairs, I bathed, and then hid Rose's dress, folding it safely on a shelf in the back of the closet. I'd have to clean it when Gunnar didn't have an eye peeled my way—get it back to her quickly before he got hold of it.

Outside, Rainey played lively notes on his violin, soothing. Soon I felt lighter and rested against the window frame, wishing

I could see him. Wishing for bigger things back in the city. Pictures of the man and woman in the photograph booth sparked thoughts as Rainey's words played my heart. *Man shouldn't have to face the world without some sort of good-luck charm and a good woman's promise.*

That was the least I could do for him . . . If I didn't have anything else, I had my promise. *A promise for a soldier who might never come home.*

In the fatness of the small hours before dawn, I pulled out a piece of tobacco paper from my desk drawer, gathered my pens and pencils, and leaned into the lamplight.

Quietly, I stared at the vase of drooping daisies in front of me and plucked through confusing thoughts. I scrawled, "Kiss Me. Kiss Me Not," across the blank page, testing. I wadded it up, snatched a clean page, and then carefully penned the words to the fortune in my best penmanship.

"Kiss Me. Kiss Me Not, Rainey," I said it seven times, too, then couldn't help but giggle, knowing my paper fortunes were about as silly as believing the truths of a daisy. But they were pretty, and an easier way for me to say things that I sometimes couldn't. It was a promise, too. A fullness. And it would lead us to what the other needed as sure as the Tiger Swallowtail flies to its mountain meadows.

Neatly, I folded the tobacco paper counterclockwise, crimped and pressed seams. Crimped and pressed some more. Then I wrote my declaration again. Several times I stopped and flexed my trembling hands.

Satisfied, I placed the fortune with Mama's inside her purse and set it on the windowsill, hoping for a favorable slice of moon, a lover's blessing, and a good curing.

I lay in bed listening to Rainey play his violin. Long, fragile notes stretched into the summer night. Rainey quivered the ghosted melody "In the Pines," snagging the stars.

> *Little girl, little girl, don't lie to me*
> *Tell me where did you sleep last night?*

In the pines, in the pines
Where the sun never shines
And shivered when the cold wind blows

" '*Tell me where did you sleep . . .*' " Rainey warbled low and lonesome.

" '*In the pines, in the pines, I stayed in the pines,*' " I hummed along softly, my eyes fixed to Mama's purse on the sill.

Chapter 25

I slept in till almost eight on Tuesday morning and Gunnar kept me inside the house all day with laundry and other chores. I tried to tell him about the fair, the shiny tractors, my tobacco, the beautiful city, and ask about him making the portraits, but, stiff-lipped, he brushed me off.

Wednesday morning I hurried out to the tobacco, watching for Rainey and hoping to see Henny. Gunnar called me over to the barn. I stood back as he muttered curses to his old tractor and tobacco wagon.

He always worried everything into the ground this time a year. It was cuttin' and stackin' time—the day we would begin to cut the tobacco and finally hang it in the barn.

"Go to the Feed and pick up your groceries," he ordered.

Reluctantly, I nodded. I knew chickens needed to be fried and hams baked for the hungry men who'd work our fields.

I turned to go and he hooked me back. "Get on the tractor and drive it up to that rock," he said, pointing to a field stone about thirty feet away.

He sighed a bothersome breath. "Go on. Quit wasting time, it's cuttin' and stackin' day."

I climbed up on the old blue Ford tractor, pulled the lever. About twenty feet away, Gunnar yelled out and I pushed in the clutch to stop it.

I jumped down and walked to the back of the tractor. "It's pulling," I said to him.

"Humph," he said, grumpy. He kicked the side links.

"There"—I pointed over his shoulder—"the pins aren't lined up on the draw bar and—"

"Lined up just fine." He leaned into the long bars, squinted, tapped a wrench on the metal that you hooked the plow up to.

I could see they weren't, and he'd taught me long ago if the pins on those two bars weren't sitting equal, the stabilizer would go wobbly and bind.

"They're not, Gunnar, stop being so pigheaded."

Rainey walked up. I pointed to the right side of the tractor, the two long bars attached behind it. "Tractor problems," I said.

Rainey bent over, inspecting.

"The lift arm's gonna keep binding," I said to Gunnar, "until you fix it right. Those pins are about an inch off. Going to pull the plow all crooked."

Gunnar struck the metal arm lift with the wrench and worked loose the hitch from the draw bar.

"Hell, Rainey," he said, "we never fixed this hitch last season. Go to town and pick me up one from Mr. Parker. Get me a can of axle grease, too."

"Not the hitch." I shook my head, knowing he was too stubborn to pay a mind and would wait until Mr. Thomas or another man came by and told him so.

Gunnar climbed up on the tractor seat. "Clean that dirt off your face and get going."

I wiped the oil off my chin. "It's not Negro Tuesday," I said.

Gunnar wrinkled his brows. "I need my hitch. You need to shop. Rainey, you wait on the Feed's back porch to tote the stuff for her. And hurry back here."

I ran to the house and washed my face and hands, then went up to my room. I opened the snakeskin purse, took out Rainey's fortune-teller and Mama's lipstick. Carefully I dragged the color lightly across my lips. I drew tobacco leaves onto the four outside folds like Mama had done to ours, sketched hearts onto the inside folds, then kissed the fortune before tucking it safely inside my dress pocket. Weren't no magic there, but a pretty prayerful pucker couldn't hurt none. Satisfied, I brushed my hair and quickly pinned it up.

We took off to the Feed & Seed with the fog lingering over us as we made our way to town.

We hadn't made it off Royal land when I pocketed his hand in mine, and blurted, "Didn't win, Rainey." I felt the disappointment build in my throat. "Didn't."

"Damn," he whistled through his teeth, gently pulling back his hand. Rainey looked behind us. "Next time, girl," he switched to an easy cheer.

We walked on as I spilled about Crockett and the time rule. Rainey snuck pats on my back through it all.

When I quieted, Rainey quieted, too.

After a few minutes, he looked up at the foggy skies, and said, "I won't miss this weather. Town's so thick with water you need a boat to make your way from one hill to the next." He stopped in the road, still a good piece from the Shake King.

I wondered what it would be like in the jungle for him.

Rainey touched my arm. "I'm going to miss you," he said softly.

I searched his solemn eyes.

"And I don't want to have to miss you," he said quietly.

My heart thumped madly.

"You okay, girl?"

I would never be okay or learn to be okay without him. I knew it deep in my bones. I fished into my pocket and pulled out his fortune. I knew I shouldn't, but I couldn't risk losing him.

"Maybe this will help you remember," I whispered, and held up the kissing fortune.

A noise stirred behind us. We stepped a safe distance away from each other and turned to watch seventeen-year-old widow, Darla Clark, pull her little red cart of youngsters toward town, the tired wheels rattling, squeaking along the road as she walked by. Her man died in a mine explosion last year over in Redstone, leaving her to fend for their two toddler boys. Darla was on her way to work the morning shift at the Kentucky Shake King. The manager arranged it so she'd have a job. Darla'd tuck the kids behind a baby gate between tubs of grease and tall barrels of rotted trash. The boys waited out her shift while she flipped burgers and scooped ice cream.

Rainey pressed the paper between his palms. "Finally," he said, taking the fortune from me and slipping it into his pocket, "I was wondering when I'd get mine."

"Takes a long time for the special ones."

He studied me a bit, patted his pocket appreciatively.

Deep in our thoughts, we walked on to the Feed, him trailing a few feet behind me. I headed around to the back where coloreds went in.

Beau Crockett stood up from one of the benches. "No shopping for niggers till Tuesday, boy. You get your days mixed up in that dumb skull?" he spat.

His son, Digit, came up behind Rainey and raised his nubby half fist. "Ain't Negro Tuesday, nigger."

Rainey set his mouth hard, stared down at the ground, and shook his head.

"See here, Mr. Crockett," I said to Beau, and cut Digit a mean look, "Rainey's in town on my uncle's fetching—"

"Shut your mouth, gal," Beau snipped, and grabbed Rainey's arm.

Rainey jerked away and drew a hard fist.

Mr. Parker poked his head out the back door. "*Beau Crockett!* Beau Crockett, you and your boy get your sorry selves on down the road unless you're spending today." He stepped outside with an ax handle he kept behind the counter. "This area is reserved for customers *and* soldiers." He pulled Rainey to his side.

Beau Crockett spit at Rainey's boots, and his son muttered a curse. Raising their hands, they mumbled more curses and backed away.

Mr. Parker held open the door. "What can I get y'all this morning?" he asked, smiling at Rainey.

Rainey hesitated. Mr. Parker nudged him, and we stepped inside.

He told Mr. Parker, "Gunnar needs a tongue hitch and axle grease, sir."

Mr. Parker walked him up to the counter, and said, "That'll be $8.79. We'll need to get the hitch out of the building out back."

Up at the cash register, Rainey stepped up beside Mrs. Stump.

Mrs. Stump stood with a naked Charles hitched to her hip and a barefoot Ada by her side, waiting. Mrs. Stump stared hotly at Rainey. "What's that nigger doing in here today?"

Mr. Parker ignored her.

Rainey paid for Gunnar's hitch and gave Mr. Parker a nickel for a package of Chuckles candy. He took out the lime and orange jellies for himself, saving the lemon, licorice, and cherry, then slid the rest across the counter to me. We both loved the little rectangle sugar-coated jellies.

Mrs. Stump slammed down her butter on the counter.

"Hester, I told your husband that I can't extend any more credit," Mr. Parker said, putting Rainey's money in the cash register. "I'm sorry."

She set Charles on the floor. "I'm here to pay off my bill and buy butter."

Mr. Parker looked at her warily. "You'll have to pay the whole amount."

"Aim to," she clipped. "But I might have to find another place to shop if you're letting *them* in on our shopping days." She jerked her head to Rainey.

The storeowner grimaced, opened his drawer, and pulled out the pay ledger to check her account.

I knew Mrs. Stump was paying for it with the baby money. Butter was too expensive, and she only used wild pig grease.

Mt. Parker nodded at Mrs. Stump, then looked at Rainey, and said, "Here, let me show you where that hitch is." He slipped out from behind the counter. To Mrs. Stump, he called over his shoulder, "I'll be right with you, Hester."

Don't forget Gunnar's grease, Rainey mouthed behind Mr. Parker.

I wandered the aisles, stopping by the new spices and seed, then went to the cooler and picked up a ham and chicken, and a can of Gunnar's grease from the ledge above it.

I set my stuff down on the counter beside Mrs. Stump and thumbed through old magazines, waiting for her to purchase her three pounds of butter. I wondered if Mr. Parker knew that babies could be sold for pats of butter—scraps of land.

Mr. Parker came back in, totaled Mrs. Stump's purchases, and bagged her stuff. Then before he could do mine, a customer turned his attention.

I looked down at Ada. She had her blond head pressed against the counter, her bottom lip rubbing back and forth across the box of penny matchbooks.

I nudged Ada and gave her a cherry Chuckles. She nabbed me a suspicious look, then huddled it in her hand a second staring before taking a tiny taste. Drooling, she shoved the whole thing into her mouth, choking it down.

I reached out to brush a piece of the sticky jelly off her chin and she shrank back, raised a fist.

"RubyLyn." Mrs. Stump turned to me. "Baby Jane gave me them seeds. And my sister over in Beauty's 'posed to send me some of them new wax beans soon. Hope to plant 'em on that field Gunnar sold us. I'll be sure and give ya some."

"Thank you, ma'am."

She lifted Charles up and smacked Ada's head away from the *Please Come Again Soon!* advertisement matches.

I opened an old edition of *Boys' Life* magazine sitting on the counter and thumbed through the pages, waiting for Mr. Parker. An advertisement for palm-sized squirrel monkeys was X'd out. Mr. Parker wouldn't let any boys order one. Ever since Billy O'Brien had bought one from the magazine for $12.95, every mountain boy, six mountains deep, had wanted one for a pet. I remembered the day Billy'd gone to the train depot over in Loyall and picked up his tiny monkey in the wooden crate.

The critter had traveled all the way from Miami Beach, Florida, with a collar and leash even. Billy toted the monkey back to the Feed and showed folks. When he opened the crate, the scared monkey ran out, bit three people, knocked over dozens of jars and several racks before Mr. Parker and a few customers could corral it.

I shut the magazine and opened the mail-order catalog, rubbed my fingers down the slick pages, turning slowly. I studied the tight sweaters, short dresses, and silky slips that reminded me of Dena's bold kiss. Rainey's soft lips. I wondered how many sweaters she owned. Maybe as many as there were Days of the Week undies. Maybe a whole month's worth . . .

Mr. Parker came up behind me and asked if I needed anything else. I paid for the food and tractor grease, thanked him, and went out the back door.

Outside, I called for Rainey and he answered back from inside the storage building. I poked my head inside and was surprised to see him lazing on a bench, feet up on the hitch, working the fortune I'd made.

"There you are," I said. "We best get back."

He raised a wicked brow, tapped the fortune-teller, and angled it toward a slice of sunlight coming through. "Says right here I get that kiss, Roo. Says so six times that I've done it."

My mind sang "Rainey" seven times. I looked over my shoulder. Across from the Feed's gravel lot, Beau Crockett stood against a flagpole, waiting for his son, I guessed.

On the sidewalk, Mrs. Stump stopped to hike Charles up on her hip. Ada clutched the worn threads of her mama's skirts, peeking back at me.

The town had burned off its early-morning bustle and had quieted with folks digging into the day's doings.

What would a few extra minutes hurt? I set down my groceries and turned back to Rainey. Grinning, I stepped inside the cool dark building. The smell of damp earth rose. Somewhere, a cricket fiddled a song to its mate.

Wisps of sunlight streamed through the chipped, gaped-hole cinder blocks. A flutter set about my bones, wobbling nerves.

I took the fortune from him and worked the folds once, then pointed. "Says seven times you're right, Rainey Ford."

That it was the most dangerous thing I could ever do, didn't matter. Not when I had something sweet like that lying in the bones, gathering its grit. I looked back over my shoulder one last time, bent over, and kissed him full and long, then stepped back breathless and wholly pleased with myself.

"Say good night, girl." He stood up, pulled me deeper into the wall's sliced shadows. "Close them kissing eyes and lend a prayer." He kissed back.

Chapter 26

I took that kiss for me, for Rainey, and for the future we could have out of here—a long kiss to other towns with proper names and with folks who saw folks fully and freely, and who didn't separate their coloreds like Monday's wash.

Weren't no barn mirror kissing either—nuh-uh—but a city kiss full of bold bigness.

The Feed & Seed's shop bell rang, parting us and sending me scurrying out of the storage's dim shelter, weak-eyed and weak-kneed.

Seconds later, Rainey came out of the building with the hitch.

Mr. Parker looked all around before spotting us.

Digit Crockett appeared around the corner of the storage building with his neck twisted toward us, glowering. He sprinted over to his daddy.

"Here, Rainey." Mr. Parker handed him a newspaper. "Don't forget Gunnar's news."

Rainey thanked him and took the paper, then picked back up the tongue hitch and my stuff, passing the groceries to me. "Think this trip to the grocery will sweeten Gunnar's mood," he teased. "Know it has mine."

"Reckon so." I blushed. My first womanly kiss and it was better than everything I'd been dreaming of in that ol' barn mirror.

We left the feed store in single file with Rainey several feet behind me, crossed through the courthouse grounds, and walked toward the Shake King's parking lot. Two shaggy-haired hippies, barefoot and in wide Mason-jar-mouth jeans, stood puffing on cigarettes, shifting back and forth, looking around and watching the road for their next high.

A burly group of men huddled around Beau Crockett, straining their necks to stab us with mean looks. Rainey tucked his chin down. Then Crockett threw a Coke bottle, yelling "coal-shitted nigger." Another man called "coon bastard," and Digit and his daddy snickered and jabbed fingers my way, snarling "white whore witch."

I didn't duck, and I would never duck for those hill scum-suckers. Instead I shot them one of Gunnar's best hurtin' looks.

From behind the Shake King building, Dusty and Dirty stepped wearily out of the shadows and sidled up to the men. The sisters cozied up to the group, scratching for a little whore pay, turning the men's attention.

Rainey muttered to keep going, then fell farther behind me.

We slowed at the tobacco rows trailing alongside Royal Road and Rainey fell into my step and grabbed my arm. He looked around, then took my sweaty hand, pulled me close. "You okay?" he asked with a little smile, setting down the hitch.

I peeked over my shoulder, too, then took a deep breath and relaxed. That was Rainey, always smiling, not letting ignorant town folk best him.

He squeezed my hand. "I love you, RubyLyn Royal Bishop. Loved you since that first day Gunnar toted you here, and with each of our good nights. And I aim to finish that kiss. Finish it with our promise."

"I love you so much, Rainey Ford, and I aim to let you." I melted.

"Then be my bride. Walk with me out of these hollars, girl, and give us that promise."

A knowing whooshed in my ears, banging itself wildly against my heart. Trembling, I tried to scrape words, then dropped the bag and flew into his arms. My answer dissolved into a burning kiss that hit low—carried us off the dusty road and into the tall, soft leaves of the tobacco field. Unpinning my hair, he pulled my hips to his, pressing, trailing his slow-talking-hands over my curls, face, and down my breasts.

"Jesus." He kissed feverishly.

Somewhere behind Rainey came a rustling in the plants, something swishing.

Then Ada walked through the rows big as Monday, her in tattered dress with one fallen sleeve, parting leaves with a long stick. The ten-year-old split a sneaky smile.

Breathless, I pushed at Rainey and nudged him to turn around. "Ada."

Rainey pulled away like he'd touched fire, moaned a tiny curse. "Ada Stump," he said, wheeling around, "don't be bruising the tobacco. Get on outta here, kid. *Get going!*" He lurched forward, wiggling a shooing hand at her.

"Let her go." I caught his shirttail. "She can't hurt anything."

Ada swept her tiny face up to the sky and kept snake-walking, beating the leaves.

The moment broke, the promise stashed away, leaving bits of Lena, her baby, Ada, and the Stumps' hidden grave.

Rainey looked around and then pulled me back to him.

"Not here," I said softly, face pinking like the tobacco flowers, and more to myself than to him. "I want to, Rainey, but I want my marrying night more."

He brushed his lips over mine, stirring, claiming the now for a few seconds longer before pulling back. "I'll see that you have it," he whispered hoarsely.

Drunk on each other, we cut through the small countryside making big-city plans.

"I'll be in Louisville a few days before they ship me out," Rainey said. "So I'll rent us a room, then come back home and get you."

"But who'll tote you back?"

"I'll find someone, don't you worry, Roo. I'll hitch if I have to. Maybe catch up with Mr. Parker before he heads back that evening."

"Gunnar will need to sign for me—"

"Once I take you to the city, I'll write him a letter and have him come up and he'll see that we are meant to marry."

"What about the money?" I had none, but he was right, Gunnar couldn't know just yet. He'd try to stop us. I'd known for years my uncle had the idea for me to get my schooling diplomas. *Two of them.* High school *and* college . . . But I couldn't let that man ship me off to Lexington to go to the College of Agriculture to study how to work *harder* for him.

'Sides, I'd be sixteen here shortly, *old in hill age,* and what Oretta always said about anyone older than twelve. *And didn't I have all the schoolin' I ever needed? I was going to be an artist. And weren't another single lesson needed to be learned than the most important one in these hills: loving my man. Til death do us part lovin', same as all women did.*

"Well, Roo," Rainey grinned, "while I was in Louisville I learned where you can rent a clean room. The army will pay us about eighty dollars a month. Heard about a place where you can get a room on credit till your first check comes in." He reached for my hand, rubbed a thumb over my knuckle.

"Rainey, eighty whole dollars! And I met some nice folks at the fair who have a store. I can drop off some art at Zachery's in Tennessee. The woman who owns it says to bring her some . . . All that money, Rainey, from my art and your army. We'll have plenty enough to get a nice place near the army base, too, so I can wait for you to come home. Gunnar won't say no to that."

That kind of money could buy snappy heels for my marrying day to go along with a set of soft baby-doll pajamas for my marrying night.

"Plenty for one of them gold bands, too." Smiling, he leaned sideways to kiss me, then bent over and pulled up a wad of clover. Expertly, his long fingers looped the stems, tying, winding the soft buds into a perfect band. "Mrs. Rainey Ford." He held it out to me.

My eyes lit upon him, exploring his coal-dark lashes, cut face, and soft swollen smile. *Mrs. Rainey Ford.* As far as I was concerned, in that moment, here amongst the tobaccos, this old

Kentucky land and open sky, a sweet promise sprung up from the earth and joined us.

I knew he felt it, too, because his eyes were shining with dampness like mine.

Back home, I put the blossom ring on my bedroom windowsill and began preparing the dinner for Gunnar and the Thomases. When I was done, I set the food in the oven to warm and hurried outside. In the barn, I gathered the bundles of tobacco sticks, hauling them to the field where they would be used to spike the tobacco plants.

I came back into the barn for more sticks and stepped over to the kissing mirror, dropped the sheet, and sowed a kiss into the dark tobacco air. Rainey snuck up behind me, fixed one on my cheek.

"Let's get these 'bacco sticks over to the field before Gunnar comes looking," I laughed, and started loading up my arms. Rainey helped me, then grabbed a bundle for himself.

We lugged them over to the fields and began driving the four-foot hickory sticks into the ground near every sixth or seventh plant.

Mr. Thomas and his son showed up an hour later, and Gunnar was sure happy to see them. He sent me back to the pump for more drinking water to sit on the gathering table for them.

When I came back with the water, Rainey placed a spear on top of a tobacco stick. "Let's lose some weight, ladies!" Rainey called out. He took the machete, cut the tobacco, driving the first stalk onto the stick. Because we'd let the cut tobacco sweat a few days in the fields before toting them into the barn, it was his favorite saying.

Gunnar would always fuss that the heavy, moisture-filled leaves had to lie in the fields to wilt perfectly, not crumbly or broken, before we'd house them in the barn and hang them on the tiers to cure.

I walked into a row behind Rainey and began spiking, too. Gunnar worked in the very back rows doing the same. Mr. Thomas and his son stayed close to the middle.

After a while, Gunnar strolled through my row, giving orders and making sure I'd picked up any fallen leaves. "There, and over there, RubyLyn . . . Pick up those leaves. Stack 'em! Leaving 'em on the ground is leaving money to rot!" He'd point and bark. "And don't forget back there." Gunnar hitched his thumb over his shoulder to the tobacco in the corner where he'd let the plants go to seed for next year. "Make sure we get those buds off for next year's seeds." He brushed past me. "And be sure and check on our workers and see that they're doing their job!" he hollered same as the next time.

In a row in front of me, Rainey laid a gravelly voice to the old spiritual slave song, "Sinner Please."

> *Sinner, please don't let the harvest pass*
> *Sinner, please don't let the harvest pass*
> *Sinner, please don't let the harvest pass*
> *And die and lose your soul at last*

Mr. Thomas and his son answered back.

> *I know that my Redeemer lives*
> *I know that my Redeemer lives*
> *I know that my Redeemer lives*
> *Sinner, please don't let this harvest pass*

Humming along, I climbed into the next verse. " '*Sinner, O see the cruel tree . . . Sinner, O see . . .*' "

The wind kicked up soft songful breezes of fresh-cut tobacco and fencerow honeysuckles.

I looked out at the land Henny worked, her daddy's field. I would love to sneak back there to talk to her about Rainey, us.

Close to noon, I got a break. Gunnar sent me to the house to fetch the dinner. I knew the men would take an hour to enjoy their meal and relax. I snatched bites here and there and waited on them. When they were settled, I hurried to the backfield with a plate for Henny.

I sat down beside her while she wolfed down chunks of chicken and cornbread. "How's Baby Jane?" I asked.

"Sister had a fever again, but she's better. Ma's been fattening her up, feeding her a'plenty with that money from the city people." She picked up a chicken leg. "What was Louisville like?" she asked in between bites. "Tell me everything about them city boys."

I told her all about it, leaving out the part about Crockett, skipping over Eve, and lightly going over my losing, while she hung on every word. Only the good things—the buildings, the art studio, the Future Farmers of America boys, the Ferris wheel, and all the city people.

She studied the land. "Y'all sure are moving fast this year." She nibbled on the chicken. " 'Bacco will be housed 'fore ya know it. First time y'all got it in 'fore September, too. You think y'all had something important to get to or something." She picked up a biscuit, munched.

"I guess I do now that Rainey's leaving . . ." I pitched her a sly smile and peered up at the sky. "A hitching maybe . . ."

Henny set down her half-eaten biscuit on the plate and placed the dish on the ground. Her eyes popped as she pulled herself up on her knees. She looked at me closely, then glanced over my shoulder to Rainey.

I nodded.

"*Oh, Roo.*"

"A *secret*. Swear?"

Henny laid her promised swear of Xs everywhere. We pressed hands together, giggling.

"Gunnar will never sign," she whispered, "unless . . ." She narrowed her eyes at my belly.

I shook my head. "I'm waiting for my marriage bed. Rainey says Gunnar'll sign once he sees we're together up in the city and making our own way."

"The city," she said wistfully. "Ya know, the law says you don't need a guardian if you're sixteen and pregnant." Henny poked my belly.

"No." I laughed. "I'm not, swear."

"That boy's been head over heels since the day you stepped on this farm and I know'd you two would get out of here one day. Just gonna have to do it quick 'fore folks find out—"

"I didn't realize it until I was losing him, Henny."

"He didn't want to lose ya neither or he wouldn't ask."

"I can have me an art studio in the city—"

"That soldier boy'll buy you two studios if ya want. Hey, what was it like kissing him? Was it same as white lips—"

"There's sweet Scripture in his kisses." I reddened and looked over at Rainey sitting on the grass eating, the sun glowing on his dark shoulders, a glistening halo above his tiny black curls. "I can still feel it . . . Feels right, Henny, and oh-so-grand. And when he asked—"

"I felt that with Carter." Henny grew a little sad.

"You'll have it again. Wait and see."

"I 'spect so," she said, suddenly brightening. "Perry Brown got out of jail a few weeks ago. Served his time for assault and growing the marijuana. Pa let him scout for ginseng on our mountain the other day and we talked. He showed back up the next morning, still looking for patches to dig this fall. I showed him some and then we took a walk down by the creek . . . Took a kiss for himself, Roo. Took myself one back."

"He's always been a handsome devil."

"Uh-huh. Gonna meet him tonight. Can I borrow your ma's jacket?"

"No, the last time you wore it you ripped the pocket." She loved the quilt jacket and had borrowed it in the past. But each time, I held my breath until its safe return. When she'd tore it a few months ago, I'd fussed and told her never again.

"I'll be real careful this time," she promised.

"I can go get my navy sweater for you."

She wrinkled her nose.

"No, I can't bear the thought of losing another stitch—"

"Okay, okay," she hushed. "Just wanted to look pretty is all."

"Never knew you to be without a beau for too long, Henny Stump, and you don't need my jacket for this one."

"Just wants me a good man, Roo . . . One that can stay out of the pokey long enough to marry and don't take the switch to me much. A man that I can love hard—love from here to Tennessee and in every one of them fancy Holiday Inn motels along the way . . ." She rubbed her bruised shoulder. "Ain't gonna be like Lena."

"I saw her at the Shake King," I said quietly.

"Whole town's seen. Sister's run off for good this time. Now I have to do all her work."

From across the fields, Gunnar hollered and waved his hat, motioning me back.

"Best get back over there," I said, standing. "Want to meet by the creek before we start tomorrow? I can tell you everything."

Henny nodded a yes, jumped up, and gave me a hug. "We's sisters?"

"Always." I patted her back.

I hurried into the tobaccos, cutting through Rainey's row. He pressed a light hold to my hand.

The rest of the day passed in a happy blur of stolen glimpses and secret smiles between us. It was nearly impossible to keep our eyes on the plants and off each other.

At 5:30, Gunnar called it a day. Nearly almost half the tobacco had been cut. I pulled myself up, amazed and relieved like I always was on cutting day.

Rainey shot me a smile and rubbed the small of his back. He took off his bandana and wiped the sweat off his forehead and neck.

We looked out at all the cut tobacco, feeling tired and grand that we had accomplished so much in one day.

"Imagine if we got this much done, what we'll do in the next few days." I marveled.

Satisfied, Gunnar worked his hands, rubbing the swollen flesh and stiff bones. I could tell he was proud, pleased. Not many of his moments could claim as much, but this time of year, it was hanging like a lit sign. Gunnar's jaw was relaxed and his stance loose. He even offered a bale of hay to Mr. Thomas for their horse back home.

Like me, Rainey lingered behind, waiting for everyone to leave, then snuck one more kiss.

Happy, I flitted inside to the kitchen and pulled out the skillet to cook. "Hey, Gunnar." I watched him fall heavily into the wooden chair. "I thought I'd fix us a quick breakfast for supper tonight."

There was plenty of ham, chicken, and beans leftover from the dinner, but we needed to save it for the men's meal tomorrow.

I turned to the stove and lit it. "Some of those biscuits spiked with bits of bacon you like so much. And white sausage gravy to slather them in." I turned back to him and saw his lids half-closed. "Gunnar?"

"Too beat to wait for a hot meal," he said, drowsy.

"Too tired to wait for me to *serve* you?" I asked, also tired and not caring if the sass stuck.

He must've been too worn out to hear because he snatched an apple and glass salt shaker off the counter and tucked himself back into the kitchen chair. Content, he salted the apple between bites, munching.

I turned off the stove, poured us a glass of sweet tea, then sliced up another apple for him and one for myself. We enjoyed the silence with the whir of the box fan whispering its own conversation. My thoughts drifted to faraway places with my husband-to-be.

Finished, Gunnar read his newspaper and had a bourbon while I got down on my knees and scrubbed the kitchen floor around him.

The kitchen was a mess from all the cooking today. I had to ask him twice to move his big feet. He grunted and lifted one heavy foot, then another, complaining how spent he was as I swiped the rag under him.

I asked him a third time and then I saw him rub his swollen, knobby hands.

"You're supposed to use Goldie's ointment every day," I scolded, "and take the Bufferin like Doc said." I got up and fetched the aspirins and balm and set them in front of him. He fumbled with the lids, grimacing, unable to get his fingers working. Pain set tracks across his weathered face.

"Let me get it for you, Gunnar."

He tried once more before slamming it down on the table, complaining. "My willow bark has the same stuff in it, and I don't have to go through this fuss."

"Doc says this is better than tea."

"*Robbery*. Mine's free."

"Here." I pried open the tin and dabbed balm across his wrists, working it in a second. Then I twisted open the aspirin cap and set two pills in front of him. It hurt seeing him like that. As much as I hated him sometimes, I didn't want to see him suffer. It was like seeing an old mountain lose its rock face and crumble.

Gunnar softened and grunted a weak thank-you growl as he worked his fingers across his red knuckles and rubbed the oily cream into his hands.

I went back to the floor.

"Why don't you use the mop I bought you?" he asked, pushing himself up from the table.

I shrugged. "Goldie says a mop is a lazy excuse for cleaning and only cleans half as good." That was true with the rag mop; it didn't take off all the stickiness when I'd tried it, spreading it to other rooms when I walked, doubling my work. I didn't tell Gunnar the other reason, lest he preach about pride: I needed to soak the tobacco off my hands. I'd been rubbing them in a brew of tansy leaves to whiten them, but the bleach was stronger than the plant—and stripped off the nasty tobacco tar, though my hands still looked at least a hundred times more wrinkly than an Oretta newborn. Now with a wedding ring coming, I wanted them cleaner than ever.

"Hurry up and get some rest. Another full day tomorrow." He yawned and stretched.

"Don't forget to take your Bufferins," I answered back.

For a second, I thought I saw a soft hand reach for my head and a tiny smile slip across his lips. Just as quick it passed and I blinked away my tiredness.

It was nearly eight by the time I finished chores and got my bath. Gunnar's light was off when I walked into my room.

I plucked Rainey's clover blossom ring off the windowsill.

"*Mrs. Rainey Ford.*" I pulled the loop over my knuckle and then picked up Mama's purse and pressed it to my cheek, inhaling the soft leathers.

I wondered if she ever went to Louisville with Daddy. Him, crafting her this fine thing to carry. Them, gussied up and shining like new silver dollars. I could see Mama there, Daddy tucked to one arm, the snakeskin purse clutched to her other, dazzling puddles of city lights shining on them as they stepped out on their evening stroll.

I ran my fingers over the worn diamond patterns, trailing the purse's tiny slant stitches. I'd take my parents with me and have them forever, wherever I'd go with Rainey. I would show them all the avenues, the fancy folks, and the Ferris wheel. I'd never leave them . . . I would never be lonely. . . .

I looked over at their photograph. *Little Miss Preach,* I mouthed, remembering her soft laugh when I'd playfully hissed and wriggled the toy telephone long ago.

When I got to Louisville I'd carry her beautiful pocketbook in grand style, arm in arm with Rainey, letting my new heels preach their tune against the city sidewalks. I held up my hand, splayed my fingers, and admired Rainey's ring.

Soft scents of tobacco, pine, and mountain magnolia drifted in with the cool breeze, swelling the curtains. I leaned out the window watching the fog crown our fields, listening to frogs call the dark. Stump Mountain slowly rose in and out of racing clouds. A burst of heat lightning laid a crooked corridor across the skies. Soon, the sun dropped behind the mountain, leaving a willowy stain of pumpkin orange.

I pulled on Mama's jacket and took her purse over to the bed, climbed in, and snugged it under my cheek. Kissed Rainey's clover ring. Once. Twice.

"Good night, sweet Rainey."

For the first time in a long while, I fell asleep quickly, with eyes tightly closed, lending a fiery prayer for my dreams and marriage bed.

Chapter 27

Long after sunset had laid fire to the fields and bedded its colors, I awoke smelling smoke.

An odd, woodsy, peppery smoke.

I flicked on the lamp, crawled out from under the covers, coughing, shrugging off my jacket.

Dazed, I looked around, then ran to my door and flung it open. Outside, the long darkened hall swayed the familiar shadows. I lifted my head and sniffed. Turning around in the threshold, I inhaled deeply, coughed again.

Then I caught it. Caught what I had first missed.

Through the tatted curtain, out my open window and in the distance, a flickering of yellowing orange rolled across the tobacco, licked at the night sky. Wisps of grayish smoke ghosted up, rode the night breeze.

"Gunnar," I mewed, then wheezed, "Gun-nar." Then again, "GUNNAR! The tobacco . . . Our fields are afire!"

I ran into the hall and pounded on his bedroom door. He opened it, groggy in his white night stockings.

I grabbed his hands. "The 'bacco." I tried to pull him. "Come quick . . . fire."

"Dear Lord," he breathed.

"*Hurry!*" I released my grip and flew down the stairs.

I fled out to the fields. Across the way, I could see Rainey running, too. "Oh no, oh God no." I emptied my prayers into the darkness.

I found my hoe near the front row and jumped into the tobacco with it, fanning, beating, pounding at the fires, dancing
all around the tobacco. I dashed to the end of the rows, looking
at the creek, searching for a bucket.

From somewhere behind Gunnar yelled, "RubyLyn, get
back . . . get back here."

I had to do something. Rushing back into the rows, I beat at
the flames' gain with the hoe.

The fire nipped at my ankles and legs.

I yelped. Whipping the hoe into the air, I swung, slashed at
the flames around me.

Out in the fields I heard Gunnar's and Rainey's distant shouts
to me.

Then I felt it, not sure of what it was. I looked down and then
all around.

Rainey called out again. Then Gunnar's hoarse cries.

I dropped the hoe.

Rainey's eyes were rounded, his mouth drawn, twisted in a
cry. He had his hands in the air, waving as he whipped toward
me in his bare feet. Gunnar was behind him.

Fearful, I took a step back, my eyes darting around.

Pain ripped through one leg. Then the other.

Rainey's shouts wrapped around mine.

Stuck to the hem of my gown, traveling up a leg, the fire tore
at my flesh. The wind lifted and twirled the ashes of my aunt's
old flower-print gown. I raised my arms and spun around.

My screams were silenced with a thud.

Rainey's body landed sideways on mine. He rolled me over
and over, slapping at my gown, me. When the fire was out he
knelt over me. Gunnar stood over his shoulder, horror fanning,
accordioning his long face.

Behind us the fire licked the grasses and scattered stalks of tobacco, spreading. Across the rows, popping melons, squash, and
tomatoes died in the vegetable patch.

"Get her over to the water, Rainey, hurry," Gunnar ordered.

I tried to stand, but my legs weren't with me.

"Need to cool the burns," Gunnar said.

Rainey swept me up and carried me over to the creek, then set me down gently in the cold waters. I winced and my whole body shook.

"I-I'm okay . . . o-okay," my teeth chattered. "Th-the f-fire."

Rainey shook his head. "Nothing—nothin' we can do now, but hope the fire department comes out. It's damn near destroyed."

"How?" I cried, knowing the tobacco had too much moisture in it to burn. "Lightning?"

"Saw trails of straw scattered everywhere. Smelled the kerosene, too," Rainey grimaced. "Won't be nothing but dead plants now."

"Kerosene—"

Gunnar leaned over the bank and peered at me. "RubyLyn, are you okay?"

"Uh-huh," I managed.

"Can you stand, Roo?" Rainey asked, gently pulling me up. Gunnar rushed down the bank and splashed through the water, nudged him aside. He reached for my arm and together we walked up the bank.

I took a ragged breath, then saw the scorched, smoldering fields of mine and Gunnar's. Flames haywired and hopped across rows. I dropped to my knees. "The tobacco," I wailed. "The food."

Gunnar booted the earth. "Nothing we can do but let it die down now."

My right leg started paining something fierce, the blisters forming on skin that couldn't be hid, and maybe would never be prettied by a silk slip. My ring finger was bare, the clover promise lost somewhere during it all.

Gunnar's sleeve was scorched. Reddening flesh popped on his arm.

"Your arm," I gasped.

A cry came across the field and latched on to mine. Rainey whirled around, glimpsing them before me.

It took every bit of muster to stand. Rainey reached for me, but I flicked at the air, urging him to go without me.

Gunnar and Rainey lingered a second, gaping toward the noise. From the lifting lights of the field fire, I saw the shadows.

One, two, maybe even three.

I squinted my eyes, blinked.

There.

And there.

Ada Stump was flying down the tree line, alongside the creek, two Crocketts on her tail.

"She caught them lighting the fields," Rainey yelled.

"Cowardly Crocketts must've been watching their fire take hold," Gunnar said. "Let's go."

Rainey tore out toward them with Gunnar not far behind.

I limped after them, nursing the pain shooting over my flesh.

Rainey caught up with Ada in a patch of grass and grabbed her arm. She hissed at him, twisting, pulling back, pummeling him.

Behind Rainey, Gunnar snatched Beau Crockett by his collar right before Crockett latched on to Ada.

Gunnar swung and his fist landed upside Crockett's head.

Crockett staggered back, sputtered, "S-stay outta my way, Gunnar," he warned with labored breaths. "I'm . . . having a'talking with that girl. She's been skulking round on my property and I—"

"*You,*" Gunnar jabbed, "are trespassing on *my* property. I told you I'd kill you if I ever caught you on it again."

Beau Crockett shook his head. "Step aside."

"You lit my field with straw. You're going to pay," Gunnar said.

Crockett shot out his arm, pointed to Ada. "Ain't got no hard business with ya today, Gunnar Royal. Just want the Stump girl . . . Stole my—"

Gunnar burst. "You gonna kill her . . . kill her like you killed that boy's pa when I refused to sell you this land and deeded it to the Fords instead . . . ? Damn you, killin's the only thing your predacious kind understands."

"The hell with them night-crawling darkies," Crockett roared. "And them Stumps—"

Gunnar pumped back, "The hell with *you*. You couldn't have my land back then when you plotted to have your boy marry my niece, and you can't have it now!" Gunnar flexed and raised his fist.

"You're a crazy old coot, Gunnar Royal. Giving land for nigger rot—and now to the Stumps," Crockett spat. "Hell, Stump's done got half his mountain land tied up in property bonds. Look, how many times have I asked ya to meet with me, friendly-like? Gots me three hundred dollars saved and—"

"And I told you I wasn't taking my church key out and having a chummy meeting with the rotted likes of you. You and your fox ways—thinking you and your likes could *ever* join my land," Gunnar stormed.

Beau raised a blaming hand to me. "Couldn't help it 'cause she got hot for my boy Cash—"

The fields smoldered. Far away, I heard faint sirens. I turned to the road, praying for the little volunteer fire department to hurry, though I knew there was little else that could help the ruined plants or any mountain farms once the devil's fiery lick took hold in these hills. And with tobacco so full of moisture, they'd likely spit fire here and there and smolder out on their own.

Still, I couldn't help but hope someone would come and douse the bigger fire happening with the men. "Gunnar, help's coming." I shook his shoulder, but he bumped me off.

"Get off my land!" Gunnar lunged forward and socked Crockett again, sending Beau's legs buckling, head wagging.

Crockett touched his lip, spit out blood. His son, Digit, bolted to Gunnar, wrapped his arms around my uncle's chest, locking the hold.

His daddy stood up and punched Gunnar in the stomach. Once, then again.

Gunnar slumped to his knees. Beau Crockett and his boy landed several booted kicks to Gunnar's belly and backside, leaving him facedown, groaning.

I ran up to the Crocketts, fists aiming for them.

Beau Crockett took his arm and swung it into my throat,

knocking the wind out of me for a second, sending me tumbling to the ground.

Rainey was somewhere behind us, fending off Ada's flailing blows. "Stop it, kid, stop . . . not going to hurt you," he yelled.

I crawled over to Gunnar's side, my burnt gown barely covering me. I kneeled beside him. "Gunnar! Gunnar, get up, get—"

The Crocketts stepped back. "Hill whore," Beau Crockett shouted, pinning his fingers to me.

The sirens grew louder. The men turned to the wail and quieted a second, taking hard breaths.

"Y'all deserved what ya got," Crockett fired back up. "Locking lips with that 'bacco nigger down at the Feed . . ."

Slowly, I shook my head. "No."

"You know'd that, Gunnar? Huh?" He bent over him and popped his eyes. "Did ya? Hell, Digit spied 'em in the storage block hooked up like two dogs in heat! You think she ain't good enough for my boys now . . . huh?"

Gunnar made a strange sound like a trapped bobcat.

"What, you actin' like you don't know?" Beau growled. "Teased Cash, then made a whore's bed an' promise with my Carter—sent my boys away, one off to his death, other to the dirty city, she did—and sent this"—he struck out his arm toward Ada—"this gawdamn little mountain witch down to tote more of her whoring letters to my boy and steal."

"Noo," I cried.

"*Liar!* Look at my boy's grave," Beau seethed. "Ya left him letters, then left flowers there like you're his *gawdamn* widow!"

From behind, Rainey cursed loudly, fought with Ada.

Beau breathed hard, shook a fist at Rainey and another to Gunnar. "Both of 'em should be whipped."

Gunnar narrowed his green eyes and moaned.

I felt the color flee my face, suddenly realizing the Crocketts knew about Henny's note to Carter and had me mixed up with her. They must've found it tacked to the fence post. Damn if I'd ever tell them different.

Then Ada lifted her head and screamed, commanding the night, everyone.

I twisted around.

Ada bit down on Rainey's hand and let out another high-pitched yell. "I lit him up, I did!" she burst. "Lit Carter's secret hiding tent down at the creek up real good . . . real good, so he'd never spawn again."

Silence wrapped the night, squeezed the heavy air.

Ada jabbed her finger at the Crocketts, me, and at Rainey, then back and forth, around and around, her hand quivering like a peach twig witching for water.

She flattened her tiny lips and brayed at me. "You . . . you gave away our baby so's you could go off and plant with that coon and have your own. Laid with that black dog in the tobaccos same as Sisters did with Crockett!"

I pressed my hand over my mouth as if it was over hers, gasping, "*No.*"

"Uh-huh," she said. "Caught Carter Crockett with Sisters—him a'planting seeds in Lena and Henny."

Low curses rammed the winds.

"Lena," I breathed. *Eve was Carter and Lena's baby. . . .*

Ada snarled. "Told Henny not to lay with Carter, but she went off a'whorin' with him, same as Lena." She lifted her arm, struck her blackened finger to the smoke-dinged skies. "No more 'bacco to whore in. No more a'planting for Sisters—Carter—*You!*" She stomped her bare foot.

A fear took hold, choking, racking my body. "*No . . . no.*"

Ada raised a blistered hand and opened her clenched fist. An empty *Please Come Again* matchbook fell out.

Chapter 28

Gunnar let out a squeezed breath, banging his head against dirt, a rasping cry fed to the charred earth, soaking my denials.

Ada sent another cackling cry across the fields.

Beside me, Beau Crockett yelled, "Bitch," and thrust a fist toward Ada. "*I will kill you.*"

Again, Rainey cursed his injury, then twisted around, stretching for Ada, but she slipped out of his grasp.

A cold fury ignited inside. Forgetting my wounds, I jumped up and lit after Ada. My feet swept across the crackling field—heels slapping close to hers—missing her by inches. Then I shot out my hand and caught her by the hair.

Ada spun around, clawed at me, her witching nails sunk into flesh. She lifted a foot, kicked my burnt legs, scraping blistered flesh.

I swung my arm, and she grabbed it and sunk her teeth into skin. I threw back my other hand to strike her, lost my footing, sending us both tumbling to the ground.

Ada rolled atop me and leaned into me and bit my check, thrashing, wild-catting her fists and feet against my burning legs.

I kicked back and raised my fist, striking her cheek.

Someone pulled me to my knees and pinned strong hands to my arms.

Ada toppled nearby.

"It's okay," Rainey said. "C'mon, come on," he urged.

"Let me go, Rainey." I jerked. "Sh-she—" I felt my body slack against him.

"Let's get you home, Roo," he pleaded.

"Everything's gone," I said. "Ruined."

Ada bared her broken teeth.

"You evil fleabag . . . you . . . you destroyed our crops . . . us . . ." I screamed and struggled to loosen Rainey's hold.

Ada scrambled to her feet, singsonging, "*Made him go a'sleep in a deep hole, a bad beau that Carter beau—a'planting girls wherever he'd go. A bad beau that Carter beau . . .*" She escaped to the woods, her ditty snagging the boughs of tall pines.

I felt Rainey tighten his grip on my arms, give a little shake. "No, girl, let her go!"

I lowered my head to my knees, rocking, sobbing a trembly hymn of denials.

Beau Crockett hollered out, "Tried to tell you 'bout them Stumps, Gunnar. Tried. Caught her two days ago tryin' to steal my kerosene cans! Ya got more to worry 'bout than your niggerlovin' whore here." He lurched after Ada.

Rainey let go of me and sprang sideways into the air. He tackled Crockett, slamming a fist into his face, once, twice. Beau's nose laid over enough for me to see it was broken.

Behind me in the distance someone laid on a horn. Crockett's son cursed, took off, barreling behind Ada, leaving his daddy to fend for himself.

I turned to see the sheriff's automobile rolling through the dying rows, coming straight at us.

On the ground, Beau Crockett growled, shot his hands up, and grabbed Rainey's throat.

Rainey drew back his fist, struck Crockett again, and then again.

"Stop, Rainey," Gunnar ordered. "You'll kill him. *Stop!*" Gunnar struggled to stand. Droplets of blood spotted his chin and splatted down onto his white night stockings. He winced and slumped over.

"*Gunnar!*" I scrambled over and shook him. "Gunnar, I—"

Slowly, Gunnar pulled himself to a kneeling stance, nailed a chilling glare to my eyes. He grimaced, then took a heavy hand and slapped me hard across the face once. Again.

My head rocked. Stunned and star-spotted, I cried out, pressed my hand to my stinging cheek.

Rainey cursed Crockett. I snapped my head upward and saw Rainey's jaw harden, a killing blood taking hold of his eyes. Same as I'd seen pass through Gunnar's when he was riled and there was no going back. His mouth set, jaw twitching. I knew Rainey would. He'd kill him, years of loss, pain, and avenging his daddy gathering deep.

"Rainey, no, please no," I cried out.

"*Rainey!*" me and Gunnar rang.

A red light whirled, slashed through the automobile's smoky headlights coming up fast. Doors slammed, and men's shouts filled the air. Behind, a small fire truck rolled through the plumes of smoke, crushing plants, spraying water from a hose hooked up to its metal tank.

Rainey dropped his fist to Crockett's face again. Fresh blood spurted out his mouth. Sheriff ran up to them and tried to pull Rainey off Crockett. "Lie still, boy!"

Rainey grunted.

"Gonna end up a dead dirt nigger like your pa if ya don't lie still. Right now, I say!" Sheriff tugged again.

Rainey landed a wild punch to Sheriff's chin, then a final hard jab to Crockett before Sheriff slammed the butt of a shotgun upside Rainey's head.

Rainey crumpled onto the ground, grasped his head, moaning. Sheriff kicked him in the side.

Rainey tried to rise, but his jaw folded down, plowed into the earth.

Crockett crawled a few feet away and lay still in the dirt.

Sheriff knelt down, rolled Rainey over, and slapped handcuffs on him. "Rainey Ford, taking you to the can for assault," Sheriff huffed. Then to Gunnar, "What happened here?" He hitched a thumb to the burnt tobacco and spit.

"Crocketts is what happened. *Him*." Gunnar raised a burnt arm. "Him and Ada Stump." Gunnar scratched out words as he slowly pulled himself up. "He's trespassing, she lit the fire. Girl's ran off into the woods."

"That wisp of a gal?" Sheriff asked.

"She got hold of kerosene and straw." Gunnar grabbed his side. "Claimed she lit up his boy's tent, too. Crockett here was trying to kill her."

Sheriff rubbed his sore jaw, narrowed his eyes. "Ada Stump done that?"

Gunnar coughed, clutched his side with his burnt arm again, nodded.

"Looks like you need Doc Sils out here," Sheriff said. "Her too." Sheriff jutted his chin my way. "I'll send him out when I get back to town."

I looked down at my nightgown, shreds of torched fabric clinging to a red blistered leg, felt my nipped cheek.

Sheriff turned to his deputy. "Get this colored boy into the car."

"No, he's hurt," I said, and stumbled over to Rainey, fearing they'd hurt him more. "It was the Crocketts and Ada—"

Rainey tried to get to his feet. "Roo, I-I'll be okay, get . . . now get on home." He pulled himself up on one knee, then collapsed.

"Rainey!" I squalled.

Gunnar snapped me back and then shoved me into the dirt.

I sprang back up. "*You.*" I stabbed at Gunnar. "You and the Crocketts are in the same bone-pickin' trash pile—"

"Silence!" Gunnar sliced his hand through the air.

I glared back. "I'm through with that. You and your tongue-burning potions and mean fireball God ain't gonna keep me silent anymore."

Gunnar looked off, like maybe he'd spent his last word with me. I didn't know whether to feel tall or sorry for him, maybe worried about what would come next.

"Get up, boy." Sheriff poked the barrel of his shotgun into Rainey's back, then gave another hard shove.

Rainey tried again, this time wobbling on both knees. I slipped his arm over my shoulder and tried to heave him up.

The sheriff nailed me a warning, poked Rainey harder with his gun.

"Now see here, Lamar," Gunnar said to the sheriff, "I'll take care of Rainey. See that he's punished for assaulting you. You go ahead and remove that Crockett trash, but leave the boy for me. He's got a date with the army soon."

A few feet away Beau Crockett rolled over, spitting out dirt, moaning.

"Hauling 'em both in. *Both*." Sheriff goosed his intent and motioned to the deputy. "C'mon, Deputy, hurry up and help me get 'em into the car. Then go find that Stump girl, bring her in, quick-like!"

Chapter 29

Dawn climbed over Stump Mountain, dissolving the night's madness and bringing a soft rain. Me and Gunnar limped into the yard just as the milk delivery service pulled away.

Clutching the milk bottles, Rainey's mama stole out of the shadows as we stepped onto the porch.

"Gunnar," she cried, "I've been waiting for you. I've been so afraid." Abby passed the milk to me, shook the rain off her long skirts. "I slept in the Parkers' storage room last night trying to finish sewing their new drape order. Someone said you were in trouble . . . The fields, they're gone! The burley and vegetables . . . And then I saw the sheriff drive up and leave with my Rainey! And him without his shoes . . . Gunnar . . . oh mercy." Abby's leaky eyes ballooned. "Just look at you two! What—"

Gunnar folded into the porch rocker. "Get my bourbon, RubyLyn."

Abby followed me inside. She found an old sheet and cut it into strips for bandages and applied some honey to our burns.

Weren't no time before old Doc Sils pulled up in his automobile.

The doctor taped Gunnar's ribs, tended to his arm while Gunnar sat stone-faced at the kitchen table. Then Doc took off my bandages and tsked at Abby's dressings.

He pulled out a bottle and lit my right leg with an iodine tincture. I wrapped my hands around flesh, gripping high on my thigh, squeezing so I wouldn't cry out as the burning liquid leeched hold of my flesh and set it ablaze, again and again. I gritted my teeth, afraid to whimper—too afraid of what else might be coming from Gunnar. I peeked over at him sitting across from me.

Abby pressed a wet rag to his face. Gunnar pushed her away with his bottle of Kentucky Gentleman and nursed himself another healthy swig. A glaze of bourbon shined his taut lips.

"Keep the dressings clean," Doc said to me after he bandaged the leg. "Other leg will heal fine without a dressing, but this one'll likely scar good, young lady."

Doc took my hand, waiting for me to say something, maybe waiting for me to admit something, and when I sucked in my breath and didn't, he preached, "You're mighty lucky . . . I've seen varnish pop off a floor like gunshot and a horse's flesh ripped clean to the bone 'cause of fire." He pressed an iodine-soaked cotton ball to my cheek where Ada had scraped the flesh with her teeth.

Gunnar took another gulp of bourbon, pulled himself up from the chair, and thudded upstairs. At the top of the stairs he bellowed down, "Clean up this pigpen, RubyLyn."

Doc reached into his toting bag, pulled out a bottle of capsules, and handed them to me. "Give these to Gunnar for his aches," he said, "twice a day if he needs it. I want him to be comfortable."

I took the bottle of ruby-red and blue capsules with the word "Tuinal" printed on the label. I waited for him to reach into the doctoring bag for me—maybe offer strong aspirin powders or ointment. Doc peered over his spectacles, and said, "See that Gunnar has bed rest and doesn't get worked up, RubyLyn." He stood and snapped his medical bag shut.

In the hall, Doc walked past Abby, stopped and flicked out his palm, and said, "Negress Ford." Abby ran back to the kitchen, grabbed his hat off the table, and gave it to him.

After his automobile rattled down the road, Abby said, "I need to try and get Rainey home."

From the top of the stairs Gunnar thumped a fist on the banister. "Not today, Abby. Think it's best if Rainey sits a while and stays away from RubyLyn."

"No," I shouted.

"Go home, Abby," he said, cutting me a sharp look.

Abby's eyes filled, but she nodded and slipped out the door.

"He can't stay in there, Gunnar, he can't!" I protested. "He could be in there weeks. He'll miss his army date. You said so yourself—"

"And I am now saying: he's staying put."

"If he lays in there he'll lose—"

"Should've thought of that before *you* lay in the fields."

"Ada Stump's laying tales. We didn't do—"

"You did enough, dammit!" he shot out, swinging a wild arm. "*Good Lord.* Look at the crop—our lives pulled from the dirt."

"I didn't do anything. Didn't. Do. It." I stacked my denial and sent the argument back up the stairs.

"And I'm going to make damn certain you don't!" Wobbly, he spun around toward his bedroom door. "Your pa's devils have taken your GodPretty, RubyLyn." His prickly words floated down the stairs, smacking skin.

The rest of the day was spent nursing wounds. By the next morning, my nerves were lit with deeper hurts. I went outside and sat on the back porch, rocking my thoughts. Here my husband-to-be was sitting in jail, without shoes even.

I stared over to the Crocketts' place, then back to the tree line, hugging myself in Mama's jacket, pulling anxiously at the threads. For a few seconds my mind played tricks and I stood to squint. It was the visit from earlier—Ada running alongside it.

Rubbing my eyes, I settled back into my seat, smacking the rocker's platform to and fro. Dizzying my thoughts. Folks said Nameless's jail only had two tiny cells. What if they put Rainey and Crockett together? What if they hurt him?

I blew on my skin around the bandage, the tingling, burning, paining me more. Soon I dozed off dreaming about crazy things—mean snakes and talking to Daddy on my old tin telephone toy.

Two hours had passed when I awoke to Sierra smacking her paw against my hurting leg. I rubbed the cat's soft ears, slowly rose in a shadow falling over me.

I took a step back.

"Y-you scared me," I breathed out.

Henny stretched out an arm and hurried up the steps. "Oh, Roo. I was scared silly. Oh! Look at ya . . . you're hurt . . . Your leg! I'm sorry about all this." She grabbed me in a hug.

I winced and stepped out of her clasp and inspected the cut on her face, her dress torn, barely covering her chest.

"Did they catch her?" I asked.

She wagged her head, then wiped her red eyes on a dirty arm. "No, th-they's got men on the mountain looking. . . ." Her words were brittle and broke. "Pa's . . . Pa's gonna kill her. And I have to leave." She sagged against me. "Ma's sending me to Beauty. She said I couldn't be trusted 'cause of Carter. Said it's all my fault. Oh, Roo, I—I have to live with old Auntie," she wailed.

"No, Henny. For good?"

"Yeah . . . Then Pa called me a whore, same as Lena. Just like that, and told me not to come back," she despaired. "I gots to leave quick 'fore they find me."

Out in the field I heard a distant shout. And another.

"I'm leaving, too, even if it kills me," I whispered, hugging her back, and then we both cried buckets.

The shouts grew closer.

"That's Pa," she said, shivering. "I—I gotta get now 'fore he takes the stick to me again."

I looked at the raised tracks on her arms, her swelling cheek.

"Gonna miss ya terribly," she whispered.

Taking off my jacket, I wrapped it around her. "Me too."

Henny widened her eyes, raised a hand to her chest. "Oh, ya knows how much I love it, Roo. But it's your ma's—"

"Mama would want my *sister* to have it."

"We's sisters," she said, her eyes shining with fresh tears.

"Always," I said, mine coming hot and fast.

"Swear?" She laid an X across her chest and two more across a shaky palm, then held up her hand to me.

"Swear." I pressed our palms together in a clasp.

Henny squeezed our hands to her cheek, and whispered, "Get your man and get outta this devil town, Roo."

"I will—"

Her daddy peeled the color off the sky with more shouts.

She dropped her hold and took off, leaving my affirmation hanging.

Leaning over the rail, I watched her, hair tatted and tangled, those bare legs whipping through the burnt tobaccos. She wouldn't be back. Likely, the last tobacco rash she would ever fuss about, too. I'd sorely miss her. I wiped my wet cheek against my shoulder. "Good night, Henny." I raised my hand and blew a kiss.

I sat back down on the rocker, piling on thoughts. When I couldn't stand it any longer, I jumped up. I had to see Rainey. Had to find a way out of here.

Gunnar ate his dinner at noon sharp, same as every day, and washed it down with two of his pain pills. When I was sure he was napping, I went to my room and changed into a clean dress.

Light as dandelion seeds and just as quiet, I slipped down the stairs and out the door. Quickly, I pulled on my shoes.

I had to get to him. But first I needed to make a stop.

Chapter 30

I rested at the bottom of the Fords' porch to collect tangled nerves. Still shaky, I grabbed the wooden rail and climbed up the steps, my raw leg tightening, pinching under its dressing.

Inside, the radio played a frayed tune. Abby's small shadow darkened a far wall as she hobbled her broken time from the sitting room to the kitchen and then back again.

She peered up at the wall that anchored family photographs. A smiling family, unlike the frowning kin that hung in Gunnar's foyer. Pictures of a dimpled Rainey, her husband, and other kin hung lopsided on cracked walls. So much love and laughter in those old photographs. All that sweet living had plumb tilted those frames crooked. More than ever I wanted that life with Rainey.

A teakettle whistled and a minute later her sewing machine's steady strum flitted out the open window, cornered the whir of a fading summer.

Watching, I rubbed my sweaty hands alongside my skirts. Abby raised her head every so often, wiping what I knew were tears from her eyes, sniffling loudly before turning back to her sewing.

Quietly, I tiptoed over to the screen door and picked up Rainey's work boots, the heavy brown leather reddened and softened from days of sun and soak. Beside them sat his old violin. I touched the worn spruce, pressed a kiss to its wood belly.

Tucking his boots under my arm, I snuck away before Abby could catch wind of my doings.

In town, I hurried past the Shake King, then crossed to the shops, folding myself into shadowed concrete lips and the town's quiet. I wanted to peek inside windows to see who was in town in case someone got word back to Gunnar I was here.

The morning bustle had long slumbered into a midday laze. My leg burned as I walked past French's bench. I gave a nod to Erbie, and he widened his eyes at my leg, then asked, "You okay, Miss RubyLyn? Need to sit a spell?"

"I'm okay, Erbie."

"Them's Rainey's boots." He pointed his whiskered chin. "Lotta stitches."

I forced a little smile, limped on past to Althea's. Then I glanced into Potter's and strolled down to the coffee shop.

I stood there a minute taking big breaths before crossing the street to the white-columned courthouse. I cut over and waited a minute in front of the small, redbrick jail beside it. Through an open window, a radio swept melodies out into the quiet.

Looking all around, I ducked into Nameless Jail, hoping no one saw, and no one wondered why I'd just walked full circle around town.

A gust of air shut the door behind me, ballooned aluminum blinds and sucked them violently back to the window, clacking my arrival.

Jailer, Bur Hancock, the tall, muscled nineteen-year-old from church, pushed himself away from the desk and stood. He was a quiet man, always buttoned beside his mama. One that I often wrote down for kissing in my fortunes just to make it fair and a little bit more exciting. Folks talked a lot about how he got this job soon after high school, saying he could be sheriff one day. And even Gunnar sniffed around him, giving a word or two, checking him out like the other mamas did for their daughters.

"Afternoon, RubyLyn," Bur said, standing, sliding his thumbs into his belt, rocking on his heels.

I looked around the small jailhouse and my eyes rested on the long, tall concrete wall alongside Bur's desk. Everyone knew the two cells were hidden somewhere behind those gunmetal-colored cinder blocks. Though I hadn't ever seen them, only heard the talk.

Thoughts of ol' Rainey Bethea whirled. Standing there made my knees knock and my heart rattle, brushing bone. The idea of my Rainey locked away here stole my greeting for a second.

Smiling, Bur quickly brushed his breadcrumb-lunch off his gray tie and sidled next to a tall filing cabinet, relaxing an arm across it. Atop the metal cabinet, a dark brown Bakelite radio scratched out a bubbly tune.

I clutched the boots and drew myself up, then took a step toward him.

"Hi, Bur. How's your mama?"

"Mama's hip's a'healing good now. Thanks for making us that fine cheddar peach pie." He patted his belly. "Tasty."

"Won't be long till it's apple pickin' time." I flashed a smile.

He grinned. "Mighty fine crust you make."

"I've come to see Rainey. I brought his shoes." I held them out.

His friendly smile popped. "Don't know that Gunnar's nigger is having visitors, RubyLyn. Sheriff didn't leave any word of such. I know the bail's been set with a fifty-dollar cash bond, though." He held out his hands. "But I'll see that he gets 'em."

My face fell flat. "Just for a minute," I pleaded, pulling the boots closer to me, "let me go in. *Please.* His mama wanted me to give them to him, and pass a few words from her . . . Gunnar too."

He looked off, like maybe he was wanting someone else to tell him what to do, but nobody else was there.

"Gunnar needs to know his worker's okay. And Rainey's mama is real worried about him, Bur. Very worried." I scooted closer, raised my skirts. "Know you heard. See this? Got my leg all burned up and walked all the way to town a'hurtin'. Mrs. Ford can't afford fifty dollars, and she'll send me right back if I don't get them to Rainey myself and tell her I talked to him," I lied.

His ears reddened when he looked down at my leg. Quickly, he scooped the keys off his desk. "Tell ya what, RubyLyn, I ought to take them boots to him, but maybe a few minutes won't hurt none . . . just a few, mind you." He crooked his finger, wagging. "The rules say I have to take a look."

I lifted up the boots for him. He peeked inside, then spun his finger around. Raising the hem of my dress to my knees, I turned slowly so he could see my shoes and legs. Satisfied I wasn't carrying anything to the prisoner, he nodded, pink-cheeked.

"Thanks, Bur." I followed him to the end of the wall.

He opened a heavy wooden door and stepped aside. "Be quick," he warned.

I bobbed my head and slipped past him into the weakly lit narrow hall.

A cloud of stale urine and bleach sweated concrete walls, smothering.

I peered into the first cell. Artie Washburn, the town drunk, lay passed out, puttering out quarrelsome snores and cloud-puffed cries to his demons.

At the next cell, someone lay on a cot near the far wall underneath a ratty brown blanket.

"Rainey?" I said quietly. "I got here as quick as I could."

He stirred, moaned. Slowly he threw back the cover. "Roo," he coughed out, "Roo." He sat up.

My hand flew to my mouth. One of Rainey's eyes was plumped shut, and his feet looked like someone had stomped on them.

"Rainey," I cried, trying to keep my voice in the cell.

He shook his head, staggered over to me, and clutched the bars. "Roo! Are you okay, Roo, are you—?"

"Fine," I assured him several times. I stared down at his swollen, blood-crusted feet. "Who did this, Rainey?"

"S'ok, Roo." He cracked a crooked smile. "Sheriff had to give me a talkin'-to, and Crockett had an itch to dance. He's gone now, got bailed out early this morning. But you should've seen *his* lively jig before he left."

Rainey was looped from the pain. I reached inside the bars and grasped his hand. He sucked in a breath, and I drew back and saw his scraped knuckles, the puffy flesh.

His gaze fell on the boots. "No," he said, and pushed off the bars. "No, no, no." He wagged a finger and wheeled around. "No, girl! You brought me shoes for jail, not for coming home."

"Rainey, Gunnar's not himself and I thought I'd do right and—"

"Tell Gunnar to take my pay and get me out of here."

"He's in a bad way."

He grabbed the bars. "Dammit, Roo, if I don't get out of here I could miss my induction. I miss my induction, I could lose everything I got, for Ma, and us."

"We won't," I whispered. "I'll find a way. *Promise.*"

Bur called out for me.

Resigned, Rainey's shoulders dipped.

"Just a little longer, Rainey," I said gently.

"Roo, thank you." He leaned his head in.

I pressed my cheek to the bars, whispered. "I'll get you out, Rainey. Get us both out."

From down the end of the hall, Bur's shadow appeared. He jangled keys and cleared his throat.

"RubyLyn," Bur called down the darkened hall, "best leave now. Sheriff's on his way in."

Rainey gave a weak nod, and I set the shoes down beside his cell and wiped my eyes. I stuck my pinky inside the bars and Rainey grabbed hold.

"Good night," we whispered.

Bur walked me to the front door of the jailhouse and looked down at his feet and all around, working his tongue loose of a stiff mouth. "Want you and Gunnar to know Sheriff caught that Stump gal. Spitfire she was."

"He did?"

"Yup, caught her behind the Feed stealing one of Mr. Parker's kerosene cans."

Relieved, my shoulders slumped.

"Yup, fought like a rabid coon. They had to take the battery cables to tie her up in the backseat of Deputy's car. Took her over to Everly County Juvenile Detention Center."

"That's good. Gunnar will be happy to hear it." I blinked to stop the sudden gush that threatened.

Wind pushed through the blinds, ruffling piles of Bur's paperwork, licking the room with dull paper-soaked breezes.

"Um, RubyLyn"—Bur reached across me, rested his big hand on the door latch and lingered, blocking my exit—"Mama . . . Mama said no one in these hills . . . heck, three counties wide, can cook as good as you, and she . . . I thought—well, I . . . maybe if Gunnar didn't have your hand set to someone else . . . I'll ask him first, but . . . maybe you'd like to . . . set a courtin' time . . . to, well . . . have a visit on the porch with me and maybe . . ."

The radio batted its static into the dead air, and for a moment it seemed like there weren't nothing left to fill it—weren't never going to be.

"RubyLyn . . ."

Again the airwaves nicked, but sharper this time.

"It's going to be a while till Gunnar gets back on his feet, and I"—I pointed to my leg—"am fit for company. Will you see that Gunnar's worker is taken care of till then? Good working man is hard to find in these parts."

He dropped his arm. "Of course, RubyLyn."

I searched his kind eyes, disappointment settling in, hating that I'd rejected him, but I could only think of Rainey in that gloomy cell—and us out of here.

I lowered my gaze and edged past him outside to the splitting elm in the middle of the parking lot. Afternoon sun streaked through the drooping branches, warming my damp face.

Darla Clark came up behind me, pulling her wagon, her little boys folded inside asleep, the metal wheels clacking loudly on the concrete. She stopped beside me to pick up a dirty, stray S&H Green Stamp to add to the ones she'd been saving to trade a baby rocker for. Ducking, she muttered a greeting and cast a weary glance back, her white-skirted uniform stained, reeking of onions and grease.

Widow Joan Marsh, sixty years old, bent and broke, dragged her splintered walking stick along the lot, tapping and talking to her two dead sons and husband all gone from another coal mishap and miner's lung. She stopped and poked her cane at my good leg, scrutinized my cut face. "Seen my menfolk at the bottom?"

I shifted, shook my head.

"See my boys down there in the bug dust tell 'em supper's on the stove. Be sure and tell 'em now, ya hear!" Widow Marsh whacked my leg. Spittle flew out of her mouth, bubbled her jaw.

Over at the Shake King, Sheriff leaned against his automobile, arms folded, chatting to Dusty and Dirty Durbin while Lena Stump hung back a few feet.

The sisters giggled at something Sheriff said. Dusty leaned into him, stretching on tiptoes to whisper in his ear—her short yellow skirt riding almost up to her hiney. Sheriff hooted and quickly rubbed his crotch, then smacked her rump. She bent over, then wriggled away.

Weren't no undies there, or even a cotton slip to cover that.

I turned my head toward the city—my attention, my heart begging for a life far from here.

Chapter 31

Friday morning, I pulled a Sunday church dress over the stylish silk slip, then went down and paced the porch boards, hoping Gunnar would soften—hoping for a trip to town for Rainey's bail.

Gunnar'd gone off into the barn, then over toward Abby's long before first light. We'd been arguing since five thirty, with me pleading for Rainey's release. When I knocked the jar of bitters out of Gunnar's hand, he'd backhanded me and stomped off to his tractor.

Still dark, I lit the porch lanterns and then stepped down into the yard. I prayed Abby would talk some sense into him, though he'd taken his tractor out to burn off his anger, not to porch-talk.

Hiding in the shadows, Baby Jane slinked out from the side of the house with her egg basket, alarming me.

"RubyLyn, b-brung you some eggs and wanted ya to know I'm r-real sorry," she stuttered, took a step closer, and held out the basket.

"Eggs ain't gonna fix this mess, Baby Jane Stump, or give back what your sister took," I snapped.

"But, I-I—"

"Don't want your damn eggs, Baby Jane!" I swung my arm and knocked the basket out of her hands.

Gasping, she shrank back. Tears sprang to her eyes and she bolted. Three cracked eggs lay glistening at my feet.

I stomped the shells, smashing, beating them into the earth. Gulping down sobs, I let the darkness fold in and carry my grief and hopelessness until it was good and spent. For a long while I stared over at the Crocketts' land.

"Done got half his mountain land tied up in property bonds . . ." Words that Mr. Crockett had flung at Gunnar looped around my head.

Property. Five prized bottomland acres my folks had passed to me.

I have to fix this now. I picked through my thoughts— thoughts about my land, Rainey, and home. There were some ugly notions rooting, but uglier ones were surely headed my way if I didn't grab hold and try.

I went to my room and gathered up the strawberry dress and washed it in the sink. Hitching the hem on my dull church dress, I pinched the silk. Wearing Rose's slip made me feel sure and strong like Emma.

I plodded down to the kitchen with the wet dress. Taking a pen to a piece of scrap paper, I wrote: *Property of Rose Law,* and pinned the note to the fabric.

Under the last burst of morning stars, I took Rose's dress out to the clothesline to dry.

Satisfied, I went back into the house, plucked the church key from the silverware drawer, and dropped it into my dress pocket.

I rummaged through my purse, tossing the pickle flyer and Future Farmers of America information onto the table. When I found what I was looking for, I hurried into the sitting room to search through Gunnar's things.

It didn't take me long to dig up the deed to my folks' five acres in Gunnar's old maple secretary. Shaking, I slipped the document into my purse, walked over to the mantel, and placed the State Fair candle cross atop Claire's wooden box. I straightened her ashes like Gunnar always did, tapped it to wake her up.

I couldn't help saying a little prayer since there was no turning back. A prayer to a kinder God I felt Claire would've known.

"Aunt Claire, I'm sorry. Please tell God to forgive me, but it's the only way. Watch over Gunnar, Abby, and the Stumps for me . . . 'specially Baby Jane and little Eve and her new family. And, oh, see that God protects Rainey, too. Tell my folks I love them."

I ran a fingertip over the smooth wood, circled my Amen into the tiny grains.

Turning to the window, I tucked Mama's purse under my arm. "Gots me three hundred dollars saved," Crockett'd said.

Once I stepped onto the porch, the mountain air calmed and erased the fevered uncertainty in my bones.

I made my way to the yard, ducked under the clothesline, the pretty strawberry dress billowing in the late summer breeze as dawn crested the hillside.

I marched across the fog-soaked field, down the property line, and straight into the devil's den.

Chapter 32

On the Crocketts' broken porch, overalls and torn long johns were clothespinned onto a nailed rope that hung below haggard eaves. Empty bottles, spilt salt shakers, and Mason jars perched beside worn rockers. Cracked raccoon skulls lined the porch railing.

I stopped about five feet away. A house sparrow flitted out of one of the coon skulls. A skinny dog raised his graying muzzle, snarled.

"Hush now, pup," I calmed, holding out a fisted hand. "Shhh, handsome boy. Shh." The dog slowly lowered its head, thumped a flea-bitten tail.

I looked over my shoulder toward home. Dawn sharpened its edge, the moon slid into its final parting.

I put a foot on the bottom board. The earth shifted. I cried out as I fell sideways to the ground. My face flattened into dewy weeds.

I twisted around. Digit Crockett was atop me, drilling one knee into my back and the other into my bad leg.

"Get off me, Digit Crockett!" I yelled, trying to bat at him. "Off!"

Digit ground his knees deeper.

I screamed.

A shot rang out, deafening. I raised my head as best I could. Beau Crockett stood on the porch with a .20 gauge shotgun, the worn stock hitched tight to his shoulder.

"Got her, Pa!" Digit said smugly, as if he'd tackled a bear.

"Get on up here, boy," Beau said to his son.

Digit scrambled away and hopped up onto the porch.

Pulling myself up, I grabbed my purse and wiped the grass from my face. Half-bent, I took a breath and raised my palm. "Got business, Mr. Crockett." I squinted up at him, the morning sun stretching its face, casting bands of pinkish orange across him and stain-darkened boards.

He touched his swollen nose, crooked, and parked to the side from the break. "Ain't got no business over here with the Crocketts, gal," Beau said, spittle draping his greasy beard. "Get on back to your likes."

I reached inside my dress pocket, pulled out the church key, and threw it onto the porch. The brass bottle opener landed near his dirty boot. "Come for a meeting," I said as big as possible.

Old man Crockett stood there a minute staring, then jutted his pointy chin to his son. Digit shot me a mean glance before slipping into their cabin.

His daddy slowly waved the gun, nudging me to climb up the porch.

When I landed on the last step, Crockett slapped a hard grip around my neck, pulled me up, then shoved me against the wall.

I crumpled to the floor, coughing, rubbing my neck, the back of my head hurting.

Crockett swung his boot, kicked my sore leg. "You got one Kentucky second to tell me what kinda meeting you is calling, gal."

I sucked in a loud yelp and tried to stand.

Crockett kicked me again.

I cried out as the blow landed to my side.

"Half second left 'fore ya never see another."

"Land," I squeezed out, clutching my side. Then louder, "*Land!*"

Inside, Digit pressed against the slits of a tattered curtain, peeking out the dirty window.

Beau pinned a suspicious gaze to my eyes, took his fist, and banged on the pane behind him, rattling glass. He set the gun beside the rocker, then plunked himself into it.

I stayed put on my knees, waiting for the nerves to climb into my bones.

A few seconds later, Digit opened the door, came out, handed his daddy two bottles of Falls City beer, and ducked back inside.

"Git on with it." Old man Crockett pointed to the opener I'd thrown and then to the empty rocker beside him.

I crawled slowly over to the church key lying near his feet and picked it up, pulled myself up, and limped back over to the rocker.

Crockett handed me a beer, and with fumbly fingers I opened it and passed him the church key. He popped off the cap, dropped the bottle opener at his feet.

Smacking his lips, he lifted a dirty jar off the board and poured his beer into it, then reached for the salt shaker on his other side. Shaking the salt into the glass, he tried to waken the piss-tired liquid.

The sun heated the morning, stickying my dress as it burned off last night's chill.

Crockett took himself a mouthful, smacked his lips again. "That's the hymnal I never get tired of opening." He kicked at the church key and bottle caps littering the floor in front of him, stretched a leg, then studied me a second, and said, "Better not be wasting my good beer, gawdammit."

I took a long drink of the warm beer. Coughed. Then choked down another. Beside Gunnar's nasty herb mix, this was my first drink of alcohol, and surprisingly, I liked the slight hum it fed my tummy before it took hold of my head. What would Gunnar think of that? Probably compare me to my drunk daddy.

I pushed the thought away and stretched a shaky hand and took another swig. One more big gulp and I set the bottle down beside the rocker. I opened my purse, fished out the deed, and snapped it in front of him. "Five acres for five hundred dollars," I said. "And it's all yours."

He snatched the deed from my hand, rubbed his potbelly as

he looked it over. He worked his mouth up tight and spit at my feet. "Worthless, ain't got the living years behind ya to sign it," he growled, and kicked another cap into the yard, scattering up a warbler sipping from a muddy bootprint.

"I will in a week when I'm a married woman." I tucked my feet under the rocker. "Just need a down payment—fifty dollars now so I can marry real quick."

"*Marry!* Who's gonna marry a nigger lover?" He guffawed through his rotting teeth. "Got ya a coon bastard coming now that you've spent my boys, that it?"

I put my hand to my belly and glared back my answer.

"White whore witch," he sneered, raising a fist.

"I'll sell it to you now."

He lowered his arm.

"If I stay, Gunnar's gonna marry me off to the jailer, and the land will be his. I need to leave quick." I ran my hand over my belly.

"Don't know," he said lazily, "that scorched land just don't seem as good as it once did. . . ." He took another swallow of beer and rocked.

"As good as it ever was. Even better. The ash will fertilize everything." I forced my back into the rocker, rocked, too.

Burping, he stuck out his thin lips, scratched his whiskered neck with the lip of the glass. "Tired land—"

"Rich soil. Four hundred, Mr. Crockett, and I'll sign it right over in seven days."

"Two hundred."

"It's worth three times more." I shifted in the rocker. "Royal land's the best around these parts. *Three hundred.*"

He leaned over his belly and spit off the porch. "Two hundred, lessen ya want to raise that skirt and show me just what else is best about the Royals . . . Eh?" He stretched out his arm, touched my dress. "Maybe we can close this meeting with a fine song . . . might could give you two dollars more for that tune . . ."

I swiped at his dirty hand. "Three hundred!" I punched the

air with a sickness twisting inside. "Anybody in Nameless will take it! And fifty now or I head to town and it goes up two hundred," I bit.

"Nobody in Nameless has two dollars to spare, much less two hundred."

"Three." I flashed fingers.

"*Three-damn-hundred!*" Crockett boomed, then leaned over and snatched me up by my hair, yanking me back to the splintered floor. "And ya sign your intention on the back of that deed, says I gave ya the fifty and leave it here, gal. And if ya ain't at the courthouse seven days from now, Gunnar's gonna find *you* buried next to a pile of deer bones, ya hear?"

A scream whistled through my teeth. "*Yesss.*"

Crockett gave one more hard tug, burning my scalp, watering my eyes, taking long strands before he finally let go.

He took another drink, stood, and flicked the fistful of hair at me.

I rubbed my head. Through blurred eyes I reached for the small nest of hair on my knees.

Noisily, Crockett downed the rest of his beer. Finished, he tossed the Mason jar out into the mud-caked yard and edged over to the end of the boards. Then the old man unzipped his pants and relieved himself off the porch. He hollered over his shoulder, "Digit, get my gawdamn pickle jar out here."

I grabbed the rocker to stand.

He turned back to me and shot out an arm. "Won't have it, gawdammit! You stay put. *Stay put.* I want that Royal land signed over to me on your gawdamn Royal knees!"

Slowly I pulled myself up, my eyes locking with his dull hazel ones. "Royals stand."

Minutes later I was behind the willow oak in our side yard heaving up beer. I stepped over to the old hand pump. Splashing my face, I cooled my neck, took big gulps, and a long drink of what had to happen next.

Feeling better, I fixed myself some dry toast and ate. An hour later, I grabbed my purse and headed down Royal Road to the town's bench.

Chapter 33

From down the street I watched Erbie Sipes doze on the bench, a crinkled paper in his hand.

For a few minutes, I rolled the First Lady's coin between my fingers, the silver Kennedy half-dollar glinting in the bright sunlight. I lifted a silent prayer and walked over to the bench.

"Hey, Erbie," I said softly. "Can I sit a spell?"

Erbie raised the brim of his ball cap, widened his sleepy blue eyes. "Morning, Miss RubyLyn. Sure can." He scooted over.

"Hey." I smiled. "Seen any new automobiles?"

He clicked his teeth. "Two—a fast-looking blue thing that sped through last Friday at three sixteen. License plate, DNY 016 . . . A '62 Chevy II it was. None this morning, and it's nearing ten. But on Monday, I saw a green Ford pickup with three baby moon hubcaps . . . The postmistress," he clicked, "had on her red shoes and took her dinner over at the Shake King at twelve thirty-six . . . Truck zipped righ' by her in the rain." His teeth clattered. "Nearly soaked them forty-six white dots off her pretty brown skirt."

"Wish I could've seen it, Erbie, but I was in Louisville with Rose Law."

"Ain't never been, but Miz Rose is righ' nice," he said. "She brings me food."

I nodded and pressed the coin into his hand.

Erbie looked at the silver half-dollar, chopped his teeth together again. "I knows when he died . . . thirty-fifth presi-

240 Kim Michele Richardson

dent"—he pointed to Kennedy—"and I knows when you got
this from the thirty-sixth president's lady. Cold day over in
Inez . . . April 24. Sure is shiny." He held it up, whistled, turning the coin slowly.

"I have something important I need you to do for me, Erbie.
You can keep it for your help. And this"—I fished the money
out of my purse and gave him the fifty dollars—"is for someone
else."

He put the bills in his lap and popped his eyes back to the coin.
"Never had me one of these, and this one's special, I knows."

"Need you to go over and bail Rainey Ford out of jail. Give
this fifty dollars to Mrs. Blackson at the courthouse. Then take
the paper she gives you over to Bur."

He clicked his teeth once again. "Rainey. Blackson. Bur," he
ticked off, wadding the money into his fist. "This is a pretty
coin, Miss RubyLyn."

"Sure is, Erbie. You keep it when Rainey walks out, hear?
Tell Rainey to meet me on your bench." I patted the wood.

"Who'll count the automobiles?" he worried.

"I will, Erbie. I've had all my schooling for arithmetic." I
took his hand, squeezed.

"Every one of them?" he asked, doubting.

I pulled the shiny red pencil out of my purse that I'd gotten
at the fair. "All of 'em."

In the first hour, the Tastee Bread truck rolled into town stopping at the Shake King first, then over to the Feed to unload. I
marked the bench twice.

Rose drove by in her Canopy and beeped. I waved and
marked the bench again.

Darla Clark rolled her wagon past. I fudged and counted.

In the second hour, I circled the bench, paced the sidewalk.
What if Erbie messed up? Lost the money? Forgot altogether? I
stared hard across the street, wishing they'd come out of the jail.

A few minutes of that and I plopped onto the bench, exhausted. The preacher rode by in his black Chevrolet.

Then I saw him. He carried his boots in the crook of an arm,
a smile cracked on his dark face. Erbie limped alongside him.

Quickly, I tucked my hands behind my back for fear of grabbing him in a kiss. "Rainey," I breathed. "*Rainey*."

"RubyLyn, let's go home." He dropped down onto the bench and wedged his swollen feet into his boots, wincing.

I gave my pencil to Erbie. "Was five, Erbie. Thank you."

When we got to Royal Road we slipped into the tobaccos. Rainey said, "Come here, girl," then gathered me into his arms.

My eyes filled and soon I was bubbling words. "Land. Marrying."

Rainey held me at arm's length. "Whoa, girl. Slow down a bit," he laughed. "How did you get me out . . . Gunnar?"

I couldn't look at him. "Sold my land."

"What?"

"Wasn't going to be much use anyhow, what with me in the city—"

"Dammit, Roo! You can't sell your land. Gunnar won't have it! I won't have it!"

I thought about Crockett wanting to keep me on my knees. "*Lordy-jones!* Crockett won't have, you won't have, Gunnar won't have! When, here, *I* have a mind!"

"You sold it to Crockett? Oh hell, Roo."

"I did. Weren't no other way. None, and you'd lose everything—us. Figured Crockett got us into this mess, his money best help us out. I'd rather lose land than you, Rainey Ford."

Rainey sighed and kissed me. "Thank you. I'll take you to bigger lands . . . Hell, girl, I will buy you a whole city if I can." He rubbed his thumb over my cheek, looked at me all serious and quiet.

I thought about the signature on the deed. "You will?" I asked softly.

"Sure 'nuff. Soon as we can get you on the city's courthouse steps." He brushed another sweet kiss over my mouth.

"But the money? I only had the fifty for bail. Rest won't come until I can sign, and I can't sign the deed until I'm a married woman." The charged word tingled my lips.

"My beautiful Roo." He put his forehead to mine. "Got fifty-two dollars coming from my pay that Gunnar owes me. 'Nuff cash to have us a fine marrying day. *A fine one.*"

"But Gunnar—"

"He won't know until it's done. And once we're in the city together, he won't stop us."

That was true. He wouldn't let us live in sin. Honor would have him laying permission real quick.

I looked out at the lost tobacco fields, the sun crackling the burnt grasses. "You're not safe here. When can we leave, Rainey?"

"I'll go home, get some clothes and my violin, and tell Ma good-bye. We'll catch a ride once we get far enough out of town . . ." He gripped my arms. "Go pick up what you need, Roo, and I'll meet you in one hour in the back of the Feed lot. We're gonna have ourselves a swell honeymoon at the Kentucky State Fair, *Mrs. Ford!*"

Oh! To have my husband there by my side instead of a nasty Crockett would be grand. I stared up at him.

He gazed into my watery eyes, and said, "I've been waiting for us forever. I love you, Roo. One hour. Okay? Now say *good night*, girl."

"I love you. One hour," I breathed, kissing him full and with the promise of more. "Good night, Rainey."

We hooked our pinkies together, lingered a second and then pressed tight, before we took off across the fields.

Ducking under the clothesline, I stopped and unpinned the strawberry dress. *I'll need a marrying dress.*

Skipping up the porch steps, I twirled around with the dress. Once, twice, imagining us finally together on the twinkly Ferris wheel and city avenues.

In mid-spin the screen door creaked open. He caught hold of the fabric, yanking the dress right from my hands.

Chapter 34

"What have you done, RubyLyn? *What?*" Gunnar threw the strawberry dress off the porch and shook me.

I choked out a cry.

"WHAT?" he boomed.

"I—I . . ."

"Crockett's been up and down this hollar, spouting off about land—*Royal* land! You took your land to get Rainey out?"

"For my—my . . . my husband."

"Silence!" He wheeled around, raised an arm.

I cringed against the wall. "We-we're getting married, Gunnar. I love him—"

Gunnar threw back a fist, pumped it twice.

I closed my eyes tight.

He barreled his big hand into the wooden board next to my head.

My legs buckled, sending me to the floor.

He punched the wall again, anger splintering the boards.

I dared to flutter my eyelids.

White-lipped and red-faced, he swung open the screen door and disappeared inside.

Piling down hard air, I sat huddled to the wall until I steadied my breathing. *I have to get my stuff and get back to Rainey.* I crept inside and ran up to my bedroom. Slamming the door, I crossed to the bed, shook loose the case from the pillow, and began stuffing it with Daddy's tin box, Mama's purse, and my brush and a clean dress.

Minutes later he kicked open my door. I saw the shotgun at his side.

"You're not going anywhere," he rasped a growl and tore the pillowcase from my hand, slinging it across the room. "Stay *put!*"

He thudded out, lit down the stairs and out the screen door.

I rushed over to my window. Gunnar pounded big strides across the fields. "Gunnar! Come back!" I banged on the top pane, pleading. "*Gunnar.*" I leaned out and shouted.

I tore down the steps and out the door.

The wind caught my skirts, tripping me twice as I ran across the field.

I caught up with Gunnar as he reached Crockett's porch.

"Gunnar, you can't do this," I shouted. "It's my land! *Mine!*" I grabbed his arm and pulled. "Mama and Daddy gave—"

He shoved me off and raised his palm.

I flinched, took a step back.

Beau Crockett sat on the rocker with his glass of beer in one hand and salt shaker in the other, leg cocked on his porch rail, watching us approach. "Well, now, come to celebrate with me I see." Crockett raised his glass, crowed. "We's kin now, with our joined lands."

"I'll never celebrate with the likes of you," Gunnar said real low, and threw crumpled money onto the porch. "Nor will any Royal! *'Specially* one who's still my charge and is a *minor.*"

Crockett curled his lip. "Ya ain't never been able to handle your women, Royal . . . Land's only fit for grave dirt anyways, nigger graves at that." He spat.

Gunnar's jaw twitched. He looked like he might raise his gun, but he only glared at him before stomping off.

I stood there for a minute, not sure what to do next.

Crockett set his glass down, picked up his shotgun, and rose slowly from his seat. "Should've known . . . Should've *known* not to waste my good beer on a gawdamn lying whore!" He pulled out the deed from his shirt pocket, wadded it into a ball, and threw it at me. "Git!" He thumped the porch board with his barrel. "Said *git* 'fore I drop ya where ya stand."

I picked up the paper and stumbled back. Glancing over my shoulder, I saw Gunnar heading toward Abby's. No telling what he'd do to Rainey. I took off.

As I neared the Fords', I saw them on the porch, hands wind-milled, mouths tightening. Catching my breath, I stopped at the tree to breathe and watched Gunnar and Abby.

Abby shook her head, once, then again. Gunnar grabbed her wrist, and she tried to jerk away but couldn't, his grip ironclad. Then he pulled her inside the tiny house.

I made it up to the side of Abby's cabin and was getting ready to barge up to the door when her words struck me.

"Tell RubyLyn . . . We have to *tell* them, Gunnar," she cried.

I ducked under the window, listening.

"I'll do no such thing. *No,*" Gunnar snarled.

"It's the only way," I heard her say inside.

"I'll not have my sins visited on them. They'll be ridiculed. Look what Rainey has to go through every day. To send him off to war with my sins? I won't! Think on it—"

"Don't you see, Gunnar . . . love. They don't need . . . for that." I only caught clipped sentences. She must've turned her back to the window.

"No, Abby. I won't have their souls die in that hate and fear."

"Love, Gunnar . . . they are—"

"No, *Lord* . . . no."

"In love." She lowered her voice to a whisper. "Just like . . . us . . . always."

Abby and Gunnar in love? I eased up slowly to hear them better and saw Abby take her small brown hands and cradle his face.

He rubbed his cheek against her palm, kissed it, and began to weep. "Abigail," he called formally, "I can't. No, Abigail, I'll lose her just like I did the others."

"Tell her everything," she pushed. "Start with the execu-tion—her parents. Claire . . ."

Parents. Claire. I soaked up more confusion.

"I can't tell her I cheated on Claire," he said.

I covered my mouth. *Cheat? He cheated? Him and his heavy words of God.*

"You must, Gunnar," she insisted. "Let her know about the hard patch with your job. How Claire always thought it was shameful work—"

"Tell her of my failings?" he cried out. "How the State called for me to electrocute a man and I *failed*? No, dammit, I won't."

"Gunnar, you couldn't help that a big storm blew through the night before and fried them switches like that."

I felt my eyes stretch and lock.

He moaned. "Damn lightning storm. I still can't believe that devil chair got a hitch in its wires and caught the prisoner on fire." He sniffled and coughed out. "I caused that poor soul a crueler death."

Oh . . . awful! I couldn't believe it—believe that Gunnar had messed up the electrocution of an inmate . . . same as ol' Rainey Bethea's hanging had been botched.

I heard him suck in a loud breath. "A damn tragedy, Abigail, and one I can never let go of—the type of cruelty I've fought against my whole life."

He'd muddled a state killin', his marriage . . .

Abby mumbled something.

"The resignation was more than I could bear." His graveled words quaked. "I was weak . . . then you . . . with child . . . Claire . . . oh, *dear Lord* . . . if only I'd been stronger . . . Claire wanting the babies so bad. And . . ."

You . . . ? What? I pressed my ear closer.

Gunnar coughed again, tears strangling the words. "And Rainey . . . After he was born, she . . . well, you saw how she folded herself up that winter. Devil's doings, my doings, Abigail."

"Pneumonia," she hushed. "You can't blame yourself—"

"I suspect it was more that made her give up her fight. It was Rainey."

I wrinkled my brow. *Rainey.*

Abby put a force in her voice. "Go, before it's too late, Gunnar. He's gone to the Feed to meet her. Tell her 'bout the law."

"Abigail, I . . . I don't know—"

"It's against Kentucky law to marry your first cousin. Go on, Gunnar, tell her about our son," she begged.

Son! I covered my mouth to hold in the scream. "My cousin . . . kin . . ." I lowered my head down and snuck away, making it to the old black locust in her yard.

I let out a whimper. Thoughts coiled around Molly and Lewis and their baby. "No." I banged my forehead against the bark. *Rainey. My husband-to-be, my kin.*

Rainey's tilt of the head when looking at me, the same as Gunnar's the times he'd looked at me when I'd done something that pleased him. Rainey's long-fingered hands that waved and wiggled with talk—same as Gunnar's before age and hard work slowed, thickened the knuckles and crooked the fingers. His walk even . . . not really a walk but more of a big sure gait like Gunnar's. How when they walked side-by-side, one shadow fit to the other. The images popped up like glints of broken glass, blinding, breaking the stretching circle of sanity.

And my foolishnesses—that I had seen none of it, blinded by deeper needs welling out from my hunger to love and be loved in this loveless life.

"No, *no-o.*" I thumped the tree with my fist. "*No,*" I shrieked, no longer caring who heard.

The quick footfalls of Gunnar and Abby closed in behind me. Gunnar latched on to my arm.

"*Let go!*" I jerked and whipped out of his hold and tumbled backward, dropping to my knees, spilling the hurt into the dark ground. "You've taken everything. Not Rainey. *Rainey,*" I wailed.

Abby tried to shush me with soft words. "Oh, dear RubyLyn, I'm so sorry, chil'."

"How could you?" I hissed.

Gunnar put a hand on my shoulder. "Get on up, RubyLyn. We need to talk about things—us here in Nameless . . ." I felt his fingers dig into my ribs, work their way under me as he tried to pull me up. "*Stand up.*"

I didn't want to get up, ever. I wanted to empty my tears—bloody the already darkened soil with more hurt. I wanted the dirt to cover me, hide me like it does its dead. I wanted nothing. And I went limp in his big, ugly hands. He tugged again and I felt him lifting me and found the strength to twist my shoulders and chest, grab one of his gnarled fingers, and bend it back.

I broke away, threw the deed in their faces. "*Nameless?* I got nothing left in Nameless!"

Gunnar grasped my elbow.

Abby put her hand on his. "Gunnar, let her go and tend to her hurtin'. Alone," she said.

"RubyLyn—" he began.

"*Don't,*" I warned.

Gunnar dropped his hold and shifted his weight back.

"Nothing left." I spit at him and tore off across the fields.

A minute later, I stood breathless in front of our house. Numbly, I bent over and picked up the strawberry dress from the yard, then climbed the porch steps.

Inside, I slung the dress over a kitchen chair. Flinging open the pantry door, I grabbed Gunnar's bourbon bottle and plopped down into the chair. Staring hard at the dress, I opened the Kentucky Gentleman and downed a big, burning gulp. Coughed. Downed more. And coughed again.

I held up the bottle, read the name, and gave a short, tight laugh. "*Gentlemen?*" I wiped my tears. "Nothing but cheaters and women beaters here."

I shoved stuff off the table, sending Mama's purse, newspaper, pens, and Gunnar's pills flying. The Tuinal lid burst off the bottle. Colorful capsules skittered across the green linoleum.

I pulled Mama's snakeskin purse onto my lap and fished out her lipstick and our fortune. I smeared the paint across my mouth, thickening, smacking my lips. I studied the flaps on the fortune-teller. Tracing my fingers over the tiny sketched portraits of me and Mama, I peered closely at the third flap with the tobacco leaf, then the fourth where Daddy should've been, instead of this poorly drawn heart with the cut down its middle.

Distant screams sawed through clouded memories. *Mama, Daddy. Daddy yelling at Mama. Me. Daddy rushing toward me, knocking me onto the floor. More screams . . . Mine. His. More crying.* I shook my head, the memory fuzzed, blurring.

I tossed back two more gulps of the bourbon and fell to my knees coughing, the bottle tipping, spilling out some of the booze. Brown liquid spread out before I caught the bottle and set it upright.

I felt the aching hum of the Patsy Cline song rub my tongue. I tipped back the bourbon to silence it, slapped the wet floor with the bottle.

Floor.

The spill had dirtied my spotless linoleum.

I stared down at it feeling trapped—aching in the darkest way—drumming the floor with the bottom of the Kentucky Gentleman.

I knew it would be hell to clean the sticky mess, but I swiped my foot over the puddles anyway, making a bigger mess for *him*. *Him* always telling me to appreciate the *living* bones in my knees. Let *him* feel the breath in his own knees and clean up this slop. If I was gone, he wouldn't have anyone . . . No one. Same as me. *No one—no more.* And *no more* Rainey and me breaking our living bones for his *dead* ones.

Rainey . . . At least he had a mama and daddy now—alive—close to his side.

I blinked, swigged more, spilt some more, and looked at the blue and red capsules scattered in the bourbon, dropping fat tears onto the floor.

The power of the booze landed low and hit me. My throat and gut felt the burn and asked for more.

Family is what I needed from Gunnar, but could never have. I guzzled down the webbed thoughts, took another long drink. All the good having one does . . . *Rainey.* Knowing about his family now would destroy him.

I stretched out an arm and touched the beautiful strawberry dress—the dress meant for us.

"Rainey," a hot breath escaped. "*Rainey.*" I howled, scooping the small capsules into my hand, rolling, jiggling them across my palm.

I looked down at the grimy floor and let out a desperate growl. "*Gunnar* . . . Damn you, Gunnar, I won't let you keep me tied to your tobaccos—alone—slowly executing me in this *godforsaken* land!"

I took another mouthful of bourbon. "I *won't* . . . and I sure as hell won't botch my own godforsaken leaving."

My fingers reached for one of the pretty pills.

"Pre-tty, pre-tty. *My GodPretty.*"

I popped the pill into my mouth. Another.

Chapter 35

Gunnar had a funny look on his face. Not his usual executioner glare or the Bible-thumping one either. I tried to pop open my eyes bigger to get a better glimpse, but they were too heavy, swimmy-like. He talked funny, too. "Go to town and telephone Doc," he was saying, smacking my cheeks.

Clipped voices crawled across the air, buzzing.

"RubyLyn, RubyLyn," he hummed, pushing my head toward the toilet. "That's right, get it all up. Up."

Abby's voice floated atop his. "*RubyLynnn.*" And Rose's over hers. I pulled a wet towel off my neck. The pink company's-coming towel. *For me?*

Gunnar smacked my cheeks again, called out, "Hurry, go to town and telephone him."

Their voices bumped like angry snakes. "*RubyLynnn . . . Hon-eee . . . Telephone-ph-phone.*" *Are they talking on my old telephone toy?*

Someone lifted me up, carried me away. *Daddy. But how?*

"M-m-m." I tried to speak, but my drug-soaked voice climbed through raw, tight pipes. "My—my . . . Da-ddy." I reached out my arm, grasping for him.

A perfumed Rose leaned in close, grabbed it, and clasped me in a hug.

Commotion.

Then I saw old Doc Sils bent, his face blurring over mine.

"All we can do is let her rest now," he said before I sped into blackness.

A pounding in my head finally stirred me awake. Night had fallen and the table lamp cast shadows across the face of my bedside clock and Gunnar's slumped body. I grabbed the top of my head, plucking off a pink towel.

Gunnar sat in a chair, perching his elbows on tall knees, hands fisted over the State Fair candle cross in prayer.

I squeezed my eyes shut. Anything to do with Gunnar and God would mean punishment.

Gunnar must've seen me move. He jumped up from the wooden chair beside my bed. "RubyLyn, you're awake. It's been fourteen hours . . . O thank you, *Merciful Lord!*" He grabbed the headboard, looked up at the ceiling, his wild-eyed expression scaring me.

I tried to get up. Weak, I slumped back down.

"Stay put. I'll bring tea." He left the bedroom.

In a few minutes, I pulled myself up and swung my legs out of bed. My feet sank into the worn rug. Shaky and a bit fuzzy, I made my way to the bathroom. I'd barely finished washing my face when I became light-headed again. I shuffled back to bed and collapsed onto the pillow.

When I stirred awake, Gunnar was there again.

"Let me warm your tea," he fussed.

In a bit he came back with the tea and some toast. "Sip slowly. And here"—he set the plate of toast beside me—"try a bite of this."

Gunnar hovered over me as I took a swallow of the hot liquid. Watching him, I nibbled on the toast, drank more tea, and soon felt less shaky.

"I-I'm fine," I trembled, pushing the plate away.

He pulled up the chair and sat down. "I'm not."

I swallowed, waiting for his hard words.

"RubyLyn, you gave me a scare . . . I have failed you and Rainey with my secrets."

"Secrets," I shivered, everything flooding back.

"Some that should've been shared. *Sins* . . . Mine and Abigail's . . . We've always loved each other, even as youngsters. But the times say you stay put with your own . . . No different than now. My weakness."

I stared at Gunnar. *Weak.* Nothing about him was weak. He was like the hundred-year oak in our side yard.

As if claiming my thoughts, he went on. "I'm ashamed to say, I was. No excuse for what I've done. Knew after Gus passed, it would be an even harder road for Rainey here if folks found out about us. *Still would.* Being colored and being a bastard in this world is damning . . . damning the already damaged that folks see and pick on. Do you understand that?"

My thoughts had pulled to it. "Yes," I barely whispered and knew he was right. At least Rainey could claim a namesake, a daddy, though it weren't the right one.

"RubyLyn," he said, "I've prayed on this every day. . . . *Every day.* I couldn't protect my women—Claire or your mama, or do much about Rainey . . . and you were my last chance. Lord knows I'd been given a few. That's why I picked you up at the orphanage. Hoping for that chance I didn't get."

My eyes widened. Gunnar never talked about this—or Mama.

"I've heard you cry out in your sleep plenty over the years," he said. "Cry out for them—for your pa. Didn't know quite what to do about it, except pray some more. I'm truly and deeply sorry for not doing right by you—for not being enough of a man . . . the *father* you needed."

Embarrassed, I looked away.

"Maybe if you know the whole truth, the nightmares will leave you be."

I squirmed. *What else?*

Gunnar gripped my hand, rubbing it, something he hadn't done but one other time that I could remember: the day we walked out the orphanage together. I couldn't help holding right back despite knowing it would fade as sure as his declarations.

"RubyLyn, you need to know that your pa died protecting you. He loved you."

"What do you mean, Gunnar?" I asked, wadding up the bed-sheet in my other hand. "It was because of the drinking. You've said it a hundred times." I untangled our hands.

He shook his head. "It was more . . . Your folks had come in late from one of their revivals. He was spent and your mama poured him a stiff drink, and after it all happened, I said the drinking killed him, when it really was the snake."

"Snake . . . But—"

"I couldn't tell you. I had to protect you. Couldn't have you blaming yourself for his death."

"What do you mean?" I asked, the fear stacking up like bricks. I pushed myself up straight.

"The men helping him at the revival didn't knot the snake bag tight when they delivered it back to your parents' house . . . Left the damn church snake sitting on the porch instead of put-ting it back in its glass cage out back in the shed . . . You picked up that old telephone you were so fond of—"

"*Telephone.*"

He rubbed the swollen burls on his knuckles. "You were just a baby, not yet five, how could you have known? You wandered onto the porch, took the toy and banged it on the sack, play-ing."

The long-ago memory burst into my brain new and bright. "Talk, talk, talk," I'd hissed long ago, tapping the plastic re-ceiver on the brown cottonseed bag. "Talk to Daddy!"

"Didn't take much." He grimaced. "The snake wriggled out and was getting ready to strike, when your pa shoved you out of the way and saved you. The snake struck his arm."

My hand flew to my mouth, tears gathered behind my closed lids. "I remember now."

"Your pa was a good man and had a strong faith. He believed God would heal him. Refused the doctor, calling on Mark . . . Mark 16:18."

I racked my brain for the Bible verse.

"He believed that verse was the word of God. '*They shall take up serpents and if they drink any deadly thing, it shall not hurt them,'* " Gunnar recited. "And I'd argued with him about it."

That's why Mama didn't sketch him on our fortune-teller. Her, saving the last flap for my memory. Frantic, I scanned the room, searching.

Seeing my distress, he lifted up the teacup. "Here, have some more."

I pushed it away. "My things—"

"I put your purse and the other things over on the dresser by those new stack of books Rose brought by this morning. She changed you into your gown."

"Rose was here?" I looked down at myself, hating that she saw me in this troublesome way.

"I couldn't keep her away."

I stared at the dresser. The crinkly fortune-teller I'd made with Mama sat unfolded beside her lipstick. The penciled sketches showing. Deep down, I must've known all along: I'd drawn the broken heart and the snake down its center to remember he'd died saving me. The memories flooded back, battering my heart.

Gunnar followed my gaze. "That damn snake . . . Too much for your young, pregnant mother. Her heart plumb busted after that. And when she got the pains in her seventh month, she wouldn't let me fetch the doc for her. Said the same thing as your pa, that the Good Lord would heal her . . . I sent for the doctor, but twice she turned him away. Never had much dealings with pregnant women. Sorry for not seeing it all then."

He wiped his own leaky eyes. "I was so busy trying to mend my own damn heart to help with her healing . . . I'm sorry."

He'd tried to save her, but her faith believed only Jesus could.

"I've been too hard on you. I can see that now. Stacking my failures on your fine art like that . . . A sore reminder of what I couldn't do. And I hated their religion. Sickened that it took them, and was hell-bent on protecting you and giving you a proper upbringing. So much, I stuck mine on you, and it's done nothing but drive you away."

Gunnar took his thumb and gently wiped a fat tear off my cheek. He stood. "Every day I pray for His forgiveness. Give me yours . . . I lost them. I can't lose you," he whispered hoarsely, and his eyes showed the troubled miles of his past and the promised road to regret. "We can start new with our land."

He flicked his hand toward the window. "It'll be tough going, but we'll get through the winter, and the fields, our fields, will rest and be better for it. We'll grow good crops. You'll make your art."

I looked past him. "And Rainey?"

"I've sent Rainey on to Louisville where he'll be safe. Become a fine soldier . . . It wasn't your fault or his. It was mine, and if you give me one more chance, I'll spend the rest of my life seeing that you have a good home and future here."

Slowly, I shook my head. "There's nothing here but useless land—worn womenfolk." I sniffed the tiredness of the house, us.

"It can happen."

"It didn't for Henny, Lena. Or Ada and Baby Jane . . . and there's Abby. Darla Clark . . . and Dirty and Dusty . . ." I said.

Gunnar swiped a hand over his eyes and walked over to the door. "There's us. Family. And, I love you," he said thickly. "Just one more chance to make it right—one more chance to be the father yours meant you to have."

He worked his knuckle over a wooden spot on the doorframe and knocked twice. "One more," he pleaded, rapping it a third time.

I looked away.

"Rest up," he called softly.

When he was gone I buried my face into the pillow and wept for the family I'd lost—wept for Rainey and the nothingness I had left.

Exhausted, I fell asleep and dreamed of a clanky Ferris wheel spinning round and round in shimmering green fields popped with tilting sunflowers and golden-eyed daisies.

Chapter 36

Ribbons of morning light spilled across tangled sheets, awakening me. Puffy-eyed, I peered at the clock, surprised to see it was almost eight, though I couldn't name the day.

A little sluggish, but I sat up feeling somewhat better. Gunnar's words had softened, and I knew he meant them. Still, my heart was heavy and thoughts were burdened.

Slowly, I stretched and tested my feet on the floor. It had been the first time in a long while that I'd slept without the nightmares. Knowing everything calmed my soul, and a quiet moment washed over me.

I wandered out into the hall. Gunnar had left a cardboard box outside my door. I kneeled down and opened it and studied the beautiful portrait of Mama holding me on her lap under an umbrella of blue skies. She'd dressed me in pretty pink ruffles and a matching bonnet that shaded my wide toothless smile. I pulled out a stack of art, sifting through the textured pages. A smaller charcoal sketch of a beaming Abby swaddling a baby in the doorway of Gunnar's barn. Another painting of a younger Mrs. Stump with her four little girls buttoned to her long skirts, hands draped along a budding belly. I recognized Henny's pouty grin, Lena's secret smile, Baby Jane's soft eyes, and Ada's fierce chin. Youthful hope brimmed in Mrs. Stump's face. Beautiful likenesses of everyone.

How hard it was for Gunnar to lay down this talent. How

hard it must've been for Claire to hang up portraits of other women's children instead of her own.

I trailed a finger over the works and examined the art again. Families that should be seen: in foyers, sitting rooms, over the Stumps' broken couch, and on Abby's paint-worn walls. Pictures that gladdened hearts and hearth.

I carried me and Mama's painting to my bed, curling up beside it. Tired, I drifted back to troubled sleep.

An hour later I woke to fresh tea on my nightstand. I gulped it down and felt more like myself. The house was quiet and I peeked out my door. Gunnar's bedroom door stood cracked, which meant he was someplace else.

I padded back to my window. The fog scratched across the fields. I stared out at the Kentucky corners of my world that could make you feel alive, forget time and other things.

Beyond, mountaintop broke through clouds as the sun birthed a new day. A new day with a startling new knowing crept into my heart.

A barefoot Baby Jane darted across the yard, dirty and unkempt. She stopped by the oak and glanced all around. Then she peeked up, catching my movement in the window. Concern crawled through her brows.

Slowly, I lifted my hand, waved, and then I remembered and held up one finger for her to wait. Hesitant, she nodded back. I plucked the ribbon I had been saving for her off my bureau and dropped it out the window.

Surprised, she scooped it up, admiring. Shyly, Baby Jane held up her basket to show me two eggs tucked inside. She took out a posy of daisies from her dress pocket and placed it atop them.

A softness took hold of my heart and I waved again.

Baby Jane set the basket under the tree and scurried away.

Beside her basket, my hoe rested against the oak's trunk. Its wood handle blackened from the fire, slick as creek stone from years of toil.

I remembered when Rainey first taught me how to hoe. So many times, we'd broken spring blisters on that old thing, toughened our winter hands. Now Rainey would be holding a gun, toughening his heart. Likely never to come back to these parts. Forever lost.

I needed to send him a *good-bye* letter. Tell him I'd changed my mind. I hoped a fitting excuse would come to me. I could never pretend it was a "good night," or tell him that he was kin—dare to let him go off to war like that, hurting. I would rather him start life anew with this small heartbreak than with the bigger hurtings of a stolen namesake. He deserved that.

"*Good night.*" I bent over and wept until I couldn't wring out another drop. "*Good night, dear Rainey. Find a safe life and a fine city woman.*"

City. Families . . . Mine.

I knew if I pushed Gunnar, I could sell my land and move away. He couldn't stop me from quitting school. I'd be sixteen in a few weeks.

I caught a glimpse of myself in the mirror, the messy hair, swollen eyes, and sloppy gown. Disgusted, I ran the brush through my tangles. I picked up Rose's slip from the bureau and pulled out a clean dress from the closet, and changed. Inspecting, I shimmied up my skirts, pinched the fabric of my silky slip.

Mountain woman, Emma had said, *educated at Centre.*

I dropped my skirts, moved over to the dresser to find some paper to write Rainey, and then I saw it. My mind jogged the jelly-jar memories, beckoned the Ferris wheel in the field. *Clanky, clanky.*

I studied the pile of things that Gunnar had brought up from downstairs, lingering on the packets of sunflower and cucumber seeds from the fair. I opened the tiny envelopes and shook some of the seeds onto my palm.

My gaze shifted to the gold eagle emblem on the Future Farmers of America booklet, the club's creed.

Slowly, I thumbed through the pages. Curling my fingers over the seeds, I spied the colorful flyer next to the booklet, studying its advertisement.

Clutching the booklet and flyer and seeds, I stepped over to the window. Dead fields lay silent. Acres of what had been, wouldn't be, and what could be.

Gunnar's beliefs and mine.

His old, ailing hands trusting mine.

Family.

I rolled the seeds over in one hand and clenched them in a fist while I tapped the flyer and booklet against my leg.

Believe, believe, believe . . . I opened my palm and blew, scattering the tiny seeds onto the sun-puddled windowsill. Setting the Farmers' booklet atop the fallen seeds, I looked at the flyer in my hand.

"I believe"—I pressed the green paper to my lips and peered down at the ledge to the words scripted onto the Farmers' pamphlet—"*with a faith born not of words but of deeds . . . in less dependence on begging and more power in bargaining; in the life abundant and enough honest wealth to help make it so—for others as well as myself . . .*" I quietly read the Future Farmers of America creed.

Without thought, I tore a square out of the bright green flyer. Folded counterclockwise, crimped, unfolded, folded again, pressing creases while staring out to the land and mountains of my birth.

"*Believe* . . ." The paper crackled over the Farmers' litany. "I believe . . . *in being happy myself and playing square with those whose happiness depends upon me . . .*"

I wiggled my fingers inside the paper pocket folds. Fresh tears splashed down on my new fortune-teller.

Believe. Believe. Believe.

No time to let it cure.

I grabbed the Future Farmers of America booklet off the windowsill and ran down the steps.

Gunnar sat hunched over the kitchen table, the candle cross pressed between his palms.

I set the fortune-teller in front of him. "This is for us." I tapped. "I think we should get a contract with them, Gunnar."

I laid the wrinkled Farmers' booklet down beside it. "And I

want to join this club that lets females in so I can learn more about agriculture and grow fine crops."

Gunnar rubbed a calloused tip over the gold eagle, nodded. Then he picked up the fortune-teller and studied it. Tears dampened his drawn cheeks. Gently, he slipped his bent thumbs and forefingers inside the tiny folds and worked the pickle-covered flaps.

Six Years Later

I'd found him.

Or maybe it was Freddy who found *us*.

"*Howdy, pretty lady . . . Howdy, howdy, soldier,*" the big wooden doll called out.

Twinkly lights painted the summer evening skies. The Kentucky State Fair bustled with all kinds of folks from all over the Commonwealth, its last night pleated with scents of tired cooking oil, stale popcorn, and spent sparkle.

We'd been bringing our twins here every year for the last three. Our daughters insisted on visiting Freddy as soon as we arrived and before we left, calling out their excited good mornings and blowing sleepy good-night kisses to him.

Gunnar'd even bought us one of those fancy Polaroid cameras to mark our visits, saying, "The Sheriff of Nameless and his family deserve a fine camera!"

I watched Bur and Gunnar carry the twins over to the balloon vendor across from Freddy. The four of them like that put a smile on my face.

Baby Jane set her cage down beside me and handed me the prize money to put back for her college. I slipped her winner's check into my purse. Excited, she wagged the shiny ribbon in front of me, waiting.

For the third year in a row I pinned the ribbon onto her Future Farmers of America jacket. Baby Jane caught my hand and squeezed, then smoothed down the purple streamers draped over the locket beneath it. I'd given her the silver locket on her sixteenth birthday, tucking inside one of the slots my sketching of the basket that I had plucked off the tobaccos that long-ago day. Baby Jane'd saved part of that old fortune-teller, too, and placed my drawing of the hen alongside it.

She kissed my cheek and hurried over to the balloon vendor to show off her award, turning heads with her bright smile and the same Siren-calling hips of her older sister Henny. Baby Jane's Grand Champion hen called after her, fussing in soft, rolling clucks.

Two teenagers strolled past, slapping Rose's musical wooden spoons against their palms. They hummed "Black Jack Davey," the song Rose taught folks to go along with their new spoons.

I tapped my foot remembering how we'd sung it in the parking lot till Crockett'd showed up. . . . At first I worried about coming back to the fair until Rose said Cash Crockett had gotten into trouble after I'd left. "They caught him in a storage barn with a thirteen-year-old 4-H girl and fired him—sent him to the city can for a while, too."

I smoothed down the day's wrinkles that puckered my old strawberry dress that Bur always teased me about. He'd laugh. "You've been wearing that old dress every year for this fair, sugar—done wore off the creases even. . . . How 'bout I buy ya a new one from the mail-order catalog?"

A quivering wind kicked up. I covered the two flapping ribbons pinned to my chest that I had won for this year's art exhibit. I'd already sold the illustrations to a book publisher in New York. A few years back, one of their businessmen had been traveling down our way and spotted my art at Zachery's in Tennessee. He'd taken a fancy, using them for a hotshot author's book covers.

The burst of air calmed. Resting my tanned hands on Freddy's white picket fence, I soaked up the night breeze.

Then he walked up alongside the small crowded fence, tall-dark-handsome as a mountain shadow over flower root. Looking smart and straight ahead at Freddy he was all decked out in a pressed uniform, polished black shoes, shiny belt buckle, and his garrison cap angled just right.

He hadn't come back to Nameless. Not once. He'd not written to me either after that long-ago good-bye letter I'd posted to him. Though he'd been sending letters and money to his mama, regular-like. She'd go off to visit him once in a great while but kept tight-lipped mostly, saying he had made the army his career.

Myself, I didn't get away from the fields much, except for this fair, and maybe once a year to see Henny and her four kids over in Beauty. She'd call, begging a ride to the penitentiary so she could visit her man, and then over to the old state insane asylum to visit Ada.

He brushed against my elbow as he eased himself into the row of people.

My insides rattled, ears filled with a whooshing—same as it did in the tobacco fields back then. I gripped the fence, a knowing banging my chest.

I was getting ready to slip away, when slowly, *a slow-talking-hands-slowly,* he stretched his pinky finger, hooked on to mine, and squeezed. Quietly, he stared up at Freddy.

I kept my eyes locked on Freddy, too, and lightly pressed back.

Soft and low, Rainey struck the words to "Sweet Kentucky Lady." " '*Honey, there's no use in sighing . . . Your eyes were not made for crying . . . Sweet Kentucky Lady . . . Just dry your little eyes . . . You're still my rose of Kentucky. No rose is sweeter to me . . .' "*

A small boy pushed up behind us, wound himself tight around Rainey's long legs. A pretty Asian lady leaned in between them, sweetened Rainey's cheek with a kiss.

"Daddy, *Daaa-dy!*" the boy shouted up at Rainey, tugging, smiling big as the moon. "Mama says it's time to tell Freddy good-bye! I don't wanna!"

Rainey dropped his hold and lifted the little boy up. "Time to go, son."

The boy shook his head. "I want to stay *forever,* Daddy," he pouted, rubbing his sleepy eyes.

"Hear, now." Rainey hoisted his son a little higher. "We don't have to say good-bye, Gunnar. How 'bout we just say good night?" he coaxed, latching on to his son's pinky finger.

Little Gunnar grinned and clamped back, then hugged his daddy's neck.

Rainey pressed a kiss into his son's tiny black curls. Resting his head atop the boy's, Rainey's tender gaze fell to mine.

"Good night," he said softly over his son's head and at me this time, and stretching his wiggling pinky.

Good night

Acknowledgments

Thank you bunches to Liz Michalski, Ann Hite, Danielle DeVore, and others who gave their valuable time, feedback, and suggestions during first drafts. Thank you, Mike Schellenberger and Homer Richardson.

Jamie Mason, thanks for being a wonderful writing friend. George Berger, thank you again for staying with me all the way.

Agents Stacy Testa and Susan Ginsburg, my wise and talented representatives and my biggest cheerleaders, you have my deepest gratitude forever.

To the folks at FoxTale Bookshop, in Atlanta, I'd be remiss if I bypassed your kindness and huge support. I love and thank you to the moon and back.

John Scognamiglio, you are the. very. best. an author can have, and I thank you for being so very good to me. To Kensington and its amazing team: Vida Engstrand, Paula Reedy, Kensington's amazing artists, and so many others behind my novels, I thank you for your dedication and endless hard work—always, always, I am grateful and indebted to you.

Joe, I love you like salt loves meat. Son Jeremiah and daughter Sierra, I love you forever.

To you, wonderful reader: Thank you for inviting me into your home.

**Please turn the page for an intimate conversation
with Kim Michele Richardson about
GodPretty in the Tobacco Field.**

GodPretty is a phrase that I made up to show starkness in the brutal and beautiful land and its people and mysteries. The term is necessarily paternalistic in the book and means to the one character, Gunnar, to keep a good and Godly soul if you are of a religious nature as he is. To Gunnar, *GodPretty* is applicable to females, while a male would be "righteous." Gunnar uses my coined phrase *GodPretty* to push his strict moral code on his fifteen-year-old niece, RubyLyn. It came out of the uncle's yearnings for his niece—wanting her to be pretty and pretty in the eyes of the Lord, so God would protect her when he no longer could, so that she would have a good life and be smiled upon by others not only because she'd be pretty but because her soul would shine, too. From the opening scene you can feel the title, the contrast with the ugly tobacco fields, giving a foreboding presence. Gunnar controls RubyLyn with this phrase, his large presence, big hands, hard ways of talking, acting. So when he punishes her, she can't resist, can't fight, until one day . . .

I wanted to write a tale of tender love and loss, the importance of land, oppression of Appalachian women in the '60s, and use a unique place. More than anything it was my hope to weave the theme of poverty's oppression on women and portray the consequences. I do this with the four Stump girls, RubyLyn, and the rest of the women in the fictional town of Nameless, Kentucky. The girls' actions show how the crushing poverty knows no gender, age, or boundaries, and how it becomes a scatterbomb, harming the person, the family, friends, and everyone in larger society—how it affects learning, choices, and notions of self-worth on life's whole journey. And again, in *GodPretty* we visit racial strife and examine difficult history from this timely subject. We also look at the last public hanging that took place in Kentucky (Rainey Bethea, August 14, 1936, Owensboro, KY).

I hoped to explore Appalachia's history, back to when President Johnson and the First Lady, Lady Bird, surprised the world and visited the tiny eastern Kentucky town Inez in 1964. Bearing witness right down to the hand-hewn porch of Tom Fletcher that Johnson squatted on, to the color of the First Lady's coat, and to the reminder of the newly minted coin commemorating President Kennedy. I wanted the reader to feel that hope and loss through the eyes of a 10-year-old RubyLyn.

GodPretty in the Tobacco Field is rich with music. I love music, particularly the violin. Though I can't play a lick, my daughter started playing strings when she was three, and my husband plays the clarinet and piano. And we have a set of simple hand-carved wooden musical spoons like those mentioned in the book.

The people of Appalachia are born to music, much of it still lost to time's passing, and I pull some lost treasures into the novel like this one I found from the National Jukebox in the Library of Congress: "Sweet Kentucky Lady" (http://www.loc.gov/jukebox/recordings/detail/id/913).

Art is important to RubyLyn, and the papers she uses for her fortune-tellers are made from the pulp of the tobacco stalk and have her intricate drawings of pastoral scenes, portraits, and her fantasy cityscapes.

The land is a vital theme, too. It is how we live, breathe. When I was young, I worked in a tobacco field one summer. *I hated it.* Now my family and I grow vegetables and fruit on our small farm to give to the elderly. But last summer I grew a tiny patch of tobacco to visit that childhood setting again for my characters.

You'll visit a State Fair in the novel, icons of summer and youth—and look at the Future Farmers of America club before it allowed female membership, the sweeping change it made in 1969, and the important role the youth organization has for our earth and our future farmers.

Making RubyLyn's Fortune-Teller

The paper RubyLyn uses for her fortune-tellers is made from the pulp of the tobacco stalk. She draws intricate scenes of rural life, portraits, and fantasy cityscapes. But you don't have to grow tobacco and produce your own pulp. You can have one by cutting out any piece of paper and following these simple instructions below. Decorate your fortune-teller any way you like.

To see other readers' fortune-tellers like the ones RubyLyn makes, please visit my Facebook page and post your photos: https://www.facebook.com/KimMicheleRichardson.

I am excited to see your works of art!

INSTRUCTIONS

1. Cut out square and fold over diagonally on both dotted lines.

2. Flatten paper and fold all four corners to the center and press in creases.

3. Unfold, flip paper over, and fold four corners to center dotted lines.

4. Fold vertically and then horizontally on dotted lines.

5. Slip thumbs and forefingers into slots.

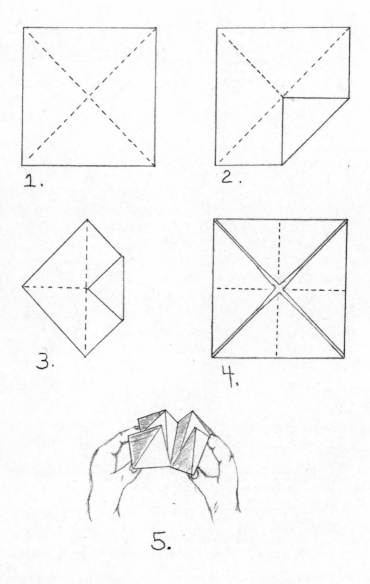

1.

2.

3.

4.

5.

GODPRETTY IN THE TOBACCO FIELD

Kim Michele Richardson

ABOUT THIS GUIDE

The suggested questions are included
to enhance your group's reading of
Kim Michele Richardson's
GodPretty in the Tobacco Field.

DISCUSSION QUESTIONS

1. In April 1964, President Johnson surprised the small Appalachian town of Inez, Kentucky, and the world by declaring his historical War on Poverty. How did this program to feed, educate, and house the poor help or hinder the poverty-ridden towns? Fifty years later, why is this area still steeped in poverty?

2. Gunnar pushes his strict moral code onto RubyLyn and uses his coined phrase *GodPretty* to keep her in line. He insists she must not only toil in his tobacco field, but keep a "GodPretty" soul while doing so. Does Gunnar believe that RubyLyn must be pretty in the eyes of God in order for his home and crops and land to be blessed? What does *GodPretty* mean?

3. Discuss Rainey and RubyLyn's relationship. Discuss marriages and relationships in the sixties and now.

4. How do you think the Labor Department's 1960s "Happy Pappy" work program would do today if paid, on-the-job training was widely available?

5. Throughout history, extended families, clans, and tribes tended to allow marriage of relatives—sometimes out of necessity, sometimes out of convenience. In 1943, Kentucky banned first-cousin marriages. Today, "Twenty-five states prohibit marriages between first cousins. Six states allow first cousin marriage under certain circumstances, and North Carolina allows first cousin marriage but prohibits double-cousin marriage," cited the National Conference of State Legislatures. Discuss.

6. As beautifully chronicled in Sharyn McCrumb's novel, later made into a movie, *The Songcatcher,* the people of Appalachia are born to music, much of it still lost to time's passing. I was fortunate enough to find the 1915 song "Sweet Kentucky Lady" and its original sheet music, along with many other treasures, and the recording on the Library of Congress Web site where they have painstakingly preserved more than 10,000 historical sound recordings for free on their online National Jukebox section. Listen to "Sweet Kentucky Lady" here: http://www.loc.gov/jukebox/recordings/detail/id/913.
What items from your past deserve to be found again, preserved, and shared with younger generations and loved ones?

7. Thinking about the lives and actions of Ada, Baby Jane, Lena, and Henny and the rest of the women of Nameless, how does abject poverty affect learning, habits, choices, and notions of self-worth on life's journey? Discuss crushing poverty's oppression on women.

8. In 1958, Freddy (also known as Freddy Farm Bureau), the eighteen-foot wooden doll of the Kentucky State Fair, was introduced and still sits proudly on his bale of hay at the State Fair. Share your icons of events that have stuck with you.

9. For decades, Future Farmers of America was strictly a boys' club. In 1969, Future Farmers of America allowed female membership. How do gender-based restrictions harm society? How does inclusion of all strengthen?

10. Discuss the Future Farmers of America creed.

11. We hardly think of the soil, oftentimes avoid treading in it, brushing it off when it sticks to us, yet it is the core

of existence. Novelist, environmentalist, and farmer Wendell Berry says:

The soil is the great connector of lives, the source and destination of all. It is the healer and restorer and resurrector, by which disease passes into health, age into youth, death into life. Without proper care for it we can have no community, because without proper care for it we can have no life.

How we nurture the soil is how we live and survive. Discuss erosion—the earth, its climate, planting, our ways of farming, our ways of harming, today versus decades ago.